PRAISE FOR THE NOVELS OF BENTLEY LITTLE

"Wonderful, fast-paced, rock-'em, jolt-'em, shock-'em contemporary terror fiction with believable characters and an unusually clever plot. Highly entertaining." —Dean Koontz

"The horror event of the year. If you like spooky stories, you must read this book." —Stephen King

"A spellbinding tale of witchcraft and vengeance. Scary and intense." —Michael Prescott

"If there's a better horror novelist working today, I don't know who it is." —*Los Angeles Times*

"Stephen King–size epic horror." —*Publishers Weekly*

"Little has the unparalleled ability to evoke surreal, satiric terror." —Horror Reader

"A singular achievement by a writer who makes the leap from the ranks of the merely talented to true distinction with this book. This one may become a classic." —DarkEcho

"Little is so wonderful that he can make the act of ordering a Coke at McDonald's take on a sinister dimension." —*Fangoria*

THE
HAUNTED

BENTLEY LITTLE

BERKLEY

New York

BERKLEY
An imprint of Penguin Random House LLC
penguinrandomhouse.com

Copyright © 2012 by Bentley Little

ISBN: 9780593199978

Signet mass-market edition / April 2012
Berkley trade paperback edition / August 2020

Printed in the United States of America
5 7 9 10 8 6

Cover image by Raland/Shutterstock
Cover design by Adam Auerbach
Book design by George Towne
Interior art: hand shadow © mantinov/Shutterstock Images

ONE

"THEY'RE HERE AGAIN, DAD."

Julian came out of the kitchen, coffee cup in hand, and walked across the living room to where his son, James, was holding on to the edge of the curtains, peeking through the crack and out the front window. Julian reached for the cord to pull open the drapes.

"What are you doing?" James cried, panicked. He flattened against the wall so as not to be seen.

Ignoring him, Julian opened the drapes. Sure enough, three skateboarders were on their driveway, one of them flipping his board into the air and then landing on it, the other two preparing to race down the sloping concrete to the street. It was the second time in two days that this had happened, and though theirs was the only driveway on the street not blocked by permanently parked cars or pickups (their vehicles went in the garage), that didn't give neighborhood punks the right to use it as their own personal skate park. Angry, he started toward the front door.

"Don't go outside, Dad. Please!"

"Get some 'nads," Megan told him. She was sitting on the couch watching TV—a tween show on the Disney Channel—and she smiled derisively at her brother before turning back to her program. The two of them fought constantly, and even before Claire had become pregnant with James, Julian had known this would happen. He and his brother had battled throughout their entire childhood, especially during the teenage years, when his dad would sometimes have to break up honest-to-God fistfights. They still didn't get along today. But Claire had read in some parenting book that it was better for siblings to be near in age, and she insisted that if they were going to have two children, the kids had to be spaced twelve to fourteen months apart. "That way," she told him, "they'll be closer. And when they grow up, they'll be friends." She'd since seen the error of her ways, although, of course, she would never admit that she'd been wrong.

"Did you hear what she said?" James cried, pointing at his sister.

"I heard. Megan, knock it off," Julian admonished.

She snickered.

"Megan," he warned.

"Ground her!" James said.

Julian opened the front door. "Both of you. Stop." Walking outside, he closed the door behind him. On the driveway, the three teenage boys were spinning in circles, the backs of their boards scraping the ground, the fronts thrusting proudly in the air. He recognized one of them as Tom Willet's kid from down the street, and though he didn't know the other two boys, they were the same ones he'd had to kick off his property yesterday. "Excuse me!" he said loudly.

The Willet boy glanced casually over at him, spinning around. "Hey, dude, where are your daughters?" He stressed the plural, laughing, and Julian hoped James wasn't listening.

"Get off my driveway."

The three skateboarders ignored him.

"Now."

"Make us." The Willet kid stared back defiantly, still spinning.

Julian felt a hot rush of anger course through him, though he knew the boy had him trapped. He could yell at the skateboarders until his voice was hoarse, but if they didn't listen, there was nothing he could do, since any attempt he made to physically remove them would have their parents calling the cops and filing assault charges. A middle solution suddenly came to him and, without saying a word, he walked over to the faucet at the end of Claire's flower bed, turned on the water and picked up the hose. He twisted the nozzle three clicks, from "shower" to "jet," and squeezed the trigger handle. A stream of water hit first one skateboard, then the others, as he swung his arm from side to side. He aimed higher, and the water shot into the boys' legs.

The skateboarders started yelling.

"Hey!"

"What are you doing?"

"What the hell?"

"I'm hosing off my driveway," he said calmly.

The boys quickly boarded down the driveway to the sidewalk.

"You squirted us!"

"On purpose!"

"I'm hosing off my driveway," he repeated. "You happened to be in the way." He smiled. "I *told* you to leave," he said innocently.

"Fuck you!"

"Douche!"

Middle fingers raised in defiance, the kids sped away, racing down the sidewalk. Still smiling, Julian remained where he was for several minutes, until he was sure that the skateboarders were gone and not coming back. Finally, he walked over to the flower bed, turned off the faucet, switched the nozzle back to "shower" and drained the rest of the water, dripping the last of it onto Claire's chrysanthemums.

When he walked back into the house, James was grinning. "That was great, Dad!"

He smiled back at his son. "That's my job."

Claire was standing in the doorway of the kitchen, looking concerned. "I don't like this," she said.

Julian nodded, saying nothing, not having to. They'd talked about the situation before. It wasn't just the teenagers. It was everything. The entire neighborhood was going downhill. There'd been several foreclosures over the past few years, and more than half of the houses were now rentals. The kids who lived in them were much rougher than the kids who had been there before.

"Maybe we should move," Claire suggested.

He'd been thinking along the same lines, though he'd hesitated to bring it up. Claire was sentimental, and not only was this the house they'd picked out together when they'd moved to Jardine, but both Megan and James had spent their entire lives in this place. There were a lot of memories here. The neighborhood *was* getting bad, however, and despite the terrible economy, their family was actually in pretty good financial shape right now. He and Claire were both employed, their house was worth much more than when they'd bought it fifteen years ago, and if they were ever going to move, this was probably the time to do it. There were bargains to be had, and they were in the fortunate position of being able to take advantage of that.

"I think we could do it if we wanted to," Julian said.

"No!" Megan shouted, overhearing the discussion. "I don't want to move!"

"I do," James said.

Julian looked over at his son, and their eyes met. A wave of sympathy washed over him. The past few years had been hard on the boy. Due to budget cuts, school boundary lines had been changed, and at the start of fifth grade, James had been plopped down in a new school, where he didn't know anyone and where he hadn't really made any friends. The year before, his two best buddies, Omar and Logan, had moved: Omar to Phoenix, where his dad had gotten a job, and Logan to Santa Fe, to live with his grandmother when his dad had *lost* his job. His other friend, Robbie, was still around, but Robbie was enrolled in a series of camps this summer because both of his parents worked and he needed someone to watch him during the day. So, since school let out, James had been spending most of his time alone, indoors, on the computer or in front of the television.

Julian could relate to his son's situation. He was out of his element as well. He'd grown up in California, in a large metropolitan area, and he'd moved here only because this was where Claire wanted to live. She was from Jardine, and since her parents were getting older, her sister lived here and many of her childhood friends had remained behind to work or get married or both, she'd been longing to return for as long as they'd known each other. As a Web designer, he could work anywhere, and after what had happened had . . . happened, after he'd quit his job at Automated Interface and gone freelance, after she'd decided to leave the Los Angeles law firm where she worked in order to set up her own private practice, he'd finally agreed to move to New Mexico with her. It meant downsizing their lifestyle, but they were both still young, and if they weren't willing to take a chance now, when would they be?

Unfortunately, Jardine didn't offer quite the bucolic rural experience he'd expected. He'd pictured himself waking up to the sound of birdsong and walking downtown with his laptop to sip flavored coffee at a cute café next to an art gallery on a tree-lined street. But the city was bigger than he'd thought it would be and resembled one of the lesser Los Angeles suburbs more than the cinematic country burg he'd imagined.

He wasn't unhappy, though, and he realized that, with two kids, their family would probably have exactly the same sort of lifestyle no matter where they lived.

"I like it here," Megan whined. "I don't want to live somewhere else."

"We're not moving," Claire reassured her daughter. "We're just talking."

But it was more than just talk, and that night in bed when Julian brought it up again, Claire admitted that she'd actually gone online the other day to look up available local properties. "I wasn't really *looking*," she said. "It was more like . . . browsing.

I was just checking to see what was out there. No real reason. But . . ." She let the thought trail off.

Julian saw in his mind those teenagers flipping him off, thought about James spending his summer hiding in the house. "Maybe we *should* start looking," he said.

She smiled, kissed him. "Maybe we should."

TWO

THEY'D NARROWED THE CHOICES DOWN TO THREE, AND THOUGH
Claire was leaning toward a foreclosed McMansion that was part
of the new DesertView development on the south end of the city,
Julian thought they should be more prudent. Just because they
were in good financial shape at the moment, it didn't mean they
always would be. Claire's office had seen a slight downturn in
clients recently, and the Web design business was notoriously
fickle. If they ended up overextended, someone might be buying
their foreclosed home in a year or two.

Personally, he liked a ranch-style house only a mile or so away
from where they lived now, in a nicer version of their present neighborhood. It was slightly smaller than their current home, with one
bedroom fewer, which meant that his office would probably have
to be moved into the garage, but it was situated in the middle of a
double-size lot, which meant they would have quite a bit of land.
On the east side of the property was what amounted to a small
orchard, with two lemon trees, two orange trees, an avocado tree
and a fig tree. The previous owner had also had a large vegetable
garden, and though it was overgrown and full of weeds, with a
little work it could easily be restored to its former glory. Claire
wasn't thrilled with the fact that the house was smaller than the

one they had now, but, as he'd been telling her, if things continued to go well for them, they could always add on.

"If we got that house, you'd be back to your old school," he told James, trying to lure the boy over to his side.

"I don't want to change schools," Megan said, overhearing them.

"*You'll* be going to the same junior high either way," Julian pointed out.

"I like Mom's house better," Megan insisted. "It has a pool."

"I like pools," James admitted.

The pool was another strike against the McMansion, as far as Julian was concerned. Maybe he was just being paranoid because all summer the Albuquerque newscasts had kept a running tally of backyard drownings, but to his mind the benefit of being able to swim and have fun was more than offset by the potential for serious injury and death.

There were three houses in the running, and the dark-horse candidate was an older two-story home within walking distance of the historic downtown district. It was big enough for Claire, had yard enough for Julian, and while it was not the first choice for either of them, it had no major drawbacks to which the other could object.

The real estate agent was the one who'd suggested they look at the property, and it was she who suggested another walk-through when, after a week, and despite her numerous high-pressure phone calls, it became obvious that they were no closer to choosing a house than they had been the first day. "I've been in this business for over ten years," she said, "and I'm pretty good at matching home to homeowner. Let me take you through the house one more time. I think, looking at it with fresh eyes, you might see some very positive attributes that you may have overlooked before."

So, Saturday morning, Julian, Claire and the kids all piled into the van to meet the realtor at the house.

"I still like the one in DesertView," Claire said.

"And I like the one with the fruit trees. But it can't hurt to check things out again. In fact, maybe we should look at all three of them today and see what we think. Besides, we don't have to decide right now. If we can't agree on one of these, we can just wait a month or so. I'm sure there'll be more homes up for sale."

It was only a five-minute drive, but Megan still brought along her iPod, and her earbuds were in before Julian even put the van into gear.

He glanced at her in the rearview mirror as he drove down the street. It occurred to him that while this generation had access to an almost unlimited amount of music over the Internet, they were much more narrowly focused in their interests than had been the kids of his day—or even his parents' day. When his mom and dad had been growing up, as they'd never failed to tell him, Top 40 radio played everything from rock to country to easy listening. They'd been exposed to the Beatles and Ray Charles and Glen Campbell and Neil Diamond, all on the same station. When Julian was a teenager, he and his friends had not only listened to music on radio, records, CDs and mix tapes borrowed from their peers, but they'd also been able to raid their parents' and grandparents' stacks of old albums and discover for themselves gems from the past. Now that avenue of discovery was completely cut off, for the simple reason that kids today did not have devices on which to play records or, in some cases, even CDs. The music could not be physically translated from those media, and that surreptitious passing down of knowledge—done behind parents' backs, which made it somehow more acceptable than when adults tried to turn kids on to a song themselves—no longer occurred.

Next to Megan, James could have been playing with his DS—but he wasn't. Instead, he stared happily out the window, and Julian smiled. As far as he was concerned, the boy was turning out okay.

Julian drove down the street. The Willet kid was skateboarding at the end of the block, and he grinned at the van as it passed, no doubt planning to head back and play in their driveway as soon as they were gone, probably with his punk friends.

Julian was going to be glad to get out of this neighborhood.

There was an accident blocking traffic on Carson Street, so they took the highway and got off two exits down. Now that he thought about it, this house did have the most convenient location of the three. And the neighborhood was nice, with well-maintained homes and people who had probably lived there forever. He could not recall seeing any teenagers or skateboards.

Claire seemed to be giving the house more serious consideration as well. "It has a good yard, as I recall. And I like the fireplace in the living room." She glanced over at him. "What do you think?"

They drove slowly up Old Main. "Good location," Julian pointed out as they drove past the brick building that housed Claire's law office. "You'd be within walking distance of work."

"It's closer to Grandma and Grandpa's, too," James said.

"That's true."

Claire was nodding in agreement, and she did not look displeased. Julian glanced around at the downtown businesses. Most people in Jardine, themselves included, bought their groceries at Safeway and shopped for everything else at The Store. The downtown district was just an area they drove through in order to reach those locations. But as his gaze took in the used-book store, the children's clothing boutique, the sandwich shop, the ice-cream parlor, the plumbing supply store, the thrift shop, the tax preparer's office, he could see himself taking a break from work and walking down here during the day, maybe meeting Claire for lunch. The idea appealed to him. *This* was close to the small-town life he'd originally imagined.

They drove past City Hall and around a park before turning onto Rainey Street. Two blocks down, they saw their realtor, Gillette Skousen, waiting next to the For Sale sign in front of the house. Julian pulled into the driveway and parked, bracing himself. Gillette gave off a distinct Up With People vibe. Blond and perky, with white teeth and perfectly smooth skin, she reminded him of a Disneyland tour guide, circa 1970. He hadn't liked her before and still didn't like her now, but she seemed competent and was a friend of Claire's sister, so he put aside his personal antipathy and got out of the van to meet her.

She was already on her way, smiling, hand extended. He shook her hand—he always felt weird shaking women's hands—as did Claire, and Gillette held forth the clipboard she was carrying. "I have some great news! The owners have agreed to come down an extra twenty-five hundred. I talked to them last night, and if you decide to take it today, they'll drop the price. How perfect is that?" Her smile grew brighter. "What say we take a look around?"

As before, they started off outside. Like many older houses, particularly the ones in this neighborhood, it had a big yard. Julian liked that. The home itself was set back from the street, and a shade tree grew in the center of the green lawn. A tire swing hung from one of the tree's lower branches, and off to the side was a birdbath in which two sparrows were loudly fighting. In the backyard, the realtor reminded them, were several blooming rose-bushes, as well as tall hedges that gave them privacy from the neighbors on either side. An alley ran behind the property, and the garage opened onto both the alley in back and the driveway in front. An adjacent storage shed provided enough room for a lawn mower, garbage cans and gardening implements, leaving the garage itself free for other uses. "You could even convert it into a rec room," Gillette had suggested last time.

Inside, the house seemed nicer than Julian remembered. There'd still been a few pieces of leftover furniture on their previous visit, as well as assorted trash and debris, but all that was gone and the place was now clean and empty. He had a much better sense of what the rooms looked like. The living room, he saw, was nearly twice the size of the one in their current house, with a hardwood floor, and a picture window that looked out on the tree in the front yard.

And Claire was right—the fireplace was impressive. Made of flagstone, it was built into the east wall and was large enough to accommodate a midsize tree stump. To either side of the hearth were rock benches, and above was a mantel, also rock. On the opposite end of the living room was the dining room and, beyond that, the kitchen. Homey, with a small, windowed breakfast nook that protruded into the backyard, the kitchen had been recently remodeled and featured plenty of cupboard space as well as a state-of-the-art gas stove.

Claire and the kids remained with the realtor, who took them outside on a reprise tour of the backyard, while Julian left to explore the upper floor of the house by himself. It, too, was bigger than he remembered, and though the master bedroom was downstairs, there were three more bedrooms up here, as well as a fullsize bathroom. One of the rooms, the one in the middle, was perfect for his office. It had a large window overlooking the backyard, was agreeably square and functional, and had multiple electrical outlets and plenty of wall space. Opening the narrow but deep closet, then walking around the room, he could envision where his computer desk would go, and his printer table, and his filing cabinets and his bookcase.

He could get a lot of work done here. Unlike his current office, it was far away from the family room with all of its attendant noise and commotion. He might actually have some privacy.

And he *needed* to get a lot of work done. Right now, he was reconfiguring a Web site for the music publishing company Darwin-Huxley, and if he wanted to keep that account, he'd better get busy. House hunting had been consuming far too much of his time over the past week, and the actual process of moving would take up even more time. The sooner he could put this all behind him, the better.

He also needed to finish the project as quickly as possible so he could get started on upgrading the interactive Web site of a midsize municipality, which had a looming deadline in less than a month.

Peeking out the window, Julian saw Gillette leading Claire and the kids from the garage onto the lawn. If he recalled correctly, the garage had a sort of attic, an A-shaped storage area accessed by a wooden ladder attached to one of the walls. James probably loved that. Just as he probably loved the basement in the house. Although it was very unusual for this area, the home had a small cellar beneath the kitchen. James had recently discovered James Bond and *The Prisoner* and a whole host of 1960s spy shows that some cable channel had been running, and was in a phase where he was fascinated by secret hideouts and underground rooms.

Through the window, Julian watched his family head back into the house, and he met them at the top of the stairs a few moments later when they came up to see the second story. Together, they accompanied the realtor through an airy corner room that Megan immediately claimed as her own, through his potential office, and through the square-walled room overlooking the front lawn that was next to the bathroom and that James announced would be perfect for his bedroom.

Julian was not one of those decisive guys who made split-second decisions on matters of major importance. He was a worrier and an incrementalist, and he liked to weigh all options, liked to study and think and play devil's advocate with himself before eventually choosing a course of action. Claire was probably the one who would have to pull the trigger on this and make the final decision. Still, he could tell that the house was not only a good bargain but a great place to live. There might be minor problems or inconveniences, small flaws that he'd probably fret over incessantly given the chance, but if they bought the house today and moved in tomorrow, he was sure he could be happy living here.

Downstairs, he walked through the backyard and garage with Gillette while Claire and the kids noisily went through the house yet again.

"You know," the realtor said as they stepped onto the rear patio, "I am so thankful I got this listing. I knew it was going on the market, but RE/MAX had it before, you know? So I figured the owners would want to go the same way again. But I was blessed that they chose me to sell their home."

"It's a nice house," he agreed.

"I'm blessed," she repeated.

Julian tried to keep a pleasant smile on his face, though already it felt strained. He was uncomfortable with people who used the word *blessed* as part of their everyday speech. The implication was that God was intervening in the minutiae of their lives, hanging around and helping them with their jobs or children or household chores as though He had nothing better to do.

Maybe it was true, Julian thought wryly. Maybe that was why there were wars and murders and earthquakes and hurricanes: God was too busy helping real estate agents find new listings to deal with those other issues.

He and Claire asked whether they could look again at the other two houses, and Gillette took them all in her car, leaving the van behind in the driveway. This time, the McMansion seemed gaudy and overly indulgent even to Claire, and Julian had to admit that while his first choice did have a lot of land, the house itself was really too small for their needs. Returning to the home on Rainey Street, Julian felt like Goldilocks. One house was too big, one was too small, but this one was just right.

"So," Gillette said brightly. "Are you ready to get the paperwork started?"

Julian hesitated. The house was great, but what if something even better came on the market next week? Or what if the neighborhood wasn't as nice as it seemed and they ended up living next to white-trash losers who were even worse than the Willets? Or what if . . .

Claire looked at him, and he read the expression on her face.

He nodded.

She smiled.

"Let's do it," he said.

THREE

JAMES SAT ON HIS BED, PLAYING A *STAR WARS* GAME ON HIS DS until his mom called him for lunch. The sun was shining through the window, illuminating his desk, bookcase and the movie posters on his wall. He loved his new room. It was away from Megan's, for one thing, and it definitely felt good to be free from her. In the old house, their rooms had been right next to each other, and she had always been walking in uninvited or pounding on the wall, yelling at him to turn down his television. This room was also bigger than his old one, with space on the floor for his beanbag chair—which had previously sat in his closet, to be brought out only for special occasions—and a built-in wall cabinet for his TV and his Wii—if he ever saved up enough money to get one.

"James!" his mom called a second time.

"Coming!" he yelled back. He finished blasting the last of the clones, then closed his game and went downstairs to the kitchen. He expected his mom to hand him a sandwich on a plate, expected to see his dad eating at the kitchen table, Megan in the living room in front of the TV. But both Megan and his dad were out in the backyard, and his mom was just carrying a dish of baked chicken drumsticks outside, pushing the screen door open with her rear as she backed out into the yard. "Wash your hands," she told him. "We're eating on the new picnic table."

James was surprised both by the type of food and by the fact that they were eating outside and all together, but he nodded and walked over to the sink, where he squirted some antibacterial soap into his hand and turned on the water. Seeing his parents and his sister through the window made him realize that he was alone in the house, and he glanced nervously to his left, toward the closed door that led to the basement.

He didn't like the basement.

James scrubbed his hands quickly. It wasn't something he'd admit to, and he was embarrassed that he even felt this way, but for the week since they'd moved in, he hadn't been able to set foot in the underground room, and though he'd successfully hidden it from everyone else, he had made a conscious effort to stay away from the door that led to it.

He'd had a nightmare about the basement when they'd first started taking things over to the new house. In order to save money, his parents had decided not to hire movers but to bring the small stuff over by themselves a little bit at a time, then rent a truck and have friends and family help them haul the beds, couches and heavy furniture. That first day, they'd made three or four trips, bringing over boxes of books, knickknacks and a lot of tools and things from the garage. His mom and Megan had stayed home, packing up more stuff for them to take, while he and his dad had ferried the boxes over, unpacking some so the cartons could be reused, leaving others in the rooms where the contents belonged. Neither of them had been sure where a grocery bag full of his mom's old cooking magazines was supposed to go, so they left it in the basement, which his dad said they were probably going to use as a storage room anyway. The basement was pretty small, approximately the size of the kitchen above, and they'd put the sack of magazines in the far right corner of the otherwise empty room.

That night, James dreamed that he was being summoned to the basement, though by whom or what he did not know. All he knew was that one moment he was lying in his bed, and the next he was walking down the street in his pajamas, making his way toward the new house because he *needed* to be there. He reached the house quickly—the city's dream topography made things closer together than they were in real life—and he strode up the walkway into the darkened, empty living room, heading straight for the kitchen, where he opened the basement door and started down. There was a dirty man standing in the corner of the room, grinning, his teeth eerily white against the dark grime of his skin. The man was as still as a statue; even his tattered clothes did not move, but he was alive and he was *hungry*. This was what had called James to the basement, and though he wanted to run away, his feet carried him forward, toward the corner, toward the grinning man.

And then he awoke.

Even thinking about the nightmare gave him chills, and he turned off the faucet and hurried outside without drying his hands, dripping water on the floor as he ran. Outside, Megan was complaining to their parents, asking why *he* got to have one of *his* friends stay overnight before she did.

"You know the Caldwells needed a babysitter for Robbie tonight," her mom told her. "Besides, Kate and Zoe are *both* coming over next week."

James sat down next to his dad and grabbed a drumstick. From across the table, Megan glared at him. He smiled back at her, taking a bite of his chicken. She turned away angrily.

He was anxious for Robbie to come over. It was the first time his friend would see the new house, and James was looking forward to showing off his room. Maybe he'd even take him into the basement. It wouldn't be that spooky with the two of them together.

Of course, they'd have to go down there in the daytime.

"What are we having for dinner tonight?" he asked. There was a lot of food on the table, and he was afraid they'd be eating leftovers. The thought embarrassed him.

His mom smiled. "Don't worry. You guys won't starve. We'll order a pizza or something."

Feeling better, James dug in, eating four drumsticks, three rolls and a bunch of sliced cucumbers, washing everything down with multiple glasses of iced tea. Ordinarily, he would have returned to his room after finishing his meal—that *Star Wars* game was addicting—but the images of the dream were still in his mind, and he did not want to go back into the house alone. So he wandered around the yard, pretended to be interested in some new flowers his mom had planted near the fence, and waited until his parents started carrying the dishes inside before finally following them into the kitchen. He hazarded a glance at the basement door as he passed by—

Had the door been ajar before?

—and hurried back up the stairs to his room.

Robbie was supposed to come over around three, but he was late, and it was after four when his family's car finally pulled into the driveway. James had spent the last hour alternately slouching in a chair in front of his computer desk, lying down reading a book on his bed, and sitting on the floor with his back against the wall while he played with his DS, unable to decide which pose would make him look cooler when his friend arrived.

He heard the parents talking downstairs, and though he wanted to wait here until Robbie came up and discovered him casually lounging in his slammin' new bedroom, James discovered after several seconds that he didn't have the patience, and he ended up hurrying downstairs and meeting his friend in the living room. He couldn't help grinning when he saw how Robbie was looking enviously up at the stairs. The Caldwells' house had only one story.

"Thank you so much for this," Robbie's mom was saying.

"We're glad to do it," his own mom replied. "James has been very excited that Robbie's coming over."

"Hey," James said, reaching the bottom of the steps and nodding hello to his friend.

"Cool house," Robbie told him.

"Right?"

"Why don't you show him around?" his dad suggested. "You could start with the basement."

Robbie's eyes widened. "You have a basement?"

James nodded, his smile fading.

His dad elbowed him playfully. "I'm surprised you didn't tell him. Wanted to keep it a secret, huh?"

"Yeah." Again James nodded, trying to maintain what was left of his smile.

"Let's check it out!"

Feigning an enthusiasm he did not feel, James led his friend through the living room, through the dining room and into the kitchen. "That's the door," he said, pointing.

"Cool!" Robbie pulled it open. "It looks like it's going to be a closet, but there's stairs!" He immediately started down, and, reluctantly, James followed, flipping on the light at the top of the steps before descending.

Maybe he'd been building it up in his mind into something it wasn't, but when he reached the bottom, James felt a distinct letdown. This wasn't the spooky chamber he'd been dreading but merely a small storage room lined with boxes and sacks filled with unpacked junk from their old house. He glanced toward the corner where the dirty man had been standing in his dream. An exercise bike was pressed against the wall.

"This is killer!" Robbie was walking up the narrow open space in the center of the cellar. "You should ask your parents if you can make this into your room!"

James shook his head. "Not enough light. Besides, I like to have a window."

"You could put extra lights in here. And you'd have tons of privacy. And if a tornado hit, you'd be totally safe."

"Come on. How often does New Mexico have tornadoes?"

"Sometimes."

"In Jardine? Never."

"But this is so great! And it's underground!"

While the basement wasn't what his mind had made it out to be, James still didn't want to stay here any longer than he had to, so he said, "You want to see great, check out my *real* bedroom. It's upstairs. You can see the street from my window."

Robbie grinned. "That's cool, too."

"We can spy on people." James led the way back up the steps to the kitchen, and the two of them hurried past the parents, still talking in the living room, and headed up to the second floor. James pushed his door open wide and stood proudly to the side as his friend entered the bedroom.

"Wow," Robbie said, taking in the posters on the wall, the built-in television cabinet, the beanbag chair on the large expanse of floor between the bed and the desk.

"Look over here." James went over to the window, pointing down. On the sidewalk in front of the house, an elderly couple was walking slowly, arm in arm. On the street beyond, two men in racing gear bicycled past, going the opposite direction.

"This is awesome."

"And they can't see us that good because the tree branches kind of block us. Even if they *were* looking in our direction—which they aren't." James grinned. "This is my room. This is where I live."

"You are so lucky."

"And when I get my Wii, the only time I'll leave my room is for meals."

"Will I be able to come over?"

James fell into the beanbag chair in a way that he thought was impressively smooth. "Sure."

Robbie leaned against the windowsill. "So, are you really coming back to Fillmore this year?"

"Yep. Thank goodness."

"Was Pierce really that bad?"

"I told you—it's a horrible school. I had no friends there.

None. The kids are all—I don't know—losers. I'm just glad to be out of there."

"Well, I'm glad you're coming back."

There was a shout from downstairs. Robbie's parents were leaving. The two of them hurried down. Robbie reddened with embarrassment when his mom gave him a hug, and he promised her he would behave. He took his suitcase and rolled-up sleeping bag from his dad, who playfully punched his shoulder and said, "We'll pick you up in the morning, sport. Have fun."

"Robbie can spend the day tomorrow if he wants," James's mother said. "We can bring him home in the afternoon or evening."

"That'd be fine, if he wants to. That sound good to you, buddy?" Robbie nodded happily.

"All right, then." His dad smiled down at him. "Come home when you want to." He looked over at James's parents. "Whenever you get tired of him. We should be home all day."

"Six o'clock at the latest," Robbie's mom said.

Good-byes were said, and after his parents left, Robbie toted his suitcase up to James's room, where the two of them hung out and played computer games for the next hour.

For dinner, they had pizza, James and Robbie going with James's dad to pick it up, and afterward they watched *The Fantastic Mr. Fox*, a movie they'd both seen a million times but that they both still thought was hilarious. Megan pretty much hid in her room for the entire evening, and that was another great thing about tonight—James hardly had to see her. BBC America was having a *Doctor Who* marathon, and they watched that until eleven, when James's mom told them it was time to go to bed.

Robbie had already unrolled his sleeping bag on the floor, and while James's mom had given him an extra pillow to use, he decided to rest his head on the beanbag chair instead. James, of course, slept in his bed. The two of them talked for a while in the dark—it was their goal to stay up until midnight—but they were tired, and within ten minutes both of them were fast asleep.

"JAMES!"

The cry sliced through sleep and into his dream, waking him.
"James!" It came again.

He sat up groggily, opening his eyes. There was an edge of an-
noyance or desperation in his friend's voice that indicated Robbie
had been trying to wake him up for a while, and he had the sense
that the other boy had been calling his name for some time.

James leaned over the side of the bed. "What is it?" he whispered.

"I want to go home." It sounded as though Robbie was about
to cry.

James squinted over at the clock Ms. Hitchens had given him
last year for reading more books than any other student in the
class. The multicolored numbers indicated that it was two thirty.
"It's the middle of the night!" James said.

Robbie did start to cry. "I want to go home!"

James felt scared. He had never seen his friend like this before
and didn't know what he was supposed to do or how to react.

But he was scared for another reason as well.

He was suddenly sure that Robbie had had a nightmare about
the basement.

It was not something he would ask about, for the simple reason that he didn't want to know, but the possibility frightened
him, and he imagined his friend dreaming about the dirty man
standing in the corner, grinning.

Maybe if they ignored the problem, it would go away. "Just go
back to sleep," James said. He felt sure that if they could just
make it to morning, everything would be all right.

"I can't!" Robbie cried.

There was a knock at the door, and James's dad gently pushed
it open. "Everything all right in here?"

"We're fine," James offered quickly.

"I want to go home," Robbie said, sniffling.

His dad turned on the light, and the room was suddenly filled with a brilliant glare that, coming after the darkness, caused James to squint. "What's the matter?" his dad asked kindly.

"I want to go home," Robbie repeated.

The look on his father's face told James that his dad thought the boy was probably just homesick. That was a possibility—but Robbie had stayed overnight at their old house before and nothing like this had happened.

"I have an idea." His dad left for a moment and came back with a cordless phone, which he handed to Robbie. "Here. Let's call your parents."

Nodding assent, Robbie took the phone. In the silence, James could hear the beeping of the numbers as his friend dialed, and then several rings before a faint voice answered.

"Dad? I want to come home." Robbie was no longer crying, but his voice still quavered with emotion. There was a pause. "I know." Robbie sniffed into the phone. "Yeah." There was a long silence. James could hear the faint chipmunk chatter of his friend's dad on the other end of the line. "Okay," Robbie said finally. "Okay. I will." He handed the phone back. "Here. My dad wants to talk to you."

"Kent?" James's dad moved into the doorway and lowered his voice so the two boys couldn't hear the conversation.

James looked at his friend quizzically. "So?"

"My dad said I have to stay." Robbie sounded resigned but no longer frightened. He'd not only stopped crying, but the panicked edge was off his voice.

James couldn't help himself. "Why do you want to go home?"

Robbie shook his head, not willing to answer.

Did you have a nightmare? James wanted to ask. *Was it about the basement?*

But he didn't say anything, and seconds later his dad came in, cheery smile in place, and told them both to go to sleep, waiting until Robbie was back in his sleeping bag, and James was in his bed and under the covers, before turning off the light. "Good night," he said. "See you in the morning."

"Night, Dad," James said.

"Good night, Mr. Perry."

James heard his dad's footsteps retreat down the hall. He almost asked Robbie if the reason he wanted to go home was because he was homesick . . . or because he was afraid of something. But once again, he didn't. Instead, he lay there silently, staring upward into the gloom.

Thinking about the basement.

And the dirty grinning man in the corner.

FOUR

CLAIRE LOOKED UP AT THE CLOCK. IT WAS JUST AFTER TEN. SHE was supposed to meet her sister, Diane, and their friend Janet for lunch at noon, but this morning's only client had canceled, and she had nothing to do for the next two hours. She considered calling and rescheduling the lunch for eleven—it would be easier to get a seat at the earlier time—but both Diane and Janet were at work, and she wasn't sure they'd be able to get off. She settled for e-mailing them, and received two quick replies, informing her that neither could meet any earlier.

Claire shook her head as she read the e-mails. She had learned to read and write before the advent of the online age and still felt out of place in the e e cummings world of the Internet, where nothing was capitalized, periods were known as *dots*, and the normal rules of grammar and punctuation did not apply.

At least her sister had spelled everything correctly.

Sighing, she leaned back in her chair. Shouldn't more people be suing one another during a recession? When times were tough, weren't people supposed to look for easy money and big payouts? The business of law didn't really work that way, but that was the common perception, and she was a little surprised herself to find just how untrue it was. Right now, all she had on her plate were a couple of divorces, a dog bite case and a property-line dispute.

She was meeting with the client disputing the property line this afternoon. The paperwork was pretty well finished on the other three cases, so there wasn't anything for her to do until she met with those clients later in the week.

Claire glanced out the window, where David Molina was carrying out a metal rack of paperbacks and putting it next to the door of his bookstore. She contemplated routing the office phone to her cell and just going home for the next hour, but the woman bitten by the dog had been a walk-in, and she couldn't take a chance that she might miss someone else coming in off the street. She needed the business.

On a whim, she e-mailed Liz Hamamoto, the only person from her old Los Angeles firm with whom she still kept in touch. She hadn't spoken or written to Liz since they'd decided to move, and she made up for that by writing a long multipage message describing the new house in detail, as well as their reasons for moving, and providing Liz with her new address.

Now David was adding new paperbacks to the rack.

She was glad they'd bought the house. Just being able to walk to and from work made a huge difference, and she felt more a part of Jardine now than she had even as a child. Over the past few weeks, she'd actually made the acquaintance of some of the newer business owners, people whose establishments she'd driven by in the past and scarcely noticed. Downtown felt more like a community to her now rather than just a work destination, and if nothing else, their new home had helped integrate her more fully into the professional life of the town, which she hoped would pay dividends in increased business down the road.

The phone rang, a woman with questions about sexual harassment, and while discussing it would have counted as a consultation back in Los Angeles—and would have required Claire to meet with the woman in person and charge for the time—things were more informal here in Jardine, and she answered questions over the phone (though as vaguely as possible), hoping the woman would retain her services. She hung up having received neither a promise nor a commitment. But she had a good feeling, which was something, at least.

Claire glanced up at the clock. Fifteen more minutes. She looked outside again. The day was nice, and though she'd originally intended to drive to the restaurant, which was several streets over, she decided to walk. If she went down to the end of the block and cut across the park, it would probably be just as fast as sitting through all of those crowded stoplights and left-turn lanes as everyone took their lunch hours. Besides, she'd get some exercise and fresh air.

She turned off her computer, switched her phone so it went to voice mail on the second ring, picked up her purse and locked up the office. Outside, she waved to David across the street, shouted a hello to Pam Lowry, who was sweeping the sidewalk in front of her Cool Kids Clothing boutique, then headed down the street toward the park.

There was a rally on the field next to the playground, an angry middle-aged man with a megaphone railing against both high taxes and the president to a group of overweight men and women wearing slogan-festooned T-shirts. Claire was tempted to point out that taxes for lower-middle-class people like them had gone *down* under the current president, but they looked like a humorless bunch, and she was sure the irony would be lost on them. She recalled, a few years back, seeing on the news a self-contradicting placard stating, KEEP YOUR GOVERNMENT HANDS OFF MY MEDICARE! The thought of it made her smile even now, and she passed by the edge of the crowd, keeping a wide berth around a red-faced older woman who was shaking her fist in the air and shouting, "I want my country back!"

When did people get so angry? Claire wondered.

Maybe they'd always been angry. Maybe her perception that things used to be calmer and more civilized was just plain wrong. But it seemed to her that people these days, even in small towns, perhaps *especially* in small towns, had lost whatever sense of tolerance had enabled America to forge a unified nation out of the diverse peoples that coexisted within its borders.

The man with the megaphone was now talking about changing the Constitution so that immigrant babies born in the United States would not automatically be citizens.

"Yeah!" a man shouted.

Claire hurried through the park.

She got to the restaurant before her sister and her friend, who were both late, and got a table. Fazio's was not only the most popular Italian restaurant in Jardine, but since the introduction of the Express Meal ("At Your Table in Five Minutes or It's Free!"), it had become the town's most popular lunch spot, period. The crowds were already starting to arrive, and Claire was lucky she got there when she did, because by the time Diane arrived, and then Janet, several minutes later, all of the tables were taken and the waiting area near the front door was filled.

They ordered—iced teas all around, small salads and different types of pasta for each of them—and while they snacked on bread and waited for their food to arrive, Diane mentioned that she'd driven by the rally in the park on her way over. "What was that all about?" she asked. "I didn't hear anything about it."

"Political rally," Claire told her sister. "Patriots who want to take back our country."

"Oh, shit." Diane rolled her eyes. "Was it that anti-Mexican group?"

"I'm sure they were there."

"How can they stand to live in this state?" Diane wondered. "This is America. And they're in New *Mexico*? That has to drive them crazy."

"There's a lot of anti-immigrant sentiment out there," Claire agreed.

"Anti-*illegal* immigrant sentiment," Janet clarified.

"Come *on*!" Diane smacked her palm down on the table, and Claire had to smile. Her sister had lost none of her political fervor over the years. "No one's worried about white people sneaking into the country, or talking about putting up a fence between us and Canada. This is racism, pure and simple."

"Not exactly—" Janet started to say.

"Are you kidding? They're talking about making it illegal for day laborers to stand in front of the hardware store. They hate Mexicans so much that in order to get rid of them they want to ban *work*!"

"It's to keep immigrants from taking American jobs."

"That's not even a concept you believe in. Do you mean to tell me that if you got offered a job with a company in Italy or Canada or France, you don't think you'd have the right to take it? Can you honestly say that you would become an Italian or Canadian or French citizen, and *then* you'd take the job? Bullshit! You'd sign up immediately, because you think you have the right to work anywhere at any time. As you *should*. As *everyone* should."

Janet clearly disagreed, but she didn't want to risk Diane's wrath, so she said nothing. Claire changed the subject. "Anybody hear from Sherry lately?" Sherry was one of their friends who had relocated to Tucson in order to move in with a man she'd met online.

"No," Diane said.

Janet shook her head. "I don't know *what* happened to her."

The food arrived, and the conversation drifted to safer topics. Claire learned that Janet's mother was finally going in for hip replacement surgery, and that Diane's supervisor at the electric company was being transferred to Bernalillo, which meant that if Diane played her cards right, she could be next in line for the position.

"Congratulations!" Claire told her sister. She held up her iced tea, and the other two followed suit, clinking their glasses together.

After lunch, both Diane and Janet offered her a ride, but Claire declined, saying she could use the exercise. She waved good-bye to her sister and their friend as the two women drove off, then decided to go home for a couple of minutes and pick up a few bottles of cold water before heading back to her office. Clients always liked bottled water. It gave the appearance of success, which instilled confidence—half the battle in the initial stages of the attorney-client relationship.

Claire cut through the park again, but the rally was basically over, and only a few stragglers stood around, reinforcing one another's opinions through heated, one-sided exchanges with imaginary adversaries. She skirted their area, going around a sandy playground where young mothers pushed small children on swings or down slides, and, once out of the park, she walked the three blocks to their house.

The kids were gone for the afternoon, Megan to her friend Zoe's, James to the community pool with Robbie's family. Julian was always home, of course, and Claire shouted a greeting up to him as she walked inside, closing the front door behind her. She had to pee and went down the hall to use the bathroom before heading into the kitchen to grab some cold bottles of Arrowhead to take back with her.

The laundry basket was sitting on the floor in front of the refrigerator.

Claire frowned. Hadn't she put that away this morning? She certainly hadn't left it in the middle of the kitchen. She glanced toward the laundry room, but neither the washer nor dryer was on, and there was no indication that Julian had done another batch of clothes. She shook her head. Maybe it *had* been her. Come to think of it, the same thing had happened the other day. She'd swept and mopped the kitchen floor and thought she'd put both the broom and mop away in the closet where they belonged— yet, an hour later, she'd found the broom leaning against a wall in the master bathroom. Obviously she'd intended to clean the bathroom and had just spaced out, but she was pretty sure she'd put both cleaning implements away. She smiled to herself. Maybe she needed to start taking ginkgo biloba. Or eating more blueberries. Weren't blueberries supposed to be good for the memory?

There was the sound of music from Julian's office upstairs. *Loud* music. One of those obscure old rock records that Julian, in his geeky way, prided himself on owning. She wasn't sure why he couldn't use earphones like everyone else and keep his music to himself, leaving the rest of them in peace, but he insisted on blasting his ancient stereo and subjecting the entire household to whatever he felt like hearing.

"Turn it down!" she shouted up at the ceiling.

He obviously didn't hear her, so she moved to the bottom of the stairs. She recognized the music now. The Men They Couldn't Hang, a group whose music he'd played incessantly when they'd first started dating.

"Julian!" she shouted as loud as she could. "Turn it down!"

The music switched off. Or was turned so low that she could no longer hear it.

"Thank you!" she called out.

Seconds later, the back door opened, and Julian came walking through the kitchen. "Were you calling me?" he asked.

Claire jumped, startled. She glanced up the stairs, then over at her husband.

He looked as confused as she felt. "What?" he asked.

"You weren't upstairs?"

"No, I was in the garage, looking for a box of old instruction manuals that I can't seem to find."

"I heard music. From upstairs."

"That's not possible."

"I heard it."

"What kind of music?"

"The Men They Couldn't Hang."

"I was listening to one of their records earlier this morning."

"Did you turn off the record player? Maybe it could've—"

"No, it couldn't. Besides, I put the record away. It's not even on the turntable."

She looked again at the stairwell, her mouth suddenly dry. "Then someone's upstairs. Because they just turned it on a few minutes ago, and then switched it off when I yelled to turn it down."

"No one's upstairs," Julian said.

"I know what I heard."

"We'll check it out." Moving carefully, walking quietly, Julian led the way upstairs. The door to his office was open, the room empty. A quick check of the other upstairs rooms revealed that they were empty as well.

They went back into Julian's office, and he strode directly over to his stereo. "Huh," he said, glancing down at the record on the turntable.

Claire looked down at the round blue-sky MCA label in the center of the black vinyl album, reading the words. The Men They Couldn't Hang. *How Green Is the Valley.*

She didn't like the unsettling feeling creeping up on her. "How could this happen?"

"I don't know." He seemed genuinely puzzled, though not as worried as she thought he should be. "I know I put that record away."

"Then how did it get here?"

He shook his head, confused. "I have no idea. Maybe I just thought I put it away. Or maybe I . . . forgot."

"But how did it—"

"I don't know. I guess I could have left it on before I went outside. There could be a problem with the sound, which is why it got loud and soft. . . ."

"Yeah," she agreed quickly. "That's probably it." But she heard the hopefulness in her own voice and realized even as she latched onto that explanation how vague it was and how many questions it still left unresolved.

She took a deep breath. "You didn't by any chance bring the laundry basket out into the kitchen, did you?" she asked.

"No," he said, frowning. "Why?"

She shook her head slowly, still staring at the record as a chill caressed the back of her neck. "No reason," she said. "No reason."

FIVE

MEGAN FROWNED AT HER IPHONE, TRYING TO MAKE SENSE OF THE
Twitter message on-screen. There was nothing she hated more
than those abbreviations made from various combinations of numbers, letters and punctuation marks. Such shorthand had probably
been convenient once upon a time, but now using that sort of code
was little more than a measure of hipness. Trends these days
changed so quickly that she had a hard time keeping up, and when
she encountered something unfamiliar, she was afraid to ask what
it meant for fear that her friends would laugh at her.

She wondered whether that was what was going on here.

MPD L2? 8LIF (XXXQ) DDF: 3907!

She read the message again, just as confused the second time.
She could not even tell who it was from, and finally she exited the
screen, deciding to ignore it.

Sighing heavily, Megan shifted on her bed and stared out the
window at the wood shake roof of the single-story house next
door. The driveway was empty, and she assumed that the people
who lived there weren't home. But, then again, they never seemed
to be home. As far as she could tell, the entire neighborhood was
filled with old people and shut-ins. The place was like a morgue,
and the only time anyone came out was in the late afternoon,
when couples walked their dogs or fitness fanatics jogged.

She hadn't seen anyone here her own age.

She wished that her family hadn't moved. *All* of her friends now lived farther away, and seeing them was not just inconvenient; it was downright difficult. That would change once school started, but this summer she felt more isolated and alone than she ever had in her life.

It was James's fault. If that little punk hadn't been such a pansy, they could've stayed in their old house and she could be at Kate's right now, watching a movie or . . . or . . . doing *something*.

In two years, she'd have her driver's license, and none of this would matter so much. But until then . . .

Her iPhone beeped, and Megan picked it up off the bedspread next to her, hoping it was a message from one of her friends.

I C U

She frowned. There was no sender name, no address.

That was weird.

The phone beeped again as another message came in.

I C U Megan

That was not just weird. It was creepy. Instinctively, she looked around. No one could possibly be watching her here, but she felt as though she was being spied upon, and she had a sudden need to make sure no one *could* see her. Carefully, she peered out the window again, checking the side yard of the house next door. Spotting no one, she shut the shade and moved to the other window, overlooking the front yard. Staying back in the shadows, so as not to be visible, she scanned the street, the sidewalk, their front yard, the yard across the street.

Nothing.

She shut that shade, too.

Turning around, Megan looked through her open doorway into the hall. It seemed more shadowy than it should, particularly for the middle of the afternoon. "Dad?" she called.

"What?" His reassuring voice answered her from across the hall, and she relaxed, the tension in her muscles dissipating.

"Nothing!" she said gratefully. She turned back toward the

center of the room. With the shades drawn, it was as dark as it could get during the daytime, and she was about to turn on the light when the iPhone beeped in her hand.

She looked down at it.

IL C U 2NITE

In one movement, she switched off the phone and threw it on the bed, crying out as she did so and shaking her hands as though to rid them of slime.

"Everything all right in there?" her dad called.

Staring at the phone on the bedspread, Megan thought about telling him, *wanted* to tell him, but she knew how he got, and she knew what he'd do. He'd take away her phone, which, as far as she was concerned, would punish her, not protect her.

It was better to keep quiet.

"Megan?" He poked his head in the doorway.

She forced herself to smile at him. "I'm fine, Dad. There's nothing wrong. Everything's fine."

HER FATHER HAD MET HIS DEADLINE AND SUCCESSFULLY COM-pleted his most recent project, so, for the first time in a long while, their family went out to dinner to celebrate. Megan was in the mood for Mexican food, while James wanted to go to Fazio's because they had pizza, but, as always, their parents were the ones who got to decide, so they ended up at that lame hippie health-food restaurant Radicchio. That was bad enough. But what made it worse was the fact that Brad Bishop was sitting with his dad two tables over. She ignored him, and he ignored her, but Megan knew he saw her, just as she saw him. It was impossible to be cool when you were with your parents, and she settled for act-ing bored and above it all, as though she'd been forced to come here. She tried not to look over at Brad but couldn't help glancing up at him periodically. Each time she did, he seemed as bored as she was pretending to be.

Dinner lasted way longer than it should have. Service, as always, was poor, and one of their parents' friends stopped by to chat, which made her want to sink into the floor with embarrassment. Luckily, Brad and his dad left soon after, and while they passed directly by her family's table on their way out, neither she nor Brad acknowledged each other.

It had been light out when they arrived, but it was dark when they left, and Megan wondered what time it was. It seemed like they'd been in that stupid restaurant for hours. "Great celebration," she said sarcastically.

"It was, wasn't it?" Her dad was either genuinely oblivious or pretending to be oblivious in order to antagonize her, but she refused to take the bait and engage him. Instead, she opened the door of the van and got in.

A few blocks later, near the park, the van's headlights illuminated a yellow sign at the side of the road: SLOW CHILDREN PLAYING.

"Look out for retarded kids," she told James.

"Megan!" her dad said sternly.

"That's what the sign says."

"I see one!" James announced.

"James!"

The two of them giggled.

They arrived home a few moments later. Her parents never let her keep her phone on when they were out in public doing family activities, so the first thing Megan did when she got inside was turn on her phone and check for messages. There was one text she'd missed, and she immediately announced that she'd be in her room and headed upstairs, not wanting James or her parents to see the message. It was probably from Zoe, and for her eyes only.

There was a split second of hesitation as she reached the top of the steps—

IL C U 2NITE

—but then she heard the sound of James's footsteps coming up the stairs behind her, she flipped on the hall light, and all was normal. Walking over and into her bedroom, she turned on both the ceiling light and the lamp on her desk before closing the door and checking the text.

?*#%$&?!

It looked like those symbols that were strung together in order to depict obscenities in comic books.

Maybe it was Zoe, she thought doubtfully, although it didn't make a whole lot of sense and didn't seem like something the other girl would send.

Megan pressed her friend's speed-dial number, but Zoe did not answer right away, like she usually did, and after six rings there was a message, Zoe talking in a subdued, dispirited voice: "I cannot use my cell phone right now. If you wish to speak to me, please call my home phone."

Megan dialed her friend's home phone, and Zoe's mom answered. "Hello?"

"Hello, Mrs. Dunbar? This is Megan. May I speak to Zoe?"

"Oh, Megan! How are you? Hold on a sec; I'll get her."

Zoe came on the line, and there were a few moments of awkward innocuous chitchat until her mother left the room. "Okay," she said finally. "What's up?"

"Did you text me earlier? About an hour ago?"

"No. How could I? My mom took my phone away because my stupid sister caught me talking to Kate when I was supposed to be pulling weeds. I can't get it back until Monday!"

"Well, *someone* texted me, but I can't tell who, and it doesn't make sense. It's like those exclamation points and question marks and apostrophes that they use instead of swear words."

"You always know if it's from me. I don't block anything."

"Yeah." She almost told Zoe about the other messages she'd received, but her friend started complaining about her sister and her mom, and it didn't seem like the right time to bring it up. Zoe went on to tell her that Kate had seen Jenny Sanchez at Dairy Queen yesterday and she had really short hair and it was blond!

"Why would she do that?" Megan wondered.

"God knows."

"Oh, that reminds me," Megan said. "I saw Brad at Radicchio."

"When?"

"Just now. We got back, like, five minutes ago."

"No one's seen him since school got out! I heard he moved."

"Obviously not."

"Who was he with?"

"His dad."

"His parents got divorced, you know. At the end of last year."

"I know. And his dad got custody. Which means that his mom must be really . . ."

"Yeah." There was a pause. "Did you talk to him?"

"No!"

"*I* would've," Zoe insisted.

From the hallway outside Megan's door came the sound of running footsteps as James hurried back downstairs.

She wished he were staying up here.

"Are you still there?" Zoe said. "Hel-*lo*?"

"I'm here."

"You should've at least waved to him or said hi. This was your chance."

Megan reddened, glad that her friend couldn't see her.

From somewhere in the background came the sound of Zoe's mom's voice: "Time's up."

"I have to go." Zoe's tone was formal and subdued. "She *times* me," she whispered into the receiver. "I can't use my phone and I can't talk for more than five minutes on *any* phone."

"Zoe," her mom said loudly.

"Gotta go. Bye."

Megan was left holding a silent phone to her ear as the connection was terminated, and she quickly shut the phone off, feeling nervous.

IL C U 2NITE

Even with all of the lights on, the room did not seem as safe as it should have, as it usually did. Looking around, she saw a poorly cleaned section on the drawn front shade, more off-white than the surrounding area, that resembled the shadow of a man's head. A seeping coolness made her wonder whether the window behind that shade was open. Atop her desk, two books were out that she could not remember leaving there. Had someone moved them to that spot while rifling through her room?

She was being stupid. She was in her own bedroom, in her own house, and it was probably the safest place on earth she could be.

Ordinarily, she would have gone online and browsed for a while, but Megan realized as she looked at her laptop that she was afraid to turn it on. She thought once more of that message she'd received this afternoon—

IL C U 2NITE

—and shivered. Her shades were all closed, but she checked them again anyway, making sure all cracks were sealed and no one could see in. The room seemed quiet, *too* quiet, and she turned on her iPod.

She knew that other sounds could hide under music, however, and rather than reassuring her, the iPod made her feel even more anxious. She was all alone up here, Megan realized, and immediately she turned off the music, dropped the iPod on her bed and sped downstairs to watch a TV show she didn't like with her surprised but happy parents. And James.

Two hours of comedies and karaoke contests later, her nerves were calmed, her sense of normalcy restored, and her earlier anxiety seemed like a horrendous overreaction. It was time for bed, and both she and James said good night to their parents and headed upstairs to their bedrooms. For once, she was glad to have her brother with her, and though they didn't speak as they trod up the steps, she was grateful for his presence and actually bade him good night before entering her bedroom and closing the door.

Often, Megan stayed up later than she was supposed to—that was the advantage of having a two-story house and a bedroom on a floor different from her parents'. She'd read or listen to music or even text her friends if they were still up. But tonight she was tired. It might have been only ten o'clock, but it felt like midnight to her. So she changed into her pajamas, walked down the hall to the bathroom, where she washed her face and brushed her teeth, then crawled into bed. Usually, she liked to sleep with the lights off, but this time she left the desk lamp on. She could hear James moving around down the hall, though he was supposed to be in bed, too. Under normal circumstances, she'd yell at him to go to sleep, threaten to tell their parents, but tonight she was grateful for the noise, and she closed her eyes and within minutes had drifted off.

She awoke in darkness.

She'd been lured out of sleep by the soft sound of an electronic beep, although she heard nothing now. Somehow her lamp had been turned off, and she chose to believe that one of her parents had come in to check on her and switched it off. The thought was comforting.

There was another beep, and Megan rolled over onto her side. She'd turned off her iPhone before going to bed, as she always did, but on the nightstand next to her she could see the light from the screen in the darkness. She sat up, leaning on her elbow, and looked over to see what was going on.

There was a message, white letters against a blue background. Bleary-eyed, she read it, her heart pounding.

☺, it said. *I C U!*

SIX

JULIAN HAD THE DREAM AGAIN, THE FIRST TIME IN OVER A YEAR, and he awoke sweaty and disoriented, not sure for a moment where he was. Then the shadowed features of the room resolved themselves into recognizable shapes—dresser, lamp, picture, chair—and he realized that he was in their bedroom, in their new house, and Claire was lying next to him. He quickly glanced over at her, and was relieved to see that she hadn't awakened. Last time she had, and when she'd questioned him, he'd been forced to invent a fake nightmare to describe.

He had never told her about the Dream.

Julian carefully pulled the covers from on top of him and slid out of bed, padding over to the bathroom. Closing the door, he turned on the light, staring at himself in the mirror. He looked as wrecked as he felt, and he took a still-damp washcloth from the towel rack and used it to wipe the sweat from his face. His heart was thumping wildly, and he was grateful that this time the fear had overpowered the sadness. For the sadness generated by the Dream was almost more than he could bear, a deep despair that negated everything good that had happened in his life, that wiped out the joy of his wife and his children and brought him back emotionally to that dark, dark day.

The fear was bad, but it was far preferable.

He experienced that fear now, an emotional vestige of the Dream even more lasting than the nightmare images that remained in his head. It was terror and panic and impotence and frustration, all knotted together in a single overwhelming feeling that would not go away. It was the way he'd actually felt on that day, and though it was something he'd never forgotten, something that was never very far from his mind, the Dream always brought it into crystal clear focus and made him relive it all over again.

His mouth was dry, and he picked up the plastic tumbler next to his electric toothbrush and got a drink of water from the faucet. He didn't like drinking bathroom water, which always seemed suspect to him, but he was grateful for it now.

Switching off the light and poking his head back into the bedroom, he saw that Claire was still asleep. He would not be able to sleep for a while, maybe not for the rest of the night, and, not wanting to disturb her, he crept through the bedroom and walked out to the living room, where he turned on the television, hoping for something to distract him. News was good, and he switched the channel to CNN. But there was no real news, only an in-depth update on a fame-seeking woman who had gained notoriety for having a lot of children. He flipped through other channels and ended up watching a documentary about ice fishing for twenty minutes or so before shutting off the TV.

Still wide-awake, he decided to go upstairs and check on the kids: a habit left over from their early childhood that still gave him comfort. At the top of the steps, he heard murmuring from Megan's room and smiled. She often talked in her sleep, one-sided conversations of several sentences, and while more often than not the words were gibberish, the sentences nonsense, occasionally he or Claire had been able to make out individual phrases that, when repeated to their daughter in the morning, jogged her memory and helped her recall her dreams. He moved quietly down the hall, careful not to wake either her or her brother.

The talking continued, and Julian frowned as he drew closer.

That didn't sound like Megan's voice. It didn't even sound like a girl's voice.

It sounded like a man's voice.

He sprinted the last few feet to his daughter's bedroom and, frantic, panicked, pushed open the door.

She was asleep, in bed, alone. Enough light shone in from the hallway for him to see that there was no one else in the room, but just to make sure, he walked around to the other side of her bed and even crouched down on the floor to look under it. The talking had stopped, and he wondered whether he had imagined it. Probably not. Megan *was* a sleep talker. But some fearful part of his brain, stimulated perhaps by the Dream, had no doubt lowered her voice a few registers in his mind and given him the impression that a man was in her room.

Moving quietly, he opened her closet and moved his hands through her clothes, feeling along the wall to make sure no one was hiding there. No one was. And the windows, when he checked them, were closed.

Megan was safe and sound.

He bent over her sleeping form and gave her a quick kiss on the cheek. If she'd awakened at that moment, she would have recoiled and told him to go away, frowning in disgust. He felt a small twinge of sadness as he recalled how she used to *like* him to kiss her, especially before she went to sleep at night. He missed that younger Megan and wished, not for the first time, that she never had to grow up and would remain his little girl forever.

He patted her back, then went over to James's room to check on his son. The boy had kicked off his blanket and was sprawled out on his bed in what looked like a very uncomfortable position. Julian drew the blanket back up and kissed his son on the forehead. James wasn't big on kissing, either, although right now he didn't mind hugs. It was going to be sad when that changed.

Just in case, he searched James's room for an intruder, too. And though there was no way anyone could have passed by in the hall without his seeing it, he looked through his office and the bathroom as well.

The upstairs was clear, all was safe, and Julian went back down the steps, returned to his bedroom, crawled in bed next to Claire and, though he expected to remain awake for at least another hour, promptly fell asleep.

In the morning, he woke late, although it was a summer Saturday and so didn't much matter. Claire was already up, her side of the bed cold, and the aroma of toasted blueberry bagel permeated the house. Julian pushed off the covers, put on his bathrobe and headed out to the kitchen, where he was greeted by empty plates in an empty breakfast nook. Through the windows, he could see Claire, still in her robe and slippers, checking out her herb garden. The kids, he assumed, were in their bedrooms getting dressed or in the family room watching TV.

The package of precut bagels was still open on the counter, and he pulled two apart and popped them into the toaster oven, pouring himself some orange juice from a carton he took out of the refrigerator. As he waited for the bagels, he glanced over at the Nature Conservancy calendar Claire had tacked up on the wall next to the door. Beneath the July photo of a mother and baby coyote was a red X marking the date on which they'd moved into the house. It had been more than three weeks already, and he realized that they had yet to meet a single one of their neighbors. There'd been no welcome wagon when they'd arrived, no one had come over to say hello, and though Claire had made an effort to stop by the houses on both sides that first week, no one had been home. Things had been so hectic ever since, what with the unpacking and settling in, that they'd kind of forgotten about introducing themselves to the neighbors.

Julian thought about the Willet boy and his skate-punk friends in their old neighborhood and decided that they really should try to get off on the right foot here. Today was as good a day as any, since they had no plans and would all be home. The toaster rang; he took out his bagels, buttered them, put them on a plate and walked barefoot into the backyard to discuss his thoughts with Claire. She, too, thought it would be a good idea to meet the neighbors, and they decided to visit the houses to either side of them around ten o'clock. It was a civilized hour, not too early, not too late.

Before taking a shower, Julian told both kids the plan, warning them not to go anywhere, and though they each moaned and complained in their own unique ways, there was no real resistance, and he could tell that they were curious about the neighbors as well. There didn't seem to be any kids on the street—a good thing, as far as he was concerned—but these days who could tell? The surrounding houses might be filled with boys and girls who spent their days bent over their DSs or playing with their Wiis or Xboxes, never seeing sunlight. In a way, he hoped that was the case. Especially for James's sake. It would be nice for the boy to have a friend next door.

Shortly after ten, all four of them walked over to the house on the north side of theirs, a single-story structure with an unimaginative but well-maintained lawn and an impressive picture window in the front. There was no vehicle in the driveway, but that didn't mean the neighbors weren't home. Maybe they parked their car in the garage. Or maybe the husband or the wife had gone to the store, and the remaining spouse was still at home. Or maybe they had a teenage son or daughter who had borrowed the family car to go somewhere with his or her friends.

Thinking over the possibilities, Julian was struck not just by how little he knew about their neighbors but by how pathetically unobservant he was. They could be living next to a ninety-year-old widow, or a twenty-five-year-old bachelor, or a gay couple or an extended family of Chinese immigrants, and he wouldn't know— even though he worked at home and was there almost all the time. It was embarrassing, really, and he vowed in the future to be a little more aware and try to pay attention to his surroundings.

He let James ring the doorbell, and as they waited for someone to answer, Julian tried to peek through the picture window. The drapes were open, but it was dark inside the house and hard to see. He could make out a pale couch and a generic-looking lamp atop an unseen table.

"I don't think anyone's home," Claire said.

Megan turned away. "Let's go."

"Wait a minute." Julian knocked on the door—loudly, in case the bell didn't work and the residents were in the back of the house—then knocked again, but after several moments it became obvious that Claire was right. There was no one home.

"Other neighbors," Julian announced, and led the way back up the footpath to the sidewalk. The house on the other side of theirs *did* have a car in the driveway, he saw as they approached. A silver Toyota sedan that told him virtually nothing about the owners. He looked over the house. It was two stories and similar in style to theirs, the only other home on this eclectic block that appeared to have been built by the same contractor.

Claire and the kids followed Julian as he strode up to the front door. Before he could even knock or ring the bell, the door was opened by a smiling bearded man his age or a little younger who was standing slightly in front of a short, chubby woman who was obviously his wife. The two must have seen them coming up the walk.

"Hello," the man said, extending a hand. "Nice to finally meet you. I'm Bob Ribiero and this is my wife, Elise. I know you moved in next door, and we've seen you around, but we didn't want to bother you, wanted to give you a chance to settle in first."

Julian was slightly thrown off by the man's earnestness, but he shook the proffered hand. "I'm Julian Perry. This is my wife, Claire, my daughter, Megan, and my son, James."

Bob remained where he was, and though he smiled and said hello to each member of the family, repeating their names as he did so, he made no effort to invite them in. His wife moved forward next to him, said hello as well, but it seemed to Julian that she had stepped up not to meet them but to block the doorway. Maybe it was nothing; maybe the house was just messy and they didn't want visitors to see, but Julian felt awkward, and it was a struggle to keep a conversation going. He told them that he was a Web designer and Claire was a lawyer, found out that Bob ran a nonemergency medical transport service ("Basically, I drive old people to and from the doctor") and that Elise did not work but volunteered a lot at their church. He also learned that the Ribieros had lived here for the past ten years, ever since they'd moved to Jardine from Alamogordo.

Megan and James were getting fidgety, and Julian used them as an excuse to leave. Everyone said good-bye, promising that they'd get together soon, and Julian and Claire headed back home, the kids running ahead, grateful to be free.

"They seem nice," Claire said finally.

Julian nodded. They did seem nice.

But . . .

But blocking the doorway was strange. And there was a reserve about everything Bob and Elise had said. It was almost as if they were hiding something, and he couldn't help wondering what that something might be.

JULIAN SAT IN HIS OFFICE, SHADES PULLED AGAINST THE SETTING sun, although orange light continued to seep between the cracks, striping the furniture and the opposite wall of the room with cinematically noirish bars. He was supposed to be working on a new project for an upscale retailer in Santa Fe, but for the past twenty minutes he'd been staring at the screen saver on his computer—twisting, multicolored, geometric designs—and zoning out. He sometimes got good ideas when allowing his mind to wander or go blank, but not today, and as the angle of the sun shifted, causing one of the orange light bars to cut across his field of vision, he thought that he might as well just call it a day. Claire's parents were coming over tonight, along with her sister's family, and he should probably head downstairs anyway.

He was dreading the visit. It was a social obligation, one of those things they had to do, although as far as he was concerned,

Claire's parents had already come over and taken a tour of the house, as had Diane and her family, and that was good enough. Claire, however, had insisted on inviting everyone for dinner, and he was going to have to put on his best face and make nice.

That was easier said than done. Her mom was all right, but her dad was an angry, hostile man who never had a good word to say about anyone, especially Julian (although, to his credit, he did seem to genuinely like his grandchildren). And Diane's husband, Rob, was a redneck jerk. Julian liked Diane, but he had never been able to figure out how she'd ended up with such a loser.

Maybe he should stay up here until they left, pretend that he had a lot of work to do and a rapidly approaching deadline to meet. Moving the mouse, he disrupted his screen saver to display a very sketchy prototype of a Web site.

Moments later, James came in quietly—as usual—entering the office as unobtrusively as possible. Neither Julian nor Claire had ever been the sort of parents to make their children knock before entering a room. Such a thing seemed too formal and distancing. But, on his own, James had developed the habit of coming into the office silently, so as not to disturb his father, waiting patiently until he was noticed.

Julian popped in a disk and saved what little work he'd done this afternoon, swiveling around to face his son. "Hey, James."

"I'm sorry to bother you. . . ."

"Knock off that craziness. Just be normal."

James smiled, moving next to him. "Okay. Sorry."

Julian took out the disk and switched off his computer, standing up.

"Dad?"

"Yeah?"

James looked at him with utter seriousness. "Is it okay if I don't like sports?"

That had come out of nowhere. But it was obvious from the expression on his face that it was something that greatly concerned the boy, and Julian, touched, put an arm around his son's shoulder. "Of course," he said. "What would make you ask something like that?"

"Megan said you think I'm a wuss and you're ashamed of me. She said it's because I don't like to play sports."

Julian suppressed a smile. "Don't listen to your sister," he told James. "You know she just says things like that to annoy you." He turned the boy to face him, putting one hand on each shoulder and looking him straight in the eye. "You are who you are. And whatever you like or don't like is fine with me. Everyone's different. As my grandma used to tell me, 'It takes all kinds to make a world.'"

James looked relieved.

Julian smiled kindly. "You're my son. I love you no matter what." His smile broadened. "Besides, if I didn't know by now that you hate PE and like playing video games, I'd be a real moron."

James grinned. "Well . . ."

He gave his son a hug, grateful once again that the boy still allowed him to do so.

"We'd better go downstairs," Julian said. "Your grandma and grandpa will be here pretty soon."

"Can I just stay with them tonight? I don't want to play with Mike and Terry."

Julian understood and sympathized. Like their father, James's cousins were wild and obnoxious. But as he explained to his son, he was closer in age to them than Megan, and a boy, and since they were coming over to his house, it was his job to be a good host and entertain them. "Tell you what, though," he said. "You don't have to stay in your room with them. I'll let you guys hang out in the living room and watch TV. Put on anything you want. Cartoons. That should keep them occupied."

"And Grandma and Grandpa can stay with us!"

"If they want to."

That seemed to satisfy him, and the two of them headed downstairs together.

Their guests began arriving soon after: Claire's parents first, then her sister's family ten minutes later. As always, they ended up separating into groups, women in the kitchen, men in the living room, and Julian saw James shoot him a look of anger and betrayal as Claire herded the kids upstairs. He vowed to make it up to his son after dinner and rescue him, allowing James to hang out with the adults and letting the bratty cousins fend for themselves.

Claire's dad criticized the furniture arrangement, then complained about the comfort level of the chair he settled into, and Julian turned on the television, switching to an Albuquerque newscast, hoping the weather or sports or whatever was on would lead to a more general discussion. He would much rather have been in the kitchen with the women—their conversation was sure to be more interesting—but he was stuck here and knew he had to make the best of it.

On the television, a reporter was standing in front of a pueblo, talking to a Zuni spokesman about recent vandalism at one of the tribe's sacred sites.

"Don't even get me started on those Indians," Rob said.

This was not a subject Julian wanted to pursue, but Claire's dad took the bait. "What happened?"

"This *college* boy who's working for us found some pieces of pottery with his backhoe, so he went and told someone, and now the entire site's shut down for two weeks until they can dig up all that Indian crap. Meanwhile, we got a whole crew's not getting paid."

"Yeah," Julian said. "Those college boys are nothing but trouble. People should never try to get a higher education. It only leads to problems."

Rob's face turned red, though from anger or embarrassment, Julian couldn't tell. Claire shot him a warning glance from the kitchen doorway, and Julian knew he'd better keep his opinions to himself for the remainder of the evening.

Which he did, as hard as it was.

After dinner, Megan immediately went back upstairs to hide

in her room. Diane told her two boys they could go play, but before James could finish pushing out his chair and dejectedly follow them, Julian told his son that he could stay if he wanted or watch something in the living room. James shot him a grateful look that made it almost worth putting up with everything else.

Almost.

Luckily, everyone left early, with mutual assurances that they'd had a wonderful time, and after putting the kids to bed, Julian helped Claire with the dishes and both of them retired to the living room. "Long day," Julian said, settling onto the couch and flipping through channels on the television. He stopped on a rerun of the original *Star Trek*.

"Thank you," Claire told him, sitting down to his left.

"For what?"

"Putting up with them." She patted her lap, motioning for him to lie down and use it for a pillow. It was something they used to do a lot but had done less and less frequently over the years. When they were first married, they would watch movies this way, Blockbuster rentals, and sometimes, after a hard day at work, he would even fall asleep with her running her fingers gently through his hair, although, generally, it was a prelude to sex.

Laying his head on her lap now, he could smell her arousal, a heavy, musky odor that permeated the crotch of her jeans. The scent of her made *him* aroused, and he turned his head to the side, pressing his face into her and breathing deeply. Neither of them had to say a word after that. Julian sat up, then stood, and both of them walked down the hall to the bedroom, where they closed the door, locked it and got undressed.

He was already naked when Claire took off her panties, rubbing them gently in his face. He could feel their dampness.

"I bet your mama doesn't know you do that," he said.

"No one does." She bent over the side of the bed, presenting herself to him, and he took her roughly from behind as she screamed her pleasure into the thick quilted comforter so the kids wouldn't hear.

SEVEN

ROBBIE WASN'T TALKING.

The two of them were sitting on the field in the park, drinking Slurpees, while Robbie's younger brother, Max, practiced baseball with his Little League team. Robbie's dad was the team's coach, and he was having the kids take turns batting. James had just asked his friend about the night he'd stayed over, about why he'd been so desperate to leave. He was hoping to hear that Robbie had felt the same thing he had, and the reason he hadn't brought up the crying was that he didn't want Robbie to get all defensive. He wanted an honest answer.

But Robbie wasn't saying a word.

James changed the subject, talked about the latest episode of a Cartoon Network show they both watched, asked about the day camp where Robbie had spent the past week, complained about his annoying cousins who'd come over the other night, wondered about whose class they'd be in this year at school. But then he brought it back again: "How come you wanted to go home so bad?"

Robbie shrugged.

James tried another tack. "Do you want to stay overnight next weekend?"

"No!" his friend said quickly, then hastily added, "Maybe you could stay over at my house this time," saying it in a way that tried to make the notion seem casual and unimportant.

Actually, that sounded like a fine idea. Although James had managed to convince himself that their new home was friendly rather than creepy (with the exception of the basement—which he would *never* like), the truth was that he was often tense inside the house. If he was with Megan or one of his parents, or if he was busy with something such as reading, watching TV or playing a game, he was fine. But when he was by himself with nothing to do and time on his hands . . . well, then he started noticing things. Like the way the stairs creaked sometimes, even though no one was on them. Or the way some of the windows didn't let in as much light as they should. Or the way he saw movement out of the corner of his eye when nothing was there.

So the thought of staying overnight at Robbie's sounded like a relaxing respite.

"That'd be fun," James admitted.

"I'll ask my dad."

Robbie refocused his attention on the batting practice, and James saw his chance at a real discussion slipping away. Glancing over at his friend, he decided to come clean. "I don't like the basement in our house," he said. He watched for a reaction but saw none. "I think it's creepy."

Robbie didn't respond, continued to watch his brother's teammates swing at softly lobbed balls.

James didn't know what more he could say. Maybe he'd been wrong all along. Maybe Robbie *hadn't* been scared by the basement.

"I thought I saw something," his friend said finally. The boy spoke so softly that at first James wasn't sure he'd heard right. Robbie refused to look at him, his eyes remaining focused on the Little Leaguers. "In the cellar. Not when we first went down there. That was cool. But later, before we went to bed, when I went into the kitchen to get a glass of water. I was the only one in the kitchen, and it was kind of dark, and the cellar door was open. I didn't think it was open before; I remembered it being closed, and then I thought maybe your mom or dad was down there, getting something. So I walked by, peeked in. . . ." Robbie's voice trailed off. He stopped talking, suddenly becoming very interested in the latest batter, and for a moment James thought he was going to have to prod his friend to continue. But then Robbie said, "It looked like there was a man down there. Maybe there wasn't, but it looked like there was, and I got scared and hurried back to where you were."

James suddenly felt cold.

"I had a nightmare about it when I fell asleep. You were right about that, but I didn't want to talk about it."

"What was it about?"

"The same thing that happened. I went to get a drink of water, the cellar door was open, and I walked past it and saw a man down there. It wasn't your dad. I couldn't see all of his face, but I could see his mouth. His smile. He was smiling up at me and it was like his teeth were glowing, and . . . and I knew he wanted me to go down into the basement. I think . . . I think he wanted to kill me. Then he said my name. . . ." Robbie sucked in his breath. "That's why I wanted to go home."

Even here in the park, in the open, surrounded by people, James was frightened. But he refused to give in to fear, forcing himself to be brave. He decided not to tell his friend that he, too, had had a nightmare about the cellar and that their two dreams were very close. *Too* close. Instead he said, "It's just a dream."

"You're afraid of the basement, too," Robbie pointed out.

"But it's *just* the basement," James insisted. "My *room's* not scary at all. In fact, it's great. I'd live in there twenty-four hours a day if I could."

"I like your room," Robbie admitted.

"See?"

"And your garage."

"Me, too!"

"Last year, my dad read me this book. It was one of *his* old books, and it was about these two kid detectives, about our age. One of them was this genius named Brains Benton, and he had a secret lab above his parents' garage. That's what yours kind of reminded me of."

"We could do something like that!" James said excitedly. "No one really goes into the garage, and I bet my dad would let us use the loft!"

"That would be cool!"

They started talking about what they could do, how they could make a secret entrance, have a couch and a TV up there, and they forgot all about the basement.

After baseball practice ended, Robbie's dad drove both of them back to James's house, telling Robbie that he'd be back to pick him up in around an hour, after he dropped Max off at home and ran a few errands. James announced to his dad that they were back; then he and Robbie went over to the garage, letting themselves in through the small side door. The garage *was* cool, he decided, looking around. Despite everything he'd said, he thought for a moment, when he first opened the door and his eyes had not yet adjusted to the darkness, that it might be scary, but it looked the same as it always had, and he gazed appreciatively at the wooden ladder attached to the far wall that led through a hole in the ceiling up to the loft.

It really was just the basement that was creepy, and James thought he could probably learn to live with that. There were plenty of people who lived in haunted houses and coexisted with ghosts. He'd seen a Discovery Channel show about celebrity ghost stories, and there were famous actors and rock stars who'd been living with ghosts for years. Some of the spirits were even friendly.

James recalled his dream of the dirty grinning man in the basement. *He* certainly wasn't friendly. But even if he existed, he was probably trapped there in the basement, and as long as James stayed out of that room, there should be no problem.

"Check it out!"

Robbie had climbed up the ladder and was peering down through the hole in the ceiling. James hurried up after him, and though he'd been up here before, he saw it now through new eyes and realized that he and Robbie really could make this into some sort of secret hideout. Maybe *they* could be detectives, he thought, and he imagined turning this room into a crime lab, with beakers and test tubes, microscopes and chemicals. Excitedly, the two of them began planning out what they needed to do to turn the loft into their crime-fighting headquarters.

Time passed quickly, and it seemed they'd been up there for only about ten minutes or so when James's dad called, "Boys!" Hurrying to the small window that looked out over the backyard, they saw both fathers standing on the back patio, waiting for them to come out of the garage.

"We need one-way glass on this window," Robbie said. "So we can see out but no one else can see in."

"Yeah," James agreed. "Coming!" he yelled down to his dad, and the two of them climbed back down the ladder and exited the building.

After Robbie left, James snagged some potato chips from the kitchen—trying not to look toward the closed door of the basement—and took them out to the living room to eat in front of the TV. But there were no good movies on, and only baby cartoons, and he soon got bored. He returned the Pringles canister to the kitchen, then headed upstairs, figuring he'd play on his computer or DS. His mom was still at work, and his dad was back in his office, but Megan was sitting on the floor of her bedroom, and, as he walked by, she asked in a voice loud enough for their dad to hear, "Want to play a game?"

That was weird.

It wasn't unheard-of—in fact, they used to play board games a lot during the summers when they were younger, before she'd turned into such a brat—but it *was* unusual, and he figured she was trying to show their dad how bored she was in order to get him to agree to let her go somewhere or do something with one of her friends. Beggars couldn't be choosers, however, and he *did* like playing games, so he agreed, stepping into her room. She pulled something off a shelf, then sat down on the rug, showing him what she held in her hands.

Old Maid.

He looked nervously at the battered red box. He'd never liked Old Maid. It wasn't the game, which was kind of fun; it was the Old Maid herself, the way she was depicted on this particular pack of cards. All of the other characters were humorous caricatures of cartoonish boys and girls. But the Old Maid was *old*, and the expression on her wrinkled face was one of barely suppressed rage: a flat hardness in the small eyes, a mouth set in a thin, angry line. He'd been afraid of that visage ever since he'd been little, and while he wanted to tell himself that he wasn't afraid of it anymore, he knew that wasn't true.

She was on the cover of the box, and even seeing her eyes peering out over Megan's fingers gave him the creeps.

He sat down on the floor as his sister took out the cards, shuffled them, then dealt them. He was directly across from her, and before picking up his own pile, he watched her sort through her cards. Megan was not good at hiding her emotions, and he knew he'd be able to tell whether or not she'd gotten the Old Maid. Seeing her smile after she'd fanned out the cards in her hand, he knew that she hadn't.

And he had.

He looked down at the flat blue backs of the cards on the floor before him, not wanting to pick them up, wishing he'd continued on to his own room, where, right now, he could be happily playing *Star Wars* on his DS, or *LEGO Harry Potter*. But he reached down, gathered up the cards from the floor and turned their faces toward him so Megan couldn't see.

There she was.

Between Hungry Henry and Sleeping Sam was the wrinkled countenance of the Old Maid. He could see only the left half of her face, but that was enough. Divorced from its twin, her left eye had an even crueler cast, and the flat portion of wrinkled mouth that was visible seemed not merely angry but malevolent. He pushed Sleeping Sam over so that the dozing boy was covering the Old Maid, then sorted through the rest of his cards, looking for doubles. He found two sets and discarded them, then, holding the remaining cards in front of him, fanned them out in his right hand and told Megan to pick.

Unfortunately, she did not pick the Old Maid. In fact, she never picked the Old Maid, and at the conclusion of a surprisingly short game, James ended up holding in his hand the one card he didn't want. He turned it facedown, placing it atop his discards, then stood. "I don't want to play anymore," he said.

Megan shrugged. "Fine. This is boring anyway." She said it loud enough for their dad to hear, and once again James thought he was probably just a pawn in his sister's bid for more freedom.

He walked over to his room, automatically closing the door as he went in, and picked up his DS. Through the window, he saw an elderly couple walking down the sidewalk. The woman turned her head to look at their house, but James quickly looked away, not wanting to see her. In his mind, she looked like the Old Maid, and, feeling cold, he walked back across the room, opening the door wide before turning on his DS and hopping onto his bed.

THEY ATE THAT EVENING IN THE DINING ROOM. EVER SINCE THEY'D moved, his mom had been on this kick, because she'd read somewhere or heard on the news that kids from families who ate dinner together every night turned out happier and more successful. In their old house, she'd been a lot more flexible. Sometimes he and Megan would eat in the living room and watch *The Simpsons* while his parents ate in the kitchen. Sometimes his dad would eat on the couch while watching the news or a basketball game. Sometimes James would play with his DS while he ate. Things weren't so rigid then. But these days, they all ate together, and more often than not, James found himself wishing that they didn't.

Tonight, Megan kept kicking him under the table while maintaining an expression of calm interest on her face as their mom endlessly described a lawsuit she was working on. Finally, he'd had enough and kicked his sister back *hard*—but his foot missed and hit the leg of the table, causing his milk to spill and everyone's chili beans to splash out of their bowls onto the tabletop. He got in trouble, despite his explanation, while across from him Megan smirked maddeningly.

They didn't speak to each other the rest of the evening, and James was happy when she went upstairs to her bedroom early. He remained with his parents, and the three of them watched TV together until his mom said, "It's getting late, and you stayed up way past your bedtime last night. I think it's time for you to go to bed."

He didn't feel tired, and, truthfully, his mom seemed sleepier than he did, but he wanted to go to bed while they were still awake, so he said good night and headed up to his room. Megan was in the bathroom, so he changed into his pajamas first and, after she got out, went in to brush his teeth. Returning to his room, he pulled down the covers—

And there, sitting on his pillow, was the Old Maid card.

He cried out, startled, jumping back and practically tripping over the shoes he'd left in the middle of the floor. He knew it was just a joke, Megan's doing, but his heart was pounding so hard that his chest hurt. He wasn't sure how she knew he was afraid of the card, but obviously she did, and she'd put it here to scare him. Which it had.

Breathing deeply, recovered from the initial shock, James took a step forward, intending to pick up the card, take it over to his sister's room and throw it in her face.

Only . . .

Only it wasn't the card from their deck. On his pillow, the creepy old woman wasn't staring angrily out at him, the way she always had. She was smiling slyly, as though she knew something about James that no one else knew, something that she was going to use to hurt him.

This grinning Old Maid was even creepier somehow, and looking at her hard eyes under arched eyebrows, he was almost afraid to pick the card up. But he did and turned it over, and the pattern on the back was exactly the same as on their deck. How was this possible? he wondered. Had his sister somehow altered the card? Had she secretly bought another deck with a different picture?

Had Megan been involved at all?

Logically, he didn't see how she could be, but any alternative was too frightening to even contemplate.

He still wanted to throw the card in her face, but instead he tore the card up, took it to the bathroom and flushed the pieces down the toilet, watching to make sure they all went down. Coming out, he saw that although Megan's door was closed, the light was on in her room, and he felt like going over there and confronting her, demanding to know how that card had ended up on his pillow.

But in the end, he went back into his bedroom without saying anything.

Because he was afraid she didn't know.

EIGHT

SATURDAY MORNING, CLAIRE DECIDED TO SLEEP IN. IT HAD BEEN a long week, and she'd stayed up late last night watching an old Audrey Hepburn movie after Julian had gone to bed. *Sabrina*. They didn't make movies like that anymore. They didn't make *stars* like that anymore. It was an old-lady thing to think, and she wondered idly whether she had been born in the wrong era, whether her taste in popular culture would have been more mainstream had she been born forty years earlier.

There was noise from the kitchen, the exaggerated sounds of annoyed children forced to make their own breakfast, and Claire smiled, closed her eyes and promptly fell back asleep.

When she finally woke up for good, the noises were gone and so, apparently, was her family. The house was quiet and felt empty, and when she called out, no one answered. She pushed off the covers, stood and picked up her bathrobe from the back of the chair next to the bed. She'd bought that chair at an antique store in Pasadena with money her parents had sent her for her twenty-fifth birthday, and she found herself wondering whether that antique store was still there. Back in California, on free Saturdays like this, she often used to go antiquing with her friends, not necessarily buying but looking, window-shopping, and that was something she genuinely missed. Although she had to admit that moving back to New Mexico had been the smartest move they'd ever made. Especially after . . .

She didn't even want to think about it.

Staring out the window at an army of billowy clouds stretched across the endless deep blue sky, she realized how much she depended on this place—the land, the sky, the town—to keep her grounded and centered. She felt at home here, and if that meant that she had to give up some of the more sophisticated pleasures of the big city . . . well, it was a small price to pay.

Although she was not sure Julian thought so. Oh, he claimed to like it here, and he never really complained, and he spent a lot of time with the kids, which seemed to make him happy. But even after all these years, he just didn't seem to fit in here. Her family saw him as someone who was here only temporarily, who was *enduring* life in Jardine until he had the chance to move back to Los Angeles, and though they'd never really discussed it, Claire thought that that was the way he saw himself, too.

She walked out to the kitchen. According to the note he left, Julian had taken the kids to play miniature golf. They'd both earned free passes in the library's summer reading program and had been begging him to take them for the past week. Claire was grateful for the time alone—there was a lot of housework she needed to catch up on—and she poured herself some orange juice, made herself some toast, and took her breakfast outside to eat on the picnic table in the backyard. The sun was shining, the birds were chirping, the clouds were rolling across the sky. It was nice not having to listen to the noise of the television or the kids bickering or Julian commenting on whatever newspaper article he was reading.

She ate slowly, leisurely, then brought her plate and glass back inside. As usual, everyone had piled their bowls and cups in the sink. She thought about putting them into the dishwasher, but it seemed like a waste to turn it on for such a small load, and she didn't feel like letting them sit in the machine until she had enough for a full load, so she did what she usually did and washed the dishes by hand.

Squeezing soap into the sink, Claire wondered whether Julian had bought refried beans yesterday when he'd gone to the store. She was planning on making tacos for lunch, and if he hadn't, she needed to give him a call and tell him to pick up a few cans on his way home. She paused to check the cupboard, saw that they were set for dinner, and immediately started to plan out the meals for the rest of the week. She'd seen a story on the nightly news a few days ago that said more husbands were helping out with the cooking these days, that more couples were sharing household responsibilities, and she wondered on which planet that survey had been taken, because it certainly wasn't true for her or anyone she knew. Even though Julian was home all day, he never lifted a finger to help around the house unless she yelled at him.

Returning to the sink, Claire turned off the water, picked up a sponge and started to wash the dishes. She stared out of the window at the empty backyard. No one was out there, but it felt as though someone was watching her, and, involuntarily, she glanced over at the door that led to the basement.

She didn't like the basement.

She knew how irrational that was, but it didn't make it any less true. From the first day they'd moved into this house, she'd found the cellar creepy. Most of it was probably cultural accumulation: all those horror movies about monsters living in basements, all those news stories about old ladies who killed their tenants and buried the bodies in their cellars, or those insane men who impregnated their own daughters and kept them chained up for years under their houses. But there seemed something off about the room itself. As a lawyer, she was used to dealing with facts. And she was not by nature a touchy-feely kind of person. But she got a *vibe* off the basement, a feeling that the room had been used in the past for unsavory purposes.

She hadn't said a word about this to Julian, who would have laughed at her, or to the kids, who would have been spooked, but she'd considered speaking to the realtor shortly after they'd moved in, to find out whether anything untoward had occurred in that spot. In the end, however, she hadn't made the effort. It would have been too embarrassing. Besides, what would she have done if something weird *had* happened in the basement? Insist to Julian that they sell the house immediately? Try to sue the realtor or the seller for lack of full disclosure? She'd have no grounds.

No doubt this was all just a result of overactive imagination. She rinsed off a cup, glanced again at the closed door.

Actually, earlier in the week, she'd had a dream about the basement, probably just a stress dream related to work and the unusually difficult Seaver divorce case she was handling, but no less unnerving for that. In the dream—nightmare, really—the basement had been used not for storage but as a pantry. This was where they kept their foodstuffs, and she was going down to get a package of spaghetti when the door slammed shut behind her. Startled, she nearly fell down the steps. "Hey!' she called out, but there was no response. She suddenly felt scared, and almost turned around, but she was close to the bottom, and instead hurriedly stepped onto the cellar floor, intending to grab the spaghetti and head back up.

The light went out.

She let out a startled cry, stumbling and nearly falling.

Within the basement, something moved. She felt it as much as heard it, but she heard it, too. A shifting, a rustling. She was about to yell for help when she saw a lightening in the darkness before her. Teeth. An eerie white smile.

And then a hard hand grabbed her wrist.

And then she woke up.

For several seconds after she awoke, Claire had difficulty determining where she was. She could still feel that hard hand holding her, still smell in her nostrils that musty cellar odor. But though the bedroom was just as dark as the basement had been, she was lying down, in her nightshirt, in her bed. Julian was next to her. Gradually, her brain sorted through the details of the two competing realities, and she came to realize that she had been asleep and dreaming. She had not been in the basement at all. It had just been a nightmare.

Ever since, however, the basement had made her even more nervous than before. She made an extra effort now to steer clear of the door that led to it.

Claire finished washing the dishes, rinsing them and setting them to dry on the plastic rack. She wasn't sure when Julian and the kids would be back, but thought she might sweep and mop the floors before they arrived, so she dried her hands on the dish towel hanging on the hook next to the stove and walked out into the hall—

Where the laundry basket was sitting on the floor.

She stopped, stared, her heart pounding. It had not been there earlier. She had walked down the hallway from the bedroom to the kitchen, and the floor had been clear. The basket had been in a cupboard in the laundry room, where she'd put it away after last washing a batch of clothes two days ago.

Claire knew the house was empty. No one else was here. No one could have done this. Still, she checked the front and back doors, went from room to room, upstairs and down, even peeking into the basement, but she was alone. She ended up in the hallway again, in front of the laundry basket, staring at the empty rectangle of white plastic.

A chill washed over her, a feeling she had not experienced since . . . since . . .

She took a deep breath.

"Miles?" she said softly.

"DO YOU *FEEL* ANYTHING AT OUR HOUSE?"

"Not this again."

Claire and her sister were standing in their parents' backyard, looking toward the mountains. Behind them, their father was weeding the garden. Their mother was in the house, preparing lunch. Claire had come over because she knew Diane would be here—it was her weekend to check in with the folks—and she hadn't wanted to remain home by herself. She'd left a note for

Julian telling him where she was, and her cell phone was on, but so far he hadn't called.

"I was alone in the house this morning," Claire told her sister, keeping her voice low so their father couldn't hear. "And I found the laundry basket in the middle of the hall. It wasn't there ten minutes before. I was the only one in the house."

"Maybe—"

"No!" Claire insisted. She lowered her voice. "It's not the first time it's happened." She explained how she'd come home last week after they'd gone to lunch and found the laundry basket in the middle of the kitchen. Then she described how Julian's record had played itself, though no one was upstairs and Julian was out of the house.

"Every time you move, you do this. Look, your new house isn't haunted, your old house wasn't haunted, and I'm beginning to think there wasn't anything at your place in California." She shot Claire a quick apologetic look. "Sorry."

Claire sighed, shook her head. "That's okay."

"You do this all the time."

"Maybe you're right. It's just—"

"I know what you're thinking. Don't even say it."

The two of them were silent, remembering. Behind them, they heard their father's trowel digging into the dirt.

"Hey," Diane said, changing the subject, "did you hear about Mr. Otano at the library? He's being laid off. Budget cuts."

"He's been there since *we* were little."

"They're only going to be open Monday, Wednesday and Friday, with one part-time librarian and the rest volunteers."

"Jesus."

"Remember when I was thinking of being a librarian?" Diane shook her head. "I'm glad I didn't go into *that* field."

"I always thought it suited you better, though."

Diane shrugged. "People don't read anymore. But the demand for electricity only goes up."

"Depressing but true."

The two of them walked back into the house to help their mother set the table for lunch. She'd told them she'd be making BLT sandwiches, but when they entered the kitchen, she was heating up barley soup on the stove. A flicker of worry crossed Claire's mind. Both she and Diane were concerned that their mother had started to forget things lately, and she hoped this was just a result of not having the right ingredients for her original meal rather than a symptom of memory loss. She shot Diane a look, received and acknowledged, and, clearing her throat, said, "I thought we were having sandwiches, Mom."

Their mother looked up, startled to see them. "Oh!" She smiled. "You're right. We were. But I found out that we were out of bacon. And tomatoes."

Relieved, Claire went over to the sink to wash her hands, and she and her sister started setting the table, Diane getting out the bowls and cups, Claire taking care of the silverware and napkins. Ten minutes later, their father was called in, and all four of them sat down.

They discussed family matters as they ate, in-laws and grand-kids, gossip, until her dad, sipping his soup, frowned at Claire. "You know," he said, "I had a dream about your house the other night."

She lowered her spoon, the skin prickling on her arms, and glanced quickly over at her sister.

"What happened?" Diane asked.

He frowned, shaking his head. "I can't remember exactly. But it was some kind of nightmare, because your mother said I was thrashing around and calling out in my sleep. She had to wake me up."

"I did!"

Claire's heart was pounding.

Her dad spoke slowly, and she wasn't sure whether the import that gave his words was intentional or not. "The only thing I remember," he said, and Claire felt cold, because she knew what was coming next, "is that it had something to do with your basement."

NINE

FINALLY, *HER* FRIENDS WERE GOING TO BE ABLE TO STAY OVER, and Megan planned for the slumber party by writing down lists of food, drinks, games, movies, everything they would need. She didn't want to leave anything to chance, and as each item was found or purchased, each task completed, she made a check next to the entry on the appropriate list. Her parents had even arranged for James to spend the night at Robbie's house, so she and her friends would have the place to themselves, and that alone was worth the wait.

James's friend might have stayed over first, but she was going to have a *party*. And it was going to be good.

The day of, everything went smoothly.

Until it didn't.

After lunch, her dad took James over to his friend's house, while Megan and her mom baked brownies and mixed together the dip for potato chips. When her dad returned, he took her over to Safeway, where she rented two *Twilight* DVDs from the Red-box. There were three girls coming over, and originally she'd planned for all of them to camp out in the living room, but her dad had put the brakes on that idea ("I'm not giving up my entire evening for your friends," was what he'd said, and she'd been tempted to respond, "Why don't you find something to do besides watch TV all night?" but she sensed that this was not the time to push back). She'd then thought about having two of her friends spend the night in James's room (that would drive her brother crazy!), but since it was her party, she knew that whoever didn't get to sleep in *her* room would feel slighted. And she didn't want to make enemies of any of her friends.

So she'd decided to rearrange her own room so there'd be enough space for everyone. It was harder than she'd thought, not just because she needed to create an area big enough for two sleeping bags and the feather mattress (she was still going to sleep in her bed), but because she needed to put away things that weren't cool and replace them with things that were. The last thing she needed was to get a reputation as a geek or a nerd.

She was removing a World Wildlife Federation poster of a herd of running horses from the wall at the head of her bed when her iPhone beeped. Putting the tacks down on top of her dresser, Megan picked up the phone and looked at the message on-screen.

Take off your pants.

She erased it, her heart thumping crazily.

The message popped up again.

Take off your pants.

A bolt of fear shot through her.

"Mom!" she yelled. "Mom!"

Her mother came hurrying up the stairs and into her room. "What is it?" Megan immediately handed over the phone. A shadow crossed over her mom's face as she read the text. "Who sent this?"

"I don't know!" Megan was almost crying.

"Have you ever gotten anything like this before?"

There was a second's pause, too short to be noticed. "No." Her mind was whirring. She was scared, and she was glad that she'd shown this to her mom—

Take off your pants.

—because it was too serious to keep to herself. Her parents needed to know about it. But if her mom found out about the other weird messages Megan had received, she would definitely take her phone away—and probably restrict her Internet access. She might do that anyway, but Megan wasn't going to *help* her.

"Who do you *think* would send you something like this? Is there a boy from one of your classes . . . ?"

"I don't *know*!" Megan insisted. And she didn't.

Only . . .

Only she didn't think it was anyone familiar, did she? No. For whatever reason, she thought it was a man, an adult, someone she didn't know but who somehow knew her. She had no idea where she'd gotten this impression or why she believed it to be true, but she did.

"Well, I'm keeping your phone until we get everything sorted out. I don't like this at all, and your father won't, either. This is scary stuff. There are all sorts of predators out there, and until we find out who's doing this, I don't want you calling, texting, tweeting, IM-ing or anything like that. Do you understand?"

Megan nodded. In a way, she was relieved. She needed to get hold of her friends and tell them not to send any texts or leave any embarrassing messages, but at least she didn't have to worry about some psycho pervert harassing her. She could just get on with her life and concentrate on her slumber party.

Maybe it was someone who found out about the party but wasn't invited. . . .

No. It was a man. Besides, she didn't have the kind of social standing that would make anyone jealous of not being invited. Her friends were probably the only ones who would *want* to sleep over.

"Thanks, Mom," she said, and smiled gratefully.

"If anything else like this comes up—"

"I'll tell you."

Her mother smiled back, and Megan returned to rearranging her room, although she could not help peeking out the window at the street outside as she took the horse poster off her wall.

Zoe arrived early, shortly after three. Her mother said that she'd been antsy all day, and she'd finally given in and brought her over. While the moms talked downstairs, Megan led Zoe up to her room and let her pick out a sleeping spot. "First come, first served."

"Where are you sleeping?"

"My bed."

"I'll sleep next to the bed, on the feather mattress."

Megan grinned. "Then I guess Julie and Kate get the floor."

Zoe went downstairs, said good-bye to her mom, and brought up her luggage, placing it next to the spot where she'd be sleeping. "I brought a Ouija board," she said, pulling the Parker Brothers box out of her suitcase.

Megan said nothing, although the idea made her uncomfortable. It was just a game, she told herself. A mass-produced product stamped out by a factory and sold in toy stores. But it still made her feel uneasy, and she changed the subject, explaining that she'd rented *two* movies for tonight, and that they were going to have not only pizza for dinner but ice cream and brownies for dessert.

Megan was glad Zoe had come early. Zoe was her best friend, and the two of them had time to talk a little, gossip and plan, before the other two girls came over.

Julie and Kate arrived together shortly after five, driven by Kate's mom. It was so nice not having James around, and the four of them ate pizza, watched one of the *Twilight* movies, ate dessert, watched the other movie, and then went upstairs, ostensibly to bed. But the moment the door was closed, Zoe got out her Ouija board.

"I don't—" Megan began.

"Cool!" Julie took the box from Zoe, opening one end and tipping it. An instruction book fell out, and she handed the box back to Zoe, picking up the instructions.

Zoe took out the board itself, putting it on her lap.

"What's a planchette?" Julie asked, reading.

"It's this pointer." Taking it out of the box, Zoe placed it on the board, a heart-shaped piece of plastic with short felt-tipped legs.

Julie continued to read the directions. "So, we . . ."

Kate pulled the booklet out of her hands. "Come on. Everyone knows how to use a Ouija board. It's not brain surgery."

"I don't."

"Okay, then," Megan said. "You're responsible for writing things down." She handed Julie a pen and a Hello Kitty notepad before sitting down on the floor next to Zoe and Kate, the three of them forming a triangle. They each placed a portion of the board on their laps, adjusting it until it was as flat as possible, then placing their curved fingers atop the planchette in the center of the board.

"So it's going to spell things out, and I just write them down?" Julie asked uncertainly.

"Yeah," Zoe told her. "Now everyone be quiet. And concentrate." She took a deep breath. "Is there anyone there?" she asked in a solemn voice.

Nothing happened. They waited a few moments; then Zoe spoke again. "Is someone there?"

The planchette started to slide slowly across the board

"You're pushing it!" Kate accused Zoe.

"No, I'm not!"

"*I'm* not moving it," Megan said.

"No one's moving it," Zoe told them. "It's working. Now just shut up and concentrate." The pointer had stopped sliding, but they all quieted down, and in a moment it started up again, moving over the board in an ever-widening circle. When it came close to the edge, the pattern changed, and it began sliding slowly to the left and right before finally stopping, its tip pointing to a letter on the top row of the alphabet.

"*I!*" Zoe announced.

Julie wrote it down.

The pointer moved again.

"*C!*"

It slid over to the opposite side of the board.

"*U!*"

I C U *Megan*

Megan lifted her hands before the device could move any farther.

"Hey!"

"What are you doing?"

"Megan!"

Her friends cried out in surprise and disappointment, but she didn't want to know where this was going, didn't want the next letter to be *M*. She still wasn't sure she believed that the Ouija board actually worked, but she was starting to, and she was afraid to see where the pointer would land.

What if it spelled out, *Take off your pants*?

"I'm not playing anymore," Megan said.

"Are you scared?" Zoe teased.

"Yes," she stated matter-of-factly, and that shut them up. Suddenly, all of them seemed a little nervous, and Megan helped Zoe put the pieces of the game back in the box. Julie handed back the instructions.

For a moment, none of them were sure of what to do.

"I know," Julie said brightly. "Let's play Truth or Dare."

"Yeah!" They all thought that was a good idea, but before they played the game, they decided to change into their pajamas, each of them taking turns in the bathroom. Megan was last, and her friends were giggling when she came back into the bedroom. She was afraid she'd missed something, but Zoe, sensing her concern, said, "We were just laughing at Kate's pj's."

Megan didn't see what was so funny. They were kind of old, yeah, and they were *Finding Nemo* pajamas, which was kind of babyish, but . . .

Julie pointed between Kate's legs, where the tail of an orange Nemo was protruding from a seam directly over Kate's crotch. Megan started laughing, too, and Kate said, "All right. That's enough. Truth or Dare: who's going first?"

"I'll go," Zoe volunteered.

"Truth or dare?"

Zoe and Julie both opted for truth, and to much delighted

squealing, they answered questions about their feelings for two of the hottest boys in school. But when it came time for Megan's turn, and she chose truth, Kate asked her, surprisingly, "Why did you stop the Ouija board?"

Startled, Megan didn't immediately respond. She briefly considered lying, but her friends had all been honest, and it wouldn't have been right for her to be the only one not telling the truth. Besides, she'd already admitted it. "Because I was scared," she said.

They all laughed, but to her relief, no further questions were asked. That was the end of it. After her, Kate chose dare, and when she refused to lift up her pajama top and show them her chest, her punishment was to go into James's room and kiss his pillow.

On the next round, Julie got to ask the questions and decide the dares, and when Megan's turn came up and she once again chose truth, Julie asked, "*Why* were you scared of the Ouija board?"

Megan looked at the faces of her friends, who were all watching her intently, as though the fate of important issues rested on her answer. She saw no trace of humor on any of their faces and wondered whether they had planned this, whether this line of questioning was intentional, an attempt to . . . to . . . what?

Nothing. She was just being paranoid. She forced herself to laugh, and they laughed, too, and the spell was broken. Once again, she decided to answer honestly. "Because I think my house might be haunted."

That did not go over the way she thought it would. Instead of being greeted with derision and laughter, her admission was met with a weak chuckle from Zoe and nervous glances around the room from Julie and Kate.

They feel it, too.

That was why they were pursuing this line of questioning.

Megan suddenly felt cold. As if on cue, the lights flickered, and all four of them jumped. Zoe, Kate and Julie tried to laugh it off, but Megan wasn't laughing. And neither were her friends. Not really. They were anxious, frightened. Megan looked around. The room seemed darker than it had a few moments prior, the corners filled with a gathering gloom. It was probably nothing, she told herself, but even as she did so, the darkness in the far corner seemed to become less amorphous, more of a . . . shape.

Zoe saw it, too. "Look," she whispered, pointing.

There was a figure in the corner now, a tall, thin form with the nebulous, wavy contours of a plume of smoke, and it twisted and turned until its vaguely humanoid shape was facing them full-on.

It moved toward them.

The girls screamed. All of them. Spontaneously. Their simultaneous cries of terror melded into a single earsplitting screech, and the figure promptly disappeared.

"Keep it down up there!" her mom ordered, calling from the foot of the stairs.

Instantly, the real world reasserted itself. Gone was the gloom in the corners, the dimness of the light. Everything reverted back to normal, and, more grateful than she had ever been for anything in her life, Megan called down, "Sorry, Mom! We will!"

She looked about the room, saw nothing out of the ordinary, nothing suspicious or unusual, only her furniture and possessions and the luggage and sleeping bags of her friends. She walked over to her bed, not wanting to meet anyone's eyes. No one said a word, and when she suggested that they go to sleep, there were no objections, only murmured agreement.

Everyone got under their covers or into their sleeping bags. Without asking any of her friends, Megan left her desk lamp on, and none of them asked her to turn it off, although, immediately, she wished she'd left *all* of the lights on. The lamp was dim, its glow yellowish and weak, the feeble illumination throwing the corners of the room into a too-familiar darkness. But she watched and waited, and the darkness never resolved itself into anything more, and after a few minutes, she allowed herself to relax and settle back, satisfied that, whatever had happened, it was all over now.

Haunted.

It was the first time she'd said the word aloud, the first time she'd even thought about it that directly, but she believed it. So did her friends. She heard surreptitious whispering from down on the floor and wondered what they were saying to one another. Probably that they were never going to come over to her house again.

She couldn't blame them. *She* didn't want to be here—and this was her home.

Why in the world had they moved?

James.

As usual, that little pansy was at the root of all her problems.

Megan stared up at the ceiling, wondering what, if anything, she should tell her parents about tonight. Would they believe any of it? Maybe they would if *all* of them described what had happened, although she wasn't sure her friends would be willing to admit to anything in the morning. Daylight somehow had the effect of making night fears seem less real.

The whispering had stopped. She wanted to ask Zoe whether she was asleep yet—Zoe was the one person who might *not* run away from all this—but didn't want to wake Kate or Julie, didn't want them to hear what she had to say. So she remained silent, trying not to think about what had happened but unable to think of anything else.

Haunted.

From downstairs came the sounds of her parents getting ready for bed. The television was shut off, doors were closed, a toilet flushed.

Gradually, the house grew silent.

Too silent.

Lying there, she began to think that she was the only living person in the house. The idea was absurd, but all attempts to convince herself of that failed, and the thought soon hardened into a conviction. Finally, she could no longer restrain herself and leaned over the side of the bed to make sure her friends were still alive. To her great relief, they were. Julie was snoring slightly, and Zoe stirred on the feather mattress. Kate coughed.

Happy to have her fears dispelled, Megan leaned back on her pillow—

And glimpsed movement out of the corner of her eye.

Her heart leaped in her chest.

Slowly, she turned her head to the right.

The monster emerged from the wall where it had been hiding, retaining some of the color and shading of not only the wall but the dresser and door. She was the only one who saw it, the only one awake, and she remained perfectly still, afraid to move, watching through squinting eyes that she hoped made it look as though she were asleep.

The creature was as wide as it was tall, and its head nearly brushed the ceiling. If that *was* its head. For the parts of its form seemed to have no correlation in the human or animal world. Indeed, its form was constantly *shifting*, what had seemed an arm retracting into a torso, the torso twisting and turning, becoming a head and then a foot.

The only constant was that there was a face. It might change position, but it was there, and it was a terrible thing to see, a raging chaos of unblinking eyes and ferociously fanged maw.

The monster hovered over her friends on the floor before gently lifting the sheet that covered Zoe. It pulled up her oversize T-shirt, but she did not awaken, and a long *tentacle*—for that was what it looked like—reached out and slipped beneath the material. Megan wanted to scream—

Didn't that work last time?

—but she was paralyzed with fear, and she watched, holding her breath, unmoving, as the tentacle withdrew and the face, now in the center of the ill-defined body, turned toward her. The mouth, with teeth the color of the objects in her room, smiled slyly.

Take off your pants.

It wanted her. She was the one it had come for, and she opened her mouth to scream for her parents.

And then it was gone.

It didn't fade again into the background, didn't fly out the window or walk through the door. It simply disappeared, winking out like a projection that had been shut off.

Megan didn't scream. She remained unmoving, ready to scream, for several moments longer, afraid it might return, afraid it might come for *her*. But it did not return, and she could see no trace of it in any area of her room, although Zoe's sheet remained pulled down and her T-shirt pulled up. Megan thought about fixing that—the assault to her friend's dignity made her sick to her stomach—but she was afraid to leave her bed, and instead she pulled the covers over her head, fingers curled tightly around the edges of the blanket, holding it down.

She waited for morning.

TEN

"LOOK WHAT I FOUND."

James stared admiringly at the traffic cone in Robbie's closet, more impressed than he was willing to admit. They had both been trying to find furnishings and decorations for their headquarters—which was what they'd agreed to call the upstairs room in James's garage—but so far James had not really come up with anything. Oh, he'd scrounged up a couple of folding chairs, and his dad had given him a junky bookcase, but he hadn't found anything *cool*.

Like the traffic cone.

"That's not all," Robbie said. "Check it out." He went over to his bed, crouched down and from underneath pulled out a life-size cardboard cutout of the stick-figure Greg Heffley from *Diary of a Wimpy Kid*.

James couldn't hide his excitement this time. "Where'd you get it?"

"The garbage. Can you believe it? Our neighbor, Mrs. Asako, works at The Store, and I guess she took this home when the last book came out. She must've got tired of it, because it was in her garbage this morning, and I snagged it before anyone else could."

"Awesome," James said, grinning.

"What I was thinking was that we could check out other people's garbage cans. We might find some good stuff."

"Especially in alleys, like the one behind *our* house. People dump a lot of things there!"

"Yeah. And even if we don't find anything today, we might next week. Or the week after that."

"I bet we can fill up our whole headquarters within a month!"

Actually, James had to admit, they'd gotten a lot done over the past few days. Robbie and his brother didn't have to go to camp this week, since their mother had taken vacation days off from work, and James and Robbie had been able to work on their headquarters. The first day had basically been spent cleaning up, and yesterday they'd started to plan out what they were going to do and where things were going to go. With his dad's help, they'd moved the bookcase to the right of the window and the two folding chairs against the opposite wall (in case they ever found a desk to go with it). He and Robbie had tried to rig up a secret entrance, connecting twine to the trapdoor at the top of the ladder and threading it back through a hole so they could pull the twine and the door would open, but it didn't work.

The most interesting thing that had happened was that they'd found the skeleton of a puppy in a small box in the corner of the loft. Robbie said that it was most likely a family pet, that someone had probably intended to bury it and forgotten to do so. But the box didn't look like a coffin, and James thought that someone had bought the skeleton and intended to display it. Either way, it was cool, and they *did* display it, setting it up on the top of the bookcase.

"We should have cards made up," Robbie said. "Business cards."

James nodded. He'd read the Brains Benton book Robbie let him borrow, and he liked the idea of the two of them starting their own detective agency. It seemed possible. It seemed like something they could do. "My dad'll let us use his computer."

"I still like the R.J. Detective Agency."

"We'll see."

They'd been trying to come up with a name for themselves, but so far had not been able to reach an agreement. Robbie wanted to call their organization the R.J. Detective Agency, the *R* standing for Robbie, the *J* for James. James preferred the FBI, the letters standing for Freelance Boy Investigators, although that was something they would never reveal to outsiders. "Besides," he'd argued, "we'd get real cases that way, because people would think they were calling the *actual* FBI."

It was going to be difficult to find a name they both agreed on.

James's dad would be picking them up in less than an hour, so they used the time to comb the street, looking for cast-off furniture or decorations that they could use in their headquarters. The only thing they found was a metal wine rack, and while they didn't really have a use for it, the object was too good to pass up, and they took it anyway. They'd figure out something to do with it later.

THEY WERE A LOT LUCKIER IN THE ALLEY BEHIND JAMES'S HOUSE. After taking the traffic cone, the Wimpy Kid cutout and the wine rack up to their headquarters, they cut through the backyard and went out to the alley, where, halfway down the block, they discovered an old exercise bike. It was standing in front of a fence, beside a trash can, with a piece of paper taped to its handlebars on which someone had written the word *Free*.

"Awesome!" James said, grabbing the handlebars and pulling the bike out farther into the alley so they could get a better look at it.

"There's no chain," Robbie pointed out.

"Big whoop." James sat on the seat, held the handlebars and pedaled. "It still works without it."

"And we could always get one."

James swung off the bike. "This would be perfect for when we're brainstorming. We could take turns riding the bike and thinking when we're working on a case. It'll help us relax and clear our minds."

"But how'll we get it up there?"

"My dad'll help us."

"Yeah, we need to talk about that," Robbie said.

"Talk about what?"

"I think we need some sort of security."

"Against my *dad*?"

"Not him specifically. Everyone. Don't you think we should get some sort of lock or something so that no one else but us can get in the headquarters?"

James nodded slowly. "Like my sister."

"Exactly."

"It's a good idea. But we'll do it after we get the place set up. We still need my dad to help us carry stuff, and we don't want him to know how to get in. We'll do it after we're all done."

"Okay," Robbie agreed.

They carried the bike back to James's house, hauling it through the gate and into the backyard, leaving it near the side of the garage while they went back out to search some more. There was nothing else in the alley, but at the end of the block, they turned and walked down the next street, glancing into open trash containers, looking for pieces of furniture set next to the curb. They were rewarded with a torn footstool that they found in front of a tan duplex. "I found it," James announced. "You carry it."

Robbie agreed with the logic and, holding the stool by one of its stubby legs, lugged it up the street while they continued to look.

Moments later, a garbage truck rounded the next corner with a loud rumble and started toward them. They were both getting tired anyway, so they decided to head back, but when James turned around, he saw a group of older kids skateboarding up the street. His heart lurched in his chest, and his first instinct was to run, but it became apparent almost immediately that these weren't the kids from his old neighborhood. Still, he stepped onto the grass of a nearby house and waited until they passed by.

Back home, he convinced his dad to take a break, and he and Robbie went upstairs in the garage and guided the exercise bike through the trapdoor while his dad pushed from below. After kicking his dad out, they began rearranging things, even finding a spot for the wine rack, which Robbie said they could fill with Coke bottles or cans. The place was gradually starting to come together, and James thought it was looking pretty good.

They still needed to figure out a way to make their entrance secret, and he let Robbie stay in the headquarters and think about it while he went into the house to snag some Pringles for them to snack on. He grabbed a couple of Capri Suns as well, and returned to find his friend bent down in front of an opening in the far wall. He had apparently pulled off a board to reveal the space behind it, and James put the drinks and snacks down on top of the bookcase, walking over. "What are you doing?"

Robbie looked up, startled. "I didn't hear you come up."

"What are you doing?" James repeated.

"There's a secret compartment back here." He motioned behind him. "I tripped over that nail sticking out of the floor, and I almost fell and my foot hit the wall, and this board came loose."

James crouched down next to his friend. "What's in it?"

"Nothing. I was hoping for treasure or a map or something, but . . ." He moved aside to let James look. "See for yourself."

James peered into the space and at first saw nothing but a small rectangular area approximately the size of a shoe box. Then he noticed that, in the center of the space, there was a low pile of dirt. It was roughly the size and shape of an anthill, but something about the smoothness of its sides made it seem deliberately constructed. It reminded James of a sculpture he'd seen an artist working on at an arts-and-crafts fair last year. The artist had used a knife to pare down and smooth out the sides of a mound of clay, and it had looked quite a bit like this.

As James watched, the right side of the piled dirt collapsed, and that triggered something in his mind. He suddenly remembered a dream he'd had the other night. He'd been in a hole, or, more accurately, a tunnel, a tunnel he had dug in the dirt. He was sliding through this tunnel on his stomach and *eating* the dirt in front of him. It was a crazy dream, but the craziest thing about it was that the dirt tasted great. He'd never encountered anything like it, and he found that he not only loved the taste but the texture. Everything about the dirt was amazing. It was the most exquisite flavor he had ever come across, and he wanted more, he wanted all of it, and seconds later he was creating a new tunnel as he ate through the wall to his left.

Now, curious, James reached into the compartment and picked up a small sample of the dirt in front of him, putting it to his lips. On his tongue, the granules felt odd, rough, dry, not enticing at all, but the flavor . . .

Was good.

"What are you *doing*?" Robbie stared at him, shocked, and James suddenly realized how completely whacked-out this must seem.

Seem?

It *was* completely whacked-out, and he didn't know what had come over him, why he'd done it. It was as though he'd been hypnotized or was in a trance, and he spit out the dirt in his mouth, grimacing as he wiped his lips with the back of his sleeve. Standing up, he hurried over to the bookcase, grabbed one of the Capri Sun pouches, yanked off the straw, shoved it in the hole and drank. He finished the whole pouch, but he could still taste the dirt, and it—

It still tasted good.

No! He shouldn't be thinking that, didn't want to think that, and he tried to force his brain to concentrate on something else.

But the mood in the loft had shifted. Robbie was looking around the room as though he didn't recognize it, as though he was a little bit afraid of it, and James, too, felt slightly spooked. He glanced toward that open hole in the wall, and it seemed somehow darker than before. Why had someone made that secret compartment? he wondered, and none of the answers he came up with were good.

Reaching for the board, he quickly covered up the space.

And everything shifted back.

The uneasiness he had felt only seconds before, the air of dread that had seemed to hang over their headquarters, disappeared. All was back to normal, and it was hard to imagine that it had ever been different. He and Robbie looked at each other.

"Who do you think made that secret compartment?" Robbie asked. "And what do you think they used it for?"

"I have no idea," James admitted.

They were both silent after that, neither of them knowing what to say, both of them embarrassed by what James, for some inexplicable reason, had done. Robbie walked over to the bookcase, opened the can of Pringles and pulled out a handful of stacked chips. James stood awkwardly in the center of the room, trying to think of something to do. Finally, he walked over to the window and looked down at the backyard, wondering whether they could put some sort of screen or shade over the glass that would allow them to see out but keep others from looking in. That way, they could spy on anyone planning to approach the headquarters.

His eye took in the grass, the bushes, the house. His gaze traveled up the side of the house to the window of his father's office on the second floor—

And he quickly sucked in his breath.

Standing in the window, staring out at him, was a dirty man wearing tattered clothes.

Grinning.

It was the man from his dream, the man from the basement, and even from here, James could see the unnatural whiteness of the teeth, the odd musculature of the not-quite-human face.

Where was his dad? James wondered. The idea that his father was also in the office, with this . . . *thing*, made James's blood run cold. "Robbie?" he said, but his voice came out a whispered croak. He cleared his throat, tried again. "Robbie?"

"What?"

James heard his friend walking over, but he refused to look, keeping his full attention on the figure in the window. A split-second before Robbie drew close enough to see him, the man disappeared, winking out of existence as though shut off by a switch.

"You just missed it!" James pointed. "There was a man standing in that window."

"Your dad?"

"No. The man who I dreamed was in the basement."

Robbie said nothing, but his face was pale.

"He was there. I saw him. He was looking at me."

Robbie didn't argue, and James knew that his friend believed him.

He didn't *want* Robbie to believe him, James suddenly realized. He wanted to be talked out of what he'd seen, wanted to be faced with a perfectly reasonable, rational explanation that was so airtight and all-encompassing he could not deny its truth. He didn't want to be left with this confusion. And fear.

But he said nothing to Robbie, and the two of them worked in silence as once more they rearranged their scavenged furniture.

THE NEXT MORNING, JAMES FOUND A BOBCAT SKELETON IN THE dirt.

He wasn't even sure why he decided to dig the hole when there was still so much work to do on their headquarters, but after breakfast there remained two hours until Robbie came over, and James went outside, took a shovel out of the storage shed and shoved its pointed end into the hard-packed earth of the backyard, using his foot to press it in more deeply, piling the loosened dirt into a mound next to one of the rosebushes. In his mind was some vague notion of making a secret tunnel, or perhaps an underground space where he could hide things, but, in truth, he had no plan, no real reason for doing what he was doing. He just . . . felt like digging.

And dig he did. Beneath the hard layer of topsoil, the dirt became looser, easier to shovel out, and he worked with increasing focus and dedication until, about three feet down, he came to the skeleton.

It was complete and unwrapped, and he didn't know how he knew it was that of a bobcat, but he did. The dirt here had started to become a little harder, firmer, and he was easily able to dig around and under the bones, removing the skeleton intact. Placing it on the ground, he studied it, wondering how it had gotten there and what had happened to the animal, what had killed it. If he could clean off the skeleton and keep it together, they could put it in the headquarters along with the puppy. The place would look like a real crime lab.

But he didn't try to clean it off now. He picked up the shovel, stepped back into the hole, and once again started digging. There were other skeletons beneath and around the bobcat: a squirrel, a rat, a rabbit. It was an odd coincidence that he'd started digging at the very spot where all of these animals had been buried, but James didn't really think about that, didn't really think about anything, just kept shoveling, placing the bones on the flat ground next to the growing mound of dirt.

He was sweating from exertion, but he didn't stop, didn't slow, in fact picked up the pace. He kept looking over his shoulder at the back door of the house, wondering whether—

hoping

—his mom or dad would see him, come out and make him stop digging.

But they didn't, and he kept on. As the bottom of the hole grew deeper, narrower, he started thinking about what it would be like to tunnel into the earth headfirst, not using the shovel but using his mouth, eating his way through the soil, carving out a smooth passageway with his body. Although he made no conscious decision to do so, James scraped out an alcove that slanted away from the main body of the hole, then tossed the shovel onto the ground above. Dropping to his knees, he placed his head into the recessed cavity. The dirt smelled good, fresh, sweet.

"What are you doing?"

James jumped at the sound of the voice, bumping his head on the roof of the alcove, causing a light sprinkle of dirt to rain about him. He noticed all of a sudden what an awkward position he was in, and he had to wiggle around, squirming backward and doing a twisted push-up in order to get himself into a squatting position in the center of the hole. He looked up to see Robbie peering down at him. His friend looked confused, disgusted, frightened.

"What is going *on*?" Robbie demanded.

James hopped up guiltily, dusting the soil from his hair as he pulled himself out of the hole. He tried to smile, but his friend didn't smile back.

"What are you *doing*?"

"Nothing," James said, trying to convince himself as much as Robbie. He brushed the dirt from his shoulders. "Nothing."

ELEVEN

CLAIRE WAS IN HER OFFICE WHEN PAM LOWRY WALKED ACROSS the street from Cool Kids Clothing, carrying a sack lunch. The two of them sometimes ate together when business was slow, but although today's heat had depressed foot traffic downtown, Claire was actually pretty busy. There was a lot of research to do, a lot of paperwork to fill out. Still, she had to eat, and she was grateful for the company. She'd spent the morning alone on her computer, typing, without so much as a single phone call to interrupt her, and it had given her a newfound respect for Julian. She didn't know how he coped with that sort of routine every single day, although he was by nature a far less social and far more solitary person than she could ever be.

"Hi," Pam said, walking into the office. "Busy?"

"No," Claire lied.

"I needed to see another human being. I've had exactly one person come into the shop so far today, and that was a guy asking if he could use my phone." Pam sat down in her usual spot in the client chair across from Claire's desk and opened her lunch sack, withdrawing a wrapped sandwich.

"And I don't even have an air conditioner like you do, just an old fan."

Claire glanced over at the humming window unit struggling to cool the office. "Oh, yeah. We're state-of-the-art here."

"Be grateful for what you have."

Claire got up and went to the square minifridge against the back wall, took out one of the Lean Cuisines she'd stored there and popped it into the microwave atop the counter.

"So," Pam said, biting into her sandwich, "do you have any juicy gossip? Any big divorces I should know about? Adulterous affairs?"

"I couldn't tell you even if I knew."

"You always say that."

"Sorry."

"I have one." Pam paused. "David."

Claire turned away from the microwave. "David Molina?"

The other woman nodded.

Claire glanced out the window and across the street. The paperback rack was on the sidewalk out front, but the bookstore door was closed, presumably to keep out the heat. "What did you hear?"

"It's not what I heard. It's what I saw. Or what I noticed." Pam took a sip from her Diet Snapple bottle. "A fairly attractive, very *buxom* blond woman has been spending a lot of time at the bookstore the past week or so. She's there every other day, at least. And she always comes around lunchtime. She stays around an hour, and as far as I can tell, she's never bought a book. I'm surprised you didn't pick up on it."

"I try not to look over there too often," Claire admitted. "David always seems a little too—"

"Flirty?"

"*Intense,*" Claire said. "Anything beyond 'hello' gets a little uncomfortable for me."

"Me, too." Pam turned around. "Oh, the door's closed. She's probably in there now."

"He's married, isn't he?"

"Oh, yeah. With three kids."

Claire offered up a wan smile. "Well, if his wife ever needs a lawyer . . ."

The microwave rang, and she took out her lunch, carrying it back to her desk. She returned to the fridge for a Mountain Dew before settling down in her chair.

"So," Pam asked, "when's the housewarming party? It's been, what, a month? How long are you going to wait?"

Things had been so hectic, what with work and settling in and the kids being off from school, that Claire hadn't even thought of having a housewarming party.

Pam must have read as much in her expression. "Come on! You have to do it!" she said. "We all want to see your new place." She leaned forward conspiratorially. "Besides, you'll get free gifts. Kitchen supplies and alcohol. It's a win-win."

Claire laughed. A party did sound like fun, and for the next twenty minutes, they discussed the prospect, bouncing ideas off each other until Claire was so enthusiastic that she had no choice but to announce that she'd do it. She set a tentative date of next Saturday for the party, but told Pam not to say anything to anyone else until she talked to Julian and everything was finalized.

Through the window behind Pam, the door to David's shop opened, and a top-heavy blonde Claire would not have pegged as a reader walked out of the bookstore onto the sidewalk, smiling happily. Seeing where Claire was looking, Pam turned around. "That's her," she confirmed. "A little out of David's league, isn't she?"

They looked at each other. And laughed.

That night, both of the kids were gone—James to Robbie's house and Megan to Zoe's—and for the first time in a very long while, Claire and Julian had an evening to themselves. They could have gone to a movie, could have gone out to eat, but domesticity had made them lazy, and they decided to stay in, eat leftovers and watch HBO, which was showing a big movie from last fall that they'd missed in theaters.

The movie was good but not as great as the hype and box-office receipts would have suggested, and afterward Julian turned off the lights and closed up the house while she went into the bedroom. She hadn't done laundry for a while and this morning had found herself without fresh underwear, so she'd continued to wear yesterday's panties. It made her feel dirty, which made her feel sexy, and she took off her clothes and sat down on the edge of the bed, waiting for Julian.

Their sex life had definitely gotten better since they'd moved to the new house. She wasn't quite sure why, although she'd read somewhere that a new environment often acted as an aphrodisiac. While that probably *was* the reason, emotionally it didn't feel quite right. There'd been an electricity to their encounters since moving here, an almost newlywedlike hunger and excitement that being in a new location could neither explain nor account for.

Seconds later, Julian walked through the door and stopped, surprised that she was naked, though he'd no doubt assumed they'd be having sex tonight.

She spread her legs wide. "Taste it," she ordered. "Taste my dirty pussy."

He did, and she held his head hard against her until she was finished, grinding into his face until his cheeks and nose and chin were glistening.

He was hard, she saw when he stood, but she wanted him harder, and she knelt down and sucked until his erection was quivering and she could taste the first salty drops of semen. Pulling her mouth away, she got on her hands and knees.

"I want it in my ass," she said.

He was too rough and it hurt, but she liked it, and when he reached around the front and cupped her crotch in his hand, rubbing it with his palm, the pain and pleasure mingled in an exhilarating crescendo that erupted in one of the strongest orgasms she'd ever had.

Afterward, she felt guilty and ashamed, embarrassed, though those were not the emotions she usually experienced after sex. Of course, this was not the type of sex she usually had, and unfamiliar feelings were probably to be expected. Still . . .

Going to the bathroom, there was blood, and she grimaced in pain, wondering what had come over her, what had come over *them*, feeling slightly uneasy about the way she'd been carried away. She spent too much time on the toilet, then too much time in the shower, and when she came out of the bathroom, Julian was dead asleep, the TV on and turned to an old Clint Eastwood movie. She switched it to the Travel Channel and got into bed beside him, making it only until the first commercial before falling asleep herself.

She dreamed of meeting a man in a basement dance club. She was younger, a teenager, and she danced with him but didn't like him, and eventually ended up giving him her cell phone number just to get him to go away. Seconds later, in that compressed time so characteristic of dreams, she was in the basement of her own house, *this* house, only she was still a teenager and she lived here with her parents. The basement was empty save for a tree stump with an ax in it.

A sudden ringing startled her, and she realized that she was carrying her cell phone. She turned her palm up, looked down and saw a text message.

Take off your pants.

Startled, frightened, she looked up from the screen.

And saw a tall, creepy man standing in the corner, grinning at her.

IN THE MORNING, SHE AWOKE EARLY, BECAUSE SHE FORGOT IT was Saturday and thought she had to go to work. She considered going into the office anyway—she *did* have a brief to write—but both Megan and James had complained lately that she wasn't around enough, and Claire realized that she ought to be here when they came home. How many summers would she have left with them? They were getting older, and soon they wouldn't even *want* her around. She should take advantage of the situation while she still could.

Julian had always been an early riser, and he was up already, no doubt making himself breakfast while watching CNN. Morning wasn't morning to him unless he could catch up on overnight world events.

Getting out of bed, Claire checked her panties, thankful to see that the bleeding had stopped, but she was still sore when she went to the bathroom. She flushed the toilet, then washed her hands and looked at herself in the mirror, moving in close. No matter how much moisturizer she used, she could not get rid of the small lines that had started to sink in around her eyes, bracket her mouth and accent her chin. Julian, she'd noticed recently, had a few gray hairs coming in not just on his head but on his chest, and what had been merely a seasonal paunch was now his permanent year-round stomach.

They were both pushing forty-five, and she realized that in a little more than five years they would be fifty. That was scary enough by itself, but what was truly frightening was that fifty no longer seemed old to her. In her mind, she felt no different than she had at twenty-five or thirty, and it seemed like only yesterday that she'd been in college and fifty had seemed like the age of a grandparent. Just last week, though, she'd read of an actor dying at the age of sixty-five and found herself thinking that that was way too young.

Her stomach growled. She was hungry, and thought she might make herself an omelet or—

Something moved behind her.

Claire swiveled around, startled. But there was nothing that *could* have moved, only the bathtub and wall. Besides, if something had been there, she would have seen it in the mirror.

So why did she feel as if she wasn't alone?

Because she wasn't.

She glanced around. There was someone in the bathroom with her. She could *feel* him, even if she couldn't see him.

Him?

Yes, it was a man. She didn't know how she knew that, but she did. Just as she knew that he was blocking the door, that she would run into him if she tried to leave the room. What would happen at that point, she had no idea, but it was definitely not something she wanted to find out.

"Julian!" she called.

And it was gone. As quickly as that. A second before, the small room had been filled with another presence, and now she was alone. Whatever had been there had disappeared. She knew it with the same unfounded certainty that had told her it had been blocking the door.

Swiftly, before it came back, she opened the door, flinging it wide. She expected to see Julian sprinting down the hall toward her, or, at the very least, to hear his stomping footsteps at the front of the house as he sped over to rescue her. But there was no sign of him and no sound save the muffled drone of television news. He hadn't heard her cry, and she wondered what would have happened to her if she had not scared the presence—

man

—away. In her mind, he looked like that creepy figure from her dream, the one in the corner of the basement, and though it was morning and light out, she shivered.

Was their house haunted?

She didn't like the basement, and James, she knew, didn't, either. Her *dad* had had a nightmare about it, and he was one of the most rational people on the planet. Then there was the record that played by itself and the laundry basket. . . .

Claire told herself to calm down. Julian was right. There was probably a rational explanation for all of it. She was just overreacting and reading import into ordinary occurrences because . . . because . . . Well, she couldn't think of a reason, but that didn't mean there wasn't one.

Her slippers were next to the toilet, and she slid her feet into them before heading out to the kitchen to make that omelet. But as she looked down at her feet, something in the corner of her eye caught her attention.

There was a face in the toilet.

Now she was being crazy.

Probably. But there was a face nevertheless: eyes formed by twin deposits of calcium from the hard water, off-white against the porcelain of the bowl, and a smiling mouth by the curved edge of the water itself. The mouth wavered as the water moved, giving the rudimentary features an unnerving semblance of life.

Had it been there moments before, when she'd used the toilet? Claire wasn't sure, but she didn't think so, and its seemingly sudden appearance upset her more than it probably should have.

Opening the cupboard doors beneath the sink, she took out the scrub brush and a spray bottle of Lime-A-Way. She coated the sides of the bowl with foaming suds, but before she could even start scrubbing, the froth began dripping irregularly down the porcelain, forming Alice Cooper eyes and an ever-widening smile, not merely maintaining the face but giving it a mocking, defiant appearance. She scrubbed the toilet as hard as she could, putting her back into it, spraying more Lime-A-Way, and more, and more, but the face remained, and though she told herself it was nothing, wasn't really a face, was just a coincidence, an arbitrary confluence of hard-water mineral stains, she realized with a sick sinking feeling in the pit of her stomach that those eyes would be looking straight up at anyone who sat on the toilet.

She was going to make sure the rest of the family did not use this bathroom.

Especially Megan.

Putting away the brush and cleanser, Claire started down the hallway toward the kitchen, intending to tell Julian everything, but her eye was caught by the newel post of the staircase, and, on impulse, she walked past the kitchen doorway and headed up the steps, wanting to make sure there was nothing . . . *strange* in the kids' bathroom upstairs.

At first glance, there wasn't.

She checked the toilet first, and while it wasn't as clean as she would have liked (she'd have to talk to the kids about that), there was no face. She looked in the sink, glanced around at the walls, peered into the mirror.

All clean.

Relieved, she exhaled deeply. She let her gaze wander over the remaining sections of the room.

The face was on the shower curtain.

It was there for only a second—long enough for her to identify it as the same one in the other bathroom, long enough to note that it was formed from abstract design elements on the curtain itself—and then it was gone, rendered invisible by a minute shift in perspective or a slight change in light. She screamed anyway, a gut reaction, and this time Julian heard her. In seconds, his heavy steps were thundering up the stairs.

"Claire!" he called.

She stepped into the hall.

"Are you all right?"

She nodded, heart still pounding. But his presence gave her courage, and she went back into the bathroom to once more examine the shower curtain. She looked at it from the left, from the right, from straight on, from a crouched position.

He followed her in. "What in the world are you doing?"

Claire stood, faced him. "Maybe we shouldn't have bought this house," she said.

"What?"

"Have you considered the idea that it might be . . . haunted?" Julian just stared at her.

"James doesn't like the basement," she continued quickly. "I don't, either—"

"It's dark," he interrupted. "It's small. It's claustrophobic. But it's not *haunted*."

"Megan and her friends were all screaming—"

"They're teenage girls on a sleepover who were playing with a Ouija board and telling ghost stories. What did you expect?"

"What about your record? And what about those things that keep getting moved around?"

"Are you serious?" He frowned at her, obviously annoyed. "You're acting like a three-year-old. First of all—"

"I saw a face in the toilet downstairs. And on the shower curtain here."

"Oh, my God . . ."

"The one in the toilet's still there!"

"Show me."

Grimly, they walked downstairs, Claire in the lead, Julian muttering disbelieving, disparaging remarks under his breath. When they reached the bathroom, the face was still there, and it looked as disturbing as ever.

Julian shook his head. "That's just a stain. It *happens* to sort of, almost, kind of, semi-look like a face. But it's like those people who claim to see Jesus in rusty drips on a water heater or Mary's outline on a fogged-up storm window. Those things aren't really there; people just want to believe that they are."

He reached for her, but she pulled away. "I don't *want* that face to be there! But it is!"

"Calm down. You got scared. You spooked yourself, and now you're all rattled. I'm just trying to explain that there's nothing *supernatural* going on here."

"Don't patronize me!"

"I'm not," he said, in a voice indicating that he was. "But our house isn't haunted, and that thing"—he gestured toward the toilet—"isn't some ghostly manifestation. It's hard-water deposits on porcelain. Whatever you saw upstairs was obviously some trick of the light. The basement—"

"The basement's creepy."

"Come on. Act like an adult, for God's sake."

"I don't see you ever going in there."

"There's no reason to."

"You know, my dad even had a nightmare about our basement."

He threw up his hands. "Oh! Well! If your *dad* had a dream, then it *must* be true!"

"There's something in this house, Julian."

"No, there isn't."

"You've felt it, too, and you're just pretending that you haven't."

She glared at him, and there was a loaded pause between them. She saw understanding dawn in his expression. He knew what she was about to say. "What if it's—"

"Don't say it!" he ordered. "Don't even *think* it!"

"We're *both* thinking it!"

"No!" Julian spun around and strode away, not looking back, heading down the hall, through the kitchen and out the back door, letting the screen slam shut behind him.

Claire stood in place, breathing heavily. That was unfair, she knew. It was the first time she'd done something like that, the first time she'd used Miles in that way, and instantly she regretted it. She didn't even know what had prompted her to go there. They'd had bigger fights before, over much more serious things, and she'd never felt compelled to drag that part of their past into it. This was merely a disagreement about weird incidents in their house. Why the hell had she brought up Miles?

She knew why, but she didn't want to admit it, even to herself.

Walking into the kitchen, Claire saw that Julian had made coffee, and she poured herself some. Her gaze was drawn to the closed door that led to the basement, but she moved next to the sink and peered out the window. She expected to see Julian pacing around the backyard, but there was no sign of him, and she wondered whether he had gone into the garage or the alley.

She wasn't the type of person who ate when she was upset—quite the opposite—but she knew she should have some food in her stomach, so she made herself some toast. She kept thinking Julian would return while she was eating, but he didn't, and he still hadn't come back into the house by the time she'd dressed. He wasn't usually one to pout—that was her province—and his absence worried her, but she knew that if she went off looking for him and found him, it would set off a new round of arguments.

Returning to the kitchen, she glanced out the window again.

No sign of him.

In her peripheral vision, she could see the basement door, and though she was still frightened, still spooked, she was determined not to be intimidated. Gathering her courage, she strode purposefully over, grasped the handle and turned it, opening the door. Before her, the steps descended into darkness, and though she could not help thinking of that—

grinning

—man she'd dreamed about, she reached for the switch, turned on the light and started down.

There was no man, of course, only the sealed cartons and sacks of junk that they'd brought down here to store. She wasn't sure what she'd expected to see, but looking around at the boxed overflow of their lives, the sense of foreboding she'd felt dissipated. Julian was right. There was nothing mysterious here. Only a small square room with a cement floor and walls that . . .

Frowning, Claire leaned forward.

Directly in front of her, above an overstuffed Hefty bag filled with James's old Hot Wheels sets, was a darkened section of wall stained with patches of mold. Not unexpected in a damp cellar, but . . .

There was a face in the mold.

The same face she'd seen in the toilet. And on the shower curtain.

Claire stared at it. She knew how crazy this would sound if she told anyone—but it was true. And though the features in the toilet and on the shower curtain had been so rudimentary as to seemingly preclude specificity, this *was* the same face.

And it was smiling at her.

To her right, atop a junky card table that Julian for some inexplicable reason had insisted on keeping, were several old tools that someone had been sorting through and left out: pliers, a hammer, a screwdriver. In one smooth move, Claire picked up the screwdriver and strode forward, between the boxes, until she stood directly in front of the face.

It grinned.

Reaching over the bag of Hot Wheels, she used the screwdriver to *scrape* the face, feeling a rush of satisfaction as the features devolved under her hand. With her first swipe, she scratched off half of one eye, then part of the mouth, then a portion of the other eye, then another part of the mouth, until the mold no longer looked like a face. But she didn't stop, and though she was pressing so hard on the screwdriver that her hand hurt, she continued scraping, bits of mold falling onto her hand, white scratches on the wall contrasting sharply with the dull gray of the surrounding cement.

Finally, Claire stepped back. She was sweating from both the exertion and the still, humid air of the basement, but she felt good as she looked at the spot where the face had been. She felt as though she'd accomplished something.

Walking back up the stairs, she found Julian in the kitchen, standing by the sink. He'd been looking through the window at the backyard, but he turned to face her as she closed the basement door. For a moment, both of them stared at each other, neither speaking. Claire saw from the look of devastation on his face how much she had hurt him, and she was about to apologize, but it was he who spoke first.

"I lied," he admitted. "I do feel it. I have felt it."

The words, completely unexpected yet gratefully welcome, acted like a ray of sunshine slicing through darkness. She felt as if a great burden had been lifted from her. She wasn't alone; she wasn't crazy. He knew what she was talking about. He understood.

But the pain in his face was almost too much to bear, and she was filled with remorse and self-loathing as she ran over and threw her arms around him. "I'm sorry," she sobbed, hugging him tightly. "I'm sorry."

"Me, too," he assured her, and there was a noticeable catch in his voice.

She wasn't sure their apologies were in any way commensurate, but she wasn't about to hurt him again by bringing up anything to do with Miles. Maybe his unbending reticence and their unspoken agreement never to broach the subject weren't psychologically healthy, but it worked for them, and the guilt she felt for crossing that line far outweighed any argumentative points she might have scored.

They remained in each other's arms, not moving, not speaking, until the phone rang several moments later and she broke the embrace to answer it. Megan was calling, and she wanted to know whether she could stay at Zoe's for the rest of the day. "They invited me to go with them to the water park," she said. "I'll be back in time for dinner," she added quickly. "I promise."

"Okay," Claire told her. "Are you going to stop by and get your swimsuit?"

"I already packed it. I have it with me—" Megan abruptly stopped speaking, as if her mother had interrupted her, though Claire hadn't said a word.

"Did you know about this ahead of time? Were you planning this all along?"

"I'm sorry. I should have told you. But I really want to go. I promise I'll be careful. Please, Mom? Please?"

Claire couldn't help smiling. "All right," she said. "But no secrets next time, okay? You tell us everything that's going on."

"I will, Mom. I will. Thanks!"

Claire hung up the phone to face a quizzical Julian. "She wants to go with Zoe's family to the water park. I said she could."

He nodded his agreement, and they hugged once more. She gave him a quick kiss. "Everything good?" she asked.

He smiled wearily. "Yeah."

Robbie's father dropped off James an hour or so later, while she was weeding the flower beds out front, and as Claire watched her son get out of the car, thank Robbie's dad for letting him stay over and then walk toward her up the driveway, she realized how big he was getting. He looked more like Julian now than he did her, though that hadn't always been the case. It made her feel sad.

She stood at his approach. "Let's go out for lunch today," she suggested.

"Where?" James asked.

She smiled at him. "Your choice."

TWELVE

SINCE IT WAS JULIAN WHO SUGGESTED THEY SHOULD INVITE THE neighbors to their housewarming party, it was his responsibility to ask them. The Allreds and the Harrisons, two older couples from across the street, agreed to come, as did two younger couples from down the block, although the only family with children, the Armados, bowed out due to a scheduling conflict.

As usual, the neighbors to either side of them weren't home.

Or weren't answering their doors.

Julian suspected the latter. Cars were parked in both driveways, but drapes were drawn and front doors were shut. He knocked, he rang, he waited, but no one came out. He had no idea why the neighbors might be trying to avoid him, and he even hinted around about it to Cole Hubbard, the single man who lived in the small house on the other side of the Ribieros. Cole said that the Ribieros, at least, were probably scared. "Ever since that homeless guy died, they've been a little freaked-out, I think."

Julian frowned. "What homeless guy?"

"You don't know?" Cole seemed surprised. "I thought real estate agents had to reveal that kind of stuff."

Julian was starting to feel uneasy. "What kind of stuff?"

"Deaths, murders, suicides." Cole sipped from the Starbucks

cup he was holding. "He died in your basement. It was all over the newspaper. I'm surprised you didn't read about it."

Our basement? Julian thought of Claire. "When was this?"

"It was a few years ago now. Before the previous owners."

"So the house was empty and this guy just—"

"No," Cole said. "That's the weird part. It *wasn't* empty. The couple was home. Robert and Shelley Gentry. They're the ones who were living there then. Nice people. They were in bed, asleep, when the homeless guy broke into their house—I keep calling him 'the homeless guy' because I don't think anyone ever found out who he was. The door was unlocked. . . . He broke a window. . . . I can't remember exactly how he got in. But the Gentrys didn't wake up, and he just went down into the basement and . . . died."

"He killed himself?"

"Not exactly. He just . . . died. He took off all his clothes, sat down in the corner, and when they found him in the morning, he was dead. There were no marks on the body; he didn't hang himself; I don't think they even found any drugs in his system. It was as if he knew he was going to die that night and for some reason wanted to die in your basement. I'm surprised you didn't hear about it. It was kind of a big deal."

Julian thought maybe he *had* read something about it in the paper, but there were so many deaths reported these days, so much crime and tabloid news not only nationally but locally, that everything kind of blurred together and he didn't really pay as close attention as he used to.

He wondered which corner of the basement the man had died in. The one where he'd stacked the boxes of the kids' old children's books?

He needed to keep this from Claire. At least for the time being. She was already stressed out and thought the house was haunted. If she found out that someone had *died* in their basement, she'd want to sell the house immediately.

"Anyway," Cole continued, "Robert and Shelley moved soon after that, and those other people bought the place. I'm not even sure anyone in the neighborhood ever met them. They *really* kept to themselves. I don't even know their names. But I gather they had some kind of run-in with the Ribieros, who were already freaked-out by the homeless guy. Bob and Elise have never talked about it, but . . . something happened."

"I got a weird vibe the one time I talked to them. The Ribieros, I mean. They were nice and all, but . . ."

Cole nodded. "They're nice. I get along with them. But I don't think you're wrong. They definitely seem weirded out by your house, and that's probably carried over to their attitude toward you. I mean, they've never said anything to me about any of this—in case you haven't noticed, we *all* kind of keep to ourselves around here—but, reading between the lines, I think they probably have a problem not just with your house but with anyone who lives there. They're a little superstitious, I think. Or more than a little superstitious."

Julian glanced down the street. "What about the people on the other side of us?" he asked. "Do you know anything about them? We've tried to go over there a couple of times and introduce ourselves, but no one's ever home."

"Oh, they're home, all right," Cole said. "But they're *very* strange. Don't even give them a second thought. They keep their yard up, their house looks nice, but they never come out and no one ever sees them. I'm not even sure when they mow their lawn or go to work, or anything about them, really. But at least they're quiet and don't bother anyone. I lived next to some hard partyers before—up at all hours of the night, stereo cranked full blast—and let me tell you, it was no picnic. Be grateful for the Boo Radleys of the world."

Julian liked Cole. He was glad that he'd invited Cole to the party, glad Cole was coming, glad they'd had a chance to talk. This was a friendship worth nurturing. Claire always said that men were much bigger gossips than women, even if they pretended to be above such pettiness, and Julian thought that was probably true. Cole obviously kept close tabs on everything going on in the neighborhood, and Julian was only too happy to be able to find out details about the neighbors from him.

He smiled. No, men didn't gossip. They shared intel.

Walking home, he wondered about the people who had owned the house before them. He and Claire had never met the previous owners, had only seen their signatures on some of the countless forms they'd been required to sign upon purchasing the property, and though he'd thought nothing of it at the time, that now seemed odd. He recalled the way the house had looked on their first visit, the trash and debris on the floor, the discarded furniture. Claire was right. Something was going on there.

And it had nothing to do with Miles.

He wished Claire had not mentioned Miles. The whole horrible incident had been on his mind ever since, and in the background, behind everything he did or said or thought, like a low hum, was an unyielding sadness, an emotional blackness that threatened to bloom into depression should he pause to examine it.

Last night he'd had the Dream again.

But this wasn't Miles; this was something else, and as he walked across the grass toward the front door, he forced those thoughts down and looked up at the house itself. Even knowing what he knew, there was nothing spooky about it. The front of the structure did not resemble a face; no spectral figure flitted through the darkness behind one of the windows. The building looked like what it was: the home of a normal, middle-class family.

Thirsty, Julian walked through the living room, through the dining room, into the kitchen, where he got a Heineken out of the refrigerator. He glanced over at the basement door. Had a man really died down there? It seemed impossible to believe. While standing on a neighbor's porch and talking about it, the idea had been incredible enough. But here, inside the house, intimately close to the location where it had occurred, the notion was truly horrifying. Though it had happened several years and two owners ago, the fact that someone had died within the walls of their home seemed like the grossest and most personal invasion of privacy.

Julian walked over, opened the basement door, switched on the light and headed down the steps. On the wall before him, he saw white scratches where Claire had scraped off the moldy face. Otherwise, the cellar appeared unexceptional, a storage room, no more, no less.

Which corner had the man died in? he wondered. The image was strange: a naked man, sitting in the corner, dead. He tried to picture it, but the jumble of boxes and bags made it nearly impossible.

He stood in place for several minutes, trying to feel something, trying to sense something, and when he didn't, he walked back upstairs, turned the light off and closed the door.

It was Sunday, and Claire and Megan had gone to Claire's parents' house for lunch, so he and James were on their own. Julian checked the clock. It was nearly noon; no wonder he was getting hungry.

Where was James? he wondered. Before Julian had gone out to issue invitations, the boy had been in the living room, watching TV, although he'd said that he might go out to his "headquarters" after the show was over. Julian smiled. He and his friends had had a secret hideout when they were James's age—a lean-to in a vacant lot, built with discarded materials from a nearby construction site—and he understood the allure. Some things never changed.

He looked out the window above the sink, intending to see whether he could spot movement in the garage's upstairs, but James was on the ground, on his knees, bent over a hole in the backyard. Was he eating dirt? It looked like it, but that didn't make any sense. Frowning, Julian walked outside. At the sound of the screen door's creaking hinges, his son looked up. There was a ring of dirt around his mouth.

"What are you doing?" Julian demanded.

"Nothing," James said, getting to his feet. But there was a guilty expression on his face, and Julian could see confusion mixed in with the guilt, confusion and fear.

"What's going on here?" he asked, less harshly this time.

"I don't know, Dad," James said, and started to cry. Julian could not remember the last time his son had just burst into tears like this. Although his initial reaction to the fact that the boy was apparently eating dirt had been one of anger, the anger shifted to concern.

Julian walked over, looked into the hole, saw nothing unusual. He put his hands on James's shoulders. "Why were you eating dirt?"

"I don't know." James was still crying.

"Well, don't do it again." He was aware that his admonition was lame and ineffectual, that he should be saying something else to his son, something more, but he was at a loss here and didn't really know what to say or how to react. Eating dirt was something that usually came up when dealing with toddlers, not twelve-year-olds. It occurred to him that there might be a deeper problem here, but he prayed that wasn't the case and that this would be the end of it.

James nodded, wiping the tears from his eyes. "I won't, Dad."

Still worried, still concerned, Julian forced himself to smile, wrapped an arm around the boy's shoulder and steered him back toward the house. "Wash your face off, then. I'll make us some lunch."

They went inside. Julian prepared macaroni and cheese, the only food he really knew how to make, and the two of them ate in the living room while they watched an episode of *The Twilight Zone*.

When Claire and Megan returned, James was upstairs in his room, playing some game. Julian didn't say anything about his eating dirt, but he did tell Claire that he'd made the rounds and invited their neighbors to the housewarming party, and that most of them would be coming. Except the Armados. And the people next door.

He did not tell her what Cole had said about the homeless man dying in their basement.

"That's great," she said happily. "I'm glad Pam talked me into this. I think it's going to be fun." She gave him a quick kiss on the nose.

"Yeah," he said. He kissed her back. He realized that he was keeping a lot of secrets from her all of a sudden.

He didn't like that.

But he had no choice.

ON MONDAY, JULIAN CALLED GILLETTE SKOUSEN, THE REALTOR who'd sold them the house. She didn't sound happy to hear from him, her chipper greeting transforming into distant formality as soon as he identified himself. "What can I do for you?" she asked coolly.

"I have a few questions about our house—" he began.

"I don't know anything about it."

That was certainly suspicious. "About what?" he challenged her. "I haven't asked you a question yet."

The realtor was silent.

"I just want to know if there's a way I can get in contact with the previous owners."

"There are privacy issues. . . ."

"You thought I was going to ask about the dead man in the basement, didn't you? The one you didn't tell us about."

She was silent again.

"I just want their e-mail or a mailing address or a phone number. That's all I'm asking for. They sold their house to us. I have the right to contact them."

Gillette sounded angry. "Fine." After spending several moments looking up the information, she gave him all three: e-mail address, mailing address, phone number.

"Thank you," Julian said.

Gillette hung up on him.

The previous owners, Bill and Maria Worden, had moved to Colorado. Although Julian initially thought about calling them, he could think of no way to ask what he had to ask without sounding . . . well, stupid. So, forgoing the instant gratification a phone call would have given him, he did the next best thing and sent an e-mail, which allowed him to compose his thoughts in a logical manner yet still transmit the communication instantly and, hopefully, receive a quick reply.

He spent the latter half of the morning carefully wording a message that started out by saying how much they loved the house and then gradually segued into a recitation of some of the odd experiences they'd had here. He mentioned that Cole Hubbard had told him how the couple who'd lived in the house before them had discovered a dead man's body in the basement, and he wondered whether *they* had ever experienced anything unusual while living in the house.

The e-mail's tone was friendly and mildly inquisitive, filled with none of the worry that he actually felt, and he sent it off immediately after proofreading it.

Instantly, a message popped up on his screen telling him that the address to which he'd sent the e-mail did not exist. He checked it against the address he'd written down, but the two were identical. He hadn't accidentally left out a letter or put in a wrong number; he'd typed exactly the same e-mail address Gillette had told him. Frowning, he thought about dialing the realtor again to double-check, but, looking at the screen, he saw his thoughts laid out logically and decided to call the Wordens directly and just read his letter to them.

After half a ring, three discordant tones rang in his ear and a woman's voice announced: "I'm sorry, but the number you have called is no longer in service. Please check the number and dial again."

This time, he did call the realtor, but she insisted that even if the information she gave him was not correct, it was the only information she had. He hung up, frustrated.

There was one option left, and Julian converted his e-mail into a Word file, added a return address and a phone number, and printed it out. He drove to the post office to mail the letter, and waited anxiously all week for a phone call or a return letter, all the time checking his e-mail.

Several days later, as he'd feared, his letter was returned, a red post office stamp on the envelope stating that it was not deliverable as addressed.

That night, he dreamed that the Wordens called to say they were coming over. They had important information to tell him. They promised to arrive by midnight, but he waited and waited and still they did not show. Claire and the kids were asleep, so he went around the house, checking doors and windows, making sure everything was locked. In the kitchen, he saw that the door to the basement was open, and he walked down the steps to make sure nothing was wrong.

At the bottom, he found the Wordens, both naked, sitting in opposite corners of the room, dead.

Maria Worden looked like Claire.

Bill Worden looked like him.

THIRTEEN

ALTHOUGH MEGAN HAD ALWAYS TAKEN BATHS AND SHOWERS BE-
fore bedtime, like her mom, lately she'd begun doing so in the
morning, like her dad. She told herself there was no real reason
for the switch, that it was merely more convenient to do it this
way, but the truth was that she no longer felt comfortable taking
showers at night.

She no longer felt comfortable taking baths at *all*.

The bathroom scared her after dark.

That was it exactly, though it embarrassed her to even think
such a thing. Still, it was better to be safe than sorry, and while
Megan might be self-conscious about the reasons for altering her
schedule, she was not at all sorry that she'd done it.

After breakfast, she went upstairs to take a shower and get
dressed.

Lately, she'd begun to think about boys while she washed herself, and today she remembered the way Brad Bishop had looked
in the restaurant when she'd seen him there with his dad. She
wondered whether he would be going to her school this year and,
if so, whether she'd have any classes with him. The thought made
her feel tingly, and she stayed under the water several minutes
longer than usual in an effort to prolong the feeling.

When she finally came out of the shower, the bathroom was steamy, the mirror all fogged up.

And there was a face on the glass.

Megan gasped, her heart thumping wildly. Instinctively, she pulled the towel around her, covering up, even though she knew there was no possible way that this . . . drawing could see her.

Except it was not exactly a drawing. It didn't look like someone had used a finger to depict a face on the glass, but rather as though a face had been pressed against the moisture on the mirror. For every feature was visible, down to a dimple on the narrow chin.

She wiped the face away with her hand, but the bathroom was still steamy, and the mirror fogged up again almost instantly.

The face reappeared.

Only it was different this time. Something about it had changed, and it took her a moment to realize what it was.

The face was smiling.

And its eyes were looking . . . lower.

She held the towel more tightly against her, wanting to run, wanting to scream, not knowing *what* to do. This wasn't really happening. Her imagination was working overtime, seeing things that weren't actually there. She was just scaring herself, her mind playing tricks on her the way it did after she saw a scary movie or TV show.

She thought of that thing—

monster

—she'd seen at night when her friends had stayed over. She'd told no one, not even Zoe or her mom, and she still wasn't a hundred percent sure that she'd really seen what she thought she'd seen. It had been late; she'd been tired; it might have been a dream. . . . There was a whole host of possibilities.

But that list of possibilities was getting shorter by the second.

Because the steam in the bathroom wasn't dissipating the way it should, wasn't going away. Instead, it was getting thicker and . . . *moving.* A long, slender section that resembled an arm moved toward her. She backed against the counter and saw the steam behind the arm thicken and coalesce into something that looked almost like a man's body.

Almost.

For there was something off about the form, a subtle mistake in proportion that resulted in a too-small head on a too-big body and an arm that resembled an anaconda. She remembered the *tentacle* that had slipped under Zoe's sheet. This reminded her of that, though the steam figure was smaller and more humanoid than that thing in the night had been.

The arm reached for her, its misty white fingers undulating and wavy, like strands of seaweed in a strong current.

Megan dashed to her left and yanked open the door, although she was wrapped in only a towel, ready to scream for her parents, ready even to accept the humiliation if James came up and saw her. But the instant the door opened, all of the steam in the bathroom shot out into the hall, pushing past her with a whoosh she could both hear and feel, as though a giant fan had turned on and propelled all of the air out of the room. The steam disappeared, evaporating in the dry atmosphere of the hallway. She turned in a circle, searching for the figure she had seen, but it was gone, and when she poked her head into the bathroom, she saw that the mirror was clear, no face.

Feeling braver, no longer needing to call for her parents, she walked back into the bathroom (though she kept the door open, just in case) and breathed on the mirror. She expected the condensation of her breath to reveal the outline of the face once again, but there were no lines on the glass at all. It was as if none of it had ever happened.

Still, she felt uneasy, and she grabbed her hairbrush and clothes and went into her bedroom, where she closed the door, quickly got dressed, then opened the door again, combing her hair as she hurried downstairs.

She wasn't sure what she should tell her parents, or whether she should tell them anything, but that problem was solved for her when she found that her mom had already left for work, James was in the garage playing in his stupid clubhouse, and her dad was on the phone, deep in conversation with some computer guy. Megan went into the living room to watch TV, and by the time her dad got off the phone and announced that he was going upstairs to work in his office, the entire experience in the bathroom seemed much less threatening and barely worth mentioning. She had a hard time believing it had happened herself.

But when ten o'clock rolled around and she decided to text Zoe and Kate about their plans for the day, the nervousness returned. Her parents had given her cell phone back a few days ago, but Megan was warier of using it than she had been before and now did so only when other people were around. With her mom at work, she went back upstairs where her dad was. She'd do the actual texting in her room, but he'd be in his office, close enough to save her if she needed help.

She didn't need help this time, but her muscles were tense when she first turned on the phone and waited to see whether there were any mysterious messages waiting for her. Luckily, there weren't, and she let out an honest-to-God sigh of relief as she typed out her texts.

As it turned out, neither Zoe nor Kate had any plans, so the three of them decided to go to a movie. Megan suggested they invite Julie to come along as well, but Julie answered neither text nor phone message, so the three of them opted to go it alone. Zoe texted that her mom could drive them, so Megan went across the hall to ask her dad whether it would be okay for her to go. "Zoe's mom's driving," she added quickly.

"When are you going?"

"Now."

"What about lunch?"

"We'll have Taco Bell."

"You have enough money?"

"Of course!"

He smiled at her. "It's okay with me. But check with your mom before you go. And make sure you're back before dinner."

"Thanks, Dad."

Megan called her mom, who of course said it was okay, and she met Zoe's van out in front of the house some fifteen minutes later. Zoe's sister, Kristi, was with them, which was kind of annoying, but she remained up front with her mom, and Zoe, Kate and Megan sat in the back and ignored her.

Since the movie didn't start until two, they had plenty of time to kill, and after they'd eaten lunch and stretched it out with endless soda refills, Zoe's mom drove them to The Store, where she and Kristi looked for shoes, leaving Megan, Kate and Zoe to wander the aisles. They ended up in the electronics department, browsing through the DVDs and covertly checking out the hot high school guy who worked behind the counter.

"I think he's looking at us," Zoe whispered as she picked up an *Avatar* DVD and pretended to read the back cover.

Megan peeked over her shoulder, but he was bending over to take a camera out of the display case for an elderly man to examine. She kept watching, though, and, sure enough, the second after he handed over the camera, he glanced in their direction. She quickly looked away, giggling. "He is!" she whispered.

Kate said nothing, but moved away from the two of them as if they weren't together. She ended up in the children's section, looking at little-kid movies, and both Megan and Zoe laughed at her.

Moments later, the old man gone, the clerk walked over. "Can I help you young ladies?"

Mortified, Megan said nothing, but stared unseeingly at the row of DVDs in front of her. She could feel the heat as her face turned red. But Zoe calmly said, "Do you have this in Blu-ray?"

"No. Only the more recent titles or the more popular older titles are in Blu-ray."

Megan had no idea which movie Zoe was asking about, and she was not brave enough to look, but she was both amazed by and envious of her friend's composure. Maybe Zoe *would* have talked to Brad if she'd been the one to see him in the restaurant. Megan suddenly felt awkward and backward and far more immature than her friend.

The clerk walked away to help another customer who was standing in front of a locked case holding smart phones, and the two of them motioned to Kate and left the electronics department, walking slowly and casually until they were in sporting goods, hidden behind a tall rack of shelves. Zoe's eyes were wide. She held a hand dramatically over her heart. "Oh. My. God!"

"I don't believe it!" Megan said. They were talking low, not wanting anyone else to overhear.

"He was interested, right? He was into us?"

"I was too scared to look!"

"He wasn't," Kate said matter-of-factly. "He was just doing his job."

Zoe ignored her. "I think he thought we were older. Do I look older? Do you think I could pass for sixteen?"

Megan didn't have a chance to answer, because Zoe's mom and Kristi suddenly appeared at the end of the aisle. The three of them immediately cut off their conversation.

"We'd better go," Zoe's mom said. "I need to make a quick stop at the library first. Then we'll stop by Circle K and get some candy for you guys to smuggle in. Those prices they charge at the theater are outrageous."

They were still early for the movie, but the theater showed some cool commercials for new movies and TV shows, so they had something entertaining to watch.

The movie itself was a horror flick, a PG-13 remake of a German art-house hit she'd read about but hadn't seen. She was the one who'd picked it—Zoe and Kate had wanted to see a romantic comedy that looked bad even in the trailers—and as she watched the film, she realized that it was the type of movie her dad would like, the kind the two of them might watch together on HBO.

They were the ones in the family who liked scary things, and when there was a clever visual reference to *Frankenstein* that only she seemed to get, Megan knew she had to tell him about this.

Zoe's mom had taken Kristi to see a Pixar movie on the next screen over, and that film had ended earlier, so the two of them were sitting on a bench, waiting, when she, Kate and Zoe came out into the lobby.

Megan arrived home after four, Zoe's mom dropping her off first, before taking Kate to her house. A monsoon had come up while they were in the theater, and thunder pealed loudly as she got out of the van. They'd missed the rain, although wet streets and a gushing gutter told her that it had really come down, but dark clouds still blocked the sun, and the occasional thunderclaps testified to the intensity of the afternoon storm.

Megan said good-bye to her friends, thanked Zoe's mom for the ride, ignored Zoe's sister, then turned toward her house. It looked creepy, she thought as she walked up the driveway toward it, and wondered if maybe they *should* have seen the romantic comedy. She walked slowly up the driveway. The gray clouds and dim light lent the house a gloominess she'd never seen before, and a chill passed through her as she noticed that none of the lights were on. There was a perfectly logical explanation for that—James liked to watch TV in the dark, and her dad's office faced the rear of the house and was not visible from here—but she could not help thinking that the house was empty, that everyone was gone.

Dead.

She refused to even go there.

Still, she stood for a moment on the front stoop, listening for sounds. If the house was empty, she was not walking in. Luckily, she heard her dad's music from upstairs—he liked to crank it up when her mom was out—and, relieved, she went inside. As she'd suspected, James was lying on the couch in the darkened living room, watching cartoons, an open package of Doritos on his chest.

"Is Dad upstairs?" she asked, though she already knew the answer.

"In his office."

Megan bounded up the steps two at a time, eager to tell him about the movie.

But her father was *not* in his office. The room was empty, and, frowning, she moved past the doorway, walking all the way in, checking to see whether he was in one of the corners or crouched down behind the desk. In the back of her mind, though she didn't want to admit it, was the fear that he had collapsed, had a stroke or heart attack or something and was lying on the floor, dead.

There was a strange clicking sound coming from his computer, and she walked around the side of his desk, grateful to see that he was not on the floor. He was probably in the bathroom, she thought reassuringly as she glanced at the monitor.

Hi, Megan!

The words were in the middle of the screen, and she might have thought her dad had typed them if they hadn't started dancing as she watched: growing, changing colors, bouncing up and down.

The words disappeared.

I saw U.

She froze, the rhythm of her heart accelerating as the new text emerged, bright red against a light blue background. In her mind, she saw the face in the mirror, the figure in the steam. She thought of the message on her phone: *I C U Megan.*

"Hi."

She jumped at the sound of her father's voice, letting out a sharp, startled yelp.

"Whoa." He was coming through the doorway, but he backed up comically in the face of her reaction. "I guess you saw that horror movie, huh?"

"Actually, we did," she admitted. "But . . ." *That's not what scared me,* she was about to say. And then she looked at the computer screen and saw only a series of free-floating icons that her dad was obviously using for his current job.

"But what?"

She shook her head. "I thought I saw something weird on your computer."

He grinned. "There's always something weird on my computer."

"That's not what I meant . . ." she began. She thought about telling him what she'd seen on his screen, thought about describing her experience this morning in the bathroom, but trying to make him believe she'd encountered something spooky right after she'd returned from seeing a horror movie was near impossible, and it was probably better if she brought it up some other time. She'd get only one shot with a story as out-there as this, and if she didn't convince him the first time, she'd never be able to do it. She didn't want to ruin her one and only chance.

So she smiled at him and changed the subject. "That was a good movie," she told him. "It was creepy."

"Did you get scared?" he teased.

"A little."

He bumped her shoulder. "Think I can convince your mom to see it?"

"Sure," she said, playing along. "And have her bring James."

They both laughed.

But she still felt chilled, and even as she was joking around with her dad, she kept her eyes on his computer.

FOURTEEN

SATURDAY.

Robbie was late coming over, so James went up to the head-quarters by himself. The place was shaping up. The skeletons he'd found had been cleaned up and arranged on a low shelf made from a wood plank balanced atop concrete cinder blocks. The shelf was to the right of the bookcase, which was now filled with unwanted magazines they'd scrounged from their respective houses. Robbie's dad had given them an old typewriter, which they'd placed on top of the bookcase next to a stack of plain white paper and a toy magnifying glass Robbie had taken from his brother's room. The exercise bike was next to the window, and the traffic cone sat in front of the secret compartment, marking it and blocking it. To-day, Robbie was bringing over his chemistry set, which would help make the headquarters look like a real crime lab.

If he ever got here.

James glanced around. They needed a clock, he decided, so they could tell what time it was.

He sat on the floor for a few minutes, thumbed through an old issue of *People* magazine, read a movie review, found a few pictures of starlets on the beach in bikinis, then stood up, restless. Standing near the window, he listened for the sound of Robbie's car, heard nothing, then opened the trapdoor and climbed the ladder downstairs.

He walked into the backyard. His parents had gone to The Store, leaving him in Megan's hands. Not an ideal situation, although if the two of them stayed out of each other's way until their mom and dad returned, there shouldn't be a problem.

James looked toward the house, where his sister was hopefully minding her own business and not spying on him.

He was about to walk out to the front yard and wait for Robbie there, when his attention was caught by the hole he had dug in the ground.

It was back.

How was that possible? His dad had made him fill it in last weekend. The work had been hard—much harder than digging it had been, for some reason—but afterward, it was as if a great responsibility had been lifted from his shoulders. The unwanted compulsion to eat dirt that had been plaguing him since the opening of that secret compartment had disappeared, and along with it the weird mixture of defensiveness and guilt that discovery of the compartment had engendered.

He'd been grateful to his dad, and the week had passed quickly and uneventfully.

But last night he'd had a dream. In it, he had dug a tunnel from the garage to the basement, *eating* the dirt as he made his way under the yard, feeling it enter his body through one end and pass out the other as though he were a worm. Now, he saw as he approached the hole, there actually *was* a tunnel, or the beginning of one, and he felt within his chest a familiar stirring.

Perfectly round, as though bored by machine, the hole was probably three feet across and went down at least that far. At the bottom were bugs, dozens of them, black, unrecognizable insects that had probably been beetles before being squished into the amorphous mass that coated the floor of the pit. A narrow passage, barely big enough for him to slide through on his stomach, had been burrowed into the side of the hole, heading toward the house.

James jumped in, hearing and feeling the bugs crunch beneath his shoes. Grimacing, he kicked them to the edges and cleared a space before the tunnel. He knew it was crazy even as he did it, but he couldn't seem to help himself, and he dropped to his knees, then ducked down and pushed his way into the opening headfirst.

It was pitch-black. He couldn't see a thing. For all he knew, there were bugs galore in the space ahead. Beetles. Worms. Or something worse.

But he pressed on, wriggling into the narrow tunnel, arms at his sides like the Grinch slithering and slinking through one of the Whos' houses. The earth smelled good, and he breathed deeply, the scent of the soil and its olfactory lure overriding the utter lack of light and helping him overcome his trepidation. He wriggled in farther—

And dirt fell on his rear end and the backs of his legs—the only parts of his body still sticking out into the hole.

He waited in place for a moment, not moving, thinking that his squirming feet must have jostled free some loose earth. But though he remained still, soil continued to rain down on the lower half of his body.

"Hey!" he cried. "Stop it!" But his voice sounded muffled even to himself, and he doubted that the sound of it even escaped the tunnel.

The dirt continued to fall. Faster.

Someone was trying to bury him.

Someone or some*thing*.

In his mind, he saw the terrible grinning man from his dreams, the one he'd spotted in the window of his dad's office, furiously throwing dirt into the hole in an effort to entomb him here forever. This was a trap, and he'd fallen for it, and he wondered whether the dirt would be packed down, the grass replaced, everything put back perfectly just the way it had been so that he would never be found. His parents would search for him, the police might think he'd been kidnapped or had run away, and all the time he would be buried here in the backyard, rotting.

Turning into a skeleton like the animals he'd found.

James tried to quell the panic rising within him.

He had to get out of here.

Now.

With a burst of energy, he shoved himself backward, using his shoulders to propel his body, since his arms were pinned uselessly to his sides. In the hole, his shoes dug into the beetle-coated earth, and he tilted his ankles, providing enough leverage for his knees to find purchase. As dirt continued to fall heavily down, he squirmed and twisted his body rearward through the confined passageway until finally his hands were out of the tunnel and able to help push him free.

He was half-submerged in loose dirt, and a huge clump of soil fell on top of his head as he emerged from the tunnel, nearly knocking him flat. Grit stung his eyes and got in his nose, and now the dirt in his mouth did not taste good at all. He shook his head to get it out of his hair and used a hand to wipe off his face. The sides of the hole were collapsing, and he clambered unsteadily to his feet. He could see no one in the yard, but he didn't have time to look around, because one entire section of the pit fell in on him, knocking him sideways and forcing him to his knees. He was pinned by the heavy earth in an awkward position, with one hand above his head and the other trapped beneath his tilted body.

He was going to die.

He knew it as surely as he knew his own name. One more shovelful of dirt or one more collapsed wall and he would be gone.

Frantic, he bent his free arm and began desperately clawing at the surrounding soil in an urgent attempt to free himself. Luckily, the side of the wall that had him pinned was solid, not loose, and he was able to pull out one chunk and then another, tossing them onto the ground above. The earth was shifting around him, almost like a miniquake, but he managed to liberate his other arm, and then both hands were feverishly yanking out hunks of dirt as his legs tried in vain to kick themselves out from under the weight holding them down. His efforts revealed a fault line in the compacted soil, and his clawed fingers pulled the two halves apart at that point, allowing him to wriggle up and out, just as the rest of the hole fell in on itself.

He emerged breathless and weak, flopping exhaustedly on the ground, alive only because he had managed to escape at the very last second. If he had been even a hairbreadth slower, he would be dead right now.

Breathing heavily, limbs shaking from both exertion and fear, he looked around the backyard, trying to see whether he could find out who—

what

—had tried to kill him, but the yard was empty.

James hurried into the house. He wanted to tell his dad what had happened. Well, he didn't *want* to, but he had to. Something was going on here, and his parents needed to know about it. Maybe they could do something; maybe they could—

Protect him.

He felt reassured just thinking the words. His mom and dad probably still weren't back, but he intended to wait for them inside, and as soon as they returned, he was going to tell them everything, from the man in the window to the secret compartment in the headquarters to the animal skeletons to the dirt eating to the mysterious hole that had lured him in and then tried to kill him. He didn't know what they could do about it, but they were adults; they would take care of it.

He walked through the back patio, pulled open the screen—

—and the kitchen door slammed shut.

It barely missed hitting him in the face, barely missed crushing his fingers against the doorjamb. If he hadn't moved his hand at the last second, he would have been seriously injured. Angrily, he turned the knob and threw the door open again, already shouting out Megan's name.

But she wasn't there.

James stopped, looking around, confused, but not as confused as he would like to have been. His sister hadn't been the one who slammed the door on him. No, someone—

something

—else had done it. And it hadn't been a prank. The door pusher had wanted to hurt him.

James stepped carefully into the kitchen, looking around. "Megan!" He called his sister's name not out of anger this time but out of need, a desire to have her nearby. Maybe she couldn't protect him the way his parents could, but she was older and braver than he was, and with two of them, they'd be better able to defend themselves against . . . against . . . whatever it was.

"Megan?"

There was no answer, and he moved forward, calling her name again. From the corner of his eye, he saw movement, and when he looked to his right, he saw the door to the basement swing slowly open. He wanted to scream, wanted to run, but he was frozen in place, and in the silence of the house, he heard footsteps, the heavy, deliberate footsteps of a man coming up the cellar stairs.

The grinning man from the corner.

Now he did run. He didn't want to leave Megan all alone, but his mind tolerated no such conscious considerations. He was acting on instinct, pure animal fear, and he dashed out the door the way he had come, filled only with the need for self-preservation. Ahead of him, past the patio, was the collapsed hole in which he'd almost been killed, and at the sight of it, a bolt of terror shot through him.

Afraid to remain in the backyard for even a second longer, he dashed around the corner of the house as fast as his legs would carry him, speeding down the driveway and out to the front yard, where, hopefully, his parents would be just pulling in. They weren't. But Megan was sitting on the front stoop, looking down at her iPhone. She looked up at him as he hurried over. She'd obviously been out here for some time, and a cold shiver passed through him.

She hadn't been inside at all.

He'd been alone in the house.

No, he hadn't.

The cold intensified.

Megan was not just looking at him, he realized. She was *staring* at him. Her face was white and her eyes wide.

Like she'd just seen a ghost.

He pushed that thought away. It was *not* what he wanted to be thinking about right now. Huffing and puffing from his brief, furious run, he stood in front of her, trying to catch his breath in order to tell her what happened. But before he could get a word out, she was standing and holding out her iPhone, that stunned look still on her face.

She showed him the message on the screen: *James will die if he tells.*

He suddenly understood her fear. He felt it, too.

"What's that mean?" she whispered. She looked furtively around, as if worried about being overheard. "Tell who? Tell what?"

The message changed.

Hi, James!

He sucked in his breath. "Who is that?" he asked her. "Who's texting you?"

"I don't know!" Her voice was still low, but there was a note of panic in it.

Whoever—*whatever*—it was, was acting in real time. It knew he was here, knew he was looking at the phone. He turned his head from left to right, hoping to spot someone on the sidewalk or in the yard of one of their neighbors. But he knew that no one on the street was sending this, didn't he? He'd nearly been buried alive, the kitchen door had almost crushed his hand, *something* had been coming up from the basement for him, and immediately after running out to the front yard so that the second after they returned he could tell his parents what had happened, Megan received the text, *James will die if he tells.*

This wasn't a joke. This wasn't a coincidence. This was a warning.

The dazed look on his sister's face told him that she knew it, too.

A new message appeared. *I will kill you both.*

"Shut it off!" James told Megan. He hadn't meant to shout at her, but his voice came out panicky and far too loud.

His alarm jolted her into action, and she turned off the device, juggling it from hand to hand as though it were hot and burning her fingers.

Before they could say a word to each other about what had happened or what to do about it, their parents pulled into the driveway. At the same time, Robbie's dad parked next to the curb to drop him off. James turned toward his sister as his dad got out of the van, but she wouldn't meet his eyes and fumblingly placed the phone in her pocket.

It was rare for James and Megan to be standing together by the front porch, rare enough to be noticed, and, walking over, their father glanced from one to the other. "What happened?" he asked suspiciously. "What's going on here?"

James shot his sister a look, imploring her to answer for them.

"Nothing," she said. Her voice sounded a lot calmer and a lot more normal than it should have.

I will kill you both.

James looked guiltily away as his dad frowned at him. "Is that dirt on your clothes? Were you digging again?"

He didn't respond.

"I'm talking to you."

I will kill you both.

He noticed his dad examining his mouth, trying to determine whether he'd been eating dirt, and James wanted to cry, filled with a frustration that could not be expressed any other way. But Robbie was here, and he and Megan had been warned, and he managed to hold the tears at bay.

Robbie started walking up just as Megan came under her father's scrutiny. The heat off for a moment, James took the opportunity to hurry over to his friend. His mom was by the curb, talking to Robbie's dad, and this was his chance to dodge both parents and avoid further scrutiny.

"Hey," Robbie said in greeting.

James nodded. "Hey."

The third degree had ended, and his dad headed out to the street to see Robbie's father. Megan remained where she was. James understood completely. Afraid to go into the backyard or over to their headquarters, he was equally leery of going back into the house. So he remained unmoving in the center of the lawn, waiting for his parents to finish talking and go inside before he took Robbie up to his room, where they could play computer games or do something *normal.*

He glanced nervously toward the side of the house. He thought about telling Robbie what had happened—and he would, eventually—but his friend seemed subdued this morning, maybe even a little frightened. James's brain was probably filtering things through its own prism, but, still, he didn't want to scare Robbie off, and he decided that this was not the time to come clean.

The parents finished talking, Robbie's father drove away, and James's mom and dad took their Store sacks out of the van before heading into the house. Megan followed, and James and Robbie went in behind her. Anxious, James looked across the living room and the dining room at the entrance to the kitchen, thinking about the slowly opening door to the basement and those terrible heavy footfalls. He watched his mom go through the kitchen doorway and waited for some type of reaction, but there was none. He heard her humming as she put away cleaning products, and he started to relax. Maybe it was over.

Closing the front door, his eye was caught by a flash of white against the dark brown of the floor. He bent down. An envelope had fallen through the mail slot, only there was no stamp on it, no postmark, no return address. The only words written on the front of the envelope were, *The R.J. Detective Agency.*

That was weird. They'd settled on the name only last night, after a long phone conversation in which he'd given in on the name in exchange for Robbie's agreeing to let James call himself "senior detective" as opposed to Robbie's regular "detective." Warily, James opened the envelope. Inside was a single sheet of lined paper on which was written a short note:

Dear Detectives,

I would like to hire you to follow a man named John Lynch. I believe he stole a very expensive bracelet given to me by my mother and have reason to believe he has stolen other items of jewelry from women in the north end of Jardine. If you can prove that he is the thief, I will reward you handsomely.

"This is great!" Robbie said excitedly, reading over his shoulder.

"I don't think we should do it," James told him.

"Why not?"

He held up the letter. "Who wrote this? Who's it from? Why didn't they sign their name? And why would they hire *us* for something like this? Besides, how did they know the name of our detective agency? In fact, how did this even get here? The mailman didn't deliver it. He hasn't even come yet."

"What are you saying?" Robbie asked, although there was more worry in his voice than defensiveness. He had obviously caught on to the fact that something was not right about this, and James saw on his face the same look of uneasiness that he'd worn when he first arrived. He might not have seen what James had seen, but he could sense that some of the things that happened in and around this house were not normal.

"I'm saying we shouldn't take this case. It's not even a case, really. Some unknown person wants us to follow some guy named John Lynch. We have no real details, and we have no way to even tell the person hiring us what we find. Don't you think that's suspicious?"

"Yeah, it is, kind of." Robbie was silent for a moment, looking at the paper in James's hand. He nodded toward it. "Was that there when you were in the house earlier?"

"I don't think so," James admitted.

"Do you think someone just put it through your mail slot?"

"I don't know."

Robbie was quiet again. "You had your mind made up even before you opened the envelope, didn't you?"

"Yeah."

"Why?"

"Because—" James began, but he stopped.

I will kill you both.

"Call it my detective's intuition," he said.

Robbie seemed impressed by that, and they left it there. James folded the letter, put it back in the envelope, and the two of them headed upstairs to his bedroom. Megan was in her own room, and the two of them locked eyes for a second as he passed by the open doorway. He was filled with a sense of helplessness. He wanted to tell Robbie what had happened, but couldn't. Wanted to talk to his parents about it, but was afraid.

What could he do? James wondered, and the only answer he came up with was expressed in a single word.

Nothing.

FIFTEEN

PAM AND HER HUSBAND, JOE, WERE THE FIRST ONES TO ARRIVE at the party. Claire greeted them warmly, accepted the expensive bottle of wine they brought, and took them on a quick tour of the house before returning them to the dining room and the food.

"This place is terrific," Pam told her. "The kitchen is amazing! And I really like the openness. And the high ceilings."

"Thank you."

"Even your kids' rooms look like something out of a magazine."

Claire laughed. "Well, we made them clean up before packing them off to Grandma's. Believe me, they don't usually look like that. Especially James's room."

"It is a nice place, though," Pam said. She punched Claire lightly on the arm. "Now aren't you glad you did this?"

The doorbell rang.

"Ask me in two hours," Claire told her.

Julian reached the door before she did and ushered in a pleasant-looking young man who had also brought a bottle of wine and whom Julian introduced as Cole Hubbard, one of their neighbors. It was his turn to give the tour, so Claire graciously accepted the gift and brought it to the kitchen while Julian took the man upstairs, no doubt to show off his office.

Julian's friend Rick was the next to arrive, and Claire forced herself to smile at him as he entered, bringing nothing. Rick was a printer, and Julian had met him years ago when he'd needed some new business cards. The two of them had hit it off for some inexplicable reason, though outwardly they would seem to have nothing in common. Jardine-born and -bred, Rick had never finished high school, let alone gone on to college, and his sole interest appeared to be beer, his favorite brands of which were advertised on the series of grimy, faded T-shirts that made up his wardrobe.

Claire had never liked Rick, and she knew that, as usual, he would end up drinking too much and railing against his ex, who'd moved to Las Cruces over three years ago. Declining to take him around their new house, she pointed him toward the food, and was saved from further conversation by the ringing of the doorbell. It was Julian's other friend, Patrick, along with his wife, Kathleen. The two of them, both workers at the hospital, were the polar opposite of Rick, and she stood with them in the entryway for a few moments, talking and catching up and apologizing for not having them over sooner. It was getting too crowded to give tours, so she bade them explore to their heart's content and answered the next ring of the doorbell, which turned out to be her friend Janet.

The floodgates opened after that, and for several minutes she did not even have a chance to close the door between arrivals. They'd decided not to invite family, only friends, and while she'd bristled at that at first, Claire was happy now that Julian had stuck to his guns. It was hard enough dealing with the disparate personalities of their respective circles without throwing relatives into the mix.

Julian had turned on some music, low and not overpowering—one of Brian Eno's ambient records, she was pretty sure—and the party seemed to be going well. People were eating and drinking, talking and laughing, her friends from work getting to know the neighbors from her street, and though her natural instinct was to hang out with her closest friends, the ones like Janet whom she'd known forever, she made a concerted effort to mingle. There was a long-haul trucker, she discovered, a retired accountant, a veterinarian, a bank teller, a contractor. It was an eclectic group, their new neighbors, and Claire was glad she and Julian had decided to host this get-together. Two of the couples from down the block were just as unfamiliar with their other neighbors as she and Julian were, and they made a special effort to let the two of them know what a great idea this was and how much fun they were having.

After spending a few moments talking to Patrick and Kathleen about recent cutbacks at the hospital and an unseasonal uptick in flu cases, Claire excused herself and maneuvered her way into the dining room to refresh her drink and grab a handful of chips. She practically bumped heads with Julian, who had arrived at the table to snag a couple of taquitos.

"It's going well," she said.

He motioned toward the table. "Do you think we have enough food?"

"We have enough drinks. So if we run out of food, it's your job to make sure everyone's drunk enough that they don't notice."

He smiled. "Deal."

In the kitchen, Rick and Cole were arguing politics. Loudly. Claire hadn't noticed before, but now their voices were carrying. She nudged Julian, nodding toward the open doorway.

"It's those damn pensions," Rick was saying. "Public employee unions have taken this nation hostage. Our tax dollars are going to pay off the retirement of those bureaucrats."

Cole shook his head. "Your dollars are going to pay off *everyone's* retirement. Oil company CEOs? That's where those extra pennies you pay at the pump go. Computer company pensions? That's why you're paying a hundred bucks for a word-processing program that cost fifty cents to mass-produce in China. You know, instead of pissing and moaning about how other people have it better than you and how their retirement systems should be as bad as yours, why don't you insist that your retirement be as *good* as theirs? Instead of trying to drag everyone else *down* to your level, try to push yourself *up* to their level."

"Don't give me that commie crap."

"Do you want to know why we're really on the hook for those pensions? Because the stock market went south, and brokerage firms pawned off toxic assets to pension fund managers, promising that they were good investments, and everyone got screwed. The pension funds lost their money due to fraud and deception, and now taxpayers are on the hook for it. That's why those executives and Wall Street types are so rich. They just take the money and let everyone else fight over the crumbs."

"Good point," Julian whispered.

"And, of course," Cole continued, "they want to eliminate retirement systems and Social Security and have *everyone* gamble their retirement money on the stock market—which is exactly what got us into this mess in the first place."

Rick's face was getting red with anger. Sensing trouble, Claire dispatched Julian to defuse the situation. "Your friend," she said. "You take care of him."

She watched with more than a little admiration as he did just that, walking between the two men and deftly changing the subject to a mash-up YouTube video he'd recently seen featuring John Wayne, a supermodel and a condom ad. Seconds later, all three of them were laughing.

But the mood of the party seemed to have shifted, and Claire was not quite sure why. She turned back toward the living room. The light, friendly tone that had dominated the gathering until now was gone, replaced by an edgier, more competitive vibe. Even the background music seemed darker, although she knew that Julian had not changed CDs.

Refilling her wineglass for the umpteenth time, Felicia, the bank teller, asked about the upstairs—perfunctorily, Claire thought—and, putting a smile on her face, Claire took her up to see the kids' bedrooms and Julian's office. An older man she didn't know was standing in James's room, staring intently at the boy's bed in a way that made her feel very uncomfortable. She wanted to order him out of her son's room *and* out of her house, but she forced herself to be polite and give the guy the benefit of the doubt, and she asked pointedly, "May I help you?"

"No," he said in a voice that implied he was offended by her very presence. He turned and, without another word, walked past her and Felicia, out of the room, down the hall and down the stairs.

"What the hell . . . ?" Claire said.

Felicia shrugged noncommittally, and Claire quickly pointed to and identified each of the rooms before ushering the other woman back downstairs.

She searched for the man unsuccessfully in the hall, dining room and living room. The front door was wide-open, and she peered outside before closing it, seeing the back of the man's jacket as he headed down the sidewalk. Who was he? she wondered. Was he one of their neighbors? Had he even been invited to the party or had he just crashed? She considered hurrying after him, confronting him, but he was already gone and it was night, and the idea of meeting up with him in the dark frightened her.

She closed the door, locking it so no one from outside could come in.

Claire looked for Julian, but he was nowhere to be found. In fact, much of the party had moved outside, to the backyard, and she walked through the kitchen and out the open door to the patio, hoping to find him somewhere in the crowd. Quite a few people were out here, but most of them were standing around silently or speaking desultorily in low, enervated voices. One man she didn't recognize was sitting on the ground, head between his knees as though he were about to throw up, atop the bare mound of dirt where James had covered up his hole. In the garage, by contrast, the lights were on, and through the dirty window she saw a couple energetically dancing, though the music from the house was not audible out here. From the alley, she could hear the sound of someone rooting around in their garbage cans.

"Julian!" she called out, but there was no answer. None of the people in the backyard even bothered to look over at her.

Where was he?

Claire was about to walk over to the garage, just in case he was in there with the dancers, when a tap on the shoulder caused her to turn around.

It was Janet.

"Do you know what's going on in there?" Janet motioned toward the kitchen doorway.

Claire was confused. "What are you talking about?"

"Come here," her friend said, grabbing her hand. Janet led her back into the house and through the kitchen, stopping before the open doorway that led to the basement. From downstairs came a series of rough male grunts accompanied by a woman's high-pitched cries.

"I don't know who they are, but it's been going on for a while," Janet whispered. "That guy *lasts*," she added. "I'm getting sore just listening to him."

"That is not right," Claire said angrily. "That's where we store our stuff. The kids' *toys* are down there." The lights in the basement were off, but she turned them on with the wall switch, and, fists clenched, stomped down the steps.

It was Pam. And her husband, Joe.

Only they weren't together.

She was on top of a box, skirt hiked up, panties down, using one of Megan's old Barbies to pleasure herself, inserting the doll's head, then pulling it out, inserting it again, pulling it out. Much of the doll's hair had been worn away, and its clothes were ragged, torn. The flesh-colored plastic looked shiny in the overhead light.

He had pushed aside some stuffed Hefty bags and cardboard boxes and cleared a space in the corner (*the corner!*), where he was standing with his pants and underwear around his ankles, grunting loudly as he thrust into what appeared to be a Christmas decoration.

"What the hell are you doing?" Claire screamed.

There was a sudden cessation of movement. Both of them blinked at her dumbly, almost as though awakening from a trance; then they grabbed and pulled on their clothes, embarrassed. No, more than embarrassed. Ashamed. Pam met her eyes for a brief second, and what Claire saw there was confusion and humiliation. It was as though she'd been completely unaware of what she'd been doing and had only now realized it.

But that did not excuse her and her husband's actions. Claire looked disgustedly at the shiny, worn-out Barbie in Pam's hand, at the fouled Christmas decoration Joe had dropped. "Get out of here!" she ordered.

She marched back up to the kitchen and stepped to the side of the door to let them pass. Janet, standing opposite her, looked shocked by what had happened down there, but, unsettlingly, also intrigued. Claire glanced away, not wanting to meet her gaze.

Pam and Joe emerged moments later, hurrying past without looking at either of them, and Claire followed the couple into the living room, watching as they rushed out toward the street and their car, slamming the front door behind them. Julian had appeared from somewhere and was sidling next to her, drink in hand. "What was that all about?"

She wanted to tell him, but not here, not now, so she shrugged it off and asked him where he'd been.

"Upstairs." He grinned. "Showing off. I convinced Cole to check out my record collection. He was suitably impressed."

Claire looked around. The house suddenly seemed much more crowded, and she saw several people who had been in the backyard only moments before. Her first thought was that something had happened out there, something that had chased them all inside, but though the men and women around her seemed subdued, they appeared neither frightened nor upset, and she supposed it was possible that they had come in because they were looking for food or drink, or perhaps preparing to leave.

The lights flickered.

Claire froze, half expecting the electricity to go off. It was rare to have a blackout unless there was a thunderstorm or a major wind, but it was not unheard-of, and she thought with resignation that this would probably be an appropriate ending for their party, which seemed to be heading rapidly and steadily downhill.

The lights continued to flicker, making the living room seem as though it were being lit by candles. Glancing through the front window, Claire saw that none of the houses across the street appeared to be affected.

Of course not.

"Do you think it's—" she started to ask Julian, but her question was interrupted by a loud roar from the rear of the house, a sudden harsh, lionlike sound that made her jump and caused Julian to spill his drink.

"What the hell was *that*?" he asked. He didn't sound frightened, but she noticed that he wasn't going back there to investigate, either. Everyone, in fact, had frozen, as though waiting to see what would happen next.

The sound came again, only lower this time, and halfway through, it began fading away until it dwindled down to nothing.

Wafting in from the rear of the house was a strong scent of burned toast.

Almost as one, the guests moved to the left in order to see down the hallway, the area from whence the noise and the smell seemed to have come. They were looking at one another, talking quietly, wondering what was going on. Claire and Julian shifted over, too.

A tall man was shuffling down the hall.

They all grew quiet.

The man was dressed in heavy clothing, inappropriate for the weather, and he moved slowly, as though his legs did not work properly. Claire tried desperately to figure out who he was, but it was hard to see his face because the hallway was so dark. *Too* dark, she thought, and she realized that once again something was wrong with the lights, although this time they were merely dim, not flickering.

The shambling figure moved slowly toward the living room.

Claire squinted into the gloom, but his features grew no clearer to her. It was as though she needed glasses, and while he continued to come nearer, his face never emerged fully enough from the shadows for him to become recognizable. His clothes were sharply defined, however, and she thought there was something familiar about them, although she could not immediately say what.

Gasps greeted his appearance as the man shuffled into the living room.

Now he could be seen. People were moving away, backing up. It was a face that should have remained in darkness. Dark, sunken eyes revealed no whites. A flattened nose seemed lost amid the swollen folds of mottled flesh that made up the forehead, cheeks and chin. The mouth, too large, was grinning, teeth inappropriately bright. Behind her, the front door opened, then closed as someone left.

Escaped.

The man stopped. She recognized him now. She still had no idea where she had seen those clothes before, but that grinning mouth was unmistakable. This was the man from her nightmare, the man from the basement.

Someone else left the house.

Claire stared in horror. That grinning mouth was opening impossibly wide, wider than the muscles of his face should have been able to stretch. From it issued that horrifying roar, only, this close, the volume was practically unbearable.

The lights went out, and the house was thrown into darkness. Someone screamed. Seconds later, the lights came on again and the figure was gone. Everyone was looking around frantically, afraid he might suddenly pop up right behind them, but there was no sign of the man.

Cole was the first one to speak. He was close by, and he turned to Julian. "That's the man who died in your house."

Claire had no idea what he was referring to, but she knew he was saying that the man was a ghost, and she looked at Julian.

"See?" she said. "What did I tell you?" She was breathing heavily, as though she'd just run up several flights of stairs. She could hear the amplified sound of her crazy-pumping heart in her ears.

The party was breaking up. People were leaving without saying good-bye, and the few who did stop to speak with them made no mention of what had happened, simply offered perfunctory congratulations before they quickly departed, like guests ashamed of a drunken host's behavior. In moments, the house was all but empty.

Rick, surprisingly, was the only one with an honest reaction. He was the last to leave, and he shook his head as he looked back toward the hall. "What the hell *was* that?" he said.

Claire and Julian shrugged helplessly.

"That was a fuckin' ghost, man. We all saw it."

It felt good to hear the word spoken, even if it was by Rick.

"Shit! Did anyone get a picture? I didn't even think about it. I shoulda whipped out my phone. Did anybody else take one?"

"I don't know," Julian admitted.

"People always wonder why those UFO photos are always grainy and shit, why no one ever gets a good picture of Bigfoot or the Loch Ness Monster or whatever. It's because when it's happening, when it's going down, you don't think of stuff like that. You're too scared to even move."

"You're right," Claire told him.

"But we were here," Rick said. "We saw it. All of us. So don't go second-guessing yourself tomorrow, telling yourself you imagined it or it didn't really happen. It happened. I'm a witness. That was no figment of your imagination. That was a ghost. And there were a good dozen or so people who stood here and watched the whole thing."

"He's right."

Surprised, Rick turned to see who had spoken. Cole Hubbard was standing on the stoop behind him, and Claire wondered whether he had gone and come back or had been there the entire time. She could not recall seeing him leave.

"That *was* a ghost," Cole said. "And we all saw it." He looked from Julian to Claire. "I can't say I'm all that surprised, and probably most of the other neighbors aren't, either. In fact, that might even be the reason some of them came." He motioned toward the two houses on either side of theirs. "Or didn't come."

"What are you talking about?" Rick said.

"A lot of old neighborhoods have a 'haunted' house. Well, this is ours."

"I told you." Claire faced Julian. "I told you."

"You want my advice?" Cole said. "Sell the house. Sell it now before the word spreads. Get out while you can."

SIXTEEN

THEY WEREN'T SAYING ANYTHING TO MEGAN OR JAMES. JULIAN was adamant about that. They didn't know what was really going on here, he argued, and he didn't want to frighten the kids needlessly.

Though initially reluctant, Claire finally agreed. "But we *do* know what's going on here," she told him pointedly. "Our house is haunted. We saw a ghost. We *all* saw a ghost."

"Not necessarily," he argued. "There were a lot of people, some of them who weren't invited. You caught that man in James's room. This guy might've been a party crasher, too. Everyone had had a little too much to drink; those lights were flickering. We might not've seen what we thought we saw. And when the lights went out, he might've just gone out the back door."

"Come on! This wasn't some teenage keg party. Guys from other neighborhoods weren't sneaking into our house to meet chicks and score free booze. This was a housewarming party with a countable number of people attending. And just because I didn't recognize that man in James's room doesn't mean you didn't invite him. I'm pretty sure he's a neighbor. But that ghost . . ." She glared at him. "Cole said it was a man who died in our house. You didn't even tell me about that."

"I didn't know," he lied.

"Right."

"I didn't."

"I don't care right now. But I do think Cole's right. I think we should sell the house."

Julian sighed. "We just bought it. We can't—"

"We can't what? Sell it? Of course we can. We'll find another house."

"We can't afford it."

"Our house is haunted! What part of that don't you understand?"

"Even if it is haunted," he told her, "and I'm not saying it is, a ghost can't hurt anyone. They might frighten people, but they can't physically harm a person."

"Fear can cause heart attacks. And ghosts can make people trip and fall if they startle them. If they can also play records and move laundry baskets . . ." She exhaled heavily, disgusted. "I'm not going to argue with you about the physical properties of ghosts. What I'm saying is, I'm not going to live in a haunted house."

"You're going to have to. Look, I don't have any jobs lined up after this one. And the town of Jardine is not exactly a hotbed of legal activity, so your phone's not ringing off the hook, either. We have to be realistic. If we were in California, we might both have enough business that we could afford a do-over. But right now, that's not an option. We have enough money coming in, and in the bank, to make our house payments and pay our monthly bills, with a little bit left over. But that's it. The down payment for this place pretty much cleaned us out. We can't afford to do it again. Or pay all those points and fees. Even if we *did* qualify for another loan. So we can't just pull up stakes and move. It's financially impossible."

He could tell from the expression on her face that he'd gotten through to her, but she wasn't going to simply give up. "Contracts are made to be broken," she said. "I should know. I'm a lawyer."

"And you can somehow weasel us out of those hundreds of pages of rules and obligations that we signed? That *you* signed?

Face it, unless we win the lottery, or Bill Gates hires you as his personal attorney and hires me to completely revamp Microsoft's Web presence, we're stuck here. At least for now."

"Fine," she said. "But we need to come up with a plan. I don't feel safe here. And even if we don't tell the kids anything—*yet*— they need to be protected."

"Agreed."

"So . . . ?"

"So we keep our eyes open. We try to find out ourselves exactly what's going on, research the house, the neighborhood, whatever, and we make sure that Megan and James are never in the house alone, especially at night."

"That's about the lamest plan I ever heard," Claire said. But she didn't have anything better, and, for the moment at least, they seemed to have called a truce.

It was daytime, though. Morning. Tonight would be a different story, and he had no doubt that, mentally and psychologically, they would each end up facing once again what had happened. Megan and James would be home as well, and as he thought about it now, it seemed to him that their bedrooms upstairs were much too far away from the master bedroom.

He wasn't about to mention that, however. He might be just as frightened as Claire, but it was his job to be strong, not only for her but for the whole family, and he needed to put a good face on everything, needed to pretend this was no big deal.

He had expected Claire to get up from the couch and leave, to get a drink or go to the bathroom or start doing the breakfast dishes or do whatever it was she would usually do when a conversation was over. But she remained in place, and there was a look on her face that he didn't trust. He knew even before she spoke that he was not going to like what she was about to say, a feeling that intensified when she met his gaze, then immediately looked away. "You know," she said, "I thought for a while that it might be Miles. Obviously, it's not," she added quickly. "But . . ." She let the thought dangle.

Julian didn't trust himself to speak.

"I've thought I've felt him before. Not just here and not just on Farris Street, but back in California, in our old house." She spoke rapidly, as though afraid he might cut her off. "I've never seen him, but there've been signs. Little indications that he was around, watching over us. I know you've seen them, too. Or heard them. Or felt them. And that last time? I wasn't trying to hurt you. I just . . . I just wanted to tell you. I guess I wanted to know if you were thinking the same thing."

She looked at him hopefully, but he turned away, unable to face her. Of course he'd thought the same thing, but he'd never allowed himself to dwell on it, and he would never admit it to her. Even now, the tears were close, and he forced his mind to change the subject, think about something else, before his eyes overflowed and he started to cry and he found himself unable to stop.

He stood.

Claire reached for his hand. "Julian? It's all right. We can talk about it."

He shook his head, unable to speak for fear that emotion might overwhelm him, and she let go of his hand, nodded. "Okay," she said.

He was the one who went into the kitchen to get a drink, and he picked up his orange juice glass from the counter, rinsed it out in the sink, filled it with water and drank it down as he stared out at the backyard.

Some feelings never went away.

Claire came in to do the dishes, and he went back out to the living room to read the newspaper, both of them pretending this was an ordinary morning and nothing unusual had happened.

He finished the paper while she was still working in the kitchen, and he called out that he was going upstairs to work, could she answer the phone if it rang. He had always been able to lose himself in a project, and today was no exception. Nearly two hours passed before Claire came upstairs and he finally looked up from his computer monitor.

He stood, stretching, and glanced down at the lower right corner of his screen. It was almost time to pick up the kids. The phone must have rung without his hearing it, because Claire said her parents had invited them over for a barbecue lunch. Luckily, Julian was behind in his work and nearing another deadline, so he had a legitimate reason not to go.

"I'll give them your regrets," Claire said dryly.

"Do that. Let them know I *wish* I could be there; I *really* do."

"You don't have to be such a jerk about it."

"Okay," he apologized, but inside he was smiling.

She walked over to his desk and gave him a kiss, a real kiss, and he understood that there was no lingering resentment from their earlier discussion; everything was all right between them. It made him feel good, and he realized how lucky he was to have Claire. He vowed to spend the afternoon researching the history of the house, as he said he would. He should have done so already, but he really did have an impending deadline, and, as usual, he'd been laser-focused on his work to the exclusion of everything else.

Claire said good-bye and was getting ready to leave when she paused in the doorway. "Do you really feel safe staying here?" she asked. "All alone?"

He didn't, but he wasn't about to admit that, so he lied, nodding. "Yeah. I'm fine."

As soon as she was gone, however, he became acutely aware of the fact that he was the only one home. The house seemed unnaturally quiet, and he could not help thinking of that shambling figure from the night before, imagining it shuffling slowly up the stairs, moving inexorably down the short hall to his office.

A car honked outside, and Julian jumped in his seat.

He wanted to laugh at himself for being so jittery but couldn't. He had legitimate reason to be nervous, and he saved what was on his screen and went through the house room by room, checking to make sure he really was alone here. He even inspected the basement, not going into it but standing at the top of the stairs, turning on the lights and looking down, although just being this close to the room made him uneasy.

As far as he could tell, the house was clean (as the psychic in *Poltergeist* so confidently and incorrectly stated), and back upstairs, he put on a record, something happy—*Beat Crazy* by Joe Jackson—cranking it up to drown out any creaking or settling sounds the building might make. Sinking into his seat, he stared for several moments at his computer screen, wondering how he should start his research. Gillette, the realtor, sure didn't want to talk to him again, and the previous owners had done everything in their power to make themselves untraceable. But if he could get a list of *previous* owners, maybe he could wrangle some information out of them.

Accessing the county recorder's Web site, he found several names and addresses, going all the way back to 1979, but when he tried to follow up, the addresses were revealed to be out-of-date, and the individuals proved impossible to track, except for one—who happened to have died.

It was after noon, and Julian was getting hungry. So he took a break and went downstairs to make himself a sandwich. Once again, the house seemed too quiet, and he turned on the television in the living room, switching the channel to CNN and boosting the volume so he could hear it in the kitchen. He'd intended to eat at the breakfast table, the way he usually did, but the closed door of the basement was in his peripheral vision, and he felt more comfortable going into the dining room. He could see the TV here as well, and watching opposing pundits, framed by red, white and blue graphics as they discussed the president's current approval ratings, made him feel relaxed and reassured.

Biting into his sandwich, Julian pondered what his next move should be. He thought he might—

A knock on the dining room window made him jump.

Looking up, he saw a man with a knife standing in the side yard and peering into the house.

Julian jerked back from his chair as though he'd been sitting on hot coals. The man staring in at him was dressed in torn jeans and a faded Willie Nelson T-shirt, wearing a yellow baseball cap with the brim anachronistically pointed in the wrong direction. He was frowning, and under his furrowed brow, his eyes were darting back and forth, taking in everything. The long knife in his hand glinted in the midday sun.

The windows were all closed to keep the coolness in, luckily, and Julian ran to the kitchen door to make sure it was locked, then ran to the front door to do the same. He grabbed the phone to call 911.

The crazy man was still at the window. The look on his face was one of dumb fascination, like Frankenstein watching a domestic scene that he didn't understand, but at least he wasn't trying to break into the house.

"I'm calling the police!" Julian announced loudly, and just at that moment, a dispatcher came on the line. Julian quickly gave his name and address, and before the woman could ask what was wrong, he told her that there was a lunatic with a knife standing in his yard and spying on him through a window. The dispatcher asked him to stay on the line, but Julian ignored her. He put the phone faceup on a table so she could hear what was going on, then ran back into the kitchen, where he opened the knife drawer, trying to find his own weapon, just in case. None of their knives were big enough to ensure victory in a fight, however, and he changed his mind, hurrying over to the broom closet, where he took out both a broom and a mop. Each of them had a long handle, and while he doubted that either of them would be able to deal any lethal blows, he could use them to bat the knife out of the man's hand, hit his head or even spear into his stomach.

Broom in his left hand, mop in his right, both of them held backward, sticks out, he hurried back into the dining room, where the man was—

Gone!

No. He had merely moved over to the other pane. He was still standing at the window. "Let me in!" he called, and his voice was neither as demanding as the request would seem to require nor as flat as the expression on his face would indicate. Indeed, the voice did not seem to match the person, and that dichotomy made the situation seem even more threatening and unnerving.

Julian remained in place, both makeshift weapons held tight.

The police arrived moments later. They came in two cars, sirens wailing, tires screeching, but nothing scared the man off. He was still there when Julian ran out the front door to meet the officers and tell them where the intruder was, and although the man did not run away, he also did not comply when a policeman, gun drawn, ordered him to drop the knife. He was still holding the weapon and staring in the window as he was subdued and the knife taken from him.

Julian had never had a reason to call the police before, and his preconceptions came entirely from movies and television shows. Although he'd expected either arrogance or hostility, he encountered neither, and he was impressed by not only the officers' levelheaded competence but the experienced efficiency with which they handled the situation.

The intruder, who refused to give his name, was handcuffed, arrested and driven away by two of the officers, while two others remained behind to take Julian's statement.

"How long is he going to stay in jail?" Julian asked. "You're not just going to book him and then let him out on bail, are you? Because I'm afraid he'd come right back here. And if my wife and kids were home . . ." He left the thought unfinished.

"He was captured during the commission of a crime," said the lead officer, George Rodriguez, a stocky young man with a thick black mustache. "So no, that's not going to happen. He might get bail, but by the looks of him, I doubt if he could make it. He also seems more than a little disturbed, so we're going to recommend a psych evaluation, which will keep him locked up for a minimum of seventy-two hours."

"Seventy-two hours? That's all? And after that . . . ?"

"My guess is that he'll fail the psych test," Rodriguez said reassuringly. "And we have him dead to rights on trespassing and threatening an officer. He's not getting out anytime soon. Don't worry about that."

Julian nodded, answering the rest of the questions he was asked. But he did worry, and after they were gone, after he was given a business card and a case number and told that he could pick up a copy of the report at the police station tomorrow, he stood in the front yard, looking at the house, trying to assess how secure it was against intruders, wondering whether he should keep some type of weapon handy. He wasn't a gun guy, but having a baseball bat next to his bed or beside the front door couldn't hurt.

Thank God Claire and the kids weren't here.

Still, he wasn't sure how he could keep this from them, or whether he should, and, instinctively, he glanced around. Had anyone else on the street noticed? If any of their neighbors were home, they certainly had. But it was the middle of the day and most people were at work, and the sirens and police cars hadn't drawn any attention. He was most likely safe. Besides, after last night's entertainment, the neighbors with whom they would have been likely to socialize were probably planning to keep a safe distance from his family *and* their house.

Julian walked back inside, his eyes drawn to the dining room window. Eventually, he decided, he *would* tell Claire. But not right away, not after what had happened last night. She needed some breathing room, some time to adjust. A one-two punch like this would just knock her flat.

He was too jittery and wound up to stay seated in front of a computer for the rest of the afternoon, and he scarfed down his sandwich, gulped down his Coke, then called Claire and told her he would be out for the next few hours, running errands. He wanted to tell her not to come home, to stay away, some primitive part of his brain believing that even with the would-be attacker arrested and in jail, their house was still not safe. But he said nothing to her about it, just said good-bye and hung up.

He actually had no errands to run, no place to go, nothing to do, so he drove over to Rick's print shop. As he'd hoped, his friend was between jobs, sitting in the office watching TV and waiting for customers, and he looked up when the buzzer sounded over the door and Julian walked in. "Dude!"

"Hey," Julian said, already wondering whether he'd made a mistake in coming here.

"Want me to print up some flyers for an exorcist? Friend's discount." He laughed, but there was an uneasiness in the laughter, and it was all Julian could do to force a smile.

Rick stood, shutting off the TV. "Seriously, is that why you're here? Because of what happened last night?"

"No. Because of what happened today."

Rick's eyes widened. "Are you shittin' me?"

Julian looked at him. "Yes. Yes, I am. I'm *shitting* you. You are emerging from my asshole even as we speak."

"You know what I mean."

"That's such a stupid phrase."

"Give me a break. I just wanted to know if you were *bullshitting* me. Is that better?"

"It is, actually." Julian allowed himself a small smile, but it faded fast. He took a deep breath. "A guy with a knife tried to break into my house at lunch."

"Holy fuck!"

Julian ran through the whole story. "They've arrested the guy. He's in jail."

"For how long? And what'll he do when he gets out?" Rick leaned forward. "Do you think this is connected to the *ghost*?"

Julian sighed. "I don't know. Everything's just a big god-damn mess. I haven't even told Claire about it yet. Not sure if I'm going to."

"You want my advice? Don't. She was genuinely freaked-out last night. Something like this . . ."

"I was thinking that, too. But she has to know. I mean, what if they release the guy and he comes back and tells her—I don't know—that he's a new neighbor or something. She needs to know enough to protect herself. And Megan and James."

"You're right, you're right."

"But maybe I should wait a few days. Maybe this isn't the right time."

"Your call, dude."

It was irresponsible of him to be here. He had work to do and a deadline to meet. But he did not want to go home, and he was glad he'd come to the print shop. It felt good to be hanging with Rick, relaxing, and he ended up staying for most of the afternoon.

Claire and the kids were home when Julian returned, and somehow having them in the house made everything seem more normal, made the craziness of last night and earlier today seem like they had happened in some other place at some other time. Both Megan and James were in the living room when he walked in, Megan lounging on the couch watching an obnoxious sitcom, James on the floor, playing with his DS. Claire was in the kitchen, cooking something that smelled delicious and that turned out to be jambalaya. She still looked worried, but she smiled at him when he entered the kitchen, and he gave her a quick peck. "Everything all right?"

She looked around, her gaze indicating the entire house surrounding them. "So far."

"How're your parents?"

"Don't even pretend to be interested," she told him.

He laughed, though he didn't really feel like laughing. In an hour or so, they would be eating dinner. In the dining room.

Where that lunatic with the knife had been staring in at him.

What would happen if the man did get out on bail, if the cops couldn't hold him, if he was let out on the streets again?

Julian didn't want to think about it. He got himself a beer from the refrigerator and walked back out to the living room, but the homey domesticity of a few moments before had disappeared, and now he saw his children as fish in a barrel, waiting to be shot.

It was all he could do to pick up a section of the newspaper that he hadn't yet read, sit down on the chair opposite the couch and scan today's headlines.

It was almost a normal evening. Maybe it *was* normal for Megan and James, but he and Claire had to work hard to maintain that surface regularity, and while several times the routine unfolded naturally enough to feel organic, by the time the kids went to bed, his muscles were tense, and he had the beginnings of a headache.

When he went into the kitchen to take an Advil, he avoided looking at the basement door.

Stress was supposed to inhibit libido, but, inexplicably, he found himself aroused, and while Claire was in the shower, Julian took off his clothes and began masturbating, stroking himself until he was hard. He thought about finishing before she came out, but then had a better idea and forced himself on her while she was brushing her teeth. She'd already showered but had not yet put on her underwear or nightgown, and when he opened the bathroom door, he saw her standing naked before the sink, her beautiful pale ass shining out at him.

Within seconds, he was across the small room and behind her, adjusting himself and shoving into the first hole available.

"Nmmmn!" she grunted through the toothpaste, trying to swat him away, but already he was thrusting, and she dropped the toothbrush in the sink, crying out, though whether from pleasure or pain he could not tell.

And did not care.

She held on to the sides of the sink with both hands to steady herself, and he plunged deep, taking her hard and fast until, finally, he exploded inside her.

Without saying a word, Claire picked up her toothbrush and resumed brushing, while he pulled a length of toilet paper from the roll and used it to wipe himself off.

Julian walked back out to the bedroom.

That definitely wasn't normal.

He lay down on the bed. What was wrong with them? He didn't know, but he didn't want to think about it. All roads led back to the house, to the man's voice in Megan's room, to James eating dirt, to that shambling horror from the party. Whatever was haunting this house—and he agreed that something was—it did not just rattle its chains and moan, like a specter in a movie. It *affected* them, their dreams, their thoughts, their actions. That made it more dangerous, but also more difficult to detect, and he wondered now whether he had done or said other things not of his own volition, things he might not have noticed or recognized at the time. Had he really wanted to stay here this afternoon instead of going with Claire to her parents' house? Had he even wanted the pancakes he'd had for breakfast? Why had he chosen the room he had for his office?

Julian forced himself to drop this line of reasoning before it headed into craziness and obsession. This was not the time to go there. He would revisit it tomorrow, when his mind was clearer. Right now, he needed to get some rest.

He thought it would be hard to fall asleep, but it wasn't. He dozed off immediately, and was dead to the world well before Claire came out of the bathroom.

He dreamed about the house.

SEVENTEEN

THE PLANTS IN THE BACKYARD WERE DEAD.

Every last one of them.

James was the first one to discover it. He saw it initially from the kitchen window while pouring himself a glass of orange juice, and if he had needed any proof that the *thing* in their house had the power to carry out its threats, the simultaneous expiration of every single living organism between the house, the garage and the alley was it. Stunned, still in pajamas and slippers, he stepped outside onto the patio, looking across the suddenly brown grass to the spiny, leafless twigs that had been the rosebushes, and the dead hedges that ringed the border of the property. It was impossible, but he could see that it had happened, and he felt a chill in his bones as he surveyed the lifeless yard.

His parents were still asleep, but Megan was up, and he went back inside, intending to show her what had happened, but at the last minute, he changed his mind. She was sitting on the floor of the living room, leaning over the coffee table as she ate her Honey Nut Cheerios, and the way she looked up at him when he walked in, the worry he saw on her face, made him decide against telling her anything.

He turned away, heading back into the kitchen, where he made his own breakfast of cocoa and toast, which he ate while staring out the window at the yard.

Both he and Megan had been walking on eggshells for the past week, spending as much time as possible at their friends' homes, not using phones or computers, not saying anything within the walls of their house that could be overheard by . . . *it*.

He was living the most stressful existence imaginable, and if he didn't have a heart attack, he was going to get an ulcer. He and Megan avoided each other, afraid to communicate by either speech or note, and for the first time in his life he was really looking forward to the beginning of school. The chance to be away from the house nearly all day, five days a week, sounded like heaven, and already he was considering joining after-school clubs, programs or teams in order to stay out even longer.

His dream was to move again—even returning to their old neighborhood would be better than this—but he could figure out no way to facilitate such an outcome. His parents seemed to like it here, and, after they'd invested so much money in the place, it was highly unlikely that they'd be willing to give it up.

He did tell his mom and dad when they woke up several minutes later, showing them through the window what had happened. Still afraid that he was being watched, that his every word and gesture were under scrutiny, James did not editorialize, did not indicate that he was frightened or that he thought anything out of the ordinary had occurred. He just stated the facts, letting them draw their own conclusions, hoping those conclusions would be the right ones. But his parents looked at each other as though they'd already known about this, or at least knew what had caused it, and instead of the shock and disbelief for which he'd been hoping, there was only a grim matter-of-factness as they talked about how much work it would be to replace the plants.

Megan came into the kitchen to rinse out her cereal bowl, heard what they were talking about and looked out the window for herself, but she said nothing, offered no opinion, simply shot James a quick frightened look and then moved on.

He had to talk to *someone*; he couldn't keep everything bottled up like this forever, and later that morning, he finally told Robbie about all that had happened.

But he told Robbie at *his* house.

They were hanging out in Robbie's room, and the conversation drifted around to the headquarters and their detective agency, which neither of them seemed to be very excited about anymore. James sensed some ambivalence in his friend, maybe even a trace of fear, and without preamble, he said, "My house is haunted," and blurted everything out. The words tumbled from his mouth as though poured from a pitcher, events out of sequence, descriptions over thoughts over feelings. He received no ridicule, just nods of acknowledgment that told him his friend had some of the same misgivings and had experienced the same sorts of feelings he had.

James had started with the text threat on Megan's phone, and he ended with it as well, explaining for probably the third or fourth time that he was afraid to even *think* bad thoughts in their house. "Like that *Twilight Zone*," he said, although Robbie didn't get the reference.

"I knew there was something wrong," Robbie admitted. "All that stuff with the dirt. It's why I didn't want to do that anymore."

James thought of their headquarters, of the displayed skeletons he had unearthed, and he shivered. "Yeah, but I have to live there."

"What are you going to do?" Robbie asked seriously.

James shook his head. "I don't know. What *can* I do?"

"I think you should tell your parents."

"I'll be dead. It said, 'I'll kill you both.' There's no room for interpretation of that."

"But can it?"

"I was almost buried alive!"

Robbie leaned forward. "But you did that to yourself. Okay, maybe it somehow got into your mind and made you want to go into that hole, but it couldn't come *out* and get you. No one in your family's been harmed. I don't think it can do it."

James remembered the panicked, desperate feeling of having the dirt fall in on him and shook his head. "No."

"Then tell them *outside* your house, like you're telling me. When you're at the store with your dad or something."

For a brief second, there was a ray of hope. But it quickly faded. "Then my dad would try to do something. Or tell my mom. And it would know. And then it would get me. Me and Megan."

"What do you think it is, anyway?" Robbie asked. "A ghost? Some sort of demon? What?"

"I don't know."

"But you must've thought about it."

"Maybe it's the house itself. Like in *Monster House* or something."

"Maybe," Robbie said thoughtfully.

"I just don't know what we can do about it. Except move. And that's not going to happen. Who knows? Maybe even if we did move, it would follow us."

"We'll think of something. Both of us are on the case now." Robbie smiled. "The R.J. Detective Agency in our first and biggest mystery."

James tried to smile back, but he didn't feel like smiling. He wasn't sure Robbie understood the *scope* of this thing. Sure, his friend believed him and was scared of the house, but this was big, this was deep, and there was no way two kids could stop something of this magnitude.

"I'm thirsty," James said. "Do you have anything to drink?"

"Hawaiian Punch."

They walked out to the kitchen, where Robbie's mom was talking on the phone. After lunch, she was going to take them to go swimming, and if he played his cards right, James thought he might be able to finagle an invitation to dinner. He wanted to put off going home for as long as possible. Especially now. Spilling his guts to Robbie made him feel as though he'd broken the rules, and he couldn't help thinking that he would be punished as soon as he got home. He dreaded the thought of returning.

He accepted a glass of Hawaiian Punch and took a big drink, then nearly choked as a terrible idea abruptly occurred to him.

What if he'd already been punished? What if Megan had just fallen down the stairs and broken her neck? What if he returned to find his parents dead? He was filled with a sudden need to call home and make sure everyone was all right. The compulsion was strong, but he resisted it. If he gave in, doubt and worry would rule him. He would never be able to leave the house without being certain that something awful was about to happen. He needed to relax, not think about it, enjoy the time he had away from home.

The fear would return soon enough.

Robbie grabbed a bag of Chips Ahoy! cookies, and the two of them returned to the bedroom, where they were planning to play games on Robbie's computer until it was time to eat. Entering the room a half step behind his friend, James saw something he hadn't noticed before. He suddenly felt cold. "What's that?" he asked, pointing. A small reddish box was protruding from the top of Robbie's bedspread, its upper third resting on the pillow.

Robbie frowned. "I don't know." He walked over, picked it up—

—and James saw the frightening face of the Old Maid on the cover of a battered box of cards. She was not smiling, as she had been on the card he'd found on his bed, but possessed instead the terrifying rage of the Old Maid he remembered from when he was little. The hag glared at him, and he felt like a kindergartner again, afraid of supposedly benign pictures that to him revealed sinister import.

"That's weird," Robbie said, but he didn't seem overly concerned. "I never saw that before." He turned the box over in his hand. "That old lady looks kind of creepy, huh?"

James nodded dumbly. He was filled once again with the urge to call home, the certainty that something horrible had befallen his family, and, finally, he gave in. His mom answered when he called, and she turned out to be fine. So did his dad. So did his sister. His mom seemed slightly confused as to why he'd called, so he made up an excuse, a weak fictional distillation of the truth, telling her that he'd heard a siren coming from the direction of their neighborhood and wanted to make sure the house hadn't burned down. She laughed. "No, nothing's burning," she told him. "Don't worry. Have a good time."

But he did worry.

Robbie's mom made them tuna sandwiches for lunch, then drove them to the Municipal Plunge, where they spent the better part of the afternoon playing in the water, leaving only when a lifeguard announced that the pool would be closing for a private party. They changed in the boys' dressing room, and on the way home, Robbie's mom stopped off at Dairy Queen, where all three of them got sundaes.

James stayed late at Robbie's, and did try to invite himself to dinner, but they were going out for pizza with Max's baseball team, and Robbie's dad politely but firmly insisted that James had to go home.

He was dropped off at his house just after five, and, looking at the front yard as he got out of the car, seeing the tree with the tire swing, the green grass and full foliage, knowing that the backyard was brown and dead, he had the uneasy feeling that the house was putting on a show, presenting a cheery false face to the public while keeping its ghastly secret self hidden. He stared up at the structure. It had a porch and a door, windows and walls, the same elements all houses had. But were they arranged in an eerie way? Could you tell the house was bad just by looking at it?

No, not really.

That was the truth. He wanted to ascribe malevolence to the building, wanted to see a face in the arrangement of windows and door. But those things weren't there. The truth was not that simple. The house was haunted, but it wasn't alive. Whatever evil resided in this place, it *lived* in his home; it was *not* his home.

And it had control over the backyard.

"See you later!" Robbie's dad called out.

"Thanks for coming over!" his mom said.

James waved at them as the car pulled away. Robbie, he noticed, hadn't said anything. He, too, had been looking at the house.

James started slowly across the lawn, walking toward the front door, feeling like a man stepping up to the gallows, a fearful heaviness settling over him the closer he got to the building. Summer was nearing its end, but though it was after five, the day was still bright, the sun still fairly high in the sky. So there was no reason for the lights in the house to be on. But the fact that they weren't made him feel anxious, and he took a deep breath before opening the front door. Would he find his sister lying on the floor of the living room in a pool of blood? Would his parents be locked in the basement, begging to be released? He didn't know, but he pushed open the door, prepared for anything.

And saw Megan and his dad on the couch, she reading a magazine, he watching the news.

His mom was in the kitchen, where a light *was* on, and she'd obviously heard the door open, because she stepped into the kitchen doorway and looked at him from across the dining room, across the living room. "Why are you so late?" she wanted to know. "Did something happen?"

"No," he said, and exhaled the breath he'd been holding.

"Is something wrong?"

He smiled at her, not a strong smile but a real one. "No, Mom. Everything's okay."

EIGHTEEN

OSCAR CORTINEZ WANTED TO SUE THE SCHOOL DISTRICT.

He was a longtime history teacher at the high school, and his contract had not been renewed for the coming school year. The district claimed it was for purely financial reasons—across-the-board budget cuts had been made throughout the district—but Oscar contended that it was the fact that he'd taught "the truth" about local history that had cost him his job. He'd gotten in hot water before for teaching off-curriculum material, but had successfully defended himself by pointing out that he had covered the required subject in the required way and had simply taught his students additional facts that inconveniently conflicted with the conventional narrative. The principal at his school had not liked that, and neither had the suits at the district office, and he and his union rep had had several more meetings with various administrators over the past few years.

He needed more than a union rep this time, though, and that was why he'd enlisted Claire.

It was easily the biggest and best case she'd had since leaving Los Angeles, and Claire was grateful that it had fallen into her lap at this time. Ever since the party, she'd been completely obsessed with monitoring everything that happened in or around their house. Every. Single. Thing. Scrutinizing the children for any unusual behavior, jumping at every stray noise, mentally cataloging the slightest shifts in the shafts of sunlight that streamed through their windows. Julian said she needed to back off and calm down or she'd go crazy, and she agreed, so it was good to have something else to focus her attention on, good to be able to direct more of her attention toward work.

Besides, if this case had a big payday—not an unreasonable expectation—they might be able to get out of the house and find someplace else to live.

The thought fueled her.

They met in her office for a consultation that lasted most of the day. Oscar explained that he believed he had been singled out and let go solely because of the subject matter he taught, a blatant infringement on his academic freedom. He'd been a model instructor until he started teaching an enhanced version of the standard syllabus, but after that he had become a pariah in the district, although his work had been recognized and rewarded by interested outside parties. He had documentation to back this up: a series of e-mails and memos covering the controversy, a stack of glowing evaluations from a period of fifteen straight years that suddenly grew harsh and critical when the current principal came on board four years ago, commendations from various teaching organizations and historical societies. His complaints seemed legitimate, and when he pointed out that no other history teachers in the district had been let go and that two of them had less seniority than he did, she told him that she thought he had a case.

Over the next two days she did some research, and the news when she saw him again wasn't encouraging. "They might have a case," she admitted. "They're claiming that test scores in your classes have been falling consistently for the past three years, and that in this era of accountability, they could not justify protecting your position at the expense of instructors whose students have been performing better on the tests."

He snorted. "Tests? What tests? That standardized pap the politicians foisted on us? *My* tests are twice as hard and three times as comprehensive as those generic multiple-guessers we're supposed to teach to." He leaned forward. "For over ten years now, America's been scapegoating teachers: 'We're falling behind the Chinese, Japanese and Koreans because there are too many bad teachers, and we can't get rid of them because they have tenure. Oh, and they're bankrupting the country because they have good pensions.' Well, the teachers in China, Japan and Korea have tenure and good pensions! Has that caused their educational systems to fail? No. Because their societies value education! They treat their teachers with respect. How do you expect American students to treat us with respect when their parents don't, when the politicians don't, when the media doesn't, when all they hear is how bad our country's teachers are? You know what? The Asian kids in *my* class do just as well on those standardized tests as the ones actually in Asia! You know why? Because their parents make them study and do their homework. If every parent did that, maybe we wouldn't be falling so far behind!"

"We're getting a little off track here," Claire said gently.

"I'm sorry," he said. "But I'm a good teacher. I always have been. And the reason I was let go is not the test scores of my students. That's just cover; that's just the excuse they're giving. The reason is, I teach *real* history. Yes, I teach the requirements. But I go deeper. And these days, if you deviate at all from the party line, you're penalized for it. Initiative used to be rewarded; now it's not only discouraged, it's punished."

"But the test scores of your students have fallen since you began teaching this 'real' history. I have them here in front of me."

"Sure," he admitted. "You know why? Because I went from teaching honors history to regular history." He leaned forward again. "You know how politicians always talk about the importance of merit pay and rewarding 'good' teachers? Well, the 'good' teachers are the ones whose students do well on the standardized tests. And here's the dirty little secret: teachers who teach the smart kids have students who do better on those tests than those who teach the low learners. I was one of those 'good' teachers.

Now I'm not. Because the principal assigned me a different class. Not because my teaching skills suddenly deserted me. And not because I've expanded the class curriculum to include information outside the scope of the textbook."

Claire nodded. "Okay."

"So we'll sue?"

"I think you have a legitimate grievance, and it's quite possible we can get your job back. But this is by no means a slam dunk. Judges and juries, if it gets to that point, are notoriously unreliable. It's not like you see on TV. There's a chance the court could rule against you. Then you'd not only be out of a job, but you'd be out quite a bit of money."

"But you think I have a shot?"

"I think you have a shot."

"Let's do it."

She nodded. "All right. We'll go after them. As long as you know the risks."

He smiled. "What's life without a little risk?"

Claire stood, and they shook on it. She hadn't had much time to delve into the substance of the teacher's lessons—she'd been focused more on the legalities of his case—but she knew from their discussions and from her brief perusal of his classroom notes that the "real" history Oscar Cortinez taught involved ethnic slaughter and very bad deeds by some very famous men. She wasn't aware of any of this. When she'd gone to school here in the mid-1980s, it was a much cheerier version of the town's history they were spoon-fed. Which meant that she was going to have to do a lot of reading up in order to familiarize herself with the issues that she planned to argue were the heart of this case.

She walked Oscar to the door and said good-bye, promising to call him as soon as she put together a rough draft of their complaint. Standing in the doorway, she saw Pam wave to her from across the street. Claire purposely looked away, walking back to her desk. One of these days, she was probably going to have to speak to Pam again, maybe even talk about what happened, but that day was not today.

She sat down, attempted to concentrate on the work before her, but the sight of Pam had brought back to her everything that had happened at the housewarming party, and she was overcome with a heavy feeling of dread. She tried to ignore it, but she couldn't, and finally she broke down and called home in order to reassure herself that Julian and the kids were all right and everything was fine.

AFTER DINNER THAT NIGHT, CLAIRE GOT ON HER LAPTOP. SHE fully intended to access some of the historical sites to which Oscar Cortinez had given her the addresses, but once her browser opened, she decided instead to look up information about their house. Julian had already attempted to research the previous owners, and while he had not been able to locate or contact any of them, he had managed to find several articles and a police report about the man who had died in their basement. There were no pictures of the man—though there was little doubt that he was the figure they had seen shuffling down the hallway and into the living room—but the background information on him was pretty complete: Jim Swanson, age fifty-six, unemployed pipe fitter, Jardine native, divorced, ex-wife living in Tucson, parents dead, no brothers or sisters, house repossessed two years prior. The one thing no one seemed able to figure out, however, was *why* Swanson had decided to break into the house, take off his clothes and go into the basement. And the cause of death was still sketchy. "Organ failure" was the official explanation listed on the coroner's report, but since the toxic screen came back clean and there was no evidence of any illness, the exact reason for the organ failure remained unclear.

What Julian had discovered was a good start, but that was all it was. A start. If they were ever going to find a way through this mess, they would need a lot more information, and Claire decided to start by seeing whether she could find Swanson's ex-wife. The woman had apparently been divorced from her husband for twelve years before his death, so it was doubtful that she could shed any light on the details of his passing, but maybe Claire would be able to discover whether he had any previous connection to the house.

She started to type in the woman's name, Elizabeth Swanson, but before she got past the *z*, her screen went black. For a second, she thought the power cord had come unplugged. Then, suddenly, the screen was filled with a single word: *Don't.*

She frowned, perplexed and, at the same time, frightened. She wanted to believe that it was a technical glitch of some sort, totally unconnected to her. But it was a command, and it applied to what she was doing, and it made it seem as though *something* was trying to stop her. She was reminded, also, of the message on Megan's phone—

Take off your pants.

—and she forced herself to calm down and breathe normally as she turned the machine off, then started it up again. The four-colored Windows logo appeared, all her little icons popped up . . . then the screen went black.

I told you.

The words appeared in the center of the screen and were instantly replaced by another message that filled the entire rectangular space.

DON'T.

Meekly, she shut off the laptop, closing it up. Her hands were shaking, and she went out to the living room, where Julian was reading *Time* magazine, James was reading a book and Megan was watching *Access Hollywood*. She tapped Julian on the shoulder, got his attention and motioned for him to follow her to the kitchen. Once there, she told him what had happened. He believed her without seeing proof, which was good, because she wasn't about to turn on that laptop again. Who could tell what type of response she'd get if she attempted to access the Internet one more time?

"Nothing from the house," he said, and she shivered, feeling cold, because he was whispering. He, too, was worried that their conversation might be overheard. "Look things up at your office or the library or one of those Wi-Fi cafés."

"You, too," she told him.

Julian nodded.

She wanted to say more. She was starting to feel like a prisoner, constantly under surveillance, and her gut reaction was to fight back, to say whatever the hell she wanted, to confront the ghost in this house by threatening it. But that wasn't a smart move, she knew, and she stared into Julian's eyes, telling him everything she could with that one meaningful look, and he nodded and kissed her, and the two of them left the kitchen and went out to the living room to watch over their children.

NINETEEN

MEGAN AWOKE WITH THE DAWN AND QUICKLY CHECKED TO MAKE sure nothing had happened to her during the night. No. She was okay. Still wrapped up like a mummy, comforter tucked into the sides of the bed, blanket and sheet tucked in below that, sleeping bag still zipped.

She emerged from her cocoon, sweating. Her parents did not know it, but she'd taken to wearing her clothes to bed rather than her pajamas. Why? Because pajama bottoms were pull-ups—pants had snaps and zippers and belts. Pajama tops were pullovers—regular shirts could be buttoned and sealed in with sweaters.

She needed the extra protection. That thing she'd seen the night her friends had come over, the formless camouflaged shape that had detached itself from the wall to examine and assault the other girls, had never been far from her mind.

Take off your pants.

Nor had the text message that had been sent to her and James.

I will kill you both.

Her life was a nightmare of fear and worry, and the worst part of it was that her options for dealing with the situation were so constricted. She could not tell her parents. She could not tell her friends. There was no one she could go to for help, and the *crea-*

ture that lived in this house could be anywhere, watching her at any time.

She had to go to the bathroom, and it was with a feeling of dread that Megan went into the one on the other side of James's bedroom. She would have preferred to use the one by her parents' room, but for some reason her mom had put that off-limits. As always, she closed and locked the door behind her, then took a towel from the rack and held it in front of her with one hand while, with the other, she pulled her pants down the bare minimum. She placed the towel on her lap while she used the toilet, so nothing could see her, then quickly pulled her pants back up when she was finished and sped downstairs, washing her hands in the kitchen.

She had never felt so much stress in her life as she had the past two weeks, and it was a wonder she hadn't snapped. This was what they never showed in movies, the contorted and convoluted rituals that had to be instituted in order to deal with everyday life in a haunted house.

After breakfast, after everyone was up and there was noise in the house, after the sun was high and night was truly vanquished, after the house was as safe as it could possibly be, it was time for Megan to take a quick sponge bath and get dressed. Six days a week, she took *only* sponge baths, not wanting to use the tub or shower, not wanting the glass in the bathroom to become fogged up. She was down to a single hot shower a week, and that one she took on Sunday afternoon, in the warmest, brightest part of the day. Her mom thought that was strange and had asked her about it, but her questioning had seemed more nervous than concerned, the queries of someone worried not because she didn't understand but because she did. Megan had almost broken down and told her mom everything. But she'd flashed on that message—

I will kill you both.

—and saw in her mind's eye an amorphous shape disengaging itself from the wall and killing both her mother and herself, and had purposefully thought up a lie, saying that she'd read that Sunday afternoon was the best time to take a shower because it required less energy to heat the water and was good for the environment.

Now she went back up to her bedroom, picked out a new T-shirt and underwear (she was planning to wear the same jeans) and carried her clothes into the bathroom. She let the tap run until the water was warm, then stopped up the sink, filled it, and tossed in a washcloth, getting everything ready so she could take her sponge bath as quickly as possible. She always bathed in shifts—bottom half, then top half—so that a portion of her body was always covered and she was never completely naked.

She did her usual swift survey, making sure nothing was out of place, confirming that there was nothing creepy or unusual within sight distance, before deciding to work today from the bottom up. Pulling down her pants, she was shocked to see cuts on her legs, long red slashes that she had not noticed earlier. Where had they come from? Had they been there while she was going to the bathroom? If so, she hadn't seen them. Her legs suddenly hurt, though they hadn't only seconds before. Seeing the wounds had made her aware of them, and she felt the pain, though the cuts were not deep and there was virtually no blood, only a thin dried line over each slash.

Using the washcloth but not using soap, she gently dabbed at the cuts with warm water before patting her legs dry with a towel. She found some Neosporin in the drawer and, using her finger, carefully smeared the medicine on the wounds. After changing her underwear and putting her pants back on, she took off her old T-shirt, washed the top half of her body, put on deodorant and quickly slipped into her new T-shirt.

The cuts bothered her.

And scared her.

Her first thought was that she was being punished, that, even though she'd obeyed orders and done nothing, the thing in the house knew what she'd been thinking and wanted to prove that it could get to her whenever it wanted, despite all her precautions. If true, what would happen to her if she dared to tell her parents about the slashes on her legs? What would happen to *them* if they knew? The safest thing would be to maintain her silence and suffer.

There was a nagging notion in the back of her mind, however, that the cuts had not been inflicted on her by some outside force but that she had made the cuts herself. In a way, this idea was even scarier. Because, try as she might, Megan could not remember doing such a thing and could think of no reason why she would.

Maybe she was losing her mind. Maybe none of the things she thought were going on were really going on. Maybe she hadn't received any of those weird texts. Maybe there'd been no camouflaged monster at her sleepover. Maybe . . .

No. Her mom had seen one of the texts—

Take off your pants.

—as had James—

I will kill you both.

—and her friends had all gotten spooked by that out-of-control Ouija board even before they'd fallen asleep. These things were real.

Megan leaned forward, looking at herself in the mirror. She wasn't crazy. She was just caught up in a crazy situation.

But what could she do about it?

She went downstairs, where her mom was already waiting for her. "Are you ready?" her mom asked.

"Yeah," Megan said.

The two of them were planning to walk downtown together, her mom to go to work, she to go to the library. She'd finished another book, and was due a prize from the summer reading program. The program was nearly over, so prizes were getting down to the bottom of the barrel, and she wanted to make sure she got something decent. Of course, the library wouldn't be open for another hour, but she could hang out at her mom's office and the two of them could get in some mother-daughter bonding time. They could talk, and maybe she could even . . .

Megan thought of the cuts on her legs.

No.

They were already out the door when her mom realized at the last minute that she'd forgotten to bring along her flash drive, so Megan waited outside, standing in the front yard while her mother went back into the house. She pushed at the tire swing, wondering why her dad hadn't taken it down, since neither she nor James used it. Then she wondered why James didn't use it. The swing was something he should have loved.

A man walked slowly past on the sidewalk, making an almost comically obvious effort not to glance at their house or yard. Megan frowned. There was something familiar about him, and she tried to remember where she'd seen him before. He was an older guy, wearing a backward yellow baseball cap, and though she was almost certain he did not live on this street, and he did not seem to have any reason to be here, he walked by, then crossed the street and walked by in the opposite direction, the way he had come, still not looking at their yard.

That was weird. But then her mom came out, and she forgot all about the man.

"Let's go," her mom said.

Away from the house, Megan felt better. The fear was still there—it was *always* there these days—but she felt lighter, physically as well as mentally. She noticed the difference only when she left, but at home there was a heaviness to everything she did. Her thoughts were slower, her movements more sluggish. It felt completely normal to her while there, but the minute she was off the premises, it was as if she'd lost twenty pounds and gained twenty IQ points.

What in the world was wrong with their house?

It was a question she carried with her, one that was always in back of every thought. She had still not come up with a satisfactory answer, but it seemed clear to her that whatever plagued their home was far more than just a simple haunting. No ghost or spirit could do all . . . this.

Her mom seemed in a better mood, too, away from the house. As they walked through the park, she began asking Megan about school. It started in only two weeks, and usually by this time they were going shopping for clothes, had started to pick up supplies and were getting ready. But this year, school didn't even seem to be on the radar. Even when they weren't distracted by other things, the subject just never came up, and it felt good to be finally talking about it. Reassuring. She herself had been so focused on events at home that she'd given very little thought to her entry into eighth grade. It was going to be her last year in middle school, and while, ordinarily, that would have made her anxious, excited or *something*, this summer it had hardly registered.

So it felt great to be talking to her mom in a normal way about normal things.

She realized that it was time to start getting seriously busy. Especially in the clothes department. She'd grown since the spring, and the only pants that didn't make her look like she was waiting for a flood were the jeans she had on now. All of her shorts still fit, but . . .

Megan was brought down to earth at the thought of the slashes on her legs.

She couldn't wear shorts, she realized.

"I noticed The Store was having a back-to-school sale," her mom was saying. "You're old enough to expand your wardrobe and not wear T-shirts every day. We should . . ."

Megan nodded, kept a smile on her face, but she wasn't really listening, and it wasn't until they reached Old Main and ran into Julie and her mom in front of the closed thrift store that Megan snapped back into the here and now.

Julie's mom greeted them with a wide smile and a friendly "Hello," but Julie's face reddened and she looked down at the sidewalk, embarrassed. Her family was poor, and it was obvious that she and her mom were waiting for the thrift store to open. Probably to look for clothes.

Megan was embarrassed, too, not because her friend had to

buy used clothing but because she was embarrassed about it, and, like Julie, Megan stared awkwardly at the ground and said nothing.

The two mothers had no such qualms, however, and Megan's mom nodded toward the closed front door of the thrift shop. "Monday morning's a good time to come here. That's when Rebecca puts out all her new items. But the first Tuesday of each month, she always has a two-for-one deal. Sometimes it's jeans, sometimes it's housewares, sometimes it's books, but if you keep your eyes open, you can get some real bargains."

Julie's mom smiled. "That's how I got this top. Three dollars. And one for Julie as well."

Mortified, Julie looked as though she wanted to sink into the ground.

Megan's mom nodded approvingly. "You know, last winter, I got a Liz Claiborne coat here that someone had given away, and it was in perfect condition. Liz Claiborne! Ten dollars! Someone must have gotten it for a present and didn't like it, because it looked like it had never been worn."

Her mom *did* sometimes buy things from the thrift store, although Megan had never felt comfortable about that. The clothes, she had to admit, were always nice—her mom had good taste—but they didn't *have* to shop there, and Megan would have much preferred if her mom bought only things that were new. Now, however, she felt proud of her mother, and she even found herself relenting about the used clothing. She knew that coat, and she thought it was very stylish. It also looked very expensive. She'd been under the impression that her mom had bought it new, and to find out that it had cost only ten dollars was very impressive.

Maybe she could stretch out her own clothing allowance if she bought some of her back-to-school things here rather than at The Store.

Julie no longer seemed so embarrassed, and she and Megan began talking about school and the classes they hoped they'd get. They'd both signed up for the ultrapopular Electronic Publishing as an elective, but neither of them had gotten their schedules yet, so they didn't know whether they'd make it in.

There was a metallic rattling of key in lock as the door to the thrift shop was opened from the inside.

"Well, I need to get to work." Megan's mom smiled and nodded at the elderly woman opening the door. "Good morning, Rebecca."

"Hello, Claire. Nice day."

"Yes, it is." She looked at Megan. "I'm going to my office. If you'd like to stay with Julie and see if you can find anything in Mrs. Fischer's store, you can."

Megan smiled, giving her mother a quick hug. She was one of the good ones. "Okay. Thanks, Mom."

All trace of embarrassment gone, Julie led the way into the thrift shop, and the two of them began searching through the shirts and blouses hanging from a series of racks on the right side of the store.

They looked through everything. Julie picked out an impressively hip outfit that one of Jardine's richer high schoolers must have recently donated, and even discovered a couple of pretty good CDs in the bargain bin. Megan found a cool top that fit her perfectly, and she told her friend to wait while she rushed over to her mom's office to get some money.

Julie had always been the most casual member of her trio of BFFs, but Megan had a newfound respect for the girl, and after this morning felt much closer to her. They emerged from the thrift shop to see that the north end of Old Main was being blocked off and vendors were starting to set up for the farmer's market. Julie's mom said she was going to go over and check it out.

"I need to go to the library," Megan told Julie. "Want to come with me?"

Julie looked at her mother, who nodded her approval.

The two girls went to the library, where Megan got her reading program form signed by one of the librarians and received her prize: a "Night at the Movies" pass, which included free entry to the theater, a free small popcorn and a free small drink. "Wow," Julie said. "I didn't know they gave out such good prizes. I'm going to do the reading program next year."

The librarian smiled. "Tell your friends."

They went on one of the library's computers, sharing it, and checked out the Facebook pages of some of their frenemies until Julie's mom found them and told Julie it was time to go.

Megan walked out with them to the parking lot, where Julie's mom had parked her car. "I had fun," she said. "We should do this more often."

Julie smiled. "Yeah."

They said good-bye, and Megan walked back to her mom's office. She expected to see a client or two, or find her mother on the phone, but her mom was alone and writing something in longhand on a yellow pad of paper. Megan went to the bathroom, and at the same time checked the cuts on her legs. Once again, there was a vague stirring in the back of her mind, a sense that she had inflicted those wounds upon herself, though she still could not remember doing so and had no idea why she would.

They looked ugly, she thought, and that was good. It made *her* look ugly. Now maybe whatever had been exhorting her to take off her pants would not want her to do it any longer. In fact, maybe if she cut herself some more, it would provide her with additional insurance and keep that thing away from her.

Was that the reason she had done it in the first place, *if* she had done it in the first place?

No.

Something told her that if she had cut herself, she had done it because she wanted to, because she liked it.

Liked it in *that* way.

Horrified, embarrassed, ashamed, Megan looked up from her bare legs and focused her eyes on the bathroom wall. That wasn't possible, was it? People didn't really do things like that for *those* reasons, did they? She didn't see how, but something about it still rang true, and she was even more afraid of the house than she had been before. She did not want to go back, and wondered whether she could camp out here in her mom's office, convince her parents to let her have a sleepover here with her friends, and then perhaps stretch that out to a week or so.

She was being ridiculous. Nothing like that would ever happen. She had to face the fact that she had to live in the house.

But maybe . . .

Reaching over, she started opening the drawers in the sink cabinet. Most of them were empty, but in one she found an old box of Band-Aids, a tube of Neosporin and a small pair of scissors. She took all of them out and placed them on the edge of the sink. The scissors, she saw upon further inspection, might be short and thin, but they were sharp, and the blades came to points. She picked them up, then looked down at her thighs. Her legs were ugly now, but she could make them even uglier, so that *nothing* would want her to pull her pants down.

She gathered her courage. Grimacing, she pressed the blade against her skin.

Pushed it in.

And, biting on her hand to keep from screaming, quickly pulled it through the flesh toward her hip.

TWENTY

THE MAN WITH THE KNIFE WAS NAMED JOHN LYNCH.

And he had been released from jail two days ago.

Julian learned about it only because he called the police station and asked to talk to Officer Rodriguez in order to find out the status of the case. Claire was at work, Megan was with her, and James was at his friend Robbie's. For the first time in three days, Julian had the house completely to himself, and, taking advantage of this temporary freedom, he decided to check on his would-be attacker and see what was happening. He was shocked to discover that, contrary to what he'd been told, the man was neither in jail nor in a psych ward but had made bail and had been released on his own recognizance.

Rodriguez was on patrol and not available, but the case was no longer his anyway and had been assigned to a Detective Pena, who was the one to take Julian's call. Pena was understanding and apologetic, but Julian was still angry that Lynch had been released, and he started lecturing the detective, describing in detail how he'd seen the man with the knife staring in at him while he was eating lunch. All of this was no doubt in the report, but Pena listened patiently before explaining that because there had been no specific verbal threats made and no overt attempts to attack, Lynch had been automatically eligible for bail.

"He was holding a knife!"

"I understand that, Mr. Perry. And he will have a trial, and even if there is a plea deal, I can guarantee you that he will serve time. But until then, he is out on bail. If you see him again, however, if he makes any attempt to contact you, let us know immediately. In that case, we may be able to do something."

"So if he terrorizes my wife or stabs my children, then you'll be able to put him away. That's good to know."

"I'm sorry, Mr. Perry—"

Julian hung up on him.

Immediately, he went outside and walked around the house, checking behind bushes, in the garage, even in the alley to make sure that that lunatic wasn't lurking about. He'd asked the detective whether the police had any idea *why* Lynch had come to his house with a knife, but Pena said that the man had offered no explanation, had seemed confused, and had claimed that he meant no harm.

The guy was clearly crazy. What if he *did* return and try to attack Claire? Or Megan? Or James?

Julian should have told Claire everything that day, as soon as she came home. What the hell was wrong with him? Now it was too late to tell her about it. He'd made a huge mistake in not coming clean right away, and there was no way he could possibly explain what had happened and why he'd kept it a secret. Probably the best thing to do at this point was maintain his silence. He seldom went anywhere, was almost always home when Claire and the kids were there. He could keep an open eye out, watch for any sign of Lynch, and if the man showed up, he'd call the police and *then* tell Claire, maybe even make it seem like it was the first time it had happened.

It was a chickenshit plan, the coward's way out, but Julian justified it by telling himself that it would be wrong to stress out Claire even more. She was already freaked about the house and practically jumping at her own shadow. She was also troubled by the fact that, despite all of the modern research options at their disposal, neither of them had been able to dig up any significant information about their home or property. Her mental and emotional plates were full to overflowing. He didn't want to add to her burden.

The garage was clear, as was the yard, and Julian closed all windows, locked the back door and walked out to the sidewalk in front of the house, scanning the neighborhood for a sign of anything unusual.

Nothing.

He went back into the house. He hadn't found a baseball bat, as he'd originally planned, although he knew there was one somewhere in the basement or garage amid the surplus clutter of their storage items, but he did go to his tool chest and take out a hammer, just in case he needed a weapon. He doubted that he would have to use it, even if Lynch came back, but it couldn't hurt to be prepared.

Julian still had that deadline and had been planning to spend the morning catching up on all the work he'd let slide lately, but the news about Lynch had thrown him off, and once upstairs in his office, he found himself staring dumbly at the screen, not an idea in his head. He reviewed the last changes he'd made to the page, thinking that a walk-through of recent work might help get his thoughts on track, and it seemed to help. He found a mistake he'd made, corrected it, and was suddenly back in the game. He knew what he needed to do next, and he knew how to get the result he wanted.

Then he heard a voice from the hallway.

A man's voice.

Julian stood, heart pounding, and grabbed his hammer, clutching the handle tightly. His first thought was that John Lynch had somehow gotten into the house, although he had no idea how that was possible. But as he cautiously approached the doorway, he could hear the voice talking—it had not *stopped* talking—and though he could not make out individual words, he recognized the tone and cadence.

It was the voice he had heard talking to Megan while she was asleep.

A chill crept up Julian's back all the way to his neck. He entered the hallway, half expecting the murmuring to be silenced, but instead it grew louder, and once again it was coming from Megan's room. He looked toward her doorway. It was daytime, but the hall was in shadow, and the hint of cool sunlight that emerged from the open doorway of his daughter's bedroom made the surrounding corridor seem that much darker.

His hand hurt, but Julian refused to loosen his grip on the hammer. He continued moving forward slowly, not wanting to alert whatever it was to his presence. He could discern every third or fourth word now, but they made no sense.

"... *comforter ... canyons ... cinnabar ... sleep ...*"

Reaching Megan's door, he peeked his head around the corner. There was movement in her mirror, a whitish blur that moved too fast for him to see, and then the voice was gone. From the opposite side of the house, not from his office but from farther out, the backyard, perhaps, came faint high laughter.

Hammer in hand, Julian explored Megan's bedroom, then James's room, then the bathroom, then his own office. But he found nothing, heard nothing, saw nothing.

Maybe they needed to find some sort of exorcist.

A month ago, a week ago even, he would have laughed at the absurdity of such a thought. But then was then and now was now, and Claire was right. Something was wrong with their house and they needed to do something about it.

If there was a ghost in Megan's room, a male ghost, did it ... *he* ... spy on her at night while she slept?

The thought was untenable, and Julian decided then and there that he and his daughter were going to exchange rooms. It might not help, it might be a complete waste of time, but this was the second instance when he had heard a man's voice in Megan's room, and this time he had also seen something in her mirror.

There was no way he was going to allow her to spend another night in there.

In the back of his mind was the idea that, as Claire had said, they should sell the house. No room was probably safe. But that thought was muted, and did not possess the urgency it should have.

Claire.

For some reason, the image in his brain was one of her naked and spread wide, shaved in the way she had not been since having kids. Suddenly, he was erect and aroused, and before doing anything else, he went into the bathroom, pulled down his pants, knelt on the floor in front of the toilet and masturbated. He finished quickly, spurting into the bowl and flushing it, and after buckling his pants, he called Rick and Patrick and asked whether they could come over to help him move some furniture.

Rick was always up for playing hooky—besides, the print shop was his own business; he could do whatever he wanted—and Patrick was planning to take an early lunch anyway, so his two friends came over, and within an hour, they had the furniture of the two rooms switched. Claire and Megan returned just as they were finishing, and though Megan reacted with shock and dismay—at least until Julian pointed out that her new room would be bigger— Claire merely looked at him with an expression indicating that, while she might not know the specifics, she did know why he was making this change.

Claire offered to feed Rick and Patrick, but Patrick said he needed to get back to work, and Rick said he was just going to grab a burger on his way to the print shop. The two men left, with Julian's heartfelt thanks, and Megan went upstairs to hang up her posters and redecorate, leaving Julian and Claire alone in the kitchen. She started making sandwiches while he explained about the voice he'd heard. He made no mention of John Lynch, but he didn't need to—this new news was frightening enough as it was.

"Maybe the kids should sleep in our room," Claire said.

"Then where would we sleep?"

"Maybe we should *all* sleep in our room."

Julian shook his head. "That's ridiculous."

"Is it? We're living in a haunted house. We should get out of here, leave and never come back. But if we don't, we need to start making some accommodations to the situation."

"That's what I'm doing."

"I don't like their being upstairs, that far away from us."

The truth was, he didn't, either. But there was little they could do about it—that was how the house was built—and while he intended to take every precaution, he said nothing to Claire, not wanting to frighten her even more.

The whole embrace of secrecy, this willingness—no, *desire*—to keep Claire out of the loop was not like him. He had never acted this way before in his life, and this line of thought seemed foreign to him, not his own. A dull pounding in his temple suddenly flared up into full-fledged pain. Thinking about this subject was giving him a headache. He squinted against the throbbing, trying at first to ignore it, then told Claire that his head hurt and he needed to take something for it. She nodded. She was grimacing herself, and they both went into the kitchen, where they found a bottle of Tylenol behind the vitamins in the spice cupboard.

The two of them made lunch together the way they used to, an assembly line of turkey sandwiches, before calling Megan to come down and eat. Now over the initial shock, Megan was excited by the possibilities of her new room, and she chatted happily through lunch, describing how she was thinking of putting a plant by the window so the bedroom would be more "green."

Lunch was nice, and his headache had subsided, but immediately afterward, Claire started opening windows around the house to let in fresh air. "This place is stuffy," she told him. "Don't you think it's stuffy?" She opened the back door so air could come in through the screen, and Julian found himself going out to the patio to scan the yard for any sign of John Lynch.

The new plants Claire had bought and planted the other day, he noticed, were all dead.

He needed to go to the hardware store and buy a lock for the gate that opened onto the alley. He should have done so after they first moved in, but it hadn't seemed very important at the time. Now anything he could do to make entry into their yard more difficult was top priority.

It occurred to Julian that a neighborhood watch might be a good idea. If he could get other people on the street to keep an eye out for Lynch, act as a sort of early warning signal, they might be able to avoid another incident. The only person he felt comfortable approaching was Cole Hubbard, and he walked through the side yard, past the dining room window where Lynch had been spying on him, and out to the front sidewalk. Cole's car was in the driveway, which meant he was home, and Julian strode past the Ribieros' house and up to Cole's front porch, where he rang the doorbell. He heard the chimes sound within the house and thought he heard movement, but though he waited for well over a minute, no one came to the door.

He rang again, waited. Knocked, waited. But there was still no answer.

That was strange.

He knew Cole was in there, and he rang again, knocked again and called out, "Hey, Cole! Open up! It's Julian!"

"Go away!"

His neighbor's voice sounded high and frightened, almost unrecognizable, and Julian was shocked as much by the tone as by the words themselves. "Cole? Are you all right?"

"I said go away!" There was an edge of anger now, mixed in with the fear.

He backed up a step, confused. He'd thought the two of them had a rapport; he'd thought they were starting to be friends. What the hell had happened?

This seemed totally out of character. Was it because of what had happened at the party? No. Cole couldn't have been so freaked-out by the ghost that he'd cut off all contact. After all, he'd stayed behind when the other neighbors had fled and had even offered them some sober, nonpanicky advice.

It could be something that had happened in Cole's personal life, although Julian didn't think so. If that were the case, Cole would have been polite but distant, perhaps begging off after a brief, generic discussion and saying he was busy. He wouldn't have been this hostile.

Or scared.

Julian was starting to get scared, too, and against his better judgment, he knocked on the door again. "What's wrong? I'm not leaving until you tell me!"

There was a short pause, and the door opened a crack. He saw unkempt hair and two days' stubble. "Go. Now."

"Why? I don't understand. What's wrong?"

"What's wrong?" The door opened a fraction of an inch wider. Cole *was* angry, Julian saw. But then that anger faded. It was as if he'd been mad at Julian and blamed him for something but had realized after setting eyes on him that Julian was not really at fault. "Go home," he said tiredly.

"Cole—"

"Your house is calling to me. And I don't know how much longer I can resist it."

Your house is calling to me? What did that even mean? Before he could ask, Cole had closed the door again, and this time it stayed closed. Julian shouted out to his neighbor, knocked on the door and rang the bell, hoping to goad him into a response, but this time Cole remained silent.

Frustrated and confused, Julian headed home, walking slowly, looking around at the other houses on both sides of the street, wondering what his other neighbors were thinking, wondering what they were doing.

The next day, Cole was gone.

The day after that, a For Sale sign went up on his lawn.

TWENTY-ONE

AT LEAST, CLAIRE THOUGHT, SHE COULD LOSE HERSELF IN HER work.

And her work on the Cortinez case was turning out to be far more compelling than she'd expected. It was not just the legal issues themselves, which were stimulating enough, but the supporting facts in the background, the alternate history that Mr. Cortinez had taught his students. These were accounts she had not heard before, a story with which she was not familiar, and she agreed with the teacher that it was something the students of Jardine, of all of New Mexico, should be taught.

At home, things might be confusing and complicated and weird and frightening, but seeking refuge in her job and in the labyrinthine logic of the law brought her calmness and a kind of peace, helped her cope with the craziness of the rest of her life. A small voice in the back of her head said that she shouldn't run away from reality like this, that her real duty was to her family, not her clients, but that voice was overridden by what appeared to be a reasonable practicality, an echo of Julian's position. She was not quite sure what had caused her to adopt such an attitude, but even at home, her fear seemed to be tempered somewhat, although she knew that if she dwelled on that anomaly, she would probably become even more frightened than she was already.

Which was why she didn't dwell on it.

Although that in itself was atypical behavior.

Claire still thought they should sell the house and move—it was the impetus behind her fierce dedication to this case—but it was not quite the urgent priority it had been. She was braver now than she had been even a few days ago.

Human beings could adapt to anything.

She was also starting to wonder whether Oscar Cortinez's version of history had some bearing on her own situation. Which was another reason she was so keen to research the particulars of this case. It might end up being nothing, but it seemed to her that the history of New Mexico and Tomasito County, Jardine in particular, provided clues as to the reasons behind the problems that were afflicting her family.

She might be able to win this case *and* figure out why their house was haunted.

And she had no doubt that she would win the case, no matter how good the lawyers turned out to be on the opposing side. The legal issues were clear. Oscar Cortinez *had* been singled out, and the layoff process had *not* been administered fairly. Beyond that, the teacher's contention that his curriculum incorporated district standards even as it exceeded those standards seemed unimpeachable.

The more Claire read, the more she talked to Oscar, the more convinced she was that his curriculum *should* supersede that of the district. She still had a lot of studying to do, but what she'd learned so far was fascinating.

She'd read all of his lecture notes and had gone to the Web sites he'd listed for her—although, in the usual way of Web sites, the information she found there was sketchy and generic, basically what a person would find in an encyclopedia entry—but the crux of his argument for a revised look at local history rested on three books that he'd provided her.

The first book, meticulously researched and heavily corroborated, was published by a small press based in Albuquerque. That did not inspire her with confidence, but when she looked up information about the publisher, she learned that it was well respected within academic circles and even had a Pulitzer prize winner on its roster (which would definitely help their case).

The second book was older and much more informal, a casual narrative written in the early 1900s by a former farmer who was also an amateur historian. He'd put together anecdotal stories from longtime residents as well as written accounts from the diaries of relatives and local law enforcement officers. Surprisingly believable and engagingly written, the self-published book not only provided an unofficial look at the history of Tomasito County and the town of Jardine, but shed light on interesting details of everyday life at the turn of the last century.

The third volume was from a different perspective altogether. A chronicle of Spain's and Mexico's adventures in the Southwest, the land's early exploration and colonization, it was based on eyewitness accounts recorded in official reports. Written by a respected Mexican historian and told from the point of view of those colonizing nations, the book had been published in Mexico in the early 1990s and recently translated by a noted professor from ASU.

All three books approached the same subject from different angles, giving, in toto, a complete picture of the area's previously unrevealed past. Oscar Cortinez had not only done a lot of research and investigation, all of which informed his teaching, but he was providing the students and future citizens of Jardine a valuable look at their own history. He deserved to be commended for his efforts, not fired, and Claire was going to make sure that this injustice did not go unpunished—as soon as she finished delving into all of the background material the teacher had provided.

Locking the door to her office and pulling down the shades so she wouldn't be disturbed—

so she couldn't see Pam

—Claire got a bottle of cold water out of the refrigerator and settled into her desk chair.

She read.

TWENTY-TWO

1598

AT NIGHT, THE HORSES SCREAMED.

The natives had warned them not to go beyond the hills, but Miguel Huerta and his men were not about to allow the primitive fears of savages to deter them from their mission, so they'd continued on, and were sleeping tonight in a wide, riverless valley that remained completely uninhabited, despite the profusion of tribes in the region. A great massacre had once occurred at this location, according to Tsictnako, their guide, and since that day, generations before, people had shunned this place, afraid of the spirit that lived here, the unseen force that had led brother to slaughter brother, that had caused madness to descend upon all survivors, be they victor or victim.

The guide had not wanted to go here, had led them over the hills only under threat of torture, and he had deserted them sometime during the night, leaving them alone in this hostile, godforsaken land, a fact Huerta discovered when he was awakened by the screaming of the horses.

It was a terrible, unholy sound, unlike anything he had ever heard. All of his men were roused out of sleep by the monstrous cries of the animals, and many of them began crossing themselves and praying, rising to their knees, begging God to protect them from the evil that was here. The more practical soldiers grabbed their swords and prepared to defend the camp, but the horses were already loose and running, still screaming, their voices like that of old women being slaughtered, and the soldiers were forced to chase after them. Huerta remained at first, to make sure that they were not under attack, but when it became clear that there was no assault, and that the crazed horses had chewed through the tethers on their own, rather than being released by men, he ordered six of the praying soldiers to stand guard while he followed the men chasing after the horses.

The night was dark, and while the moon was out, little of its light illuminated the world below. The group of men who had started off before him had brought a torch with them, and after picking up one for himself as well, Huerta followed their bobbing, weaving light through the weeds and low brush, over small knolls and hollows.

Twenty horses. They had twenty horses altogether, and every one of them had taken off in the same direction, as though chased by something.

Or drawn by something.

He caught up to his men before they found the horses, and all of them stumbled upon the animals together. The steeds were still screaming, but the sound here carried strangely, and it seemed that they remained quite a way off. So it was a surprise when Huerta, who was in the lead, passed between two unusually full and prickly bushes, only to see his torchlight fall on the animals' bodies.

They had set upon one another. They were rolling on the ground, fighting, a writhing mass of muscle, hair and hoof that in the flickering orange light looked like one giant multiheaded monster. Some of the horses were already dead, their stomachs bloody and bitten open, chunks ripped out of their necks and flanks, their flesh being eaten by the snapping mouths of their fellow steeds. It was an aberrant and unnatural sight, one so shocking and sickening that the men who happened upon it stood motionless for several precious moments, unsure of what to do. It was Huerta alone who retained his wits, who rushed forward and ordered his men to do the same, to grab whatever they could—tether or mane— and try to separate the furiously battling animals. But that was easier said than done. The horses were larger than men, and, struggling, biting, kicking, rolling over one another in the darkness, screaming, they were nearly impossible to separate. By the time the soldiers had pulled two of them away from the heap, the others were either dying or dead.

With their last breaths, some of the fading horses were viciously biting into their brethren, their flat, square teeth cannibalistically ripping into the rough flesh surrounding them.

Huerta ordered the men holding the ropes that had been lassoed around the necks of the two rescued horses to take the animals back to camp. He had no idea how they were to continue on with nearly all of their pack animals dead, but he would find a way, even if soldiers had to act as slaves.

The dust that had been kicked up by the melee had started to settle, and his eyes peered into the slowly clearing gloom. He was not sure he was seeing what he thought he was seeing. For behind the sluggishly stirring mound of dying horses was a small hut, the first sign of man they had seen since coming over the hills. It was a strange sort of structure, made from dead branches and sticks, a primitive shelter more akin to the wild growth of the surrounding wilderness than any form of human habitation. Had it not been for the reddish glow emanating from within, he might not have even noticed it.

He did notice it, though, and he did not like it. The unusual construction of the hut bothered him in a way he could not explain, and that reddish light seemed hellish. His first instinct was to turn away and take his men as far from this place as possible. But he was a leader, entrusted by the king to explore this northern land, and it was his duty to investigate all that he encountered, no matter how unnatural.

Still, it would be imprudent for him to further endanger any of his men. This was something unknown and very likely dangerous. The best approach would be for him to enter the structure and determine whether any peril awaited, and for his men to wait outside, ready to respond should he require them to do so.

Huerta handed off his torch, gave his instructions, then, sword drawn, crouched down and entered the hut.

The glow, he noticed immediately, was coming from a fire pit in the center of the single room. There was no one in here, and the only piece of furniture was a small table made from twigs, next to a large flattened rock that obviously served as a chair. On the hard dirt floor lay bones, human bones, and in the smoldering fire pit was a man's blackened hand with the flesh still on it.

What was this place? Huerta knew not, but it was evil; of that he was certain. He could feel here the presence of an unholy spirit, and he quickly exited the hut, feeling afraid, hoping he had not been corrupted by exposure to such malevolence.

Outside, two of his men were fighting. How this had happened in the few moments he had been inside the hut, Huerta could not understand, but as he emerged, he saw a line of soldiers, their backs facing him, while from the other side of the line he heard a metallic clash of swords. Pushing through the row of men, he saw Ferdinand de la Cruz and Hector Barbara, his best and most loyal warriors, engaged in an intense duel, apparently to the finish.

This was neither the time nor the place for swordplay, and even if the two men had a grudge against each other—which Huerta did not believe the case—it was not the appropriate occasion. They were aligned against other forces, engaged in a dark battle against an unseen evil, and they must put their personal differences aside until these other, more important matters were settled.

But Ferdinand and Hector showed no sign of ending their conflict. They each had seen him, they both knew he was there, and ordinarily his mere presence would cause them to leave off. A kind of fever seemed to have gotten into the soldiers, however, and their focus was entirely on each other. How this had come to pass in such a short span of time and why the other men stood watching dumbly rather than intervening could not be adequately explained by conventional reason. This, Huerta was certain, was connected to the madness of the horses and the horror inside that hut, and he knew in his soul that if he did not put a stop to it now, this evil would spread.

He stepped forward. "Halt!" he ordered. "Cease this fighting!" But the men paid him no heed. He felt the anger growing within him. He bade them stop yet again, and when they refused to obey, he grew enraged and held forth his own weapon. "I order you to put down your swords!" he shouted.

He was by far the most accomplished swordsman in his company. It was one of the reasons he was the captain of this expedition. He had had occasion to use his blade skills before, and all of his men knew that he had both the will and the ability to mete out punishment for any transgressions.

Yet these two continued fighting.

Although they were evenly matched, Ferdinand seemed to have gained the upper hand, due primarily to his position on the slight upslope of the land. He had sliced open Hector's right arm, inflicting serious injury, a fairly deep wound that was bleeding out through slashed clothing. The blood looked black in the flickering light of the torches, and shiny. Hector, for his part, had become enraged by his adversary's successful penetration of defenses, and, holding his sword with both hands, was making up for his disadvantages with passion and vigor. He stabbed forward zealously, crying out in triumph as his blade sank into the flesh of his rival's leg.

Ferdinand listed sideways but did not fall, and once again, Huerta ordered both men to stop the fight.

They ignored him.

Filled with an anger so black that he could feel its searing intensity in the tightness of every muscle, Huerta stepped forward, and with a scream of fury he sliced at Hector's head. He was strong and his blade sharp, his blow powerful, but the head was not severed in a single slice. His sword was caught in the other soldier's neck, and he had to pull it out and hack again. This time, Hector's head fell backward, spurting copious amounts of blood but still tenuously connected to the body. One more stroke, however, and the head was off, falling to the ground and bouncing once even as the body crumpled behind it.

Ferdinand, by this time, had fallen, though whether from the stab wound to his leg or as a reaction to his captain's intervention, Huerta knew not. What he did know was that Ferdinand had to die, and as the other man tried to push himself up from the ground, Huerta ran him through with his sword, twice in quick succession, both times through the chest. The soldier collapsed backward, lifeless, but even though he was dead, Huerta continued to chop at the body, hacking off hands and feet, arms and legs, until what was left of Ferdinand was little more than a bloody stump surrounded by chunks of chopped flesh.

Finally, Huerta stopped, breathing hard and wiping his face, though his hand was bloodier than his cheeks and only smeared the wetness around. The other soldiers were staring at him in shock. Shock but not disapproval. They seemed surprised by what he had done, but not judgmental, and though they had watched him slaughter their compadres, though he himself knew that he had gone too far, that what he had done was not only wrong and sinful but utterly mad, their faces retained the same placidity they had worn while watching the two soldiers duel.

He let the sword fall from his hand, then dropped to his knees in supplication, putting his hands together in prayer. He was damned and he knew he was damned, but that did not stop him from tearfully begging the Lord for forgiveness.

His men stood there, staring.

From far away, from the camp where the others had returned, Huerta heard a familiar sound, carried easily on the soft night breeze.

The sound of horses screaming.

He looked up, eyes stinging. The stars could not be seen from here. Above, there was only blackness.

The savages were right. Men should not live in this place, he thought.

Ever.

1777

NO CHURCH HAD BEEN BUILT, EVEN AFTER ALL THIS TIME, AND Father Juarez grew angry as his horse entered the village. He had consecrated the site five years ago, founding the church on a spot where its stained-glass windows would hold and transfer the light of the sun into the glowing colors of God's glory. He had done so with the understanding that the men left behind would induce local natives to construct the physical building in his absence. Such a strategy had led to the completion of three of the other four churches he had founded. The fourth, located in an inhospitable plain far from convenient resources, was nearly finished.

Yet here his church had not even a foundation, and the men he had assigned to this post were still living in tents and crude temporary buildings amid the primitive homes of the natives.

His horse, and the other horses, carts and pack animals of his party, trudged through the deep, sucking mud that served as a street. News of their arrival traveled fast, and before they reached the makeshift structure that was to serve as their barracks, a semiformal welcoming committee had assembled. From atop his horse, Father Juarez scanned the faces of those who waited to greet him. "Where is Brother Francisco?" he asked.

The men looked at one another, averting their gazes from his, and none of them answered his question.

"Where is Brother Francisco?" he repeated.

Jacinto Paredes stepped forward. He was the leader of the soldiers left behind to assist the friars in their mission. "Brother Francisco is gone," he said.

Father Juarez frowned. "What do you mean, he is gone?"

"Five days ago, we awoke to find that Brother Francisco was not in his quarters. We thought at first that he had gone for a walk, to meditate before prayers. He had done so before on several occasions, though not without telling someone of his intentions. But he did not return for the midday meal, and he still had not returned by nightfall. We called for him and conducted a search of the land about the village, but he was nowhere to be found. In the morning, I myself led a party into the surrounding wilderness, and there have never been less than two men out since, but we have not been able to locate either Brother Francisco or his body." The soldier made a gesture of confused helplessness. "He is gone."

Father Juarez dismounted, the rest of his party following suit. "This is unacceptable."

"I apologize, Your Holiness."

"You are assuming that Brother Francisco *left* of his own accord, wandering into the wilderness and disappearing. Have you not considered the possibility that he was *taken* by one of these savages and killed as part of some beastly ritual?"

"We assume nothing, Your Holiness. But we know these people. They are extremely peaceful and docile. The friars have succeeded in converting nearly all of them to Christianity. And there are none unaccounted for, none who would have had the opportunity to carry out such an abduction. It appears far more likely that Brother Francisco became lost on a trek and could not find his way back, was injured and unable to return, or was harmed by a wild animal."

There was an awkward pause, and once again the men who had lined up to greet him looked away, unable to meet Father Juarez's gaze.

He narrowed his eyes suspiciously. "There is something you are not telling me."

"Forgive me, Your Holiness, but the truth is that Brother Francisco has not been of sound mind. He has claimed to have visions of spirits and demons, and asserts that the ground you have consecrated is evil and unclean. He has fallen prey to local superstitions and has grown afraid of this place. He has refused for weeks to perform even the most basic of his duties, and, in truth, none of us were surprised to find him gone. And, yes, I believe the most likely reason is that Brother Francisco has fled."

"Is this why my church has not been built? Is this why it has not even been *started*?" The anger came out now, and Father Juarez lashed out at the men he had left behind in this village, excoriating them for not carrying out the will of God, for forsaking His church and their Christian duty, for indulging in the sin of sloth. He wished Brother Francisco were here so he could upbraid the friar to his face, but he unleashed a verbal attack on the man before going on to denounce those who had not had the fortitude to stand up to such blatant defiance of Church and country.

"You appointed Brother Francisco and gave him authority over all of us," Jacinto Paredes reminded him gently. "It was not our place to question his decisions."

Father Juarez stared at the man, fuming. Such insubordination would not have been tolerated in the civilized world, but here in the wild, apparently all decency and respect had been forgotten. Despite his anger, however, he recognized the truth of the soldier's words. It had been Brother Francisco's duty to see that the church was built; it was his fault that it had not been, and Father Juarez stated to all who had gathered that if Brother Francisco was captured—and *captured* was the word he used—he would not only be stripped of all authority but punished severely for failing to follow orders.

When he had finished, another man stepped forward, Brother Rodrigo, the friar appointed to succeed Brother Francisco in the event of death or incapacitation. "It is not all the fault of Brother Francisco," the friar said. "Even before he began succumbing to these delusions, he was unable to convince the natives to work on the church, though most of them had been converted. They were frightened of this ground, and I fear he may have surrendered to their superstitions."

Father Juarez frowned. It was not this man's place to speak.

Was insubordination tolerated by everyone here? Still, once again
he recognized the truth in these words. He looked back across the
muddy stretch of ground that served as the village's main road
and saw natives tentatively approaching in small groups of two or
three. He turned toward Jacinto Paredes. "I want you to gather
all of the savages in this village, as well as a translator who can
impart my words to them. I am going to give them direction myself, and order them to do God's bidding and build this church.
After I eat and freshen up, I shall address the local populace, and
you and your men will begin leading teams who will take turns
excavating the site and constructing the foundation. They will
work from sunup to sundown on all but the Lord's day, and we
will have our church before another year is past."

The soldier bowed his acquiescence. "Yes, Your Holiness."

Father Juarez spoke to the men who had accompanied him and
bade them have the slaves unpack his belongings. After choosing
the least mean house to occupy for the length of his stay, he was
presented with food, and while it was not unlike the repasts he
had had in similar outposts, it seemed all the more satisfying for
being delivered amid such wretched surroundings.

Finally, he was ready to address the converts, and he stood on
a raised cart before the spot where the church was to be built,
facing the friars, soldiers and natives who had gathered on the
adjoining field, the location where Father Juarez foresaw the in-
stallation of a rectory garden. He began with a prayer, an invoca-
tion, and with his words being translated by Brother Augusto, all
bowed their heads in unison. He went on to stress the importance
of erecting a church in the village, a physical building dedicated
to worship. The other churches had already been built, he said, or
were currently under construction, and the workers here needed
to get busy and follow suit or risk the wrath of God.

There was nervous muttering at the translation of this last,
worried looks exchanged by the natives, and Father Juarez nodded in satisfaction. Finally, his point was getting across.

"Brother Francisco is gone," he concluded. "I am in charge

now, and I hereby order you to begin construction on God's church under the direction of myself and Brother Rodrigo."

To this, there was an answer from a man who seemed to be the leader of the savages.

Insubordination again.

"He says they cannot," Brother Augusto translated. "He says the place where the church is to be built is bad land. They will build the church if it is moved to another location but will not do so if it remains at this site."

Father Juarez felt his anger rising. He and his men had been nothing but kind to these natives, had brought them God and culture and farming techniques more advanced than any seen before in this heathen land. And how were they rewarded? How were they repaid? By defiance, not gratitude.

He was not about to have his decisions second-guessed by savages, to have terms dictated by half-naked primitives, and, trying to hold in his fury, he said, "Inform them that this site has been chosen by *God*, that, as men, they may not question His will nor defy His edict. They will build the church, and they will do so on the consecrated land. It is so ordered, and any unwillingness, any disobedience, will meet with swift and sure justice."

Brother Augusto spoke for a moment in the native tongue. The leader of the savages turned to his people and spoke. The reply he received was a short, ugly word that he repeated to Brother Augusto with what seemed to be a smug satisfaction.

"They will not do it, Your Holiness."

"What?" Father Juarez felt the heat in his face.

"They refuse," the translator said.

"Then kill them all. As a lesson to those who would defy the Church and the will of God."

"Should I warn them of that punishment?" Brother Augusto asked. "Should I tell them that if they—"

"No," Father Juarez said. "Kill them."

There was hesitation, and soldiers looked to one another as though for guidance.

"Kill them all!" Father Juarez ordered.

The rifles began firing. There was smoke and screaming, the sound of explosions, savages running and falling, the smell of gunpowder, blood and excrement. When it was all over, when the smoke and dust had cleared, when the chaos had ended and the screaming stopped, there was an eerie silence. Standing on his cart, Father Juarez overlooked the scene. Bloody bodies lay in irregular heaps upon the ground, dozens of them, men, women and children, chests blown open, limbs torn apart.

He remained unmoved.

"Bury them," he ordered. "We will build the church upon their bones."

IN THE YEARS THAT FOLLOWED, FATHER JUAREZ CAME TO REGRET his decision, which had been made in anger and haste. His charge was to tame these savages, to teach them, to convert them from their pagan ways. They were like children and should be punished as such, as he'd learned during the time intervening. His penalty for disobedience and sloth had been too harsh, and he had decided to make his home here at San Jardine to atone for his mistake.

For a mistake it had been. Whether or not this land really had been bad or cursed or evil, as the natives had insisted, it had certainly been stained and tainted by the slaughter he had authorized, and was now as corrupted and debased as the savages had claimed it to be.

The spirits here were not at rest.

Was that his fault? Father Juarez knew not. But more than one good man had been taken from them in the prime of life, felled by spirits unseen, the victim of an unexplainable accident or a suspicious unknown illness. Earlier this week Brother Ignatio, unable to cope with the pressures placed upon him, had taken his own life, drowning himself in the cistern by weighting himself down with rocks and ropes. Father Juarez was grief-stricken and filled with remorse. Brother Ignatio had been his best friend and closest confidant, a studious, industrious servant of God who had dedicated himself to bringing others to the light. As a student of Scripture and a scholar of the Catholic philosophers and theologians, he, more than anyone, had known that to take his own life would keep him eternally from God's grace. Yet he had died by his own hand.

Father Juarez could not understand such behavior. It made no sense. And for such a devout man to so thoroughly reject his own beliefs, to so flagrantly and irrevocably defy his God . . . It was beyond his comprehension.

Unless Brother Ignatio had *not* taken his own life.

Those were the rumors Father Juarez had heard. And it was why he feared for himself. It was wrong of him to have such a focus, and blasphemous to be afraid while under God's protection in His own church, but when he retired at night to his chamber, when he lay upon his cot and stared up at the painted adobe ceiling, he saw shadows that should not be there, shadows that had no source. Shapes darker than the darkness seemed to move about the room, and he would say his prayers loudly so as to drown out the whispers that called to him, the whispers that knew his name.

Now he worried that if Brother Ignatio had been compelled by demons or spirits to take his own life—or, far worse, if demons or spirits had taken life *from* him—a similar fate might befall himself.

Already there were reports that Brother Ignatio's spirit had been seen in the bell tower and in the library, two of the places he haunted most in life. If it were merely the natives, or even the soldiers, who had reported seeing this, Father Juarez might well have dismissed the claims. But two of the friars had seen him as well, Brother Martin up close, and the friar recalled with genuine terror espying a face filled with such anger and hate that it distorted the features into something monstrous.

"Are you sure it was Brother Ignatio?" Father Juarez pressed him.

"I am certain," he replied. "It could be no other."

On Sunday, Father Juarez presided over Mass, and for the first time in a very long while, he was acutely aware of the fact that the foundation of this building was filled with bones. The bodies of those he'd had killed lay here beneath the nave, and he wondered, not for the first time, whether it was his own intemperate and misguided decision to inter them there that had led to this pass.

What did God think of his actions? Father Juarez wondered. He had prayed for forgiveness times too numerous to count and had often asked for a sign, though none had been provided. *Was* he forgiven? Did the Lord look into his heart and see contrition there, repentance?

Maybe Brother Ignatio *had* taken his own life.

Maybe he had known he would not get into heaven.

That night, Father Juarez made his rounds, checked to make sure the slaves were locked in, then went into the chapel, where he lit another candle for Brother Ignatio before kneeling in front of the altar to pray. The chapel was cold and dark, lit only by the flickering votive candles in the alcove. He was halfway through his prayer, reciting the litany of individuals for whom he was asking blessings, when he heard a noise behind him.

The shuffling of sandaled feet on the floor.

He continued with his litany, willing himself not to speed through the names of those to be blessed. It was probably one of the other friars come to pray or perhaps light a candle. But he did not really think that, and it took all of the self-discipline he possessed to concentrate on his entreaty to God and not open his eyes to see who was coming up behind him.

The shuffling feet drew closer.

His focus was not on his prayer. His attention was divided, and he knew that God knew, and he made the decision to start over again and devote his mind, heart and soul to speaking with the Lord to the complete exclusion of all else—after he opened his eyes and turned around to see who was there.

Father Juarez did stop praying, and he did open his eyes, and he did turn around. Despite the fears lurking at the back of his mind, he really did expect to see one of the friars or, at the very worst, Brother Ignatio's wavery, transparent shade. He was not prepared for what he actually saw, a horror so unexpected that it caused him to cry out and cross himself even as he stepped backward toward the safety of the altar.

For while the spirit before him *was* Brother Ignatio, or had been, it was disfigured almost beyond recognition. The entire form possessed the color and consistency of shadow, save for the whiteness of the wildly grinning mouth, which was Brother Ignatio's mouth but corrupted, just as the faintly glowing eyes deep within the recesses of the distended face were Brother Ignatio's eyes, augmented by . . . something else.

The effect was ghastly, a dreadful abomination so far from God's conception of human that he felt damned just gazing upon it.

The figure spoke to him in a voice aged and cracked and filled with the knowledge of hell, and even as Father Juarez ran out the side door of the chapel, crying out in terror, he heard the threats made against him, atrocities of the flesh he could never have imagined. He expected to be followed but was not, and in the courtyard he stopped, breathing heavily, and looked to the heavens, begging the Lord for deliverance from this evil.

No stars could be seen from this spot. It was as if those lights of heaven winking in the firmament had been extinguished. He knew that was not the case; they no doubt could be seen elsewhere in the world. But they were invisible from this location, and the darkness above the church was complete.

He realized he was babbling as he pleaded with God to put an end to this horror, but he realized as well that he had brought it upon himself, that it was his retributive decision to order the deaths of those natives that had led to this torment. He had usurped the authority of the divine and was being punished for his sins, and God would not hear his pleas, no matter how much he implored the Almighty to spare him.

The wind whispered his name, laughingly, and Father Juarez

turned to see from whence the voice had come. All was still, all was dark, but the wind returned and with it the whisper of his name.

All was not as still as it seemed, however. There was a lantern hung from a post holding up the roof of the soldiers' barracks. It creaked in the wind, drawing his attention, and by its faint yellow light, he saw something slithering on the ground, a monster of mud and leaf, twig and clay, a cousin to the Serpent. It maneuvered through the garden toward him, and it was this that was the source of the whispers, this that was calling his name. As it approached, it began to rise up, this unholy atrocity, and on its elongated head, even in the gloom, Father Juarez saw features of the face that he recognized, that he knew.

The monster whispered his name. Laughed.

He ran to his quarters, awakening all, screaming with the onset of madness.

TWENTY-THREE

THERE WAS NO COURTHOUSE IN JARDINE, SO ANYTIME CLAIRE
was required to appear before a judge, whether for a hearing or a
trial, she had to drive the fifty miles to Amarejo, the county seat,
an arduous trip that inevitably consumed the better part of a
working day. Even early morning appearances required an hour's
drive there and back, in addition to the waiting time in court and
the length of the meeting itself, so the best she could hope for was
a return to Jardine by noon or one o'clock.

Today's preliminary hearing for Oscar Cortinez was *not*
scheduled for the early morning. It was set for eleven thirty, which
meant it would probably be postponed until after lunch. In court
parlance, that meant two o'clock. So she doubted she'd be home
before five. To make matters worse, she had to attend an eight-
o'clock deposition for the Seaver divorce, which the lawyer of her
client's soon-to-be-ex-husband refused to conduct in Jardine. So
she needed to get up early, leave the house early, and spend the
entire day in Amarejo, with probably a significant amount of
downtime between the deposition and the hearing.

She let the kids sleep in, but if *she* had to get up early, *Julian*
had to get up early, and she prodded him awake, telling him to
make coffee and get breakfast ready while she dressed and put on
her makeup. Breakfast consisted of an overtoasted bagel, but at

least the coffee was good, and she drank two cups to ensure that she would remain awake for the long, boring drive. "I may be back late," she warned Julian. "So if I don't get back in time, or the kids get hungry, there's leftover chicken in the refrigerator and fish sticks in the freezer. If you guys want, you can make Pasta Roni or macaroni and cheese."

"We'll figure something out," Julian told her.

She double-checked her briefcase to make sure she had all pertinent forms and paperwork for both the deposition and the hearing, packed her laptop in its case, made sure she had enough money to buy lunch, turned on her cell phone and gave Julian a kiss before stepping outside. "Be careful," she told him. She wasn't exactly sure what she meant by that, but he nodded, and that reassurance buoyed her as she walked out to the van in the driveway and pushed the button on her key to remotely unlock the doors. She waved good-bye to Julian one last time before he went back into the house.

To her left, Claire sensed movement, and she quickly turned her head in that direction. There was a man walking down the sidewalk toward her, an average-size man of medium build wearing a backward yellow baseball cap. She'd seen him around before, but it seemed odd for him to be out this early in the morning. He *could* be exercising, she thought, but he was not running, jogging or even walking fast, and the closer he came, the more uncomfortable Claire felt.

She quickly got in the van and locked the doors before starting the engine.

The man passed by without even glancing in her direction, and Claire relaxed a little.

She watched him walk away. She was so worked up that these days anything even slightly off from the usual routine had her seeing threats where none existed. Arranging her purse, briefcase and laptop on the passenger seat next to her, she turned on the satellite radio, tuned in CNN, then started off.

The sun was up, but the day was still young, and much of the morning's light hid behind clouds that stretched from horizon to horizon, creating billowing silhouettes that stood out sharply against the gradations of pink and orange behind them. More vehicles than she'd expected were on the road, and that caused a slowdown where the highway narrowed to two lanes in Yucca River Canyon. Truth be told, she was glad for the company, happy she was not all alone on the road. For the thoughts in her head were the type that inspired fear and dread. She was not planning out questions and exceptions for the deposition, was not going over in her mind opening statements for the hearing. She was going over the history she had read about in Oscar Cortinez's books, the tales told by Spanish explorers and Mexican missionaries.

She found the supernatural aspects of the various accounts disturbing. She knew that most of it could be put down to the superstitions of the time and the fears that probably befell all sojourners through what were then unexplored lands.

But . . .

But in her mind, as she read, she imagined the area as it must have appeared back then, without the buildings, without the people, without the roads, and in her conception, the focal point of the horrific events was the land on which their house now stood.

Of course, that was ridiculous. No church had ever been constructed on that spot. Still, the events described in those histories possessed an unnerving correlation to the events that were transpiring between the walls of her own home, and thinking about them left her feeling cold and anxious.

She was determined to bring it up to Oscar when she saw him, and, luckily, they both arrived early to the courthouse, which gave them a chance to talk. He, of course, wanted to go over the particulars of the hearing, wanted her to once again walk him through everything that was going to happen, as well as reassure him that they would eventually emerge victorious. Hand-holding was an important component of the practice of law, and though they'd had the exact same conversation just last night, they did it again until his nerves were soothed and he was ready to play his role.

With some extra time to kill, Claire saw her opportunity and cleared her throat. "Oscar," she said cautiously. "I've been reading the material you provided me. These stories about evil spirits and haunted places . . ."

He waved her away. "Justifications. A way to rationalize the murder, brutality and atrocities committed by first the Spanish against the native Americans and then the English against the Spanish. Don't worry. They won't hurt our credibility. History texts are full of references to ghosts and demons and the supernatural. It was how the people in those days explained events and phenomena they did not understand—if you read some of the accounts of the California Gold Rush written by the men of that time, they would curl your hair. Often such stories are excuses for bad behavior, defenses for violent societal overreactions that seem indefensible to us today. And, in this case, they were used to justify the slaughter of opposing societies."

Claire nodded, as though in agreement. She wanted to pursue this line of questioning, but chose to wait until after the case had been decided before probing any deeper. She could not afford to engender any doubt in her client, and she knew that by asking what she really wanted to ask, she would risk losing Oscar's confidence. It was clear that he disbelieved in the supernatural and put no stock in any paranormal explanations. If she indicated that she felt otherwise, it might make him think that she was unstable.

Maybe she was.

AT HOME, JULIAN AND THE KIDS HAD EATEN BY THE TIME SHE RE-turned.

"How'd it go?" Julian asked.

"Good," she said. "The deposition went well, and the district is already indicating that they might be willing to settle. We have a strong case, and they know it."

"That's great," he said.

"Yeah," she said, though without much enthusiasm. She opened the door of the refrigerator and took out a head of lettuce, intending to make herself a salad.

"What's wrong?" Julian asked.

She looked at him. "You know what's wrong."

"There hasn't been anything—"

"Don't," she told him. She chopped the lettuce, got out some tomatoes and carrots, and he wandered back out to the living room, where Megan and James were fighting over control of the TV.

Both of the kids went to bed early, while it was still a little light out. Granted, the days were long and it didn't get dark until sometime between eight and nine, but it was totally out of character for either of them to voluntarily go to bed at this hour, and Claire had a sneaking suspicion that they wanted to be asleep before night truly fell.

She didn't blame them.

Julian was watching a movie on HBO. She watched it with him for a while, and when she was sure the kids were asleep, she told him about what she'd been reading, the historical accounts of ghosts and demons and unexplainable phenomena. He was skeptical, of course, but not that skeptical, and she knew that while he wanted to disbelieve, he probably did not.

"It has to be connected to what's happening here, to us," she said. "It makes sense that if those sorts of things were occurring on this land hundreds of years ago, they're probably affecting what's going on now."

"What is this, a monster movie?" he tried to joke. But he knew as well as she did that what was going on was closer to that reality than anything else, and when she stared at him disapprovingly and said nothing, he apologized.

They were too far along to pretend that they were overreacting to a settling of the house or similarly rational events that could explain what they were going through. This was bigger than that, more concrete. Multiple people had seen a ghost walk down their hallway and into the living room. It was time to look for real answers, not logical explanations.

They talked about it for a while, not really coming to any conclusions, agreeing only that they needed to investigate the situation more, watch the kids carefully and be very, very cautious.

Julian was tired, had a headache, and went to bed early, but Claire was wired and wide-awake. She worked on a few pretrial motions for the Seaver divorce and tried to determine the starting point for a settlement with the school district. Her mind wandered, though, and she found herself thinking about something she'd read, a strange small detail she'd come across in two of the books, the one written by the farmer and the one penned by the Mexican historian.

As a test, Claire went outside. Everyone in the house was asleep, so she unlocked and opened the front door very quietly, closing it behind her. She walked onto the lawn, then to the sidewalk. She had been out after dark before, but she'd never had any reason to study the sky. Now, however, she looked up.

The night was black.

No stars.

She tried to recall whether she'd seen the moon since moving to their new home and couldn't.

Shivering, she walked down the sidewalk until she was in front of the Ribieros' house, where she stopped, looking up.

The Little Dipper and Orion's belt were right where they were supposed to be, and a half-moon hovered just above the roofline of a house across the street.

She'd been afraid this would happen, on some level had *known* it would happen, but the sheer concrete fact of it took her breath away. This wasn't some nebulous experience that could be interpreted in many different ways. It was a measurable truth: the moon and stars could not be seen from their house.

Why this was the case, she had no idea, but she walked very slowly along the sidewalk, looking up all the while. The sky was clear and beautiful, the kind she remembered from childhood. She expected to find a specific cutoff point beyond which the stars and moon could no longer be seen, but instead the lights in the sky did a slow fade, as though they were gradually being obscured or turned off. By the time she reached the boundary of her yard, the sky was jet-black.

What did this mean? No answers suggested themselves, but the scope of the phenomenon left her feeling small and helpless. This was far bigger than just having a ghost in their house. She walked down the sidewalk in the opposite direction, and the same thing recurred: the moon and stars gradually reappeared as she moved away from her yard.

She returned to her driveway and stood there for a moment, not sure whether she wanted to go back inside. At the moment, however, she felt safer inside than out, and she stepped onto the porch, opened the front door and walked into the living room—where the lights suddenly turned on, revealing the laundry basket sitting in the center of the floor.

From the kitchen area, she heard a door swing open and hit the wall. Hard.

The door to the basement.

She couldn't deal with this now, and she ran quickly down the hall to the bedroom, not bothering to check the cellar door, not bothering to turn off the lights in the living room. Breathing hard, she closed the door behind her and instinctively pressed her back against it to prevent anything from getting in. She thought about waking Julian, thought about telling him to go upstairs and get the kids and have them sleep with them for the night, but she saw him on the bed, and both her fear and those thoughts fled instantly from her mind. For he had decided to sleep naked, and had kicked off the sheet and blanket. He was on his back and his erection stuck straight up in the air.

Forgetting everything else, she walked forward, stripping off her clothes before climbing onto the bed.

She sucked him while he slept, working feverishly on his erection, and he came in her mouth, still asleep.

She swallowed, masturbated, then closed her eyes and dreamed of a world where there were no stars, no moon, no sun, and the sky was always black.

TWENTY-FOUR

ONCE AGAIN, JULIAN SPENT THE BETTER PART OF THE MORNING trying to look up information about their house, their street, the town. His deadline was real and it was nearly here, but Claire wanted him to investigate further and try to find out what he could about the history of their property. She wouldn't specify what she hoped to do with such knowledge, but he knew how her mind worked, and knew she probably had a plan. Although whether that plan was to sue the realtor and the seller for not revealing that their house was haunted, or whether it was to perform some sort of ritual to exorcise the ghost, he couldn't say.

She was smart, though, and tenacious, and she had a much better chance of figuring a way out of their predicament than he did.

Of course, she didn't want him to be looking up things here, in the house, not after what had happened to her. But it was daytime and he was feeling brave.

Besides, part of him *wanted* something like that to happen to him.

As was often the case with Internet research, Julian ended up scrolling through a list of articles and sites that had nothing whatsoever to do with the subject at hand. And chances were that when he did find pertinent information, it would be a brief generic overview, the equivalent of a *Reader's Digest* article.

It was his job to design Web pages, but even he had to admit that there was a lot of useless crap out there on the Web.

After fifty fruitless minutes, Julian reset his parameters to narrow down the search, but there were still some twenty-eight thousand hits, and it wasn't until the fifth page that he found one that even applied: an official town Web site sponsored by the chamber of commerce that, in a bid for tourist dollars, played up the local history angle. There was nothing mentioned about hauntings (although with the popularity of so many ghost-hunter shows on cable, that would definitely have been a draw), but the site did describe Jardine as a former frontier town populated by the likes of the legendary Kit Carson and originally founded by the Spanish.

It wasn't much, but it was a beginning, and Julian hoped to expand upon that with subsequent references in other linked sites.

No such luck.

He scrolled through Web page after Web page for the next hour without encountering anything even remotely helpful. Finally he decided to take a break, and he went downstairs, where, miraculously, Megan and James had found a show to both of their liking and were lying down on the living room couch and floor, respectively, watching television.

Julian did his fatherly duty and chided them for watching too much TV, telling them that, when this show was over, they had to turn off the television and find something else to do. They muttered their assent, and he went into the kitchen, where he grabbed an apple and a can of Dr Pepper.

Back in his office, he took some time off to write an e-mail to his client, detailing everything he'd accomplished so far, setting up an excuse for himself should he miss the deadline, which looked increasingly likely. He paused, reread what he wrote before sending it, took a sip of Dr Pepper—

—and the text on the screen *moved*.

As he watched, uncomprehending, individual letters separated themselves from words, moving up, moving down, moving out, the pixels that created them flattening and shifting, coming together in a dark mass that slowly resolved itself into a face.

The face of the ghost who had crashed their party.

The man who had died in their basement.

Julian pushed his chair away from the desk as the face looked up, looked down, looked around, then pressed against the monitor, grinning. It looked for all the world as though someone were actually trapped behind the screen, and Julian recoiled at the unnerving reality of the illusion.

Then the face became pixilated, broke apart, losing mass, losing color, fracturing into fragments that once again rearranged themselves into his e-mail message.

Julian reached over and quickly turned off his computer before backing away again, more unnerved than he would have expected to be by such an experience. He stood, then paced around the room, taking deep breaths, thinking. Maybe Claire was on the right track. Maybe there *was* something connecting the haunting of their house to events in the past, and maybe the thing in this house saw what he was trying to look up and wanted to scare him away.

Just as it had her.

He *was* scared. No doubt about that. But he also didn't seem to be getting anywhere with his research, and it occurred to him that a more fruitful approach might be to check the library. Public libraries often had books and documents pertaining to local history, as well as reference librarians who themselves were repositories of information. He glanced at the Beatles clock on his bookcase. It was just after eleven. Julian paused for a moment, deciding what to do, then headed downstairs.

The kids were still camped out in the living room. "All right," he told them. "Turn it off."

"But the show's not over," Megan complained. "You said we could wait until it was over."

James had already used the remote to shut off the TV.

"Come on. Let's go." Julian took the key ring out of his pocket, jingling it so both kids could hear.

"Okay," James said, getting up off the floor.

"Where?" Megan asked, suspicious.

"Out for lunch. We'll go to McDonald's. Then I need to stop by the library and look a few things up."

Megan wrinkled her nose in distaste. "McDonald's?"

"Taco Bell, then."

"*I* want McDonald's!" James announced.

"We'll flip for it. But come on; we gotta go."

"*I* gotta go," Megan said, and headed down the hallway to the bathroom.

Julian found himself still jingling his keys. He hadn't realized how nervous he was, how much he wanted to get out of the house, until his daughter said she had to use the bathroom. James looked in that direction and started to say something, but Julian cut him off. "*You* can go at Taco Bell."

"McDonald's!"

"Whatever."

As soon as Megan finished, he ushered the kids out of the house, not relaxing until they were safely in the van.

"You said we were going to flip a coin," James said.

Julian nodded. "We will."

"But how will we know where we're going unless we do it first?"

Julian pushed himself up from the seat in order to get a hand in his pocket. He pulled out a dime. "Okay, call it."

"Heads!" they both said in unison.

"One person gets heads; one person gets tails," he said patiently.

"I want heads," James insisted.

Megan sighed melodramatically. "Fine."

Julian flipped the coin, called it. "Tails."

"Ha!" Megan said, pointing a finger in her brother's face and grinning.

"Taco Bell it is." Julian drove to the fast-food restaurant, where they ate a reasonably harmonious meal before heading over to the library. James parked himself in front of one of the computers and Megan wandered into the young-adult stacks, while Julian went over to the reference desk to talk to the librarian. As he'd suspected, the library did have a lot of items dealing with local history. There was actually a closet-size "history room" that held nothing but books, brochures, pamphlets and magazines related to the history of Jardine and Tomasito County. Most of the items could not be checked out, but they could be studied in the library, and Julian pulled out two volumes that looked promising: the relatively recent *New Mexico Ghost Stories* and the considerably older *Tales of Tomasito County*. Behind a glass case were stacks of old newspapers, and he asked the librarian whether he could look through them, but she said the papers were in fragile condition and were kept in the case for protection. There was microfiche of the newspapers available, however, and a viewer near the computers, and she showed him the file cabinet containing the microfiche, explaining how they were organized by year.

Julian couldn't spend all day in the library, and even if he could, he still wouldn't be able to read everything. So he skimmed the books, neither of which was as helpful as he'd hoped, before grabbing a handful of microfiche and sitting down to scroll through the headlines of Jardine's early days. The newspapers didn't go back as far as he wanted—maybe not enough people could read back then—but he began at 1900 and started working forward.

Megan came up while he was still halfway through the year 1901 and asked whether she could go to her friend Kate's house for the afternoon. Kate was standing next to her; the two had obviously run into each other.

Or they had purposely planned to meet here.

It was impossible to keep up with the cell phone shenanigans of teenage girls.

Kate smiled shyly. "Hi, Mr. Perry."

Julian looked from one to the other. "You can go," he told Megan. "If your mom is home," he said to Kate.

"My mom's right here. Mom!" she called.

There was a chorus of shushing from annoyed patrons, and the librarian at the front counter frowned at her, but seconds later, Kate's mother was standing before him, and the two of them talked over logistics. She and Kate were going to The Store first, but then they were going home, and Megan was welcome to come with them.

"What time should I pick her up?" Julian asked.

"Oh, I'll drop her off. What time do you want her back?"

"Five o'clock," Julian decided.

After saying their good-byes, his daughter happily went off with her friend, and Julian paused for a moment to check on James and make sure he was all right. Sitting between two other boys, his son was deeply engrossed in the cartoony mayhem of a computer game, and, satisfied, Julian went back to his microfiche.

Sometime later, Julian became aware that a person was standing behind him. Assuming it was another patron who wanted to use the microfiche reader, he was all set to apologize for hogging the equipment when he turned to see James standing there. In a first, James said he was tired of playing games and wanted to leave. Usually it was the other way around, and Julian glanced at his watch, shocked to see that it was almost three o'clock. He hadn't really come across anything useful yet, and didn't want to feel as though he'd wasted the entire afternoon, so he said, "Ten more minutes."

"I'm bored, Dad."

"I know. But . . ." He had a sudden idea. "Hey, do you want to hang out at Mom's office?"

James's face lit up. "Yeah!"

Perfect. Claire could watch James, while he could continue looking through these old newspapers. Julian took out his cell phone. He wasn't supposed to use it in the library, but he leaned into his carrel, close to the microfiche reader, and called Claire, speaking softly. He explained the situation, and she agreed to come by the library to pick up their son.

While he waited, James checked his summer reading program

status on the wall chart and picked out another book to read. Julian continued to scroll through headlines, but before he'd gotten past another month, Claire was there. James hurried over with his new book. "You rescued me," he declared with exaggerated gratitude.

Julian stood. "Thanks," he told Claire.

"Any luck?" she asked.

"There might be something. That's why I want to stay a little longer."

"I don't," James announced.

Smiling, Claire put an arm around her son. "Why don't we get some ice cream?" she suggested.

He grinned. "Excellent!"

"Do you want me to pick him up when I'm finished?" Julian asked.

Claire shook her head. "We'll meet you at home."

She gave him a quick kiss on the cheek; then the two of them were off, and Julian turned back to his newspapers. The "something" he had told her about turned out to be a pattern. It wasn't anything specific, probably not anything they could even use, but for a period of years in the early 1900s, the majority of murders and violent crimes seemed to take place on their street. He didn't think it was a pattern that had continued through the present day, but he thought about the man who'd died in their basement and wondered whether other deaths—mysterious or not—had occurred in or around their house over the decades, unrecognized by the newspapers.

It was getting late, and since he finally had something he could show to Claire, Julian decided to call it a day. He shut off the machine, picked up the pieces of scratch paper on which he'd scribbled notes, and started to put away the stack of microfiche.

"I'll take care of that," the reference librarian said, walking over. "We like to refile everything ourselves, just to make sure it's all in the right order."

"Okay. Thanks." He handed over the microfiche sleeves, as well as the two books he'd looked at, and left the library, heading home.

He was the first one back, and he was glad of that. Before Claire and James returned, before Megan was dropped off, he went through every room in the house, even the basement, looking for anything even slightly out of the ordinary. He was more creeped out than he wanted to be or than he would ever let on, but he was the husband, he was the father, and he needed to make sure that it was safe for his family to be here. He even went into his office and turned on the computer again, waiting to see whether anything weird showed up on his monitor, and he was gratified when, after he accessed several different screens and re-typed his e-mail message, nothing did.

Downstairs, he heard the front door open and close, heard the happy voices of Claire and James, and he shut off the computer, satisfied that—for the moment, at least—the house was clear. He took the steps two at a time, and—

The first floor was empty.

There was no one else home.

Julian heard voices again, from the living room, and goose bumps prickled on his neck and the skin of his arms, making him shiver. Even this close, the voices *still* sounded like Claire and James, and a wave of despair washed over him as he wondered whether that meant they were dead. Claire had walked to work this morning, and in his mind he saw the two of them crossing the street on the way home and being hit by a drunk driver or a car with bad brakes, James flying forward and cracking his head open on the asphalt, Claire crumpling as the bumper forced her down, tires rolling over her midsection, crushing her organs and bones.

Numbly, he stepped into the living room. His worries about Claire and James vanished. Whatever spirit was here, it was not one of them. There was a heaviness to the atmosphere, a palpable malevolence that would never be associated with either his wife or his son. He could imagine this thing *imitating* them, though, trying to make him believe they were here, trying to torture him.

His first instinct was to flee, but he forced himself to stand his ground, and he looked carefully around the room. There was nothing to be seen, nothing out of place, no visible apparition, but there was a bad energy suffusing the living room, making the light seem darker, making the furniture seem old and creepy.

And it appeared to be emanating from the fireplace.

Once the most impressive aspect of the living room, perhaps of the entire house, the oversize fireplace now just seemed threatening. The opening was like a maw, and it was much blacker than it should have been at this time of day, black enough that it seemed to go back farther than the wall of the house, black enough to hide the presence of unspeakable creatures. Julian reached out and switched on the ceiling light, but it did nothing to further reveal what lay hidden in that space.

Slowly, nervously, cautiously, he stepped forward.

He heard the voices. They were male and female, young and old, but they weren't James and Claire. They weren't even speaking real sentences. Like the man's voice he had heard in Megan's room, they were saying actual words but not in a way that made sense.

"... *mail slot luggage* ..."

"... *first come table slime* ..."

It was a conversation between crazy people, delivered in competing monotones, and it was coming from within the fireplace. Close now to the hearth, Julian crouched down to peer into the opening.

A whoosh of air flew over him, around him, past him.

Only ...

It wasn't air. There was volume to it, heft, and a sentience that he sensed but did not understand.

Then it was over. The room was back to normal; the fireplace was just a fireplace; there were no more voices. Seconds later, the front door opened, and Claire and James *did* walk in. Julian went over to greet them, grateful and unexpectedly elated that they were here and alive.

Claire frowned at him. "What's wrong with your hair?"

James laughed.

Julian reached up and patted the top of his head. His hair was sticking up where that *thing* had blown over him. He used his fingers to comb it back down. "Wind," he lied.

"It wasn't windy—" Claire started to say, but she caught his look over James's head and cut herself off. "Oh."

They discussed it later, though he downplayed his description of the event and left out his real reaction completely. The kids were in another room, and before Claire could quiz him further, he quickly told her what he had learned at the library. She seemed excited to hear that there was a history of death and violence on their street, though he had no idea how she could possibly use that information to help solve their problem, and for the first time her sense of hope seemed stronger than her fear.

He almost told her about the face on his computer screen, but at the last moment decided against it. Enough had happened today already, and he chose to let it go.

They made love that night, and it was normal, tender, comfortable, the way it used to be. There were no bizarre urges, no inexplicable compulsions, no external pressure of any kind. He could almost believe some of their more recent encounters had never happened, and they fell asleep holding each other, happy.

JULIAN WAS AWAKENED AFTER MIDNIGHT BY THE SOUND OF laughing. It was soft, whispery, and might in other circumstances have been mistaken for the rustling of wind outside. But he knew it for what it was and sat up in bed, listening to the eerie laughter as it swirled around their bedroom, then left through the door and moved down the hall.

There was nothing he wanted more than to hide his head under the covers, the way he had as a child, and wait for morning. But Megan and James were upstairs alone, and he immediately pushed off the covers and hurried after the noise.

It was in the kitchen now, and he went there, turning on the lights as he did so. He saw nothing in the kitchen, but the door to the basement was open, and from the room down there he heard laughter. It was louder now, less whispery, and though he had not been able to determine anything about its character before, the laughter definitely sounded masculine to him now.

Julian looked around for a weapon. It obviously wouldn't help against something unseen, but it would make him feel braver, and he opened the middle drawer and settled on that old standby: the carving knife.

He was about to proceed to the basement door when something outside caught his eye. Through the window above the sink he saw movement, and he flipped on the patio lights just in time to see the little garage door close. He stood there for a moment, unsure of what to do. The smart thing would be to call the police. But he wasn't sure this was something the police could help with, wasn't sure that whatever had gone into the garage was . . . human. Of course, if it *wasn't* human, the smartest thing to do would be to stay here in the house.

But he had a knife in his hand, his adrenaline was up, and Julian unlocked the back door and stepped outside. He was barefoot and in his pajamas, but that didn't slow him down. The dead grass was cool beneath his toes as he moved stealthily toward the garage. He glanced from side to side as he approached, making sure nothing else was out here, looking up to see whether the lights in the garage had been turned on.

He opened the door, then stepped back quickly, knife extended, but nothing leaped out at him. After waiting a beat, he moved forward, walking into the garage and turning on the light. He glanced around. Everything seemed to be in order; nothing looked out of place. Since the van was parked in the driveway, and the lawn mower and most of the gardening implements were in the storage shed, the garage was relatively bare. With the light on, it was easy to see everything within the open area, and Julian wondered whether he had been lured in here purposely. His grip on the knife tightened.

No. Whoever—*whatever*—had gone into the garage had not known that he was watching. He'd caught someone—*something*—sneaking in and closing the door. It had not been part of some elaborate show put on for his benefit.

Although the laughter had lured him into the kitchen . . .

No. Something was here in the garage. He just couldn't figure out where it had gone.

His eyes alighted on the ladder.

Upstairs.

Julian's heart started thumping. He knew he shouldn't go up there. It was stupid. Possibly dangerous. He didn't even *want* to do it. But he found himself walking over to the wall where the wooden ladder was attached. He looked up.

The trapdoor was open.

Why hadn't he noticed that before?

Upstairs it was dark. Beyond the square entrance to the loft, he could see nothing, only blackness. It was impossible for him to climb the ladder and still hold the knife in such a manner that it could be used, and he had decided to quit, go back to the house, and return in the morning, when he could see and it would be safer. But he felt a drop of warm wetness hit his forehead, and he touched it with his finger and it was blood.

Someone or something was bleeding up there.

What if it's James?

The thought had not even occurred to him before this moment, but he realized with a sinking feeling in the pit of his stomach that he had not checked on the children after being awakened by the laughter. It *could* be James. The area upstairs was where he and his friend played, their "headquarters." He could have been the one sneaking into the garage and closing the door behind him.

Julian wiped the blood from his forehead with his palm. A

half-formed plan to wake Claire and call 911 was jettisoned immediately, and he quickly shifted the knife to his left hand, placing it in the crook next to his thumb so he could use his other fingers to grasp the ladder's rungs. He sped up to the top, and only then, only when his head and shoulders were protruding from the floor of the loft and he was at his most vulnerable, did he realize that it couldn't have been James. The back door of the house had been locked. If James had gone out first, the door would have been unlocked.

Julian braced himself for a blow, but even as he winced in expectation, he was pushing himself up into the loft and frantically searching for a light switch or a pull chain attached to a bulb. He'd been up here only in the daytime, and only on a few occasions, so he didn't even know whether there *was* a light in the loft.

Nothing hit him as he got to his feet, and since he was next to a wall already, he pressed his right hand against it, feeling around, even as his left hand gripped hard the handle of the knife. Amazingly, his fingers encountered a switch, and he pushed it up as a shielded bulb in the center of the room turned on, bathing the loft in a light that was probably soft and weak, but that after the blackness of a moment before seemed as bright as the sun.

Julian stood where he was, rubbing his eyes, and as soon as they adjusted to the brightness, he saw where the blood had come from.

A dead body on the floor.

It was John Lynch, the intruder he'd seen through the dining room window. Julian recognized the yellow baseball cap.

"Oh, my God," he whispered.

The man had stabbed himself. Not just once but multiple times. In the face. A slice through his left cheek had widened his mouth to clown proportions; another in his forehead revealed skull beneath skin. What was left of his nose resembled chopped raw hamburger, and a hard stab near his right eye had continued down the side of his head and taken off a sliver of skin with hair, as well as a piece of ear. He had finished himself off by plunging the knife into his own throat, from whence it protruded now, the wound around the blade revealing a thin, ragged strip of ripped cartilage, blood covering not just the remnants of his neck but his arms, his chest and the surrounding floor. A thin rivulet ran across the uneven floorboards to the trapdoor opening, which was where it had dripped onto Julian's head.

There was even blood splattered five feet away on a stand-alone cardboard cutout for *Diary of a Wimpy Kid*, and the stench in the loft was so strong Julian marveled that he had not noticed it immediately upon coming up.

He gulped in air, trying not to gag.

How had there been no screams? How had the entire neighborhood not been awakened by Lynch's shrieks of pain?

Julian felt like screaming himself, and even as his brain was logically processing the information being fed to it by his eyes, he was scrambling back down the ladder. Halfway to the bottom, the lights winked off above him, and he realized that somewhere along the line he had dropped his knife.

All the lights in the garage went out.

Willing himself not to panic, he reached the bottom of the ladder. Stumbling over his feet in the darkness, he found his way out of the garage and ran back to the house to call the police.

TWENTY-FIVE

"WE'RE MOVING," CLAIRE SAID FLATLY.

"We can't—"

"Can't what? Sell the house? Oh, yes, we can. I don't want to hear any more of your rationalizing bullshit. I'm not spending another night in this place. We're taking the kids, and we're going to my parents'."

The police had just left, after several hours of questioning and investigation, and the four of them were gathered in the living room, sitting on the couch and the love seat, though Claire didn't feel comfortable even doing that. She wanted no part of this house, and even if they had to unload it at a loss, even if they had to live in an apartment, she wanted to get rid of it. There was no way she was going to live in a place where someone had killed himself. And in such a gruesome way. Neither she nor the kids had seen the body—she had not allowed Megan or James to even look out the window when the covered gurney was wheeled out—but they all knew what had happened, and the very thought of such violence made her queasy.

The fact that this was the *second* person to have died here in the past few years was even more disturbing. Of course, when you came down to it, unless you were moving into a new home, some-one had probably died in virtually every house in the country, especially in those that were more than fifty years old. These days, a lot of people died in hospitals, but in her grandparents' day, *most* people had probably died at home.

Their house was not merely haunted, though. It seemed to be a death magnet, attracting people who were about to die or wanted to kill themselves, and there was no way in hell she would allow her children to be exposed to such an influence. Beyond the immediate fears, it was only a small stretch to imagine that influence expanding to include violence against others rather than just oneself. It might seem ridiculous to imagine Julian stabbing the kids in their sleep, or Megan or James beating their parents' brains in with a baseball bat, but she was not willing to take any chances.

"I understand how you feel," Julian said. "I don't think it's good for the kids to be here, either. I think you should pack up, and I'll take you guys over. But—"

"No 'buts'!" Claire shouted at him.

"But I think I should stay here," Julian finished.

"What the hell for? You're just being an asshole! We need to get out of here! All of us! Right. Fucking. Now!"

She was aware that she was swearing in front of the kids, something that she had never really done before, something both she and Julian had always taken pains to avoid. She was aware, also, that they were staring at her in shock because of it. But the most important thing at this moment was to get far away from the house as quickly as possible, and she was willing to do whatever she needed to do to make that happen.

"I think I might be able to—" Julian began.

"You're not going to be able to do shit! It's over. We're done. A man just killed himself in our garage. We have ghosts walking down our hall. There's nothing to do but get out."

She hazarded a glance toward Megan and James. Neither of the kids looked surprised by news of the ghost, but they looked both frightened and worried, and that made her wonder whether they'd witnessed more than they'd told her. She faced them straight on. "Have either of you . . . seen anything here before?" she asked carefully.

"I want to go," James quickly responded.

"Me, too," Megan said emphatically.

"Yes." Claire nodded. She stood. "Come on," she told Julian. "Let's go."

She actually wasn't sure how long she could spend at her parents' house before their smothering drove her out, but even if she had to endure a week or two of her mother's nagging or her father's complaining before they found someplace else to stay, it would be worth it.

She was not going to live in a place where a man had committed suicide.

"I'll drop you off," Julian said. "Then I need to come back and clean up—"

"The blood?" Megan said, horrified.

"No," he assured her. "The police'll do that. I just need to check things out and make sure everything's okay."

"And then you'll come over to Grandma and Grandpa's." James's voice was at once insistent, worried and hopeful.

"We'll see," Julian said, but Claire could tell from the expression on his face that he had no intention of doing any such thing.

"Stay if you want," she said, her mouth set in a hard, straight line. "But we're leaving."

WHEN SHE ARRIVED AT HER PARENTS' HOUSE JUST BEFORE DAWN, after calling ahead to explain the situation and tell them that she and the kids were coming over to stay for a while, both her mom and dad thought that she and Julian were separating. Especially when Julian dropped them off and unloaded the luggage but did not remain himself. Neither of them said anything in front of Megan or James, but they both brought it up when the kids went into the guest rooms to unpack their suitcases. Her mom was worried, her dad happy, and though she told them, specifically, that there were no marital problems, she could tell they didn't believe her.

Claire understood why. She and Julian were not a perfect couple; they fought like everyone else. And back in Los Angeles, they'd gone through some pretty rough times. But they had never slept apart, not once since getting married, and even to her this felt emotionally like a separation. Her anger toward Julian only emphasized that feeling. She was furious at him for continuing to put himself in danger, even as she was afraid for him—and worried that the decision was not completely his.

But all of this she kept hidden from her children and her parents. She had to be strong right now.

Megan and James were in the two small guest rooms at the back of the house, which meant that she would have her old bedroom back. It was her mom's sewing room now, but there was still a twin bed against one wall, maintained for emergencies, and Claire brought her own luggage in and closed the door. She sat down hard on the bed, taking a deep breath, thankful, for the moment at least, to be alone. She had never been even remotely religious, but this entire situation had caused her to examine her core beliefs in a way that she hadn't since . . .

Since Miles died.

Claire looked out the window at the gradually lightening sky. What *did* happen to people after they passed away? It seemed pretty obvious that lives were not merely extinguished, that some of them, at least, lived on in another form. But nothing about that implied a coordinating higher power, though she wished it did, and the idea of an anarchic afterlife filled with ghosts trying to return to the order and comfort of this world left her feeling low. She thought of Miles, wondering, for what was probably the millionth time, what had happened to him after death. She had always liked to think that he was still with them, hanging around. The idea had been consoling to her, but it was no longer, and when she considered everything going on at their house, she thought that maybe she preferred for him to have simply stopped living. The idea made her depressed, and she was grateful when Megan and James pushed open her door and came into the room.

"Are you going to work today?" Megan wanted to know.

"I have to," Claire said.

"Can we stay here at Grandma and Grandpa's?" James asked.

"Of course," she told them. "You can even invite your cousins if—"

"No!" they both said in unison.

"Okay. But I don't understand why—"

"No!" they repeated.

"Fine."

She moved her suitcase to the floor by the foot of the bed, and together they went into the kitchen, where her mother had already started making French toast for breakfast.

JULIAN MET HER FOR LUNCH AT HER OFFICE, AND THE MEETING was surprisingly awkward. It was as though they *were* actually separated, and though, after the fight they'd had this morning, such a feeling was understandable, it still made the encounter stilted and odd.

He brought Chinese takeout, which they ate at her desk, and of course they talked about the kids. She told him that both Megan and James were upset, but that being at their grandparents' house rather than home seemed to make them feel more secure. He was glad of that and seemed relieved, as though it was something that had been weighing heavily on his mind, but when she broached the idea that he should sleep tonight at her parents' house as well, he quickly changed the subject.

As it turned out, the police would *not* clean up the loft, but they recommended a cleaning service in town that would wash floors, scour walls and remove all traces of blood from the site of a murder, suicide or accident. Julian had contacted them earlier this morning, and they were scheduled to come by in an hour. He had no idea how long such a process would take, but he'd been assured that with the steam cleaning and chemical solvents they employed, the loft would be spotless.

"And after that, you'll come to my parents'," she said.

There was a long pause. "I'm going to stay."

"Still?" The anger was audible in her voice. "Why?"

He shrugged, as though it was something he could not explain and perhaps didn't understand himself. Claire felt chilled, and she looked into his eyes, searching for a trace of anything unfamiliar, wondering once again whether he had been contaminated or corrupted by whatever was in that house.

"Julian—" she began.

"I don't *know* why."

"Doesn't that scare you?"

He shrugged again, and what frightened her more than anything was the realization that she knew of no way to get through to him.

Shortly after he left, she received a call from one of the school district's attorneys, wanting to talk settlement in the Cortinez case. She switched easily to lawyer mode, grateful for the distraction. She'd done a pretty good job of laying out her case for them at the hearing, if she did say so herself. She'd kept a few big guns in reserve, just in case, but she'd always thought this could be settled without a trial, and she'd purposely spelled out her best and strongest arguments in the hopes that they would see that if they took this all the way to trial they would lose. Apparently they had seen it, and after hanging up, she called Oscar and set up a meeting with the district and its lawyers for tomorrow at ten.

It seemed weird, doing such prosaic work when everything at home was so crazy, but it was also calming, in a way, and it kept her from dwelling on the events of the previous night and the impossible situation in which she now found herself.

On her desk was the stack of books and monographs Oscar had given her, the raw material of his curriculum. She was convinced there was a connection between those atrocities of the past and the violence that had happened at her house, though the exact linkage remained elusive.

Soon she wouldn't need to worry about it anymore. Soon the house would no longer be theirs, and someone else would inherit all of the responsibilities.

But could she do that, in good conscience? Could she fob off the house on some unsuspecting sucker when she knew the horrors it contained?

She began sorting through Oscar's materials, finding several monographs and one book that she had not yet read. There was work still to be done on her few pending cases, and she knew that should be her priority, but it wouldn't hurt to take a short break and . . . look. Glancing over at the clock, she decided to give herself a half hour, and she picked up the book, flipped to the back and started scanning through the index, thinking that there were probably a lot of details that even the most exhaustive historical accounts left out.

TWENTY-SIX

1855

KIT CARSON DISMOUNTED FROM HIS HORSE, FILLED WITH A SAT-isfying sense of accomplishment. He looked around at the cluster of adobe buildings, wooden corrals and barns. He had heard of this village but had not thought he would find it, as, to his knowledge, it existed on no map. Both as a scout and an Indian agent, he had come across rumors of a community built where the land was cursed, where murder and death were the consequences of occupation and where, over the years, countless massacres had taken place. It had seemed to him that such a location would be of invaluable strategic importance. If it was charted and known, enemy combatants could be led to this site, assured of imminent destruction. But he had come to believe that this place was merely a myth, a folktale created to frighten travelers in the territory, and it was only last week, when he ran into Utah Pete by the Rio Grande, that he discovered that San Jardine did indeed exist. Pete gave directions, even drew him a map, and, along with the other Utes camping along the river, insisted that the Mexicans who populated the village needed to be exterminated.

Kit's own wife was Mexican, so he wasn't necessarily disposed to agree with such a sentiment, but in order to obtain the directions to this place, he gave his word as a government agent that he would assess the situation, and he had brought with him a couple of Ute soldiers and a raft of volunteers. It was a small concession to make if the rumors about the location turned out to be true.

The volunteers had remained behind at the camp this afternoon, but the Utes were with him, and when he glanced over at their faces, he could see they were scared. He, too, felt an uneasiness here, but it was more than made up for by the feeling of triumph he experienced. That very uneasiness, in fact, was behind the triumph, for it indicated to him that the stories he had heard over the years were most likely accurate.

The three of them tied their horses to a post and walked down the single street. San Jardine looked like one of a dozen other villages he had come across in his travels, rather typical for this area, in fact, with its single store and bar, its collection of small, poor homes and its outlying farms.

The only feature that made it different was what stood at the far end of town, the one building he had avoided looking at, and the reason he had come.

A man carrying a rifle stopped to question him, obviously the person in charge of whatever passed for law hereabouts. The man spoke no English, but Kit's Spanish was good, and he explained who he was and why he was here. At first, the man denied that there was anything unusual about the village and told Kit that his information was mistaken. If there was such a place as he described, San Jardine was not it. But when Kit asked what the building was that lay at the end of the street, and why no homes or farms or other buildings stood anywhere near it, the man broke down, admitting that that land was *malo*, bad. His reticence turned into effusiveness, and he explained that everyone in the village shunned that area, neither went there nor spoke of it, and that avoidance of the site came naturally to even children and animals.

Word had it that, fifty years ago, there'd been a church on the spot, and that it had been destroyed by a band of marauders, one of a historical procession that had decimated the population of what had at one time been a thriving community.

Kit looked to the end of the street. Even a church couldn't change the nature of that land, and this to him was a powerful realization.

Why had people remained here? Kit asked. Why hadn't all of the families left and moved elsewhere?

The man had no answer, and somehow that seemed the most disturbing thing of all.

There had been no one on the street when he'd arrived, but behind the man to whom he'd been talking, other men with guns had gathered. Kit had the impression that they'd heard the topic of discussion and come out to make sure that he did not try to walk to the end of the street. They seemed fearful of the small building there, as of a primitive god, and bent on keeping people away so as not to rile the forces within.

Kit spoke to the Ute soldiers to either side of him in their own language, and they pulled out their guns and got a bead on the head honcho before them.

"Now I am going to inspect that location," Kit announced to the villagers, "and I do not wish to be impeded. Do I make myself clear? If any attempt is made to stop me, my men will immediately start firing. They are expert soldiers and will be able to kill several of you before you are able to kill them."

The man who'd been talking to him looked angry and frightened at the same time. But he lowered his weapon and lowered his head, allowing Kit and the Utes to pass. The other men dispersed, leaving the street, going back into their homes. In moments, the street was clear. The village might as well have been abandoned.

Kit looked over at the Utes. Once again, he saw the fear on their faces. He felt it, too, and the air grew colder as the sun hid behind a cloud. A shadow fell over the land.

They walked past the store. The village, he saw now, was bigger than he had originally thought. Its size was deceptive, because it was shaped like a horseshoe, spread out and back, leaving a short center, everything built away from and around that small structure at the end of the street. He still was not sure what that building could be, but as he approached, as he grew close, he saw that it was a ramshackle cabin, windowless, with a tattered cloth hung over its rough doorway. Smoke seeped out from around the cloth's edges, smelling of lives, smelling of death, and behind the smoke was an eerie light, a colorless glow that was unlike anything he had ever seen.

He stopped several lengths in front of it. The street had ended, and he was standing before an overgrown patch of brush-covered ground. A narrow footpath led through the scrub and to the cabin door.

As brave as he was, he found himself afraid to enter the cabin. Something lived in there.

The tattered cloth billowed in an unfelt breeze, and the glow behind the creeping smoke flickered. For the first time in his life, his urge was to turn tail and run, to get away from this village as quickly as he could. But that meant only that this place did have power, that the stories he had heard were true, and he would be forfeiting his duty as an agent of the government if he did not follow through, enter that building and find out whether that power could be used to promote the interests of the United States.

Gathering his courage, he stepped onto the footpath. But when he announced to the Utes that they were going in, the Indian soldiers shook their heads and remained in place. They would do anything else he asked, they said, ride into battle with him against overwhelming forces, but they refused to enter that cabin. He understood, and though he could have had them both executed for such insubordination, he had no intention of doing so. This was beyond the limit for almost any man, and he told them to wait by the end of the street with their guns drawn to make sure that none of the villagers attempted to interfere. This they promised to do, and he steeled himself and strode briskly up the path toward the cabin, his own pistol out and ready.

This close, the smell of the smoke was stronger, an odor heavy with the knowledge of mortality, with the weight of years and places long gone. He was afraid of the smoke, afraid of the smell, afraid of the colorless light within the dilapidated structure that could not have come from any lamp or fire. If he paused, he knew he would not have the fortitude to continue, so Kit marched directly up to the cabin, pushed the tattered cloth aside and stepped over the threshold.

Inside, it was dark, that eerie glow nowhere in evidence, the windowless interior so dim he would have sworn that it was night outside. There did not even seem to be any smoke, though the air was filled with whispers, soft words spoken by unseen presences that came from nowhere, came from everywhere, and made no sense to him at all.

Before him, the single room was meanly furnished—cot, table, chair—though he could make out little more than outlines in the gloom. The only aspect of the cabin that struck him as unusual, beyond the absence of any visible resident, was the odd sense that the interior of the ramshackle structure was older than the outside, and that the room in which he stood stretched far beyond the walls that enclosed it.

Near his ear, one of the whispers spoke his name.

"Hello!" he called. His voice seemed to echo, as though he were in a cave, and it took his brain a moment to realize that the whispers were repeating his cry, mocking him.

This was not what he had expected, and it was not something he could understand. Until this very second, the tactical value of this site in combat had been his sole focus, the idea that had led him here and that had lain in his mind since the first rumors of this village had reached him all those years ago. But his plans seemed foolish now, small. He suddenly realized that the power here could not be used, harnessed or contained. It was too big, too deep, too dangerous. He understood why the villagers kept away from this spot, and he wanted more than anything to get out of this cabin and as far away from here as possible.

A colorless fire sprang up in the center of the room, in a shallow hole he had not been able to see in the dark. It had no fuel, no kindling, but seemed to come from the earth itself, a blaze of indeterminate origin and pallid illumination that revealed words scrawled on the wall in what appeared to be blood, words he had never seen before and did not understand. On the cot, he saw now, was a low mound of whitish powder in the shape of a man's body.

"*Kit*," something whispered. And then his given name: "*Christopher.*"

Panic welled within him as he recognized that the thought on which his mind was focusing was not his own.

Using all of the strength and will he possessed, he stumbled back through the doorway, becoming tangled for one terrifying, heart-stopping moment in the tattered cloth before staggering up the footpath to where the Utes still stood.

It was dark now. He had been inside the cabin for a few minutes only, but in the open air it appeared as though more than an hour had passed. He was breathing heavily, and, grabbing the canteen from its strap around his neck and shoulder, he unscrewed the cap with trembling fingers and drank.

One of the Utes asked him what had gone on inside the cabin, why he had been in there for so long, but Kit shook his head, not wanting to answer. He stared before him at the buildings of the village, arranged *around* the cabin, the way hunters surrounded a bear or some other dangerous predator. Motioning for the Utes to follow him, he marched back down the empty street to the center of San Jardine.

In the windows of each adobe house, he saw as he drew close, were statues, figures carved from rock or molded from mud, sitting or standing behind small burning candles. He had not noticed them earlier, and they looked to him to have been placed there to guard the homes and protect the inhabitants within.

From him?

He felt a stirring of anger. As he knew from his wife, Mexicans proclaimed themselves Catholic, but this was even more pagan than that. It was bad enough worshiping all those graven images, all those "saints." Hell, they'd even turned Jesus' mother, Mary, into some kind of *goddess* that they prayed to. But what they had here had no connection to Christianity. It was primitive even beyond the religions practiced by Indians, and the figures in the windows looked like little monsters: creatures with oversize heads and spiky teeth, triangular bodies and multiple claws. From inside one of the homes, he heard the whimper of a woman, then a slap to shut her up, then silence.

The Utes were right. These Mexicans deserved to die.

He'd known it the moment he emerged from the cabin, but the feeling grew stronger as he looked at the various statues in the windows, those little blasphemies against God.

There was the thundering of hooves from far away, faint yelps of exhilaration that grew louder and closer by the second. As instructed, if he did not return by sundown, the volunteers were to come after him. And they had. Horses galloping, torches flaring, voices hollering, they came riding into the village from the opposite end, and Kit met them in front of the mercantile. He bade them dismount, then explained what they were to do.

A man emerged from the store, the man he had spoken to earlier, the law. The man had his gun drawn, and Kit shot him where he stood. The man fell, not dying right away, screaming in Spanish, and then the shooting really started. Other men came out of their homes, and volunteers took them down, moving quickly on to other houses and busting in doors, guns blazing.

In the end, they surrounded the remaining villagers, herding them into a corral, women and children mostly, but a few old men as well. The younger men, the husbands and fathers, were all dead, and their families were crying, screaming, wailing. A young girl, no more than twelve, tears streaming down her face, raised her arms to him, begging for mercy for herself and her mother. The volunteers paused, looked at him questioningly.

Kit glanced back at the tumbledown cabin at the far end of town.

"Open fire, boys," he ordered.

1921

NEW MEXICO HAD BEEN A STATE FOR NEARLY A DECADE NOW, but the civilizing influence that should have come with the change had not made it to Jardine. As sheriff, Luther Dunlop was in a perfect position to judge such things, and in his considered opinion, the town was more lawless now than it had been while still part of a territory.

Particularly on Rainey Street.

Sitting at his desk, Luther thought about the murder that had just occurred there, about the man whose body had been taken away to the mortician's. He had never seen such savagery before. And the fact that a beautiful young woman had done it—to her own husband, no less—made his blood run cold. For when they had found the gentleman, his manhood had been severed and shoved into a sort of *pouch* that she had carved into his stomach. His nipples had been sliced off and placed there as well. Apparently, the man had bled to death, but what none of them could yet figure out was why he had not fought back against his wife, why he had allowed her to do such a thing. For he had not been restrained in any way, and even the worst of the injuries might not have been fatal if treated in time.

The fact that she had been able to do this at all defied common logic.

Luther sighed. He didn't like Rainey Street. He would never admit that to any man alive, but it was true. Something about the road made him feel uneasy. There'd been three killings and fifteen fights resulting in injuries on Rainey over only the last three months, a statistic that would give even lawmen in Chicago pause.

But it wasn't just the violence that bothered him. He could handle violence; it came with the job. No, it was the *feel* of the place. Sometimes when he drove down that street, he grew nervous for no reason, and more than once, when no one else was in the motorcar, he purposely took a detour down another street, when taking Rainey would have been more convenient.

The telephone rang just as Luther was taking his flask out of the bottom drawer of his desk. He quickly unstopped the cork and took a quick drink before answering: "This is Luther Dunlop."

There was no one on the other end of the line.

"Hello?" he said, but was greeted by silence.

Luther hung up immediately, jerking his hand away from the telephone as though it were contaminated, convinced that the call had come from the murder house, though there was no evidence to even suggest such a thing.

Had it been silent on the other end of the line, or had he heard whispers? The more he thought about it, the more he was certain that someone had been whispering, though he could not for the life of him figure out who or why.

The young wife who had committed the murder, Angie Daniels, had been arrested and was safe in a cell, but just to make sure, he went back into the jail to check on her.

He stopped at the edge of the doorway, shocked.

Mrs. Daniels had taken off all of her clothes and was standing in the center of her cell, completely naked. There were two other prisoners in the jail—both men, both drunks—and he would have expected them to be whooping it up, egging her on, or, at the very least, *staring*. But they had both turned away and were backed into the far corners of their own cells, facing the walls as though frightened.

She turned her head to look at Luther, and what she said made no sense, though it scared him.

"I was in the room where things grow old."

She did seem older to him now than she had when he'd arrested her, and though ordinarily he would have given her a stern warning and ordered her to put her clothes back on, this time he turned around, closing and locking the jail door behind him.

The telephone rang again, but he was afraid to answer it, and let it ring.

He walked outside to clear his head. In his mind, he went over the way Mrs. Daniels looked at the house and the way she looked just now in her cell, trying to figure out what seemed different about her, why he thought she now looked older. Was it because of what she'd said? That bizarre nonsensical statement?

I was in the room where things grow old.

Or was it because she was naked, because, without her dress and girdle, parts that had been held in were allowed to fall out?

No. It wasn't just her body. Her face looked more lined. And her hair seemed grayer. Luther had no idea how that was possible, but it was true, and the fact that the other prisoners were afraid of her made him think that they'd noticed the same change in her that he had.

Inside the station, the phone stopped ringing, and moments later, his deputy returned from accompanying Mr. Daniels's body to the mortician's. Jim Sacks wasn't much of a deputy and was as dumb as dirt, but Luther was sure happy to see him now. He explained what was going on in the jail, and Jim had a reaction that was completely and utterly normal: he grinned and said, "I want to see that!"

The deputy's response gave him courage, and Luther followed Jim into the building. Jim got his eyeful, then turned official and ordered Mrs. Daniels to put her clothes back on, which she did. Out in the office, the deputy winked, slapped him on the back and said, "Thanks for waiting for me. That's some woman, huh?"

Luther had a difficult time sleeping that night. He had no dreams, but he kept waking up, and each time he did, he was filled with the growing certainty that he had done something he should not have or had forgotten to do something that he *should* have. It was a vague worry but a very real one, and he awoke in the morning tired and unrested, the feeling still hanging over him.

Later that week, Mrs. Daniels was transferred to the county seat at Amarejo, and for that Luther was grateful. She'd kept her clothes on after that first incident and hadn't done anything strange since—he even thought she looked young again—but he was glad to see the last of her just the same, and around town things began to seem calmer, more pleasant.

Until the following Tuesday.

Jim was the one to take the call. Luther was eating lunch at Bob's Diner, and he knew from Jim's face when he saw the deputy hurry in, looking for him, that this was bad. Jim didn't even want to explain what had happened in front of the other customers, and Luther accompanied him outside, getting quickly into the car as Jim told him that a woman had been seen *hanging* her children from her front porch.

Luther didn't believe it at first. As more and more homes were fitted with telephones, young men and unstable adults had begun using the instrument for pranks, and this sounded to him like one of those instances.

But when they turned onto Rainey Street, Luther knew instantly that it was true, and it was he who spotted the house. "There!" he said, pointing. Jim pulled the car to a stop at the front yard of the house.

The woman had already strung up two of her children. They hung from ropes attached to a beam on the wraparound porch, twisting slightly in opposite directions, eyes bulging and mouths open in dark purplish faces. The remaining three children sat on a porch swing, sobbing. She was tying a rope around the neck of the smallest one, preparing to hang him, too.

Why weren't those kids running away? Luther wondered. Why weren't they screaming for help?

He knew why, though.

It was Rainey Street.

Both Luther and Jim leaped out of the car and ran up the porch steps, pistols drawn. "Stop right there!" Luther ordered.

The woman ignored him and tightened the noose around her son's neck.

Luther pushed her to the floor, away from the boy, grabbing the rope from her hands, and Jim held her down. She was screaming incoherently, spit flying from her mouth as she jerked her head from side to side, yelling out nonsensical words. Her hair was wild, her eyes wilder, and she looked like someone who had escaped from an insane asylum. He recognized her, though, had seen her about town, and he wondered what had happened to turn her like this.

Other neighbors were gathering around to see what all the commotion was about. The two children—one boy, one girl—were still hanging from the beam, but the sight of the dead kids did not generate the reaction he thought it should. There was very little reaction at all, in fact. The purple-faced corpses might as well have been duffel bags for all the interest that was shown in them.

Luther looked down the street in both directions. It was an evil place, he thought, though the nature of that evil seemed different every time he was here. It was as though each killing, each death, changed the street, gave it a new character. Last week, after Mrs. Daniels had murdered her husband, the street had seemed angry, a location where rage ruled and violence was the accepted response to any misunderstanding. Today, however, it was a realm of craziness, where it seemed perfectly reasonable for a mother to hang her children in front of her house and leave them dangling like butchered lambs.

But the uneasiness he felt here remained constant. Luther liked nothing about this place, not the street nor the sidewalk nor the yards nor the houses.

Especially one house.

He glanced over at it now. It was an address at which nothing illegal had ever happened, a quiet, nondescript residence where an old widow lived by herself. That widow, Mrs. Hernandez, was the one who had called in about the Daniels murder. He had talked to her afterward, asking what she had seen, and she'd seemed a nice enough old lady, but he had conducted the interview on her porch because he did not want to go into her house.

The house frightened him.

The weird part was that he wasn't frightened by any one particular thing. No, it was the overall atmosphere of the house that made his skin crawl, that set his nerves on edge. It wasn't what had happened here but what *could* happen here that scared him. If there was a source for the evil on this street, an origin point from which everything else spread out, it was this house. He didn't know how he knew that, but he did, and he was glad that he wouldn't have to go over there today.

Jim had handcuffed the woman, who was still spitting and screaming, and hauled her to her feet. "Do you want me to take her in?" the deputy asked.

"No. I'll do it. You watch those kids. Take them into the house or the backyard. I'll send Mrs. Biederman over to get them; then I'll come back and we'll cut those other kids down, take them over to Jake's."

"Why do you think she did that?" Jim wondered, looking at the two hanging children.

Luther shook his head, said nothing.

But he knew the answer

It was Rainey Street.

TWENTY-SEVEN

AFTER CALLING TO MAKE SURE CLAIRE AND THE KIDS WERE ALL right, talking to each of them in turn and assuring them he was okay, Julian made himself a turkey sandwich for dinner and ate in front of the TV while he watched the nightly news. He missed his family, but he was glad they weren't here. If he had any sense at all, would have left as well, shoving a For Sale sign into the grass of the front yard and hightailing it out of the neighborhood as quickly as he could.

But he could not do that.

Why? What did he have to prove?

That he wasn't a coward.

Julian carried his plate and cup into the kitchen, placing the dishes in the sink. He thought of Miles, and had the sudden urge to see a picture of his son, to once again look upon the little boy's face. He could see it in his mind, of course—the blond bowl cut, the wide green eyes, the mouth that was almost always smiling— but he wanted to look at a photograph, to view not just a memory but a tangible object, a real recording of the boy in a specific place at a specific time.

No one was home, so there was no need to be discreet, and he went down to the basement and began digging through boxes, searching for the photo albums that they kept hidden, the ones they never showed Megan or James, the ones they wanted to save but never looked at.

It took him a while to find the photo albums, and halfway through his search, he realized that the basement did not seem scary to him. Had it ever—or had he just accepted the verdict of the rest of his family? He wasn't sure, but he knew that he was alone in the house, it was night, and he was down here and not afraid. There was something reassuring about that, and he found himself able to fully concentrate on his search for Miles's picture without being troubled by any of the usual distractions.

Finally, after what could have been one hour, could have been two—he'd lost track of the time—Julian found, at the bottom of a Hefty bag, beneath Claire's old maternity clothes, a familiar green album with the gold-embossed word *Photos* on the cover. Even the sight of the photo album made his heart lurch in his chest, caused him to catch his breath, and he stared for a few moments at the green cover, steadying himself, building up his courage. Finally, he took a deep breath and opened it.

Miles was right there on the first page.

He'd thought he'd have to go a little way in, past pictures of Claire that he'd taken while they were dating, past their wedding and their first apartment. But nothing was in chronological order, and the photo that greeted him immediately upon opening the album was one of Miles that he'd taken at the beach that last summer, when his son was four. Miles was sitting in a hole that they'd both dug together in the sand, looking up at the camera and grinning. He was holding his little blue plastic pail, and there was a smear of sand on his cheek where he'd rubbed it with his dirty hand. He had on his Thomas the Tank Engine bathing suit, and his blond hair was sticking out in every direction. In the upper right corner of the photo, just past the rim of the hole, were Claire's feet.

Julian didn't realize he was crying until it became hard to see, and when he wiped his blurry eyes, he felt wetness on his cheeks as well.

He turned the pages until he found another picture of Miles, this one taken at his fourth birthday party. Miles was wearing his little suit, hair neatly combed, standing behind a pile of wrapped presents, and smiling. This was the way Julian saw his son in his mind. He used his fingernail to pull up the edge of the clear plastic sheet that covered the photos on the page, and drew the sheet back, peeled off the photograph and put it in his shirt pocket.

He missed Miles. It was a loss that time had not softened or made easier, and there was a physical pain in his chest right now, as though his heart actually ached. The depth of the hurt was why he and Claire never discussed their first son, why he tried so hard to live in the present and not think about the past. He knew from a lifetime of media exposure that such an attitude was probably unhealthy, that it was always better to let emotions out than keep them in, but he didn't feel that way. This was the approach that seemed to work best for him, and while it might not be politically correct or socially acceptable, it was how he had chosen to do it.

It kept the guilt at bay.

He'd thought more about Miles in the past month than he had in the last thirteen years. It was the house's doing, and Claire was right: once or twice, at the beginning, he *had* considered the idea that it was the ghost of their son who was haunting them. But that was obviously not the case, and with that possibility excluded, he was left with the discomforting memories that thoughts of Miles dredged up within him.

Memories of Miles's death.

Julian closed the photo album, closed his eyes, tried to get his mind to go somewhere else.

It wouldn't.

"*Daddy!*"

It was the last word Miles ever said, and it remained as fresh in his mind today as it had when his son shouted it, two terrified syllables that cut straight through his heart and would be perfectly preserved in his brain until the day he died.

As a college student, as a young man, Julian had enjoyed hiking. He'd belonged to the Sierra Club, had met one of his former girlfriends on a club-sponsored hiking trip, and had enjoyed taking Claire on backpacking excursions to various wilderness areas throughout the state. Even after they had Miles, they'd continued hiking on weekends, although, necessarily, closer to home.

It was on one of these treks, into the Santa Monica Mountains, that it had happened.

They'd been stupid to go that day at all. It was a Sunday, and though the Saturday before had been nice, for the entire week prior it had been raining. They should have known better.

But it had been a hard few days at work for both of them, and they'd wanted to get away from the city and out in the open air, if only for a couple of hours. Griffith Park would be too crowded, they knew, Angeles Crest too treacherous, so they'd opted for the Santa Monicas. They'd hiked there before, many times, liked the views and were familiar with many of the trails.

They were an hour in and pretty high up, Claire ahead, he moving more slowly, at Miles's speed. He was letting Miles walk on the outside of the trail, though he'd never done that before. He'd also allowed the boy to walk without holding on to his hand, and he'd never done that before, either. Afterward, Julian asked himself why he'd been so negligent, asked himself a thousand times, but he had never been able to come up with an answer.

He remembered they'd been talking, he and Miles, laughing about something Oscar the Grouch had said on *Sesame Street* earlier that morning. And then, not more than a foot away from where he stood, the saturated ground under Miles's shoes had given way, and Julian had watched in impotent horror as an entire section of trail slid down the side of the mountain, taking his son with it.

"*Miles!*"

Crying out, Julian dropped to his knees, leaning over the newly formed edge, expecting to see his son's body sprawled at the bottom of the ravine below.

But Miles was only a few feet down, lying flat against the collapsed section of muddy trail, arms raised instinctively as though grasping for purchase.

"Daddy!"

He would never forget the look on his son's face at that last second, the pleading, the fear, underpinned by the hope and belief that Daddy would be able to stop this and save him. It was a look that would haunt him until the end of his life, an expression of complete and utter trust, the purest faith he had ever experienced or ever would experience. But he had hesitated. He could have reached down and grabbed his son's hands, but he'd been afraid that the section of ground on which he knelt would give way, claiming him, too, and he'd thought that it would be safer if he moved a little to the right first.

Then the mud had slipped, and Miles was swept away, tumbling down the slope, buried under an avalanche of sludge.

Claire was screaming, her piercing cries echoing off the walls of the canyon. He had no idea what she was doing, could only hope she had the presence of mind to go for help or call 911 on her cell phone. But he had no time for any of that. He was rushing down the side of the mountain, in defiance of all safety precautions and common sense, stumbling, falling, getting up again, crying out himself, keeping his eye on the sliding section of trail, trying to determine where under all of that mud and rubble Miles was located. He was pretty sure he knew the right spot, and when the slide stopped at the bottom of the ravine, he dropped to his knees and began digging frantically, using both hands to scoop up as much mud as he could, flinging it aside and immediately scooping up some more. He kept expecting to see his son's fingers or glimpse the blue of his shirt, but he didn't, and he dug deeper, aware in the back of his mind that the boy had been down there for too long, and filled with the growing fear that he was searching in the wrong spot.

He'd still been digging through the mud, sobbing, when the rescuers arrived, though he didn't know when that was or how long he'd been there. Sometime later, someone had found Miles's body, but it hadn't been him, and all he remembered after that was kissing Miles's cheek before the stretcher carrying him was lifted to a helicopter, the gritty, bitter taste of mud on his lips.

And Miles had been gone.

The next time Julian had seen him had been at the morgue, where he and Claire had been required to identify the body.

Pressing the palms of his hands against his eyes and taking a deep, shuddering breath, Julian willed himself not to cry. It took a while, but he managed to stem the tears, and, breathing slowly and evenly, he placed the photo album in the Hefty bag underneath the maternity clothes, putting everything back the way it was.

He reached into his shirt pocket and pulled out the photo he had put in there, looking at it.

"Miles," he said aloud, and it felt good to say the name again. "Miles."

JULIAN DREAMED THAT NIGHT OF THE GARAGE, AND IN HIS DREAM he climbed up the ladder to the loft, where dozens of animal skeletons were arranged over the crimson-soaked floor. The stick-figure cardboard cutout of the *Wimpy Kid*, still splattered with blood, was smiling at him and winking, pointing toward the broken exercise bike, on which sat a small human skeleton, pedaling slowly.

The skeleton was Miles.

Awakening to the fading sound of his own scream, Julian sat up, disoriented for a moment by the fact that he was alone in bed. Then he remembered where he was, where Claire and the kids were, and he settled back onto the pillow, wondering why he had decided to stay here, why he hadn't gone with them. He'd had a reason, he knew, something besides the fact that he didn't get along with her dad, but at the moment that rationale eluded him, and he worried that, as Claire had suggested, it was the house that had kept him here.

Or the garage.

For he sensed now that the locus of power, the source of whatever was going on, had relocated there from the basement.

Thinking about the nightmare he'd just had, he got out of bed, walked over to the window, pulled the curtains aside and looked across the backyard toward the garage.

Where the man who had killed himself was standing behind the window of the loft, staring back at him.

Julian let the curtain drop and ducked out of the way, moving to the side, heart hammering in his chest. He waited a moment, then pulled the curtain back and peeked around the edge of the window frame, hoping the figure would be gone. It wasn't. The ghost of John Lynch, still wearing that backward yellow baseball cap, remained in place, staring at him across the yard, and in an attempt to prove his bravery, Julian opened the curtains all the way and stood directly before the window, staring back himself. He waited there for several minutes, expecting the figure to fade and disappear, but it did not, and the ghost staring back at him looked as solid as the man himself had been.

More annoyed now than scared, Julian closed the curtains again and decided to go back to bed. He should have been too terrified to sleep, but staring at Lynch's ghost had given him courage. The breach across which they'd regarded each other seemed uncrossable, and he was pretty sure that the ghost was stuck in the garage and could not come into the house. The idea gave him comfort, and while it might not signal an end to their problems, it was at least a step in the right direction.

Climbing into bed, Julian put his head down on the pillow and pulled the top sheet over himself. He fell asleep almost instantly.

He did not dream.

HE WAS AWAKENED IN THE MORNING BY THE SOUND OF A SIREN. It was loud, close, and then it abruptly shut off, and Julian went into the living room and peeked out the window to see a fire truck parked in the street, halfway in front of his house. In the Ribieros' driveway, next door, was an ambulance with its back doors open, and red and blue roof lights still flashing.

Julian hurried back to the bedroom, slipped on some jeans and a Hawaiian shirt, quickly put on his tennis shoes, then walked outside just as two paramedics wheeled a gurney out of the Ribie-ros' house and into the back of the ambulance. He couldn't tell from this angle whether Bob or Elise was on the gurney, but he got his answer moments later when Bob emerged from the house with another paramedic who was jotting something down on a clipboard.

Julian didn't want to intrude, so he stayed where he was, watching from the sidelines.

The surprising thing was that he was the only person from the neighborhood out here. Glancing around, he didn't even see any-one peeking through their windows or out from behind a parted curtain. His neighbors, apparently, had no interest in what hap-pened on their street, and he remembered how no one had come out to see what was going on when the police arrived to arrest John Lynch.

The ambulance left, siren off, which was hopefully a good sign, and the remaining firemen and paramedics put on their helmets and got onto the fire engine. Bob Ribiero locked up his house, saw Julian, glared at him, then got into his car and followed the am-bulance down the street.

What was that about?

Frowning, Julian walked out to the sidewalk just as the fire engine pulled away. He'd wanted to ask one of the men what had happened, but he missed the chance by a few seconds and ended up watching the fire truck leave.

Once again, he looked around at the neighborhood houses and, this time, across the street, he saw Spencer Allred standing on his front porch. Finally, *someone*. Julian waved, walking over. At the sight of him, the old man looked as though he wanted to go back inside his house and hide, but he didn't; he waited, and Julian walked up to the porch, stopping at the bottom step. He gestured toward the Ribieros' place. "That was Elise," he said. "I wonder what happened. Heart attack?"

"Your house," Spencer replied.

Julian looked at him, startled. "What?"

"Your house happened to her."

Julian didn't know how to respond to that.

Spencer sighed. "It's not your fault. It might not even be your house, exactly. This whole street is . . . off. But your house is at the center of it, and the Ribieros live right next door." He thought for a moment, as though not sure whether he should say what he wanted to say. "You know, the reason some of us, a *lot* of us, came to your party, your housewarming party, was because we wanted to see the inside of it for ourselves. And when it . . . when it ended the way it did . . . Well, let's just say that most of us weren't that surprised."

Julian felt a thrill of excitement. "So you know something!"

The old man shook his head, backed away. "I don't know anything."

"You weren't surprised? Why not? You *do* know something." Julian moved up a step. "What's going on here? What's wrong with our house?"

Spencer reached the door. "I don't know, and I don't want to know. Forty years I lived here, minding my own business. That's the only way to survive: don't get involved." He pulled open the screen door, stepping inside. "Now go home. Get away from here."

"Spencer?" his wife called from inside the house.

"Coming!" he answered.

He closed the door.

Julian turned around. From this vantage point, there seemed nothing wrong with his house. Or the garage. But he knew better, and Spencer Allred did, too. Probably most of the homeowners on this street did, and as he walked back home, he wondered whether the ambulance siren had been off because Elise Ribiero was already dead.

TWENTY-EIGHT

MEGAN AWOKE IN THE MORNING REFRESHED. SHE WAS USED TO feeling tense and stressed when she emerged from sleep, and this was such a pleasant change that she lay there for a few extra moments, staring up at the bands of light formed on the ceiling by the sun shining through slats in the shades, enjoying the sensation of freedom.

Freedom from the house.

It felt over, all of it, despite what had happened the night before last, and she reached over to the nightstand and turned on her iPhone, not afraid of it anymore. She might even text her friends today, and just thinking that made her feel good. Putting on her robe, she walked across the hall to go to the bathroom and was embarrassed when she pulled down her pajama bottoms and saw the cuts on her legs.

That ended today, too.

She was not much of a breakfast eater, but once again her grandma had made a big breakfast—pancakes and bacon—and out of politeness, Megan forced herself to eat.

For some reason she could not explain, she wanted to go back home. Not to stay, of course. And definitely not at night. But in the daytime, when it was safe.

When her dad was there.

Part of it was that, of course. It had been only one night, but she missed her dad, and it didn't feel right without him here. James had worriedly asked before breakfast whether their parents were going to get a divorce, and she'd told him no, but she wasn't sure that was true. It didn't make any sense for the family to be separated like this, and she knew that Grandma and Grandpa thought there was something wrong, which they tried to make up for by being especially nice to her and her brother. She hoped that wasn't the case, but she thought of how angry her mom had been—

We need to get out of here! All of us! Right. Fucking. Now!

—and it troubled her. Talking to her dad might help. He was always more honest with her and James than their mom was, and he might be willing to give some honest answers.

But that was not the only reason she wanted to go back.

No. She also wanted to return home to see whether things had changed.

By all rights, their house should have been the *last* place she wanted to go. She was finally brave enough to use her phone again, finally felt free to text, and it made no sense to go back to where she'd been so threatened and terrified.

I will kill you both.

But, for some reason, she had the impression that whatever had been in the house was gone—and she wanted to check it out for herself. The feeling of freedom and liberation that had been hers this morning since awakening was not one she had felt when she'd left the house before. In fact, the black cloud that had hovered over her at home had previously accompanied her no matter where she went. Now, however, it was gone, and she didn't think that would be possible unless whatever had been living in their house had left.

It was important for Megan to find out for herself whether that was the case, and she was hopeful that if the house really was free of all . . . ghosts . . . demons . . . whatever they were, things might be able to go back to normal.

At first, she planned to call her dad and tell him she was coming over, but after everything that had happened, he might not want her in the house, so it would probably be better if she just showed up. And while she'd considered asking her mom whether she could go, she knew the answer would be no, so instead she texted Zoe, asking her friend to call her back immediately and pretend to invite her somewhere. It was a ploy they had used before, on both of their mothers, and it worked every time.

Zoe was either busy or her phone wasn't on, because it was nearly a half hour later, as her mom was getting ready to say goodbye to them before going to her office, that Zoe finally called. Megan made sure she picked up in front of her mother and grandparents, spoke loudly enough for everyone to hear, and in response to Zoe's question, "So, what's the plan?" she replied, "I'd love to! Let me ask my mom."

Megan turned to her mother. "Zoe wants to know if I can go with her to the Kachina festival at the park."

James was glaring at her, letting her know that he thought she was a traitor for leaving him alone. Grandma and Grandpa had strict rules against daytime television, and severe restrictions on when and where James could play with his DS. Without Megan, he was looking forward to a long, slow day of dominoes and gin rummy.

She was taking a big chance here. The park was within sight of her mom's office, and it would be very easy for her mother to find out she was not really there. But the brazenness of the lie was what might make it work. Besides, there really *was* a Kachina festival at the park, and if called on the carpet, she could always claim to be in a part of the crowd that her mom had not seen.

She was suddenly struck by an even better idea: after going home and checking the place out, she *would* go to the park. And she and Zoe would stop by her mom's office to say hello.

All bases covered.

"Sure," her mom said. "You can go. It sounds like fun. Do you want me to drive you two?"

"No," Megan said quickly. "We're riding bikes."

"But your bike's still at the house."

"I mean, Zoe's riding her bike over here. Then we're going to walk."

Her mom frowned. "It's kind of far. I'm not sure I want you to—"

"I'm going to be in eighth grade, Mom. Jeez! You think I'm such a baby that I can't walk down the street by myself?"

"No. I'm just saying that it's a little far away. And maybe the streets of Jardine aren't as safe as we thought they were."

Megan knew her mom was thinking about what had happened at their house, and she had no ready answer for that. On impulse, she put the phone back to her ear. "My mom says I can go, but she's worried about me walking there. Can your mom drive us?"

"Where are we really going?" Zoe asked.

"Zoe says sure, her mom'll take us."

"Okay, then."

Megan gave Zoe her grandparents' address, then hung up, smiling her thanks at her mom and ignoring James's hostility. She felt guilty for the deception but was determined not to show it.

It occurred to her that this was a trap, that she was being lured back to the house deliberately, but that worry was fleeting, displaced almost instantly by the need to ascertain whether or not the house was still haunted.

I will kill you both.

Zoe lived only a few blocks away from her grandparents' place, and she showed up on the doorstep less than ten minutes later. Megan had taken the key to her house from her purse and put it in her pocket, which was hard to accomplish surreptitiously with James following her like a puppy everywhere she went, begging her to take him with her. Ordinarily, she would be taking great delight in his suffering and would be milking it for all it was worth, making him dance through hoops before finally telling him that he could not accompany her, but she had more important things on her mind this morning and ignored him completely, pretending he wasn't there.

Her grandma offered Zoe some orange juice, but Megan said they had to get going, and after promising to be careful and to be back for lunch, she and Zoe finally made it out the door.

It *was* a long way to their house and the old downtown, and though to do so was unsafe and wobbly, the two of them rode together on Zoe's bike, which, luckily, had a retro banana seat that could accommodate both of them. Zoe pedaled slowly, staying on sidewalks as much as possible, and it was nearly a half hour before they turned onto Rainey and pulled to a stop in the driveway of Megan's house.

She hopped off the bike. The van was gone, which meant that her dad wasn't home. She didn't like that. She thought about waiting outside for him, or even coming back later, but it had taken a lot of subterfuge to get here, and this might be her only chance. She'd known that already, which was why she'd brought her key, but the prospect of going in alone still made her nervous, and she looked from window to window, trying to spot anything out of the ordinary.

"So, why are we here?" Zoe asked. They hadn't been able to talk on the bike, and while that should have given Megan enough time to come up with a plausible explanation, she hadn't done it. Although she didn't want to lie to her friend, she didn't want to spell everything out, either. She wanted Zoe to go in cold, wanted to get her honest, unbiased opinion of the house.

"I need to . . . get something out of my room," Megan said lamely.

Zoe looked at her. "Really?" she said dryly. "You called me up, lied to your mom about where you were going, had me sneak you out here on my bike . . . so you could get something out of your room." She was about to say something else sarcastic when a strange expression crossed her face. "Wait a minute. You're not . . . I mean . . ." Zoe looked at once worried and suspicious, shocked and scared. "We're not here to get *drugs* or something, are we? Marijuana?"

"No!"

"What is it, then? You didn't go through all this effort for nothing."

"I can't tell you yet. Just . . . just trust me." Before her friend could respond, Megan was taking out her key and walking up to the front door. Her heart was pounding. She really didn't want to go in, but . . .

She turned the key in the lock, opened the door.

The two of them walked inside.

Everything was where it was supposed to be. Nothing had been moved. She wasn't sure why this surprised her, but it did. The morning was bright, and sunlight streamed through the windows, but Megan turned on the light in the living room anyway.

Something about the house had changed.

She couldn't put her finger on it, but the feeling she got from being here was different from what it had been before. Not better, necessarily. But different. The discomfort she felt now seemed less intimate, less immediately threatening, although it was still there. She said nothing to Zoe, not wanting to frighten her friend, but she could tell that Zoe felt something, too.

It wasn't gone.

She'd been hoping everything would be back to normal and they could all return and live happily under one roof. Her disappointment was overwhelming, and it was all she could do not to cry in frustration. But fear overpowered disappointment, and Megan realized that even with the light on, the living room still seemed dark. She had no desire to go deeper into the house, to go upstairs or down the hall or into the kitchen. She wanted only to get out of here, and was about to tell Zoe that they should do just that, when the lights went on in the dining room. And then the kitchen.

"Megan?" Zoe said nervously.

Upstairs, something heavy fell to the floor, shaking the whole house.

"Megan?"

The danger was palpable. She wasn't supposed to be here and

would get in trouble for coming over, especially when no one was home, but that didn't matter. She was worried for her dad, and she immediately sent Zoe outside while she wrote her dad a quick note, using a pen and the back of an envelope she found in a pile of mail on the coffee table:

Dad,

Zoe and I stopped by while you were gone. Don't tell Mom. We heard a loud noise upstairs and the lights came on by themselves.

You need to get out of here. You can't stay. It's dangerous. Please!

I'll call you when I get back to Grandma and Grandpa's. Leave your cell on. Don't stay here, Dad.

Please! I don't want anything to happen to you. I'm scared. I love you.

—Megan

She left it where he would be sure to see it, leaning the envelope against the TV screen in the living room.

There was another loud noise from upstairs, a thump, followed by a high-pitched whistle that could have been a teakettle, could have been a bird, but was undoubtedly something else.

She hurried outside, closing and locking the door behind her, then looked around for Zoe. Her friend was nowhere to be seen, and, worried, Megan called her name. "Zoe!"

There was an answer from the backyard, and it was with a feeling of dread that Megan walked up the driveway and around the side of the house. It had been wrong to come here, and she wished now that she had just listened to her parents and stayed away. Something could happen, and if it did, no one knew where she was.

Zoe was standing by the back fence, by the gate that led out to the alley. "Your yard's dead," Zoe said, motioning in front of her. "Don't you guys ever water it? All your plants . . ."

"They died overnight. We don't know what happened." She was about to say that it was probably some disease, but she decided not to lie. She wanted Zoe to know what was going on, wanted someone besides her family to be a witness.

Her friend seemed to sense that it was something serious and significant, and it was with a solemn expression that she walked over the dead grass to meet Megan.

Megan told all. Well, not all. There wasn't time for that. She wanted to get out of the backyard and away from the house as quickly as possible, so she didn't go into too much detail. But she told Zoe that the house was haunted and hit the highlights, including the guy who'd committed suicide in their garage. Zoe had been frightened enough by the Ouija board and the sleepover that she didn't require a lot of convincing, and when Megan said that she'd tell her the whole story later but that right now they needed to get out of there, Zoe didn't argue.

She did, however, pause. "Wait. I hear music. Maybe your dad's home."

Megan heard it, too. It was coming from the house, and it sounded like one of her dad's records. Joe Jackson? Elvis Costello? Graham Parker? Someone like that, someone he'd taught her about. But her dad wasn't home, and there was no way—no *logical* way—that his stereo could have been turned on. She listened carefully, and the lilting tune wafting from the open upstairs window of her dad's office gave her chills. She recognized it now. Joe Jackson. "It's Different for Girls."

Was that some sort of message?

The music disappeared.

The *open* upstairs window? Whenever her dad left the house, he always made sure all doors and windows were closed and locked. She looked up, sensing movement behind the screen. A figure was standing there, looking down at them. It was too dark to see any details, but she could make out a backward yellow baseball cap.

It was the man who'd killed himself in their garage.

Screaming, Megan ran down the driveway toward the street. Zoe was screaming right behind her, and she grabbed the handlebars of the bike, kicked up the kickstand, leaped onto the seat and started pedaling. Megan kept running. Neither of them slowed down until they reached the park.

Zoe reached the park first, and was already off her bike, walking it, when Megan caught up.

"Told you," Megan said, breathing heavily.

Zoe, trying to catch her breath, just nodded.

They stood there for several moments, staring at each other, frightened, and it was not until a Hopi woman on the outskirts of the Kachina festival smiled at them, motioning toward a table full of little wooden dolls representing demigods and demons, that they started moving again, passing through the festival to the other side of the park and Old Main.

TWENTY-NINE

JULIAN MET CLAIRE FOR LUNCH AGAIN AT HER OFFICE, BRINGING takeout tacos this time, and it felt just as awkward as it had the day before. He didn't think she was still mad at him, but there was not much talk while they ate, and when they did talk, the conversation seemed forced. He hated this feeling of estrangement, but he knew that the only cure would be for him to leave the house and stay with her and the kids at her parents' place, and that he was not willing to do.

At least, not yet.

Although . . . he was not sure why. After his experience last night—an experience he was definitely *not* going to tell her about—he should have been falling over himself to get out of there. But something was keeping him in the house. He told himself that it was the hope, the possibility, that he was close to finding out what was really going on and figuring out a way to stop it. But he didn't believe that, and whenever his mind even approached the subject, he quickly steered it in another direction. He didn't want to think about what he was doing or why.

Lunch today didn't last as long as it had yesterday. They both avoided talking about the big-ticket items, and their efforts to discuss small stuff were downright painful. Julian didn't jump up and leave immediately after finishing his tacos, but shortly after *she* finished and he sucked the last of his Coke through the straw, he stood, wadding up his napkin and throwing it in the wastepaper basket. He told Claire he still had to finish work on that Web site and had better get going, and they parted amicably but without hugging.

He was outside and had just unlocked the driver's door of the van when Claire stopped him. "Julian?"

He looked up to see her standing in the doorway of her office. "Yeah?"

"I don't want you to stay there. You've proved your point. Whatever it was. You're a big macho guy, and you're not afraid of anything."

He felt himself hardening against her. She must have sensed his antipathy, because she quickly added, "I'm just afraid for you. It's dangerous there. And you have two kids, you know. *They* should be your priority."

That hit him where he lived, and he tried to come up with a response that made sense, but she was right. Nothing was more important than Megan and James.

Still . . .

"Something's happened," he told her. "Something's changed. You're not there, so you haven't noticed it, but it's like . . ." He tried to verbalize what he'd been feeling. "You know how the basement used to be creepy? It's not anymore. The garage is. It's like this new ghost somehow deposed the old one. I don't know what it is about our house that makes the spirits of dead people hang around, but it seems like the people who die there stay there. At least until someone else takes their place. And right now, the guy who killed himself in the garage is our ghost du jour."

Claire gave him a hard stare. "You think that's cute? You think you're being funny?"

"I'm not trying to be. I'm sorry. But I think I'm onto something here. I think I might be able to—"

"I don't care if you find a way to exorcise every single ghost in every haunted house in the country. It's not worth the risk. You have two kids who need you. *I* need you. That house is just a house. We sell it, get rid of it, find another. People do it all the time for all sorts of different reasons. It's not a big deal. Let it go."

They'd attracted attention. A couple who'd just exited the sandwich shop were walking slowly down the sidewalk, pretending not to look or listen but doing both. In the van's side mirror, he could see the owner of the used-book store across the street pausing in his rearrangement of the outside paperback rack to watch.

Julian didn't want to talk in front of them, and he moved back onto the sidewalk, where he stood in front of Claire, putting his hands on her shoulders. "I'm close," he told her.

"No!"

"Yes."

She pulled away from him and went back into her office. He thought of following her, but she wasn't going to change his mind, he wasn't going to change her mind, and it was probably better if they didn't get into a shouting match right now.

He walked back to the van and got in. The bookseller was arranging his paperbacks again; the couple from the sandwich shop had left. Julian backed into the street. Intellectually, he knew Claire was probably right, but emotionally, it felt wrong, and he drove home convinced that he had made the correct decision.

The sight that greeted him when he pulled onto Rainey Street was completely unexpected.

Every single house was up for sale.

Except theirs.

He'd been gone for a little under an hour, which hardly seemed to be enough time for something like this to have happened. Of course, every For Sale sign was from the same real estate agent at the same real estate office—Randolph Wilson at RE/MAX—so it would have been easy for the agent to have simply gone down the sidewalk planting signs. And for all Julian knew, some of these sales may have been in the planning stages for days or weeks or even months, and the realtor may have just found it more convenient to list them all at the same time. But that hardly seemed likely. What seemed most probable was that, like Cole, the rest of his neighbors had been frightened and had all decided to move at once.

Julian drove slowly, looking to see whether anyone was home. A lot of people weren't. The Allreds' car was still in their driveway, but he doubted that either Spencer or Barb would talk to him. Harlan Owens's red Jeep was parked in his driveway, and his pickup was on the street in front of the house, so he was definitely home. Julian didn't know Harlan well, but he knew him enough to speak to, and after parking the van in his own driveway, he walked down the street to Harlan's house.

"Go away!" was the response he received when he knocked on Harlan's door, and the words were spoken with such force and anger that Julian didn't even try to argue. He stepped off his neighbor's porch and headed back to his own house, glancing down the street in disbelief at the row of identical For Sale signs in each yard.

Maybe Claire was right, he thought. Maybe they *should* get out now. Leave and not look back.

But Randolph Wilson of RE/MAX had just made that harder. Who was going to want to buy a house on a street where *every* home was for sale? They wouldn't be able to get back anywhere near the amount of money they'd sunk into the place. *If* they could sell it at all.

Julian unlocked the door and stepped inside. The mail had arrived in his absence, and he bent down to scoop the envelopes off the floor, where they'd fallen after coming through the slot. He glanced at the return addresses to see whether any of them were checks rather than bills, then went into the living room to dump them on the coffee table with yesterday's mail.

Someone had been here. There was a note written on the back of an envelope, leaning against the TV screen, and with a pounding heart he walked over, picked it up and read it:

I will cut off Megan's head and use it to decorate my mantel.
I will stuff James with straw and use him as a scarecrow in
the garden. I will rape Claire until she likes it. And I will kill
you when I am finished.

THERE WAS A SCRIBBLED SIGNATURE AT THE BOTTOM OF THE
message, though it was indecipherable and he could not even tell
with which letter it started. Was it from John Lynch? His gut feeling was yes, which meant that apparently he'd been wrong:
Lynch's ghost was not confined to the garage where he had killed
himself.

Or *had* he killed himself?

Despite the unbelievable brutality of Lynch's death, Julian had
assumed from the beginning that all of his wounds were self-
inflicted, an opinion with which the police seemed to concur. It
was hard to believe that anyone could stab himself in the face the
way he had and then go on to thrust the knife into his own throat.
But there'd been no evidence whatsoever that anyone else had
been involved or even present, and as one of the detectives had
told Julian, a man committed to killing himself will go to incredible extremes in order to accomplish his goal.

The police had been looking for *human* assailants, however,
and Julian wondered whether the killer of John Lynch *had* been
human.

He should get out of here now, right now, head over to Randolph Wilson's office—or even Gillette Skousen's—and put this
place up for sale immediately.

But he didn't.

Music was coming from his office upstairs, a record he recognized but had not played in a long time. The Smiths. He caught a
stray piece of lyric: "*. . . such a heavenly way to die . . .*"

Again, he knew he should leave. But he remained where he
was, not fleeing the house, not going upstairs to investigate the
mysterious music, but just . . . waiting.

And then the music shut off and everything was back to normal. Julian stood in place for several moments, but when he saw nothing, heard nothing, felt nothing, he began searching each room for anything that might be amiss. He started upstairs, but his office was clean, as were the kids' bedrooms and the bathroom. The Smiths record *was* out and on the turntable, the orange album cover with its haunted-eyed street urchin staring up at him from the floor, where it had been tossed, but nothing else seemed out of place, and the room was quiet. He went downstairs, through the living room again, the dining room, the kitchen, the hallway, the bedroom, the bathroom. All clear. He saved the basement for last, but it, too, seemed completely normal, entirely free from all evil influences.

Evil?

It was a word and concept that had been floating around the periphery of his thoughts for a while, but he had never allowed it concrete residence in his mind until now. It fit, though. It was the word that best applied, and he had never felt so relieved as he did when he stood in the basement, looking around at the bags and boxes, sensing nothing unusual, feeling no fear.

Julian walked back up the steps, shutting the door behind him. He was thirsty, and he got himself a glass of water from the sink in the kitchen. As he drank, he looked out the window at the backyard. He knew what was next—the garage—and for the first time since starting his search, he felt real trepidation. Putting down his glass, he considered taking out a knife and bringing it with him, but a weapon wouldn't be much use against a ghost, and he decided it would probably be better to leave his hands free.

He needn't have worried. There was nothing out of the ordinary in either the main body of the garage or the upstairs loft.

Was it over?

That seemed too much to hope for, and, indeed, the note left by the TV and the Smiths record playing by itself indicated that whatever haunted this house was simply taking a breather. But he was encouraged by the fact that he hadn't felt anything in any room he'd checked, and he thought it was possible that the ghost—or ghosts—had gone. Or perhaps writing the note and putting on the record had used up too much energy, and any entity was dormant now and had to recharge.

That was information that might be useful in the future.

He spent the rest of the afternoon actually working on the Web page he was supposed to be finishing, and was able to do so unmolested. There were no creepy messages on his computer screen, no mysterious noises in the house, no flickering lights, no murderous intruders, and after the first hour, he was almost able to forget that anything weird had happened here at all.

Almost.

For dinner, Julian heated up a frozen burrito in the microwave and ate it while he watched the news. Afterward, he phoned Claire and the kids, but the call did not go as well as it had the night before. Claire was still angry with him, and both Megan and James seemed resentful and withdrawn. He was hurt by their reaction, and after the conversation dwindled and sputtered to a stop prematurely, he almost went over to see them. But something kept him from it, and he sat there with the phone in his hand, staring into space, and by the time he put it back down, the news was over and *Access Hollywood* was on TV. He looked over at the clock, shocked to discover that a half hour had passed.

Where had the time gone? It was nearly night outside now. He had not yet closed the shades, and as he looked out at the darkness of the street, he realized that most, if not all, of his neighbors were gone. He might very well be the only person on the street.

Suddenly grateful for the noise and companionship of the television, Julian turned up the volume. From the corner of his eye, he saw that the light was on in the kitchen. He had taken his plate and glass in there after eating, but he could not remember whether he had left the light on. Ordinarily, he turned off the lights automatically as he left a room—habit—but he might have left them on this time.

Or he might not have.

Julian decided he would feel more comfortable if *all* of the lights in the house were on, and he stood and went from room to room, downstairs and up, until the entire house was illuminated. As an added precaution, he checked to make sure that all windows were closed and that both the front and back doors were locked.

He'd intended to work a little more on the Web site before going to bed, but now he decided that he wasn't in the mood—

was afraid

—to do that, so he sat down on the couch, picked up the remote and flipped through channels until he found *The Daily Show* on Comedy Central. He needed a comedy right now, something he could laugh at, and he put down the remote and settled back on the couch to watch.

He was asleep before the first commercial.

When he awoke, another commercial was on, so he wasn't sure how much time had passed. He glanced toward the clock, but his attention was drawn by movement outside the window.

James.

Julian leaped to his feet as his son hurried across the front yard to the side of the house. He knew exactly where the boy was going, though he had no idea how James had sneaked out of his grandparents' house and made it all the way over here, and Julian sped through the living room, through the dining room, into the kitchen, where he quickly unlocked and opened the back door.

There was no sign of James—he must have already gone into the garage—and Julian dashed across the patio and through the backyard. He reached the small door of the darkened garage and was about to pull it open when there was a sharp cry behind him. He turned to see a deep, wide hole in the center of the dead grass. How could he have missed it before? Julian didn't know, but he ran the few feet over to it and peered down. An arm's length below the surface, holding desperately on to a small protruding root, was his son.

Instantly, Julian flopped onto the ground on his stomach,

stretching his arm down in an effort to grab the boy's hand. But his fingers would not reach. There were still several feet between them, and he inched forward until he was overhanging the ledge at a dangerous angle, but the distance remained insurmountable. The pit beneath his son's dangling legs appeared bottomless.

"Don't move!" Julian ordered. "Hang on! I'm going to get a rope!"

"*Daddy!*" James's voice sounded exactly like an older version of Miles's, and Julian cried out in alarm as the boy slipped several inches, the root he was grasping pulling out from the sidewall, dropping dirt onto his face.

"*Daddy!*"

Julian's heart sank in his chest as he realized that history was about to repeat itself. He was filled with a despair so deep and black that it rendered him immobile, and he did not even reach down again and *try* to grab his son's flailing arms as the boy screamed and disappeared into the depths.

And then—

He was sitting, and he felt the couch cushion against his back. It had been a dream, just a dream, though it took his brutalized mind a moment to process that fact, and when he opened his eyes, he was not sure at first that they *were* open. He swiveled his head around, used a finger to check that his eyelids were up. They were. It was just that all of the lights were off, and it was impossible to see anything. The entire house seemed to be dark—the entire *neighborhood* seemed to be dark—and Julian reached under the coffee table for the flashlight he kept on the shelf there in case of blackouts. His searching fingers couldn't find it, but seconds later, a lamp atop the end table opposite the couch switched on, bathing the area in a weak yellowish glow.

He was not alone in the living room.

There were shadows galore in the dim light, but there was one shadow that did not correspond to any object in the room. It lurked next to the fireplace, a formless, undulating darkness that appeared flat but somehow had heft.

He stood slowly, observing it. He was afraid, but also fascinated, and as he watched, the formlessness took on a shape, folding in on itself and wobbling crazily from side to side until it resembled nothing so much as a sideshow fat man with multiple arms and a thick tubelike tail that extended into and up the fireplace. Julian backed slowly away, moving toward the front door.

And the shadow thing was right there, an inch in front of his face.

He started, gasped.

The shadow smelled. An odor of mold and dirt that seemed almost familiar. One of the waving arms reached out and touched him, and in that moment, Julian had a clear sense of it. This wasn't the ghost of John Lynch, although Lynch's spirit was there and dominant. This was something else. It *wanted* him to know what it was, and though he did not fully understand, he knew that this was a being comprised of spirits and souls, one that absorbed the dead but was *of* them, not separate. It was a creature that was ancient but evolving, that changed and grew with each addition, and though his comprehension of its complexities was imperfect, he knew that, at its core, this thing was evil.

And it wanted him dead.

It didn't want to kill him, though. It wanted him to kill himself. He wasn't sure why, didn't get the distinction, but the knowledge was sure and definite, delivered directly to his brain by the cold, shadowy appendage that lay against his forearm. He was supposed to commit suicide. That impulse, however, was one he'd never had, and he jerked away, stood in the center of the room, pulled himself to his full height and loudly said, "No."

The attack was immediate.

The lamp on the end table flew toward him, its cord pulling out of the wall socket and throwing the room into darkness. He lurched to the right and felt the object whiz past, heard it smash into the coffee table. All around was the sound of movement—squeaks, scrapes, creaks, crashes, thumps, thuds, knocks, bangs—

and Julian dropped to the floor and began crawling toward the area where he thought the front door should be. He ran into something heavy and immobile—the Southwestern pot containing Claire's ficus tree—hitting the vessel with his head, pausing for a second to get his bearings, relieved not to feel the wetness of blood on his face.

This is what it's like to be blind, he thought, and scurried as fast as he could across the floor, angling left.

He hadn't realized until this moment how powerful a being this was, hadn't known it could wield physical objects against him, although, in a weird way, such a real-world concern took some of the edge off the fear he felt, giving a tangible specificity to the more primal terror he'd experienced until now.

Something brushed past him, something *hairy*, and in an instant that primal fear was back. He let out an involuntary cry of horror and revulsion, and then he was kicked in the side, the air knocked out of him as he was sent flying. But he was kicked in the right direction, and he rolled over, gasping for breath, discovering that he was lying against the front door. Forcing himself to ignore the pain, even as a sharp blow was delivered to the small of his back, he found the door handle, pulled himself to his feet and flung open the door, staggering forward.

He made it out of the house, slammed the door behind him.

And collapsed.

HE AWOKE HALF ON THE FRONT LAWN, HIS HEAD RESTING ON THE cement of the driveway, one arm twisted under and used as a pillow. He knew where he was and what had happened, was not groggy at all, although his back, neck, side and shoulders all hurt, and immediately upon wakening, he got in the van and drove to Claire's parents' house. Her dad, Roger, answered the door, greeting him with a frown, but over the old man's shoulder, Julian saw Claire, Megan and James eating breakfast in the kitchen, and with only the most perfunctory of greetings, he pushed his way past Roger into the house and hurried over to his family, filled with gratitude that they were all here and all right.

James looked up as he entered, and the expression of joy and relief on his son's face—joy that he was here, relief that nothing had happened to him—made Julian rush over and give his son a big hug. The strong hug he was given in return almost made him feel like crying. "I love you," Julian said.

"I love you, too," James said instantly.

It was something they had always said to each other, but its usage had fallen off in the past year, and Julian vowed to himself that he would never stop saying it to his son.

Or his daughter.

He let go of James and grabbed Megan, holding her close. "Love you," he said.

"Love you, too, Dad." Megan *was* crying, and he pulled back and used his index finger to wipe the tears from her cheeks, the way he'd done since she was a baby.

Claire was looking at him over Megan's shoulder, and her eyes were tearing up as well. He pulled out a chair and sat down next to her. "You were right," he said. "I'm not staying there anymore, either. We'll sell the house, take the loss if we have to, and find someplace else to live."

"Hold on a sec. Did I hear what I think I heard?" Claire's dad stood in the kitchen doorway, glaring at him disapprovingly. "Are you actually going to sell your *house* because you think it's *haunted*?"

Julian faced him. "Yes," he said calmly.

"Well, I'll be—"

"Dad," Claire warned.

"That's the stupidest thing I ever heard."

"You read the article in the paper. And I told you what else happened there."

He waved her away, still glaring at Julian.

"Roger . . ." Claire's mother said warningly.

Julian ignored them both. "I'll work there in the daytime," he told Claire. "Like a regular office. But I'll sleep here at night. With you."

"Why do you have to go there at all?"

"Yeah, Dad," Megan chimed in.

"Because my computer and all my work's there."

"You have a laptop," Claire said.

"I need *all* my stuff. I'm down to the wire and have to get this done. Afterward, I'll quit."

She looked at him. "The house is still manipulating you. You think you're thinking for yourself, but you're not."

"I'm not being manipulated. I know exactly what I'm doing."

"You're not thinking of keeping the house?"

"No," he assured her. "Of course not."

"Because it sounds like—"

"No. I told you. But it's not the house that's the problem. It's what lives in the house." He didn't want to describe in front of her parents and the kids what had happened, so he took her arm and led her out of the kitchen, down the hall to the room in which she'd been sleeping. He closed the door. In the mirror above the dresser, he saw his reflection: he looked like a homeless man, his clothes wrinkled, his hair disheveled, his entire appearance one of unruliness and disarray. He *looked* like he'd spent the night on the front lawn.

He sat her down on the bed, took a deep breath. "I saw it," he said. "I felt it. I don't know what it is, exactly, but the thing that's haunting our house is much bigger than a ghost. It's *made up* of ghosts. It's . . . it's an entity of some kind that . . . that takes the people who died at our house or on our property and . . . and they become part of it. I don't know how to explain it, but it's big, it's old, it's dangerous, it's evil."

She was nodding. "So those massacres, those suicides, those murders, all those men who died there over the years, they're part of this."

"Yes!" he said, relieved that she understood despite his stumbling description. "Exactly!"

She looked at him. "Is there any way to get rid of it? Exorcise it?"

"I don't know," he admitted. "I don't think so."

Claire took a deep breath. "You are *not* going back there to work." She fixed him with a face that brooked no disagreement.

He nodded. Thinking about what he'd been through, he realized that he didn't want to go back to the house. Maybe she was right; maybe he *had* still been under the influence when he'd arrived. But he wasn't any longer, and he readily agreed to do his work here at her parents' house. "I still need my disks and files and CDs," he told her. "But I'll call Rick and have him go over with me this morning. The two of us should be able to get everything I need in a few minutes. Is there anything you need? You or the kids?"

"Not right now, but we will have to start moving our stuff out of there sometime soon," she said.

"I'll look around, see if there's anything else I can bring with me."

"No. Things are too . . . hot there right now. Just get your equipment and go. We'll let things cool down for a few days, then decide what to do."

Julian offered her a half smile. "We can't stay at your parents' forever."

She smiled back. "Nor do we want to. But let's just take it easy for a few days. Think about things. We shouldn't make any rash decisions. You just get your Web site done. I'll work my way through this district settlement; then we'll figure out where to go."

"I love you," he said. He realized he hadn't said it to her when he first came over.

"I love you, too," she replied, and kissed him on the nose. "But let's get out there now and rescue the kids from my dad."

Julian took a shower, then had breakfast. Claire went to work shortly after eight, and as soon as she was gone, he gave Rick a call. The print shop didn't open until ten, which gave them plenty of time, and Rick promised to meet him there in fifteen minutes.

"Can I go?" James asked as soon as he hung up the phone.

Julian put a hand on his son's shoulder. "No," he said. "It's too dangerous." He heard Roger's snort of derision from the couch and chose to ignore it. "But don't worry. I'll be back pretty quickly."

It *was* quick. Rick must have been able to tell that he wasn't really needed, as there was no heavy lifting and everything they took out of the house could have been just as easily carried by one person, but he had seen the ghost that night of the party and had no doubt read between the lines and figured out that something else had gone down. He didn't ask any questions, though, and for that Julian was grateful.

"I'll explain it all later," Julian promised when they were finished.

Rick nodded, looked down the street, then over at the house. "Whatever it is, I think you made the right decision," he said.

Julian spent the rest of the morning setting up his equipment in the room he'd be sharing with Claire, using her mother's sewing machine table as a desk. He spent the afternoon working, trying to ignore all the distracting intrusions, taking occasional breaks to hang out with the kids. To thank her parents for their hospitality, he took everyone out to Fazio's for dinner, and afterward all six of them sat in the living room watching television until, one by one, they drifted away.

The last thing he wanted was to be left alone with his father-in-law, but it was nine o'clock and the kids were in bed, Claire was in the bathroom taking a shower, and Claire's mother went into the kitchen. Julian pretended to be concentrating on the procedural crime show that was on TV, but Roger leaned forward, blocking his view. "You pathetic fruit fly," he said disgustedly. "I always knew you weren't a man, but now you're afraid of your own *house*? Because you think it's *haunted*? What are you, three?"

Julian said nothing. He didn't want to get into it right now. They were going to be living at Claire's parents' for a little while, and it would not be a good idea to antagonize her father on his first day here.

Still, the old man kept pushing. "Is this how you take care of your family? Huh? I'll put up with this sort of talk from my daughter and my grandkids. But I want you to know that I have no respect for you at all—"

"You think you're brave enough to stay in that house alone?" Julian confronted him. "One night in there, you old buzzard, and you'll be weeping like the scared little girl you really are."

"Get out!" Roger bellowed. "I will not be treated this way in my own house!"

Julian stood. "Fine," he said. "We'll leave."

"Not them, you!"

"*We'll* leave," Julian repeated. "And we're going to move back to California, where you most definitely will *not* be welcome in our home."

Claire's mother had come in from the kitchen and heard the last of this. "Julian! Roger! I won't have that kind of talk in my house. You two apologize and make up right this minute!" She glared at her husband. "And you be a gracious host, or so help me God I'll . . ." She left the thought unfinished.

The two men looked away from each other, focused their attention on the television and sat silently. But moments after Marian returned to the kitchen, Roger's grumbling started again, snide asides to himself that Julian was obviously meant to hear. Julian tuned him out, ignoring him completely, and finally, unable to put up with it anymore, Roger stood, taking out his keys. "Come on," he said disdainfully. "Let's see your house. Prove to me that it's haunted."

Claire had just returned, wearing pajamas and a robe, and she stepped between them. "No one's going there. Especially at night!" She turned to her father. "You can check it out tomorrow, Dad. It's safer in the daytime."

"Jesus Christ!"

"Roger!" Claire's mom called out. She stood in the kitchen doorway, frowning at him. "The Lord's name."

"Hell's bells, Marian. I'm supposed to put up with this . . . childishness *and* be polite?"

"Yes!"

He threw up his hands. "Fine." But as soon as the two women left the room, Claire following her mother into the kitchen, the old man turned on Julian. "This is idiocy. You two are going to lose a fortune; then you'll come crawling to me, and . . ." He must have seen from the look in Julian's eyes that continuing along this line of reasoning would cause big trouble, because he let the sentence trail off.

"Go," Julian said. "Check the house out. Try to prove me wrong."

"I will."

Julian looked straight into his father-in-law's eyes. "It's your funeral," he said flatly.

THIRTY

AS ALWAYS, ROGER WAS THE FIRST ONE AWAKE, AND THE HOUSE was silent as he got out of bed to do his business. By the time he came out of the bathroom, Marian was in the kitchen, starting the coffee, though Claire, Julian and the kids were still asleep.

"You're not really planning to go over to their house, are you?" Marian asked worriedly as he sat down at the kitchen table.

"Of course. Why not?"

"I just think—"

"Their house isn't haunted, Marian. Jeez Louise."

She didn't respond, but the stiffness of her back told him that she disagreed, and she remained silent as she started making the waffle batter.

Claire entered the kitchen a few moments later, wide-awake and wearing a bathrobe, and Marian said, "I don't want him going over to your house."

"It's not a good idea, Dad," Claire agreed. She sat down next to him at the table.

"There's no such thing as a haunted house."

"Whether you believe it or not, we saw what we saw. And we're selling the place no matter what you say."

"That's just stupid. You're going to take a bath because—"

"Because we have to get rid of that house."

At the counter, Marian turned around. "Don't do it, Roger."

"I'm going," he said stubbornly.

"Then take Julian with you," Claire said. "He can show you where everything happened, explain it to you."

Roger grunted. He knew what her plan was. If he went with Julian, that fairy probably wouldn't even let him into the house. They'd walk around the yard, look into windows and leave.

"That's a good idea," Marian seconded.

He nodded, pretending to agree. But after they'd all finished eating and Claire had gone off to work, the first thing he did was sneak into the bedroom and call Rob. If he was going to go with a son-in-law, it might as well be the one he liked. The line was busy, though, and he hung up, sat down on the edge of his bed and watched the *Today* show for a while. He liked that Ann Curry.

He got distracted, lost track of time, and by the time Marian came in looking for him, nearly a half hour had passed. "Why are you hiding in here?" she demanded.

"I'm busy," he told her.

Huffing with disapproval, she made the bed around him, then took her clothes out of the closet and went into the bathroom to change. He picked up the phone, tried to call again, but Rob wasn't home, and he got Diane instead. He told his daughter to have her husband call him back, because he wanted Rob to go with him to Claire's house, then changed his mind and said he'd go over there alone.

"Dad—" she began.

"Good-bye," he said, and hung up on her before she could give him a lecture.

He turned off the TV, then picked up his keys and wallet from the dresser.

"Roger?" Marian called from the bathroom.

Hurrying out before she could quiz him about where he was going, he passed through the living room, where Julian was playing some kind of card game with his kids. Roger smiled and waved at Megan and James, but he and Julian ignored each other as he walked out the door.

Driving side streets instead of main roads, he was there in five minutes. He parked the car in the driveway and got out to check the lay of the land. All of the houses except theirs were for sale, and all of the yards, including theirs, were dead. Weird, he had to admit, but except for the lawn problem, nothing about Claire's house looked unusual at all. He walked up to the front door and took out his key, thinking about Julian. How could that pansy be afraid of his own house? Roger was embarrassed that his daughter had married such a pantywaist. No wonder their boy was turning out the way he was.

Unlocking the door, he stepped inside. It looked like a tornado had hit the place. Lamps were broken, tables and chairs overturned. Broken glass littered the floor. That gave him pause. Julian had described this, but hearing about it and seeing it were two different things. He recalled that nightmare he'd had about their basement, and though he hated to admit it, he felt less secure than he should have because of the dream.

He was getting to be as bad as they were.

Dreams weren't real. He had nothing to be afraid of. The only thing that had happened here was that there'd been a blackout, and Julian had stumbled around in the dark like an asshole, knocking things over.

Roger made his way through the debris. In the dining room, the table was covered with a fine white powder that looked like flour but, considering his hippie son-in-law, could just as easily have been cocaine. Although there was no way Julian and Claire could afford *this* much cocaine.

Frowning, he walked around the side of the table to the opposite end. Someone had drawn in the powder with a finger, and it wasn't until he was looking at it from the proper angle that he could read what it said: *Sniff some, you stupid old fuck.*

Roger felt his face grow hot with anger. Julian had written this and had left it here for *him*, knowing he would come by the house to investigate, knowing it would cross his mind that the powder resembled cocaine. He bent over, put his face near the tabletop and breathed in.

It smelled like rat poison.

Sniff some, you stupid old fuck.

Julian was trying to kill him.

Roger felt chilled. He and his son-in-law didn't like each other, but he never would have thought Julian capable of such cold-bloodedness, and he straightened up, looking around, seeing the entire house as one gigantic booby trap. What waited for him in the kitchen? Upstairs? In the basement?

Roger shook his head to clear it. That made no sense. Julian had fled the house because he was afraid, because he thought the house was haunted. He hadn't been pretending. And he certainly hadn't poured rat poison all over the dining room table on the off chance that Roger would come over alone and inhale a big nostrilful to test whether it was cocaine.

Maybe the house *was* haunted.

That made no sense, either.

Roger had no explanation for anything that was going on, but he was warier now than he had been when he'd first arrived. He felt uncomfortable here, and while he still wasn't willing to concede that Julian and Claire might be right about the house being dangerous, he was starting to think that it might be a good idea to leave and come back later, maybe with Rob.

Suddenly there seemed to be a smoky smell in the air, one that was faint but growing stronger. At first he thought it was coming from somewhere outside, but when he turned around, sniffing, trying to determine its origin, he saw a small plume creeping out from the fireplace in the living room. The sight made the hair stand up on the back of his neck. It was not just that there'd been no fire in the fireplace a moment ago and there was no way one could have been lit; it was the behavior of the plume of smoke itself. For rather than emerging from the flue and dissipating, or floating up toward the ceiling, the thin gray tendril moved out and into the room, solid and well-defined, turning left, then right, like a snake exploring a new environment. There was something *alive* about the smoke, and Roger was gripped by the certainty that it was searching for him.

All thoughts of showing Julian to be a pathetic coward with an overactive imagination had fled. Roger was filled with the single-minded desire to get out of the house as quickly as possible. There was no way he was going back through that living room. Which meant that in order to get out of the house, he had to exit through the back door.

The tendril of smoke was five feet long now and nosing its way toward the dining room.

Feeling the panic well within him, Roger turned and hurried into the kitchen.

Except it wasn't the kitchen.

He was in a dark, low-ceilinged space that looked like the interior of a tent. Before him, in an indentation, was a fire, and though the smoke issuing from the blaze was wafting upward, it looked completely normal and not tendril-like at all. It was the only thing that looked normal, however. The floor was bare ground, dirt, and the material of the tent walls seemed to be dried skin, skin that looked too smooth and light to be animal.

He whirled around, intending to run back through the doorway, but the doorway was no longer there.

A stifled sob escaped his throat. He thought of what Julian had told him—

You'll be weeping like the scared little girl you really are.

—and wondered whether his son-in-law had planned this. Maybe that powder on the tabletop *had* been cocaine, and he had accidentally snorted some and now he was hallucinating. The timing was right, and it would explain everything that had happened afterward, including this.

But he didn't really believe that. He *wanted* to believe it, and right now he hated Julian more than he ever had, but somehow

Roger knew in his heart that this was really happening, that Julian and Claire were right about this house, and all he wanted at this moment was to escape and go back home, to see his wife again, to spend the rest of the morning reading the paper and watching TV before having lunch with his grandkids.

He *was* weeping now, was nothing more than a frightened old man, but he focused on the situation before him, forced himself to think through it. Maybe all of this was illusion. If so, if he was in the kitchen but simply couldn't see it, the door that led outside was . . .

He stood in place to get his bearings.

There.

Roger faced a section of tent wall, stepped around the fire in the center of the room and moved forward to reach out and touch the flesh-colored material in front of him. He half expected his hand to pass through it, for it to be nothing but illusion. It was real, though, very real, and his fingers pressed against a smooth, springy substance that reminded him of his own upper arm. Instinctively, he recoiled, grimacing in disgust. His touch revealed a parting in the tent wall, however, and this close he saw that there was a seam in the material. There *was* a door in front of him, albeit a tent door, and though the feel of the material made him sick to his stomach, he took another half step forward and, using both hands, pulled apart the flaps.

Behind the flap was a man standing in front of a space that was pitch-black and lifeless, a man wearing a backward yellow baseball cap and holding a knife.

"Hello, Roger," he said in a voice that sounded impossibly old. "Glad you could join us."

THIRTY-ONE

CLAIRE WAS AT HER OFFICE AND HAD JUST ANSWERED AN E-MAIL from the school district's attorneys when the phone rang. It was Diane. Her sister was calling to tell her that their father had phoned, asking Rob to go with him to Claire's house. "You know Dad. He said he needed a witness to prove to, quote, that pansy Julian, end quote, that your house wasn't haunted. Luckily, Rob was at work and wasn't home, so I answered the phone. I told him not to go, but . . ."

"Yes. We know Dad."

"I'm with you on this, Claire. I don't like that house. Now, after everything that's happened . . ." She drew in a loud breath. "I don't think Dad should go there. He's getting old, and . . . I just think it might be dangerous."

"It is dangerous. But it's daytime and he'll only be there for a few minutes. I think he'll be okay."

There was a weird pause on the other end of the line, and Claire's heart lurched in her chest. "Di? There's something you're not telling me."

"After Dad hung up, the phone rang again, and when I answered it, there was this *voice*. It was all deep and spooky, and it said, 'He's a stupid old fuck.' That's it. That's all it said. Then the person hung up. I checked the caller ID, and . . . it was your number. At your house."

Claire was filled with a sensation of panic, but she managed to keep her voice calm. "You stay there. I'll get Julian, and we'll go and see what's up."

"I'm going, too."

"Di . . ."

"I'm going, too. I'll call Mom; then I'll meet you there."

"Okay, but if you get there before we do, just wait until we arrive. I think it's better if all three of us go in together. Safer."

"Gotcha."

There was no way Diane would make it there before she did. Their house was the next street over on the other side of the park. *Call Mom?* "Shit," Claire said aloud, and quickly dialed her parents' number, hoping to get through before her sister. She did. Her mom answered the phone and Claire asked to speak with Julian. She kept all traces of worry out of her voice—she'd let Diane explain to their mother what was going on—but as soon as Julian came on the line, she told him exactly what had happened and asked him to meet her in front of the house. She was expecting an argument, probably because it involved her dad, but Julian agreed right away. His voice had changed its tone after she'd repeated what Diane had said about the phone call from their house—

He's a stupid old fuck

—and she could tell that he was as worried as she was.

"I love you," she said before she hung up, and meant it.

Claire *was* the first person to arrive at the house, and when she saw her parents' car in the driveway, she knew she couldn't wait around for Julian and Diane to show up. She had to rush in there and get her dad out.

For some reason, however, her key didn't seem to fit in the lock, and she was still fumbling with it—in between bouts of pounding on the door and yelling, "Dad!"—when Julian swerved next to the curb in front of the house, driving her father's old truck. Diane was mere seconds behind him.

Julian tried her key, then his, but when neither seemed to work, he led them around the side of the house to the backyard.

Where the kitchen door was not only unlocked, but open.

Claire's heart skipped a beat, restarting its rhythm at a much more rapid pace. This couldn't be good. "Dad!" she called.

She hadn't expected an answer, and she didn't get one. On the white cement of the patio, she saw muddy footprints. Or muddy prints of *some* sort. They were clumpy and ill defined, and it was impossible to tell whether they came from a shoe, a foot, a claw, a hoof or something else.

They led into the house.

Julian and Diane had to have seen them, too, but neither of them said a word. Claire stepped past her husband. "Dad?" She walked inside, Julian and Diane right behind her.

The mud disappeared. Before her, the kitchen seemed perfectly normal, nothing out of place, exactly as it should have been. Despite the promise of the muddy prints, the clean kitchen was not really a surprise. What was a surprise was that the living room appeared to be in impeccable shape as well. She could see it through the doorway, past the dining room. From Julian's description, she had expected broken lamps and overturned furniture, but from what she could tell, the room was immaculate.

Julian noticed it, too. "What the hell . . . ?" He hurried over, turning about, an expression of complete confusion on his face.

That should have been good news, Claire supposed, but somehow it scared her far more than a trashed room would have. They were dealing with something here that could *change* things. Julian was right. It wasn't a ghost. Or wasn't *just* a ghost. For the being that occupied this house was able to destroy objects and put them back together again. Its powers were not merely supernatural but godlike, and she realized that there was no way they could ever hope to fight against something like that. She discarded once and for all any thought of vanquishing the spirit. She just wanted to find her dad and get him out of here. After that, she didn't care what happened to this place. It could burn to the ground for all she cared. In fact, burning to the ground would be the *best* possible outcome. She wouldn't have to live with the guilt of palming this evil place off on another unsuspecting soul, and they might even get some insurance money out of it. But what would happen after that? The land itself was cursed. Any new home built on the same spot would have the same problem. And what if the entire neighborhood was razed? What would the city do with the land? Expand the park? Put in a shopping center? Each of those was a disaster in waiting. The only useful possibility she could foresee would be a landfill, but the council certainly wouldn't have one in the center of town.

Diane tapped her shoulder, and she jumped, startled out of her reverie.

"I'm checking upstairs," her sister said.

"Not alone you're not."

"No one's going upstairs," Julian said, coming back into the kitchen. "We check the ground floor first. Together. If we don't find him here, *then* we'll go upstairs."

"Dad!" Diane called at the top of her lungs.

There was no answer.

"He's not in the dining room or the living room," Julian said. "I was just there. We'll check the basement, then our bedroom and the bathroom. After that, we'll go upstairs. If we don't find anything in the house, we'll check the garage."

"Dad!" Diane called again.

Julian walked over to the basement door, pulling it open. "I don't understand it," he told Claire as he flipped the switch to turn on the cellar lights. "The living room was trashed. That lamp on the end table was thrown at me, and it smashed on the coffee table. Pieces were everywhere. . . ."

"I believe you," she said honestly, and that was all she needed to say.

Julian walked down the steps while Claire and Diane waited at the top. "Roger?" he called.

"Dad?" they yelled together.

There was no response, but Julian spent several minutes moving boxes aside to make sure he—

his body

—wasn't hiding somewhere down there.

The basement was empty, and Julian came back up. The three of them passed by the deserted laundry room, then moved out into the hallway and on to the master bedroom. It was daytime, but the drapes were drawn, and Claire turned on the lights. They were all calling for her father yet receiving no response.

"The bed," Claire said, pointing.

"That was me," Julian said, embarrassed. "I didn't make it." He flipped up the covers, though, just to make sure no one was under there, then dropped to his knees, lifted the ruffled skirt and checked beneath the bed, shaking his head as he stood to indicate there was nothing.

Claire moved over to the bathroom and turned on the light in there as well.

Her heart leaped. On the floor, she saw the muddy prints again, threateningly brown against the lightness of the white tile. The mirror was fogged up, as though someone had just come out of the shower, and on the clouded glass was the imprint of . . . a face, she supposed, although it did not look like any face she'd ever seen. The elements were all there—eyes, nose, mouth—but they were in the wrong place, in the wrong order, and the scary thing was that for a brief moment she didn't know why they were wrong, because she couldn't remember where those parts were supposed to go. It was not until she saw the blurry contours of her own face in the corner of the mirror that she remembered the nose went over the mouth, and the two eyes were above that. For a terrible second, that awful face had seemed . . . right.

Behind her, Diane saw the same thing and let out a short, sharp cry, which sent Julian running over from the closet where he'd been searching.

"What *is* that?" Diane wanted to know, but neither Claire nor Julian had an answer.

"Let's just find your dad and get out of here," Julian said grimly, and the three of them hurried out of the bedroom and up the stairs.

"Roger!" Julian called.

"Dad!"

"Dad!"

He was not in Julian's office, James's room, Megan's room or the bathroom. They saw nothing unusual upstairs, and though Claire thought she heard a weird tapping in Julian's office, it might have been her imagination, since neither Julian nor Diane heard a thing.

As agreed, they went out to the garage together, but by now what little hope remained in Claire of finding her father had vanished. She didn't know where he was or what had happened to him, but something had certainly occurred, because he seemed to have disappeared.

He was not on the ground floor of the garage, they saw instantly. Julian went up to the loft by himself, and though he stayed up there several minutes longer than she thought he should have and returned looking pale and shaken, he claimed that he'd seen nothing out of the ordinary.

"So he's not here," Claire said.

"Maybe he went home," Julian suggested.

"His car's still in the driveway."

"Maybe he walked away. Or got scared and ran."

"We need to go to the police," Diane announced.

"The police aren't going to believe—" Julian began.

"I don't give a shit what they believe. My dad is missing, and it's their job to find him, and if they happen to discover the existence of ghosts on the way, well, good for them. But Dad's gone. And we need to get him back, no matter what it takes."

Claire agreed, and instead of arguing the point, she grabbed her sister's arm with one hand, Julian's with the other, and pulled them both out of the garage. Just in case. Once in the driveway, she took out her cell phone and dialed 911. She looked up at the sky, wondering why the sun and clouds were visible from here but the moon and the stars were not. Did it mean something?

A police dispatcher came on the line. "What is your emergency?"

"My father's missing. He disappeared about an hour ago—"

"Excuse me, ma'am," the dispatcher said, and there seemed to be a tone of smirking condescension in her voice, "but an adult male is not considered missing until he has been gone for forty-eight hours. Your father has been out of contact for one. I suggest you wait. I'm sure he will turn up later this morning."

"You don't understand," Claire said. She saw the anxious expression on her sister's face. "He disappeared *inside* our house." She hadn't intended to bring any of this up, hadn't wanted the police to think her crazy and not take her seriously. But there wasn't going to be any action taken to find her father for two full days, and she knew she needed to spell everything out. Still, she had to be careful what she said. "We've had some incidents at our home recently," she began.

"Vandalism," Julian whispered.

"Incidents of vandalism," she said more confidently. "Someone shut off our lights and attacked my husband in our living room. This is the same house," she added with sudden inspiration, "where an intruder named John Lynch committed suicide several days ago."

Julian gave her a thumbs-up.

Now it was her turn to be condescending. "I'm sure that crime is in your records," Claire told the dispatcher.

"You may report the assault and file a claim regarding the vandalism. Although, since they occurred previously, neither incident is considered an emergency. I can transfer you to an officer who will take your statement and arrange a meeting. As for your father, a person has to be missing for forty-eight hours before the police can open an investigation."

"Transfer me," Claire ordered.

She spent the next five minutes trying in vain to convince a

Lieutenant Weiss that he needed to come out to their house to investigate, finally giving up and handing the phone over to Julian, who alienated the officer in record time and ended up turning off the phone in anger and disgust.

Diane was crying. "What do we do?"

"I don't know," Julian said helplessly. "Does Rob know anyone who has contacts at the police department? Maybe we can get some help through a back channel—"

"I don't think so," Diane said, taking out her own phone, "but I'll ask."

Rob didn't, and, from Diane's side of the conversation, it didn't sound as though he believed a word of what she was telling him, but he promised to ask around and see whether maybe someone he knew knew someone who could help them get some traction with the cops.

Diane hung up. "What do we do now?" she asked.

Claire looked over at the house. "Let's get out of here," she said.

As they passed by her dad's car, she felt a pang, wondering whether she would ever see her father again. He was rough, and he was mean sometimes, and he hated Julian, but she loved him, and she didn't know what she would do without him. Her parents were both getting on in years, but she had never really considered, *seriously* considered, what she'd do if one of them died. Now she realized that if her dad died, it would not just affect her emotionally, but would require her and Diane to take care of their mom. Her dad was the one who ran the household, did all the shopping, paid all the bills and made most of the decisions. If something happened to her dad, she and her sister would have to take up the slack.

Claire immediately felt guilty for even contemplating such mundane, practical considerations, and she pushed all such thoughts from her mind before telling Julian and Diane to meet her at her parents' house, and climbing into the van. She wanted to cry, wanted to dwell on her unhappiness and wallow in it, but luckily driving required concentration, and her emotions were once again under control as she pulled into her parents' driveway.

All that hard-won discipline threatened to crumble, however, as soon as she walked into the house, saw her mom and knew she would have to explain that her dad was missing. A more enlightened parent might let her kids in on the conversation, too, but Claire's instinct was to keep them away from this as much as possible, and she told Megan and James to go into their rooms while she talked to Grandma.

She didn't know where to start. Diane was already crying, but Julian stepped into the breach and informed her mom that they'd just come back from their house. "We were looking for Roger. He went over there this morning to prove me wrong, I guess, and show me that our house isn't really haunted. He called Diane first to ask whether Rob wanted to go with him, but Rob was at work. After he hung up, she got another call, a weird call, and we went out there to make sure he was all right. His car was parked in the driveway, but he wasn't in the house or in the yard or in the garage. We couldn't find him."

"He disappeared," Claire said, touching her mom's arm. "He was just . . . gone."

Her mother seemed confused. "He can't have just disappeared."

"He did, Mom. I don't know how, but he did."

Diane was nodding. "That house *is* haunted. I've never experienced anything like it. The bathroom was all fogged up, and there was a . . . a *face* in the mirror."

Their mom started to cry.

"We called the police," Claire said, "but they can't do anything until he's been missing for forty-eight hours."

"What do we do?" her mom asked.

That was the question. Claire had been going over possibilities in her head, but the truth was that there weren't a whole lot of options. This wasn't a situation where the choices were self-evident. She'd never encountered anything even remotely similar, and doubted that anyone else had, either. Even if the police *were* to get involved, she doubted that they would be able to find her dad. He had been taken by the same creature that had attacked Julian, and whether her father was alive or dead, they would never discover what had happened to him unless they figured out how to stop whatever lived in that house.

Whether he was alive or dead.

Her vision grew blurry as the tears threatened to come. She forced them back. She needed to be strong right now. For her kids, for her mom, for herself.

"Maybe he'll be back later," her mom said. "Maybe he'll be back in time for dinner."

Either she didn't understand what was happening or didn't want to face it. Claire nodded. "Maybe," she said.

"Maybe," Diane echoed.

But he wasn't.

THIRTY-TWO

"WHAT THE HELL ARE YOU DOING?"

Jumping at the sound of her mother's voice, Megan cut herself. Deep.

She'd thought the bathroom door had been locked, and she was sitting on the toilet, pants down, steak knife in hand, making small, light incisions on the inside of her thigh, just above the knee, when the door swung open. Startled by her mother's shout, Megan let her hand slip, the knife drawing not just across the surface of the skin but slicing through fat into muscle. The pain was incredible, and she cried out, her eyes tearing up even as they caught the stricken look of horror on her mom's face.

"Megan!"

She hadn't been doing it to make herself unattractive this time. She'd been doing it . . . Well, she didn't know why she'd been doing it. It had seemed like a good idea ten minutes ago, but now, with the blood gushing down her leg onto the linoleum, she realized how crazy it was. She reached for the toilet paper, pulled and pulled until she'd unspooled enough for it to pile into folds on the floor, then grabbed the entire mass of tissue and shoved it against the flowing cut, shocked to see how quickly the blood soaked through.

Her mom was screaming, calling for her grandma and her dad,

and in seconds they were there. Megan was in so much pain that she wasn't even embarrassed for them to see her with her pants down.

"Oh, my God," her dad said.

By this time, her mom had soaked a washcloth in cold water from the sink and was pressing it against the wound, having tossed the toilet paper aside.

"I'll get ice," her grandma said quickly, and now Megan knew she was really hurt, because James was standing in the doorway and she didn't even care.

She'd never felt such intense agony, and she was no longer crying, because she was gritting her teeth against the pain, squinting her eyes so tightly she could not see.

"We're taking her to the hospital!" she heard her mom tell her grandma, and Megan opened her eyes to see her grandmother handing over a fresh hand towel filled with ice cubes. Her mom let the bloody wet washcloth she'd been pressing against the wound drop onto the floor, replacing it with the ice-filled hand towel. "Hold this," her mom ordered. "Press it hard to stop the bleeding. Do you think you can stand?"

Grimacing, Megan nodded. The cold ice made the cut feel a little better.

"Stay here with James!" her mother said. Her grandma nodded.

With her dad on one side and her mom on the other, each holding a hand under her armpit to support her, Megan got off the toilet, still bent over, keeping the makeshift ice pack pressed firmly against the slice on her leg. "Make sure she doesn't fall," her mom said to her dad, and crouched down, taking over ice-pack duty and encouraging her to stand up straight. Megan pulled up her pants, pausing as her mom adjusted the hand holding the ice. She let out a sharp yelp as a flash of pain stabbed through her.

"Do you want me to carry you?" her dad asked.

Megan nodded.

"Maybe that would be better," her mom said quickly. "I'm not sure we want that blood to be pumping."

"Start the van and open the door," her dad replied, grunting as he picked her up, one hand under her neck, the other under her knees.

Megan saw a steady stream of blood streaming over her father's arm, saw a frightening amount of red puddled and smeared on the floor. She reached out and held the ice-filled hand towel against the cut while her mom ran through the house and outside.

"Megan?" James said worriedly.

"I'll be okay," she reassured him, though she had no idea whether that was true or not. The bleeding hadn't stopped or even slowed down, and that was getting very scary. Had she sliced open a vein or something? Was she going to die?

"Where's Grandpa?" she asked as her dad carried her down the hall.

"We don't know," he admitted.

"Is he dead?" Maybe that was why she'd been cutting herself.

It was an uncharacteristically blunt question to have asked, and her dad's answer was equally blunt. "We don't know."

The house was reaching out, Megan thought. She and James should have kept quiet.

I will kill you both.

Even though they were away from it, they should not have revealed its secrets. Now they were going to have to pay. She started to cry, though whether it was over her grandpa or because of the pain or it was simply a reaction to the totality of everything that was going on, she could not say.

The van's engine was running and the side door was open. Her mom was inside, laying towels over the back bench seat. Between both parents, they got her onto the seat and laid her down on the towels. They weren't sure how to hook up the shoulder harness and didn't have the time to figure it out, so her mom sat on the floor next to her, holding her in place and making sure she didn't move while her dad slammed the side door shut, got in the front, backed quickly out of the driveway and took off.

Megan started feeling woozy on the way to the hospital. It

suddenly seemed hard to keep her eyes open, and she closed them for a moment.

After that, sounds and images came in short staccato bursts, some of which remained in her brain, others of which were forgotten as soon as they appeared. A wheelchair. A bed. A curtain. A doctor. "She's lost a lot of blood." A shot. Her mom crying. A television. A Geico commercial. A nurse. A plastic bag hanging from a hook with a tube coming out of it. Beeping. Her dad in a chair, watching her. James. Grandma. Two doctors talking. Mom. Dad. Mom.

Eventually, things sorted themselves out. She was in a hospital room, and it was daytime. Sunlight streamed through a window to her left, above a bed in which an old man lay snoring.

"She's awake!" her mom said excitedly, and as weak as she felt, Megan had to smile. It was nice to hear her mom's voice. Her dad was there, looking down at her, and a moment later a nurse was there, too, smiling, telling her everything was going to be okay.

Apparently she had lost a lot of blood because she *had* hit a vein, although, luckily, it was a small one; otherwise she would probably be dead. Doctors had repaired the damage and sewn everything up. The lost blood had been replaced, and she was being given some kind of medicine to make sure no dangerous clots formed. She would have to remain in the hospital under observation for a few more days.

"How . . . ?" She tried to speak, but her throat was dry and the word came out a croak. The nurse picked up a plastic cup from a tray that sat suspended to the right of the bed and placed a straw in Megan's mouth. She sipped water through the straw, the coolest, freshest, best-tasting water she had ever had. Her throat felt better, and she swallowed before trying to speak again. This time her voice was weak but clear. "How long have I been here?"

"Since last night," the nurse told her.

Last night? She'd been knocked out for most of the time she'd been here, but still, it felt like days.

After the nurse left and the three of them were alone, save for the snoring man in the next bed, they were silent for a moment. Her parents looked at each other; then her mom cleared her throat, speaking in a careful, considered way that indicated she had spent time preparing her topic of conversation. "Honey? I know you don't want to be here. I know this is hard for you, and I don't want to make it any harder, but your dad and I have a few questions we'd like to ask you."

Megan knew what was coming next.

"This was all an accident, I know. And I'm sorry I startled you and made you slice your leg open. I should have knocked first. But, sweetie, why were you cutting yourself in the first place?"

She wished she had an answer, but she didn't. "I don't know," she admitted, and started to cry.

Her mom came over to the bed. She couldn't give Megan a hug—there were too many tubes and monitors in the way—but she did the best she could and curled an arm around Megan's shoulder on the pillow. "It's all right," she said, and used a finger to wipe away tears. "We'll talk about it some other time, when you're feeling better."

Megan didn't want to talk about it at all. Postponing the conversation would give her time to come up with better answers, but she doubted whether she would ever be able to come up with a real reason. *The house was reaching out,* she thought again, and that was probably as close as she would ever come to the truth.

She had just awakened, but she was feeling tired already—it was most likely the medicine—and she asked her parents whether it would be okay if she took a short nap.

"Of course," her dad said.

Her mom gave her shoulder a squeeze and then went back to her chair. "Go ahead, honey."

When she awoke, it was dinnertime. A nurse was using a button on the remote-control panel at her bedside to raise her into a sitting position so she could eat the wretched-looking meal placed on a tray that was attached to her bed by a metal arm. Both of her parents were still in the same seats, although her dad was watching CNN on the TV mounted to the wall and wasn't aware that she'd woken up until her mom nudged him with an elbow.

The nurse left, and they all had a good laugh about the awful food as Megan attempted to eat it. No mention was made of her cutting herself, and everything that was happening outside this hospital room seemed distant and unconnected. The snoring man had awakened and was eating his dinner. Loudly. Her dad saw her glancing over there, distracted, and he stood up from his chair to pull the curtain between the beds, blocking her view. Megan smiled at him. "Thanks."

There was nothing to do and there wasn't much to say, so after eating as much as she could, Megan used the remote-control panel attached to the armrest of her bed to flip through the channels and see what kind of cable the hospital had. It wasn't very good. There were the networks, several news channels, several sports channels and a bunch of other stations she wasn't much interested in. She finally gave up and switched it back to CNN. "It's my TV and I was going to make you watch one of my shows," she told her dad, "but there's nothing on. So it's all yours."

It was boring just lying there in bed, and after a while Megan felt guilty for making her parents be bored, too, so she told them they should go home. They both looked at each other uncertainly. "I'm tired anyway," she lied. "I want to go to bed. You can come back in the morning."

"I'm spending the night," her mom said.

"In that chair? Go home. I'll be fine. Check on James and make sure he's staying out of trouble." She'd meant it as a joke, but the second after she said it, a host of unwanted images sprang up in her brain: James cutting himself in the same way she had . . . James returning to their house to dig a hole in their backyard . . . James wearing a backward yellow baseball cap and holding a knife.

Her parents, too, looked worried.

She decided to be honest. "I'll be safe here," she said softly. "Look after James. And Grandma."

Her mom nodded grimly. "Julian," she said. "Go."

"What about you?"

"I'll sleep here."

"Mom . . ."

"Megan's right," her dad said.

"It's just a cut—" Megan began.

"It's not just a cut. That's why you're here. They had to replace over a liter of your blood. And they're monitoring you to make sure you don't develop any blood clots." She gestured around. "Although I don't see a whole lot of monitoring going on. I don't know whether they're understaffed or what, but these nurses and doctors don't come by anywhere near as often as they should, and I need to be here in case something happens."

"Actually, ma'am, we check your daughter on a very specific schedule, and the likelihood of her developing blood clots while being administered the medication that's in her IV drip is highly unlikely."

The nurse appeared behind her mom, and her mom's face turned red. "I'm sorry. I didn't mean to—"

The nurse smiled kindly. "Nothing to be sorry for. I know you're concerned. I just want to put your mind at rest. This is a precaution against a very remote possibility. Your daughter's going to be fine. She's only here right now because we want to make sure we guard against all potentialities."

"See?" Megan said.

"Besides, visitors are not allowed to stay overnight in the rooms. All visitors must leave at ten. You're welcome to remain in the lobby, but it's probably better if you go home, get some sleep and return in the morning."

"I'll be fine," Megan said.

"I'm staying until ten," her mom announced.

"You know your mother." Standing up, her dad gave her the closest thing to a hug that was possible in the bed, kissing her on the forehead. "I'll be back to pick your mom up later," he said. "I'll see you then."

"Give me a kiss if I'm asleep," she told him.

He smiled, nodded. "And I'll be back for breakfast," he promised. "Love you."

"Love you," she returned, and felt the tears well up as he headed out the door, waving.

The nurse checked the monitors, wrote some information down on a chart, drew some blood and changed the drip bag. Her mom talked to the nurse for a few minutes in the hallway, beyond her hearing range, and Megan flipped once again through the television channels. There was nothing good, so she left it on *Jeopardy!*, and the game show remained on in the background while she and her mom talked. She asked whether any of her friends had been told that she was in the hospital, and her mom said no, not yet, but she'd let them know tomorrow so they could come and visit. Megan asked whether there was any news about Grandpa, and her mom grew quiet and sad and merely shook her head.

That opened the floodgates, and they talked about the house, *really* talked about it, for the first time. She held back a little, afraid that if she told everything it might endanger the rest of her family—

I will kill you both.

—and she was pretty sure her mom held back a little, too, probably for the same reason, but they did discuss their feelings about the house, little things they'd seen and heard, and the way it had all sort of built up until it was what it was today. Her mom said that Mr. Cortinez at the high school had given her a lot of information about the history of Jardine and that it seemed as though people had been dying there, killing themselves and killing others, since before the town was a town.

"We should have moved as soon as you found that out."

"That's what I told your dad. Although it was only a week or two ago, to be fair. Besides, who knew that some lunatic would kill himself in our garage."

"It happened before," Megan pointed out.

"That's true."

"So are we going to sell the house now?"

"I guess so. If we can." Her mom paused. "But I'd feel guilty palming it off on someone else, wouldn't you?"

"No!" Megan said instantly, and out of the corner of her eye she saw the numbers of her heart rate accelerate on the monitor. If the nurse hadn't turned down the sound, it would probably be beeping. She took a deep breath, forcing herself to calm down, not wanting a team of doctors and nurses to rush into the room to see what was wrong with her. "No," she said more softly. "We can't live there again."

"We won't," her mom assured her. "It's just . . ." She shook her head, tried to smile. "We'll think of something to do with it."

Megan wanted to ask about her grandpa. It was the big question hovering over everything. But whether it was because she was just a kid or because her mother wasn't ready to face the subject, Megan understood that it was something her mom would not discuss. She hadn't gotten any details from either of her parents, but she could tell by the way they'd been acting that his disappearance was unexplainable and frightening and somehow involved their house.

Maybe—hopefully—things would just work out and her grandpa would return on his own, none the worse for wear.

But she doubted it.

They'd gone as deep as they were going to go. Besides, *Glee* was about to be on, and Megan wanted to watch it. Her brain hurt from worrying, and right now she just wanted to relax and enjoy some mindless entertainment. It was a two-hour episode, and for those two hours she forgot everything else, even enjoying the commercials when they came on. After that, she flipped through channels before stopping on back-to-back reruns of *The Office*, which she and her mom both liked.

At ten o'clock, an orderly arrived to escort her mom out. Promising to return first thing in the morning, she gave Megan a kiss on each cheek and a kiss on the forehead "for protection," the way she had when Megan was small, and they both blew each other another kiss as she backed out the door.

Feeling alone and a little sad, Megan sniffled, wiping tears from her eyes. But a nurse arrived almost immediately to administer a checkup, and after using the bedpan, Megan found that she was suddenly extremely tired. There was nothing she wanted to watch, but she left the television on anyway, turning down the volume until it was white noise.

She closed her eyes, letting the indistinct murmuring lull her to sleep.

She awoke in the middle of the night, the curtains pulled not only on her left but on her right, to block the sights and sounds of the corridor outside her room so she might sleep in peace. High on the wall, her television was still on, but no movie or show was being broadcast. Instead, the monitor was white with black letters moving from left to right across the screen.

It looked like the screen of her cell phone.

Megan squinted at the message through bleary eyes, then quickly reached for the remote control. She pushed the red "off" button, pressing it over and over again, but the television refused to obey.

I told you, Megan, the words repeated, *I will kill you both.*

Frantic, she pressed the button that called for the nurse.

It didn't seem to be working, because no one came. She wanted to get up and out of bed, walk down the hallway until she found someone to help her, but she was connected to the monitors, and a plastic tube dripped medicine into her wrist.

On the other side of the curtain, the snoring had stopped.

Was the man dead?

She needed to calm down. The words on the TV were just that: words. They couldn't hurt her. They might frighten her, but they couldn't cause her any harm. She took stock. Did she feel like cutting herself or hurting herself in any way? Did she have any suspicious or unusual thoughts? No.

Megan glanced up at the screen again, and the words were gone. An infomercial was being broadcast, some type of cleaning product.

Maybe she'd imagined the whole thing.

She closed her eyes, settled back down. Just the possibility that it had all been in her head allowed her to forget about it and fall back asleep. Which she did almost immediately.

She dreamed of the man with the yellow baseball cap. He was in a small, primitive shack, a wooden hut with no furniture and no windows, and he was roasting her grandpa over a fire in the center of the floor, preparing to eat him. Her grandpa was screaming, his clothes and hair burned off, sweat and blood oozing from his reddening skin, falling sizzling onto the flames. He was tied to a spit of some sort, and every so often, the man in the yellow cap would turn him over and poke him with a fork to see whether he was done.

When she awoke, the curtains had been pulled back, the snoring man's bed was empty, and sunlight was streaming through the window. She called for a nurse, used the bedpan, ordered breakfast, endured a checkup and was told she was doing well.

The chairs next to her bed were empty and remained empty. She kept looking from them to the doorway. Ten minutes passed. Fifteen. Twenty. A half hour. Forty-five minutes.

Her breakfast arrived—cereal, toast and orange juice—and she started eating. She was worried but pretended to herself that she wasn't.

Finally, just after her tray had been removed, her mom arrived.

Alone.

Crying.

THIRTY-THREE

HIS GRANDPARENTS' HOUSE SEEMED LONELY. GRANDPA WAS missing, Megan was in the hospital, and his mom was staying with her. Only he, his dad and his grandma were home for dinner. His dad bought pizza in an effort to cheer him up, and let him watch *The Simpsons* instead of the news, but it didn't really work. It made him feel sadder, in fact, made him more aware that things weren't normal, that everything was out of whack.

He didn't really understand what had happened to Megan. He'd seen her in the bathroom before her parents rushed her to the hospital, and it looked like she'd stolen a steak knife from the kitchen and was using it to cut up her legs. Had she been trying to kill herself? What would have happened if Mom hadn't walked in on her? Would she be dead?

Did the house make her do it?

That was what he really wanted to know, but she hadn't been awake when he went to see her, so he'd been unable to ask. He remembered what it had felt like when he'd been compelled to dig, when he'd obsessed over holes in the backyard, and he needed to let her know that he understood, that he knew what she was going through.

He didn't like the fact that she'd been cutting herself here at Grandma and Grandpa's. As far as he was concerned, that meant there were two possibilities, neither of them good. Either whatever lived in their house had the power to reach all the way out here to make them do what it wanted. Or they'd been infected and carried within themselves a part of that *thing*, which could manifest itself at any time.

Both thoughts terrified him.

Throughout dinner and afterward, he kept examining his every thought and movement, as well as the words and actions of his dad and grandma, looking for any sign that they had been influenced or corrupted in any way. He saw no evidence of it, but that didn't assuage him. It could happen at any moment, and he became more and more worried as time passed and nothing weird happened. It had been almost twenty-four hours since his mom had found Megan bleeding in the bathroom, and he was on edge, waiting for something like that to happen again.

After *The Simpsons*, *King of the Hill* came on, then *Family Guy*, then *The Simpsons* again; then his dad told him it was time for bed.

James got up from the couch and looked down the long, dark hallway. The guest room he'd been using was at the far end. "I don't want to sleep in that room," he said.

His dad started to say something, probably that there was nothing for him to be afraid of, but they all knew that wasn't true, and when his grandma spoke up and said that he could sleep in her room—she and his grandpa had separate beds—James looked over at his dad, and his dad didn't object.

His dad went with him while he got his pajamas out of the guest room, and stood outside the bathroom while he changed. His grandma had put new sheets on the bed and had brought over the blanket he'd been using from the other room. He said good night to both his dad and grandma, giving each of them a hug, then got into bed, leaving the door open and the hall light on. It took him a long time to fall asleep, and he was still awake an hour later when his grandma came in and got into her bed. He pretended to be asleep, however, and eventually he did drift off.

In his nightmare, it was midnight and he was back at their house. He had gotten up, thirsty, and walked downstairs to the kitchen to get a drink of water, which made no sense because he always kept a water bottle next to his bed. But he got a drink from the kitchen sink nevertheless, then went over to the basement door, opened it and walked down the stairs. Only the basement wasn't scary. There was no sign of that grinning man in the corner, and whatever it was that had made the cellar creepy seemed to be gone.

It was the garage that was scary now.

He knew it instantly, and he walked up the stairs and outside, through the backyard, past small holes packed tightly with the bodies of dead animals, and plants so desiccated they resembled the skeletons of misshapen creatures. Both garage doors were open and the building was filled with light, but even the light was scary, and he knew that he should not go in there alone. He did, though, walking through the lighted open area straight to the ladder against the wall. There was darkness at the top of the ladder, and he didn't want to go up to the headquarters, but he couldn't stop himself, and, putting one hand over the other, he climbed the rungs. The trapdoor was already open, and he poked his head up through the space.

Headquarters had changed since the last time he and Robbie had been up here. All of the junk they had collected was gone, and instead of the items they had scrounged from alleys and garbage cans, the room was filled with primitive furniture that looked like it had come out of some settler's cabin two hundred years ago. There was a bench made from a split log, a table of hand-hewn wood, a copper bathtub filled with water, a rocking chair made from the branches of trees, a low wooden bed with a homemade quilt thrown atop the mattress. There were no lamps, but light seeped in from below through cracks in the floor, making everything look even older and spookier than it already was.

James wanted to climb back down, but there was something he knew he had to do, and he pulled himself through the trapdoor and onto the floor, standing. The light from below created weird shadows on the walls and ceiling, and at first he thought that was what was making him feel slightly off balance. But then he realized that something in the room was moving. He glanced around, trying to figure out what it was.

The rocking chair.

Slowly, almost imperceptibly, the rocking chair was rocking. No one sat in it, but it was rocking nevertheless, its slatted shadow swinging like a pendulum among the others on the ceiling, back and forth, back and forth. The wood creaked, the only sound in the stillness save for his own breathing.

The last thing in the world he wanted was to pass by that chair, but there was something he had to do, and he gathered his courage and walked forward, not looking at the rocking chair, though he could see its movement in his peripheral vision, and he could hear it.

Creak.

His focus was on the wall ahead, on the rectangular board that he would have to pull out in order to get to the secret compartment.

Creak.

Then he was past the rocking chair and could no longer see it, not even in his peripheral vision. He crouched down near the wall, used his fist to tap the board, and pulled it aside when it came loose. Bending down, he looked into the secret compartment.

And saw, inside, on top of the small hill of dirt, his grandpa's bloody head.

James awoke—

—in his bedroom, at home.

It was night, it was dark, and he was confused, disoriented. He was supposed to be in his grandma's room, and for a moment he thought he was still dreaming. Then he sat up, felt the familiar reality of his bed below him, saw the outlines in the darkness of his movie posters on the wall, smelled the musty odor that his room got sometimes when their house was closed up for too long, and he knew that he was really back home.

Was he alone in here?

The thought terrified him. Their house was scary enough when everyone was home. But if he was the only one in it . . .

Maybe this was just another dream.

No. Why try to fool himself? He knew it wasn't. How he had come to be here and why, James had no idea. The only thing he did know was that he needed to get out of the house as quickly as possible. He was in his pajamas and wasn't wearing shoes, but though he still had some clothes in his closet and could probably find an old pair of sneakers to wear, he didn't want to waste the time it would take to find them. He had to get out of here *now*, and he jumped out of bed, running through the darkness, down the hall, down the stairs, to the front door—

And he couldn't open it.

He turned the lock, jiggled the handle, pulled as hard as he could, but no matter what he did, the door wouldn't budge.

To his left, a light switched on, and the suddenness of it made him jump. He looked to his left, toward the living room. A single lamp was on, and it shone on only one section of wall, illuminating what should have been his mom's framed Vincent van Gogh poster from the Los Angeles County Museum of Art.

Should have been . . . but wasn't.

For inside the frame was a giant picture of the Old Maid, a poster-size version of the most dreaded card in that terrible game, and she was staring directly at him, her eyes scowling, her mouth grinning, a juxtaposition that made her look completely and utterly insane.

A low noise came from somewhere, constant and cracked and high-pitched, and it took him a moment to realize that it was coming from the picture.

And that it was laughter.

As he watched, the Old Maid began rocking back and forth, and her scowling eyes lightened, her eyebrows moving up until she looked downright jolly. Somehow that was worse, and James jiggled the door handle one last time before heading into the kitchen to try the back door. If he couldn't open it, he'd break a window and get out that way.

Did the phone work? he wondered. Maybe he should call his dad and—

He tripped over something lying in the doorway between the hall and the laundry room, his arms flailing wildly to keep himself from falling. He ran into the washing machine and quickly put his hands on it to steady himself before turning around to see what he'd stumbled over.

It was his grandpa.

James let out a shocked cry. The old man wasn't headless, the way he had been in his dream, but he was unmoving and curled up on the ground. Was he dead? James thought so, but was afraid to find out.

His grandpa stirred, moaned.

James jumped, startled. Immediately he went back to the doorway and dropped to his knees, touching the old man's shoulder. "Grandpa?" Maybe they'd both be able to get out of here together. "Grandpa?"

A skinny arm shot out, a dry, cold hand grabbing James's wrist and holding tight. He tried to pull away, but the grip was strong, and then his grandfather sat up, grinning crazily. Struggling to free himself, James made a fist and used it to pound on the hand that was holding him.

His grandpa's other hand swung in from the right and slapped James hard on the side of the head.

James burst into tears. He couldn't help it. The pain was tremendous, but that wasn't the only reason he was crying. There were emotions at work, emotions he didn't even understand. But that didn't stop him from hitting his grandfather, moving from hand to arm, trying anything he could to get away, curving his fingers into claws and trying to scratch that old, cold skin.

The other hand hit the side of his head again, causing his right ear to ring.

The hand holding his wrist let go, but now both of the old

man's hands were slapping him. Hard. Left side of the head, right side of the head, left side of the head, right side of the head . . .

Still sobbing, James tried to scramble backward, but his grandpa kept coming at him, hitting, smiling.

Only it wasn't really his grandpa. He didn't know how he knew that, but he did, and it made it much easier to do what he had to do.

James threw himself backward, landing hard on his butt, then jumped instantly to his feet and kicked the old man hard in the face. He felt the nose give way beneath his heel, and he expected to see blood, but there was none. Only a crooked nose above that crazy grin.

Blood *was* coming out of his own ears. Both of them. He could feel it trickling down. His hearing was muffled, although that didn't matter much right now, and he wondered whether he'd been hit hard enough to do permanent damage.

His grandpa started to stand, and James kicked him again, then ran into the kitchen. As he'd expected, as he should have known, the back door was jammed, too, just like the front door. He didn't have as much time to try to get it open, because his grandpa was coming after him, but he wiggled and pulled hard enough to know that even if he did have more time, it probably wouldn't make much difference.

James ran into the dining room, aware that the house had become an enclosed box. He was trapped in here. There was no way for him to escape, and eventually his grandpa would probably catch him. If he could only break a window or use the phone . . . But the old man was right behind him, and all James had time to do was run.

The last thing he wanted was to go through the living room, but he had no choice, and he sped past the framed picture of the Old Maid, not looking at it but hearing beneath his slapping footsteps and ragged breathing the Old Maid's cracked, high-pitched laugh. He was determined not to go upstairs—*that* would be a trap—so he ran back into the hallway, making a circle. Except the hallway was different. It had changed since he'd hurried through here only a few moments before. The walls were darker, as was the floor, and there was an extra door just before the one to his parents' bedroom—which had been open but now was closed.

He was afraid to go anywhere that he hadn't been already, so, like a little kid, he stayed on the same track—hallway, laundry room, kitchen, dining room, living room, hallway—although he checked behind him to make sure that his grandpa was still giving chase. He didn't want to turn a corner and find that the old man had switched directions and was waiting for him. No, his grandpa was still back there, and James sped up, dashing through the laundry room into the kitchen.

He could see through the window that it was already starting to get light outside, which meant it was nearly morning. When his dad discovered that he was gone, he'd figure out where he was and come and rescue him.

All James had to do was stay alive until then.

His dad would save him.

He was still running, moving through the dining room again and toward the living room and the Old Maid. The basement door had a lock, he remembered suddenly. Whatever had taken over his grandpa might be able to pick locks or ignore them or even walk through doors, but there was a chance that it couldn't, and if James could get over there and lock himself in, he might be safe. At least for a little while.

It was worth a shot.

He ran into the hallway again, as fast as he could, sliding around the corner, and this time the door that led to the laundry room was the *only* door. He sped through it, and instead of passing by the entrance to the basement, he stopped and tried the knob. It opened easily, and he turned on the light and stepped inside, quickly closing the door and fumblingly turning the latch until he heard the lock click.

Any hope James had had that he'd been able to slip into the basement unnoticed disappeared instantly when the doorknob rattled loudly behind him as he hurried down the stairs. He reached the bottom just as his grandpa—or whatever had taken over his grandpa—slammed into the door, trying to break it down. It was an old house, and the door was thick and solid, so James didn't really think the old man's body would be able to break in. But he remembered the steely hardness of the cold hand that had gripped his wrist, and he knew that while it wasn't *likely*, it was still *possible*, and he looked around frantically until he found a box big enough to hide behind. He moved an overstuffed Hefty bag aside, got behind the box, moved the Hefty bag back and crouched down, waiting.

His dad would come. His dad would find him. His dad would save him.

He knew he would.

He knew he would.

THIRTY-FOUR

"WHERE IS HE?" CLAIRE SCREAMED AT HER MOTHER.

"I don't know!" the old woman sobbed.

Julian stepped between them. "I think we all know where he probably is."

"I'm going over there!" A string of saliva flew out of Claire's mouth as she spun hysterically around and ran toward the front door. "I'm going to get him! I—"

Julian grabbed her shoulders. "Stop it!" he ordered. "Get a grip!" His own hold on sanity was little more than tenuous, but someone had to be in charge. "Megan needs you! Go over to the hospital and stay with her and make sure she's all right!" He turned to his mother-in-law. "You stay here, in case he comes back or Roger comes back or . . ." His brain couldn't think of a way to finish the sentence, and he just let it trail off.

Marian was wiping her eyes. "And you?"

"*I'm* going over there. I'll find James and bring him back."

Claire was still hysterical. "We couldn't find Dad there! What if you can't find James? What if you—"

"The longer I stay here, the more time we're wasting. Go! Take the van. I'll take the car." He didn't wait for a response, and somehow the decisiveness of his words and the determination of his actions seemed to grant him authority. Claire didn't argue with him but started talking to her mother, telling her mom to call the hospital the second James came back. He wanted to say good-bye to her, give her a kiss, tell her that he loved her, but any indication that this wasn't going to go perfectly would undermine her confidence and might send her over the edge, so he said nothing as he closed the door behind him.

His last glimpse was of Claire giving her mom a hug.

Then he was hurrying out to the driveway, out to his in-laws' Civic. He got in, backed out and sped away, hoping he'd be able to find James. And hoping that, if he did, his son would be alive.

Daddy!

Julian pushed that thought out of his mind.

There was far more traffic than there should have been, and he seemed to hit every red light along the way. Several times, he ended up hitting the steering wheel in frustration as he just missed a yellow light, wondering whether the delay would cost him or whether, if he had sped through the red light, he would have been stopped by a cop and ticketed, wasting even more time.

Julian played it safe, just in case, but he grew increasingly agitated as he drove, the short trip seeming to take forever.

Finally, he turned onto Rainey. The houses looked like they'd been abandoned for months instead of days. There were no cars in any driveway, and every tree, shrub, plant or blade of grass was dead. In the middle of the block was his own house, and while he understood that all of the homes here were haunted or corrupted, he knew that his house was at the center of it; in his house lived the source.

He pulled into his driveway, opened the car door. The neighborhood was silent, and the second he got out of the vehicle, he heard his son's cry. *"Daddy!"*

It was just like in his dream, and, horrified, thinking he'd been granted a glimpse of things to come, he ran up the driveway, past the side of the house. But there was no hole in the center of the backyard.

"Daddy!"

The voice was coming from inside the house, though how it could be so clear and loud Julian did not understand. It occurred to him that it was not James at all, but he'd never know whether that was true unless he checked, and he ran across the patio and opened the back door, bursting into the kitchen.

"Daddy!"

James's voice was coming from the basement, and Julian rushed over to the door with a sinking feeling in his gut, remembering what Claire had seen Pam and her husband, Joe, doing down there.

"James!" he called. "I'm coming!"

The basement door was locked. He had no key for it—he wasn't sure there *was* a key—so he began kicking the door as hard as he could, aiming the heel of his shoe at the metal plate framing the knob and the lock. He wasn't sure what good that would do, since the door opened outward, but after two good hard kicks, he heard a metallic clank, and when he tried opening the door again, there was wiggle room.

"Daddy!"

"I'm coming!" Julian yelled. He kicked the door again. And again. And this time when he tried to twist the knob, it turned, and the door swung open. The light was already on downstairs, and as he hurried down the steps, he saw that all of the bags and boxes, all of the odds and ends they'd stored down here, were gone. There was only one thing on that basement floor.

The hole.

It was the same hole as in his dream, though it was inside rather than outside. That made no logical sense, but it was true, and Julian rushed down the remaining steps, acutely aware of the fact that his son's screams had stopped, that the basement was silent. He could hear his own footfalls and the thumping of blood in his ears, but nothing else.

Reaching the bottom, he crossed the few feet it took to get to the edge of the hole and peered down. An arm's length below the surface, not holding desperately on to a small protruding root, as in his dream, but caught on that root by the back of his pajamas, was James.

Instantly, Julian flopped onto the ground on his stomach, stretching his arm down in an effort to grab the boy. Unlike in the dream, he was able to reach, and his fingers grasped the curved collarless pajama top. He started to pull but realized that James might be too heavy for him to hold with one hand. The material of the pajama top might rip as well. Adjusting himself, scooting forward, Julian used both hands, getting one under each of his son's armpits, and, wiggling backward, managed to pull him up and out.

He fell backward onto the hard cement floor, holding the boy to him, tears rolling down his cheeks. It took him a moment to realize that James was limp in his arms, and for a brief, heart-stopping second, he thought that he'd failed, that he *hadn't* saved his son, that the boy was dead. But then he felt movement beneath his hands, looked into James's face, saw the fluttering of his eyelids and knew he was alive. The boy was hurt, though. There were bruises on his face and dried blood in his ears, and while he might be alive, he wasn't conscious.

Julian stood, reached down and picked his son up, the way he had when he was a baby. He wasn't a baby anymore, though, was almost too heavy to carry up the stairs, but Julian did it.

He expected to be stopped, expected roadblocks to be put up, expected some sort of opposition, but he was allowed to reach the top of the steps, walk through the kitchen and leave the house without incident. James was getting *really* heavy, and Julian kept talking to him as he staggered down the driveway toward the car, hoping for a response. There was none, but that didn't stop him from trying, and he continued asking James whether he was all right, kept on begging him to wake up, even as he placed him temporarily upright and leaned the boy's weight against himself so he could get the rear door of the car open.

Déjà vu. This was twice in two days he'd had to do this with one of his children, and it was just as awful and frightening the second time around. After maneuvering his son onto the backseat and quickly closing the door, Julian immediately got in, started the car, swerved backward onto the street and headed for the hospital.

It was déjà vu in more ways than one. He thought of the way James had been calling for him, crying out desperately for help.

"Daddy!"

He had sounded almost exactly like Miles.

But he wasn't Miles.

And he was alive.

JULIAN LIED.

As soon as he knew that both kids were going to be all right, he left Claire at the hospital, telling her that he was going to get Megan's iPhone and James's DS so that the two of them would have something to do besides watch TV. But he had no intention of returning to his in-laws' place or picking up anything.

He was heading back to *his* house.

He had no plan, didn't know what he was going to do, but for the past twenty-four hours everything he knew, everything he'd learned, everything he'd seen, everything that had happened had all been swirling around in his mind, and he was sure the answer was in there somewhere, if only he could find the key to unlock it. Maybe if he went back to the house, it might trigger something in his brain, give him an idea, help him figure out what to do. Because his father-in-law was missing, and both his son and daughter were in the hospital. It needed to end here. He had to put a stop to this. Now. Before something even worse happened.

He'd considered asking Rick to come with him. He would have liked some moral support as well as the additional muscle, but he refused to drag another person into this. Enough people had been put in harm's way already. This was something he needed to do himself. Although even as the thought occurred to him, Julian recognized its essential stupidity. Police didn't go after criminals alone. Firemen didn't fight fires alone. He recognized also that the idea that he should go into that house by himself was not his own. It had been placed in his brain, implanted there. He did not fight it, though, did not slow down or call Rick or Patrick for help, but increased his speed so he would get to the house faster.

His cell phone rang. Julian picked it up, glanced down at the number of the caller, then automatically answered and said, "Hello," before it registered that the call was coming from their house.

"I'll get both of them next time. Megan and James. And your little wifey, too. Did you get my note? I'll rape her good and hard. In the ass, the way she likes it best—"

Julian clicked off, threw the phone on the passenger seat next to him. He didn't recognize the voice, but he thought it might have been John Lynch's. Whoever it was, it did not scare him off but cemented his resolve to return to the house as quickly as possible.

That's the intention, a small, logical part of his brain told him, but he ignored it and, moments later, turned onto Rainey Street. He pulled into his driveway—

déjà vu

—and got out of the car.

He went through the front door this time. Inside, the house was dark, like a cave. It took his eyes a moment to adjust, and when they finally did, he saw that the interior had changed. Not only had the furnishings been moved and swapped, but the location of the rooms themselves was different. He should have been in the entryway, facing the living room and the hall. Instead, he was looking into his office. Through a doorway in the opposite wall, he could see the kitchen.

He stepped into the room. It was a mess. Books and papers, records and CDs had been strewn all over the floor. The walls were smeared with wide streaks of brown that he hoped to God were chocolate. On his desk, amid a small mound of rubble, his computer was on. The monitor glowed white in the dimness, and there appeared to be words written on it, though when he drew closer, he saw that it was merely a random collection of letters. Nonsense.

Or maybe not. There seemed to be a kind of pattern in the arrangement of the vowels and consonants, and it occurred to him that maybe it was another language, the true language of the being that lived here.

Yesssss.

Julian looked up, startled. Had the word actually been spoken, or had he heard it only in his head? Either way, it had accompanied a rush of wind that blew out from the fireplace, which for some reason was now in his office across from his desk, rather than in the living room. Squinting into the gloom, he tried to see what was in the fireplace, which seemed to stretch back far beyond the width of the house, though that was only an impression, as the darkness within the square opening was complete.

Another rush of air blew out from the fireplace, only this one he could see. It was not smoke, exactly, though it had a billowing quality that reminded him of smoke. Rather, it resembled an arm or a tentacle, one of the liquid, flowing protuberances of an amoeba, perhaps. It had no color of its own but matched precisely the hue and shading of its surroundings, its lower portion the same color as the floor, its upper half corresponding precisely to the appearance of the wall, down to those unexplainable brown streaks.

It was the same formless entity that had assaulted him in the living room before he had moved out, the same evil creature that had tried to get him to kill himself. It didn't look like a fat man's shadow anymore, and he had the feeling that this was closer to its true appearance. Although maybe not. He remembered from the cold touch of that shadowy arm that this being was constantly evolving, was always in the process of becoming, that it took on the properties of its latest acquisition. Maybe it had changed since the other day. Maybe this was what it looked like now.

Was Claire's dad part of it?

"Roger?" he said tentatively.

There was no answer, no change. The breeze kept blowing,

and the billowing, liquidy tentacle kept moving forward, causing Julian to back up until he was against the wall and had no place left to go.

He smelled the familiar odor of mold and dirt, and then the creature touched him. *Cold.* Once again, he sensed the age of it. And the newness of it. The ghost of John Lynch was there, although it wasn't as dominant this time. It was being assimilated. He detected no sign of Claire's dad. He wondered why, and an answer was given to him: because Roger had been killed; he had not committed suicide.

Julian understood now why the entity had revealed itself to him, why it had given him a glimpse into its makeup. It had been trying to lure him, letting him know that if he killed himself and joined with it, he would become top dog, offering him power as an incentive.

Of course, once again, his first instinct was to say no, but . . .

But he paused, pulling himself away from that cold touch and moving around to the side of the desk. It could have held on to him, could have maintained contact, but it knew the direction in which his thoughts had been heading and gave him space, let him think.

His mind was racing. It was a kamikaze solution that had just occurred to him, a flash of either brilliance or insanity, but he thought that if he could be the one driving the bus, if he could take control of this thing, he could kill it. He could make *it* commit suicide. He had no idea whether that was even possible or how it would be done, but it was worth taking the chance. He certainly didn't want to die. He had too much to live for. But this thing had already murdered his father-in-law and attacked his kids. He had to stop it. Besides, Julian remembered the last time he had been presented with this choice. He had been pressured into trying to kill himself, and when he had refused, he'd been attacked unmercifully. This creature wanted him for some unknown reason, but he knew that it would not allow him to escape a second time. If he refused again, it would finish him off.

He was going to die today no matter what.

He was going to die.

Intellectually, James understood what that meant. But emotionally it didn't really register—which was probably a good thing.

Wind blew out of the fireplace again, and the billowing tentacle approached him, apparently deciding that he'd had enough time to think. He moved away, stepping on papers, stepping on books, stepping on records. It followed him, the color of his desk, the color of his computer, the color of the debris.

He might not be able to kill it, but at the very least he'd be able to prevent it from attacking his family.

I'll get both of them next time. Megan and James. And your little wifey, too.

That would never happen. He'd make sure of it.

In fact, he could stop it from going after *anyone*. He could make sure the entity stayed dormant, didn't touch another person, didn't haunt another house.

He had no choice. There was no other way to do it, no one else who *could* do it.

It was worth the sacrifice.

The tentacle touched his arm, colder than ice, and the second it sensed his decision, the house was back to normal. Better than normal. It was if a professional cleaning service had instantly gone over every inch of their home. Everything was in its place, the windows were clear, the wood gleamed, the metal shone. He was no longer in that cockeyed version of his office but was standing in the entryway, looking at an idealized version of their living room. Nothing was coming out of the fireplace, and he sensed no other presence in the house. If he had not known better, he would have thought this was the model home of a model family and there were no such things as ghosts or monsters or things that went bump in the night.

On an impulse, he moved into the living room, peeked out the front window. The grass on the lawn was green; the tree was leafy and shadier than it had ever been.

The yards across the street had been restored as well.

Julian turned around, seeing the spotless dining room and kitchen beyond. Now that he had made his decision, he was reluctant to carry it out. The emotional weight of what he was about to do came crashing down on him, and the only thing he wanted was to see his family. But if he tried to leave, he would be killed. He knew that intuitively and for a fact. Despite the deceptive calm in the eye of this storm, the picture-perfect fiction surrounding him now would be maintained only as long as he cooperated, as long as he did what he said he would do. Any deviation would result in death.

Still, he had a little time, and he went over to the cupboard in the dining room where Claire kept the boxes of photos that she had not had time to put into albums. He pulled out the top box and put it on the table, sorting through the pictures. He saw a photo of Megan when she was five, dressed as Princess Jasmine for Halloween; saw James at three, standing proudly in front of a fort he had built out of couch cushions. There were photos from a visit with Santa, from a trip they'd taken to the Albuquerque Zoo, from various birthday parties. He found one he'd forgotten about: himself and James at the county fair, going down the Super Slide side by side. Julian's vision blurred as the tears came, and he'd never loved his wife or his children as much as he did at that moment.

He would never get to see Megan and James grow up, he realized, never get to go to their weddings, never get to show them these photos when they were adults, never get to see *their* children. It was a whole world he was going to miss, a whole life, and he was overwhelmed by a sense of loss so profound that he dropped the picture on the table, refusing to look at any more photos.

It was time, he decided.

He just had to figure out how to do it.

Hanging was out. He was afraid to go that way, and it was probably the rudest, cruelest thing he could do to his family. One of them would have to find his body, and that would be an image that would remain with the person for the rest of his or her life.

Likewise stabbing himself, which he probably wouldn't even be able to get through.

The old *M*A*S*H* song was wrong, he thought. Suicide *wasn't* painless.

Poison was probably the best. Or an overdose. He went into the kitchen, looking through the cupboard where they kept the medicine and vitamins. There were a couple of leftover prescription bottles from some of the kids' winter illnesses, but they weren't a family that kept sleeping pills around or had any heavy-duty medications. Under the sink he found Drano, and in the laundry room was bleach, but both of those would be nasty, and he wasn't sure whether they would kill him or he would throw them up and find himself in the hospital with a lot of explaining to do.

He returned to the cupboard to check again and found a full bottle of Advil as well as a bottle of the baby aspirin that Claire had him take with his vitamins. Could he overdose on those? He read the Advil warning label: "The risk of heart attack or stroke may increase if you use more than directed."

Yessss.

It was the voice he'd heard before.

Apparently, he was being watched more closely than he thought.

Julian picked up the Advil bottle, then paused. Was his mind being read? It seemed that way. Which meant that it knew what he was planning to do and wasn't worried about it. Did that mean his scheme wouldn't work?

He didn't dwell on it, thought about something else, the price of gas, the president's poll numbers, trying to keep his mind clear so he wouldn't be found out. Briefly, he considered running away, dashing out of the house and hauling ass down the street. But he knew that wouldn't work. He'd *felt* the power of that thing. It had grown so strong that it had physically changed the interior of his house. It would kill him before he got out the door this time.

Then it would go after Claire, Megan and James.

He needed to put an end to it once and for all.

Julian got a glass out of the dish rack, filled it with water and opened the Advil bottle. It was almost new. The label said it contained a hundred tablets. He poured several into his hand, washed them down with water. Did it again. And again, and again, until the bottle was empty. Feeling nothing yet, he wandered through the dining room and into the living room.

He thought of leaving a detailed note, being completely clear and unambiguous, because he didn't want there to be any questions or misunderstandings, didn't want Claire or the kids to blame themselves. This was going to be tough enough for them without the added burdens of guilt and confusion. There was no time to sit down and write a letter, however. He needed to act quickly before *it* figured out his plan. That was why he was still trying to shield his thoughts, trying not to think about what he was thinking, trying to concentrate on superfluous matters. His plan would work only if he was allowed to carry it out, if he maintained the element of surprise. He couldn't waste time penning a letter to his family—and he couldn't explain in the letter what he wanted to explain, because then *it* would know, too.

Besides, Claire and the kids wouldn't know he had committed suicide. They would think that the creature in their house had killed him. As hard as that would be for them to accept, it was still better than the truth.

He looked to his left. On the sideboard was a photo he had taken of Claire and the kids at the hot-air-balloon festival a few years back. Claire had had longer hair, and was wearing jeans shorts that no longer fit her and a T-shirt that her sister had brought back from Santa Fe. James was missing his two front teeth, and Megan was smiling in that innocent way she used to have but that she'd lost sometime in the past few years. The picture made him sad, not only for what he was going to miss but for what was already gone.

He took out the picture of Miles he'd been carrying in his pocket, leaning it up against the balloon-festival photo. Miles was next to James, and when seen together, it was obvious the two of them were brothers.

Julian started crying. The tears burned hot on his cheeks, and he plopped down on the couch, feeling an odd lurch in his chest as he did so.

What was the last thing he had said to Claire? he wondered. It hadn't been, "I love you," though it should have been. It was something more mundane, like, "I'll be back as soon as I can," or, "Is there anything else you want me to bring back?"

He should call her now, say it to her, tell her that he loved her, but his cell phone was still in the car, where he'd thrown it on the seat, and even if the phones in the house worked, which was doubtful, his fingers weren't up to the task of dialing. They felt fat, like overstuffed sausages, and when he tried to wiggle them, he found that he couldn't.

He couldn't move his left arm at all.

As his vision blurred, as he started to fade, he looked over at the pictures of his wife, his daughter, his sons. A final tear rolled down his cheek.

Good-bye, he thought.

THIRTY-FIVE

STRUGGLING.

He was not himself anymore. There was no himself anymore. He grasped for purchase, trying to remember what he had been and figure out what he was now. He was a part of something but he was lost in it, sightless, adrift, with only the most rudimentary senses to guide him. Then he was touched and touching, energy flowing into him, through him, connecting him to everything, to all of it. The form he had taken was enormous and powerful, and he could sense within it the competing wills of the thousands who had come before him. He was them, they were he, and while this new form was unwieldy, almost ungovernable, he was determined to take charge, to be in control. It was imperative that he do so, though he could not remember why it was so important.

He stretched out.

There was no time here. Seconds could have passed or minutes or hours or days or months or years. It could be today, tomorrow or yesterday.

And suddenly . . .

He could see the house. He was in it, around it, part of it. He knew where he was and what he was and why he was here. In the living room, his body was still on the couch, where it had died, *and he took care of it, made it disappear so no one would be able to find it, so his family would not have to see his corpse.*

His family.

Claire.

Megan.

James.

He knew instantly what had been done to them and what was planned for them. For the first time since becoming, he understood what he was supposed to do, what he had to do.

He remembered.

But he didn't know how to go about it. He couldn't shoot himself, couldn't jump off a bridge, couldn't even take pills or poison, the way he had before.

How powerful was he? he wondered. He reached out, saw the street outside, felt the other houses on the block. A police car drove by, and he touched the man inside, made sure that as he drove on he thought there was nothing unusual in the sight of all these empty homes and dead yards.

How far could he spread out? Could he reach all the way to the hospital? Of course he could. Megan had been made to cut herself and James had been taken, both in their grandparents' house. So he needed to go farther than that, needed to stretch as far as he could.

To the breaking point.

That was it. He knew from everything he was and everyone who was here that it was the link to this spot that kept his form alive, that granted it power. He needed to leave, to sever all ties. If he could move from this location, he could break the connection off at the source. It would be like pulling the plug on an appliance. Whatever was left would dissipate, float away.

Already he felt resistance. John Lynch. Jim Swanson. The man before him. And the man before him, and the man before him . . .

He needed to maintain control. It was hard, but it was possible. He was the newest and the strongest, and what he had be-

come was what it had become. They were one and the same; that was how it worked, and he tamped down the other voices even as he moved away from the house, away from the neighborhood, through the town.

Stretching.

THIRTY-SIX

THE LIGHTS IN THE HOSPITAL FLICKERED.

Claire had been about to fall asleep. Maybe she *had* been asleep. But the sudden sputtering of the overhead fluorescents in what almost looked like a lightning flash jerked her wide-awake. She was in a modern hospital, in a room filled with expensive diagnostic equipment, with medical professionals hard at work throughout the building, yet she was filled with the same sense of dread she'd felt back at their house.

Frightened, she checked on James, lying asleep on the bed before her, then dashed down the corridor to Megan's room in order to make sure her daughter was all right. She passed two nurses at the station between the rooms, but that didn't make her feel any less uneasy. She knew what was going on. She'd experienced this before.

The hospital was haunted.

Where was Julian? He should have been back—she looked at her watch, shocked at the time—hours ago! Her heart felt like it stopped for a second. Something had happened to him. She didn't know how, didn't know where, didn't know when, but it had, and she was almost hysterical as she ran back to the nurses' station.

She stopped, taking a deep breath before she spoke so she wouldn't seem crazy. "I need one of you to go into room one twenty-eight and watch my daughter, Megan Perry. I'm with my son in one twenty-four. I'm afraid something might happen to one of them."

The lights flickered again, the ones in the corridor, the ones above the nurses' station, the ones in the rooms, and the nurses looked at each other worriedly. "I'm sorry," the older one told her. "But we need to stay here and monitor all the patients. If there's a power outage and the emergency backup comes on, we need to make sure there are no glitches or disruptions that could endanger one of them."

There was no flickering this time, but Claire saw something worse, something that the nurses, looking down at the screens before them, did not see at all.

A twisted shadow, folding in on itself, moving from ceiling to wall to floor before sliding through the open doorway to James's room.

"James!" she cried, running over. She screamed his name at the top of her lungs in the hope that one of the nurses would follow, but she heard no footsteps or cries behind her, and when she rounded the corner of the doorway, James was still sound asleep in his bed.

Couldn't anyone hear her?

The atmosphere in the room was heavy, and though the lights remained on, they seemed dim and were unable to penetrate the darkness that had enveloped the walls and corners. James's bed and the empty bed next to his were little islands of visibility amid the growing gloom. *Things* were moving, unidentifiable entities that were glimpsed only out of the corner of her eye. Below the beeps and pulsations of the machines were whispers, sibilant sounds that were not quite words but that still seemed to carry meaning.

She should have been more afraid than she was. But there was familiarity in the horror, a pattern or signature or underlying unity that was almost recognizable.

Was recognizable.

"Julian?" she whispered.

Everything stopped. The movement, the sound, all of it.

She knew at that instant that he was dead, though she didn't want to believe it, refused to let herself believe it. "No," she said, wiping her nose. "It's not true."

"What's not true, Mom?" James sat up, rubbing his eyes. He froze, looked around, instantly aware of the changed nature of the environment, knowing they were not alone in the room. Claire moved next to him, reaching out to hold his hand.

A figure detached itself from the gloom, a vague dark shape composed of swirling shadows that nevertheless stood there, watching them, perfectly still.

"Is that Dad?" James's voice was hushed, and she heard the devastation in it. She had never in her life seen a look of such complete and utter despair on another human being.

It mirrored exactly the way she felt.

But no, that was not true. She was older; she was an adult. She had lived through a death before and come out the other side. She could handle this. She had done it before. But James was just a boy, an unusually sensitive boy, a boy who was much closer to his father than most children his age. Julian, too, had been closer to James than most fathers were to their sons. Probably because of Miles. He had been there for James every hour of every day of his life, the buffer between his son and the world, and the two of them stood staring at each other now, the shadow and the child, each suffused with a sadness so overwhelming it was palpable.

"Mom!"

Megan came through the doorway, a look of confused determination on her face, as though she'd done everything in her power to get here—but didn't know why. Claire had no idea how her daughter had gotten out of bed, but she had, removing the monitoring clips from her fingers but leaving in the IV and dragging the rolling IV stand with her.

Where were the nurses?

It didn't matter, Claire realized. Physically, medically, her children were fine, and what was happening here was so far beyond the scope of everyday reality that such a question was meaningless. The reason the nurses weren't here was because they weren't a part of this. It was not for them.

For a brief moment, the shadow in the center of the room grew less vague, more solid.

"Dad?" Megan said.

There were no details visible, and Claire could barely see through her tears, but she recognized the contours of the form. "Yes," she told her children.

And then . . .

It was gone.

THIRTY-SEVEN

CLAIRE. MEGAN. JAMES.

He saw all three of them. Megan and James were asleep, but the arrival of his presence awakened Claire.

She saw him, too. She knew him.

He remained in the hospital, calling to them, gathering them to him, watching them, even as the rest of him moved outward, spreading thin, past the boundaries of the town, past the surrounding plain, into the desert, into the sky, into the earth. It was a nanosecond. It was a year. The others, all of them, fought him every step of the way, the power that bound him to the place of origin refusing to let go.

Stretching.

Stretching . . .

And then the link was cut.

He snapped back, all of him. His family was safe. And for the briefest fraction of a second, he saw them again.

And he knew they saw him.

For the last time.

Before he was gone.

THIRTY-EIGHT

JUST LIKE THAT, THE HOSPITAL ROOM WAS BACK TO NORMAL. *Everything* was back to normal, and a nurse came in to escort Megan to her room, apparently oblivious to all that had just occurred. Megan and James were crying. Claire was crying. Was it over? Was all of it over? She was filled with the certainty that it was, and she called Diane and her mom, asking whether they could watch the kids. As soon as they arrived at the hospital and she'd told them what had happened, and Diane was safely ensconced in Megan's room, her mom in James's, Claire drove the van over to their house, her heart sinking as she saw her parents' Civic in the driveway.

She knew Julian had come here.

The front door was unlocked and wide-open. The second she stepped through it, she heard music. Julian's music. A record was playing. She didn't remember the name of the album, but she recognized the song—"Girl of My Dreams" by Bram Tchaikovsky—and she ran upstairs, buoyed by a sudden hope.

Dashing down the short hall, she ran into Julian's office. The room was empty. The stereo was on, but it had obviously been on for a long time, probably for hours. It was just that the "repeat" button had been pushed—she saw the little red light—which meant that each time the needle reached the end of the record, the arm lifted up, moved back and started again at the beginning.

"She's the girl of my dreams. . . ."

Claire turned off the stereo.

The house felt . . . empty. There was nothing here, no spirit, no monster, no creature, no consciousness. She was all alone, and she was filled with the certainty that it was Julian who had done this, who had exorcised the house. How, she had no idea. But in the end he had figured something out.

And it had killed him.

Even thinking the thought was like a stab through her heart.

Claire wandered into James's room, then Megan's, overwhelmed by the prospect before her. How was she supposed to raise them both by herself, without any help? Despite her frequent complaints that she did everything, she knew in a way that she never had before that it wasn't true, that they had always *both* raised the kids together.

Until now.

"You bastard," Claire sobbed, though she didn't know whether she was speaking to Julian or to the house that had taken him.

She knew it was wrong to be mad at Julian, but she *was* mad at him. There'd been no reason for him to come over here. They could have taken off, moved to another town, another state, someplace where they could not be found. Even if they had left the house untouched, abandoned all of their furnishings and belongings, lost every dime they had, ended up poor and living in a cramped apartment, they still would have been together. They would have still been a family.

"Fuck you!" she yelled, stomping down the stairs. This time she *was* addressing Julian. "Fuck you, you selfish bastard!"

She went through the first floor of the house, room by room. On the dining room table was a box of pictures, and next to the box was a photo of Julian and James taken at the county fair, the two of them sitting on canvas sacks and speeding down a giant slide in adjoining lanes: Julian laughing, James screaming. She would never see Julian laugh again, Claire realized, and she stared at his face in the picture as though trying to burn the image into her brain so she would never forget it. Picking it up, she brought it to her mouth and kissed it.

She felt guilty for being mad at him, and though she had no idea whether his ghost or spirit or whatever part of him lived on after death could hear her or was even around, she spoke to it, addressed it, as she began running from room to room.

"I'm sorry," she cried. "I'm sorry, I'm sorry, I'm sorry. . . ."

EPILOGUE

THEY SOLD THE HOUSE. THEY LEFT NEW MEXICO. THEY MOVED TO California, where the weather was mild, the cities were large and the ocean was close. Where Julian had been born and raised and had always wanted to live.

The horror was over, James knew, but it had not ended. Not for them. They had to live with the consequences on a daily basis, and while it was not something they ever discussed, maybe not even a conscious decision that had been made, they did not return to Jardine. And when Grandma or Aunt Diane, Uncle Rob and the cousins wanted to see them, those relatives had to come out to the coast, where his mom took everyone on sightseeing trips to the beach and Disneyland and Knott's Berry Farm and Universal Studios.

But the family did not fall apart. Megan did not become promiscuous, and neither she nor James turned to drugs. They both did well in school and graduated near the top of their classes, and if they were a little more subdued than most of their peers, a little more introverted and introspective, it did not impact their lives either socially or academically. They actually ended up being closer than most siblings, certainly much closer than they had been before.

When James was a senior in high school, he and Megan and

his mom made a pilgrimage to Jardine. Enough time had passed, and while he wasn't sure which one of them had come up with the idea, all of them were curious to go back.

They drove, taking turns, making it into a three-day road trip, stopping off and spending one night in Tucson, one night in Ruidoso, seeing sights along the way. It was as though they were preparing themselves, psyching themselves up for the return, and James, for one, was grateful for the extra time.

Jardine had grown, and he didn't remember it as well as he thought he did. The streets seemed unfamiliar, and even the old downtown, where his mom had had her office, was not as he recalled. In his mind, one of the buildings had been on the opposite side of the street, and the city hall at the end of the block had not been there at all, even though, clearly, it had.

His mom was driving, and she went around the edge of the park (smaller than he remembered) and pulled onto Rainey Street.

James recognized their house immediately. Like everything else, it looked different in person than it did in his memory, but though it had been painted another color and now had a wraparound porch, the old tree was still in front, restored to its former glory, and there was a tire swing hanging from one of the lower branches, just like in the old days.

They parked on the street and got out of the car, none of them saying a word, and he looked up at what used to be the window of his bedroom, recalling how he and Robbie had stood there and spied on the passersby. He wondered what had happened to Robbie and whether his friend still lived in town.

His gaze moved to the right, to the garage. What had happened to the salvaged items they'd left in the loft when they'd moved, those furnishings and knickknacks he and Robbie had scavenged for their headquarters? Probably the people who'd bought the house from them had thrown everything away, thinking it junk.

It *was* junk, James supposed.

To everyone except two twelve-year-old boys planning to start a detective agency.

He was filled with an almost overpowering sadness as he thought about the time his dad had helped them bring the broken exercise bike up the wooden ladder through the trapdoor.

He looked around. Memories of his dad were all over the house and yard. He'd known that already, of course. It was one of the reasons they were here. But he hadn't expected it to feel so immediate or so emotional.

He remembered the time Megan had told him that his dad was ashamed of him because he didn't like sports. In his mind, he could hear his dad's voice, telling him, "You are who you are. And whatever you like or don't like is fine with me. Everyone's different." It had been the perfect thing to say, and he recalled how his father had smiled and said, "If I didn't know by now that you hate PE and like playing video games, I'd be a real moron."

He had not thought about his dad's voice in years, was not sure he would have been able to call it to mind before this moment, but now it was as clear to him as if he'd heard it yesterday. In his mind, he could see every detail of that scene: the way his dad had been sitting at his desk, the clothes he'd been wearing, the light in the room, the smell of the house. He was transported back all those years, and the feeling was at once wonderful and awful.

"You're my son," his dad had said. "I love you no matter what."

James wiped the tears from his eyes.

His mom grabbed one hand, Megan the other, and, grateful, he squeezed both.

"Should we go up to the door?" Megan asked. "Tell them we used to live here and see if they'll let us look around?"

"No," their mom said, "this is fine," and her voice was calmer than James would have expected, as calm as he had ever heard it. *Content,* he thought, and that was not a description that usually applied to his mother. Coming back here, seeing the house, had done something for her, and he was glad that they had made the trip.

"We'd better get going," his mom said a few moments later, after they'd had time to take it all in. "Your grandma's waiting for us."